SNATCHED

Pamela Burford

RADICAL POODLE
PRESS

Paperback edition published 2018 by Radical Poodle Press
Copyright © 2011 by Pamela Burford

Paperback ISBN 978-1-939215-76-5
Ebook ISBN 978-1-452469-64-5

Interior design by BB eBooks
Cover design copyright © 2011 Patricia Ryan
Author photograph copyright © Jeff Loeser

www.pamelaburford.com

BOOKS BY PAMELA BURFORD

Jane Delaney Mysteries
Undertaking Irene
Uprooting Ernie
Perforating Pierre
Icing Allison
Preserving Peaches
Simmering Stu
Liquidating Larry
Scrapping Scarlett
Jane Delaney Humorous Mystery Series: Books 1-3 Box Set

Romantic Suspense
Snatched
Going Commando
Storming Meg
A Case of You
Twice Burned (Double Dare book 2)

Contemporary Romance
Rags to Bitches
In the Dark
Snowed
Too Darn Hot
The Boss's Runaway Bride (a novella)

The Wedding Ring matchmaking series:
Love's Funny That Way
I Do, But Here's the Catch
One Eager Bride To Go
Fiancé for Hire
The Wedding Ring Matchmaker Series: Complete Four-Book Romantic Comedy Box Set

1

L UCY WOKE WITH the munchies the night the kidnappers came for her. She padded down the curved staircase to her dark kitchen, where the stove clock's LED display informed her it was 2:23 in the a.m.

"Happy birthday, kiddo." She flicked on the overhead fluorescent. "You made it to the big four-oh."

She poured a double small-batch bourbon on the rocks, nuked a bag of 94 percent fat-free popcorn, and polished off a partial pint of Cherry Garcia just as the last kernel detonated. She smiled. Timing is everything.

She located the paperback thriller she was reading in Frank's library— her library now, she supposed, at least until the marital assets were sorted into His and Her piles. The His pile would include the centerpiece of this room, the bloated, pigskin-upholstered "chair and a half" Frank had had custom-made over her dogged objections. God knew she'd never wanted the damn thing, any more than she'd wanted the puffed-up McMansion that surrounded it, yet five weeks after she'd asked Frank to move out—the hardest thing she'd ever had to do—there sat his throne in all its swinish glory.

And the sick thing was, she'd gotten kind of used to it. The chair was as comfortable as it was ugly, squatting before the fireplace like a sumo wrestler with seams. It was also absurdly comforting in the dead-ass middle of the night when every sigh and rattle of the huge house reminded her how alone she was. She called the chair Babe, after the movie pig.

The house would probably be sold, which suited her just fine, though that would be one more heartbreak for Frank—something else for her to feel guilty about. But all that would take time, and meanwhile there was nothing and no one to stop her from moving her home office up here from the basement.

Frank had dubbed this space his "library," going so far as to order forty linear feet of "important" used books from some salvage outfit, plus the built-in shelves to display them. But it had been constructed as a sunroom, with skylights and a wall of south-facing windows and French doors. During the day this room was flooded with buttery light, in contrast to the windowless catacombs where Lucy had pounded out the first thirteen books of her Johnny Sherlock children's mystery series.

She experienced a naughty thrill thinking about the unfinished fourteenth book languishing on her computer's hard drive. With her contractual deadline less than a week away, every waking minute ought to be devoted to finishing *Johnny Sherlock and the Painted Poodle*. Legions of prepubescent fans were counting on her, more and more each year according to her royalty statements. And Lord knew Lucy Narby—Lucille Moss to her readers—had never missed a deadline. Dependable, responsible Lucy? It was unthinkable. Logically she should be down there right now, cranking out that sucker.

But it was 2:23 in the a.m., and the rules of logic were officially suspended at 2:23 in the a.m.

The bag of popcorn emitted a burst of fragrant steam as she yanked it open. There it was again, the stab of guilt—not over the calorie count, but the label. It was ridiculous, really. Every time she chowed down on a snack food that didn't bear the familiar KrunchWorks logo, she felt like a traitor. Frank was nearly as devoted to KrunchWorks as he was to his family, a company man through and through. He'd forbidden her to bring a competing brand into this house, and she never had. Until now.

Lucy set her whiskey glass and the illicit popcorn within reach, lifted Grandma Willie's freakishly unique hand-crafted quilt from its display rack, and submitted herself to Babe's wide-load embrace. She set aside the emery board that served as a bookmark, hoping reading might nudge her toward the restorative coma she so badly needed.

She read for twenty minutes until the faint snick of a door lock brought her head up. She recognized the squeak of the exterior side door that led into the kitchen. Her pulse stuttered for several seconds until the alarm system's warning tone stopped, telling her the code had been correctly entered on the keypad. Muted footfalls followed, moving toward the stairway. Stair treads groaned under multiple pairs of feet, ascending with unhurried caution in the dark. Overhead a floor joist creaked. Then another.

Lucy threw back her head and shouted, "Points off for inept skulking. I am so disappointed."

All movement upstairs ceased. Lucy chuckled and sipped her bourbon. She'd raised John to be sneakier than that.

She hadn't expected to see him until spring break. Of course, Long Island was only about a six-hour drive from Ithaca, and he'd surprised her on weekends before. She hoped this particular visit had been prompted by her birthday. His father had no doubt nagged him, as usual, reminding him to send a gift.

Frank had called *her*, too. He'd wanted to take her to Paris for a long birthday weekend or, failing that, at least a romantic excursion to Manhattan: *La Bohème* at the Met, dinner at her favorite Northern Italian restaurant, and a champagne-drenched suite at the Plaza. She'd declined as gently as she knew how, wondering how long it would take him to realize they weren't getting back together, that their marriage was really and truly over.

John had one or two buddies in tow, by the sound of it. Possibly the paramour du jour, too. Ashleigh. The girl possessed a pretty head unburdened by deep cogitation, but at least she chose clothing that flaunted the dainty barbells skewering her nipples. Then again, what would be the point of enduring such a disagreeable procedure only to hide the result under a Playtex Cross Your Heart?

John was a discerning kid. It wouldn't last. Meanwhile Lucy squelched any hint of maternal disapproval. That hard-won bit of wisdom had eluded her own mother.

Her visitors descended the stairs, making no effort at stealth now that they knew she was awake. She wished she'd thrown on a robe, but at least she had on matronly pj's and not some peek-a-boo nightie. John shouldn't get *too* embarrassed.

She slipped the emery board back in her book as she heard them approach. "I'm a hard gal to surprise."

"I wouldn't be so sure."

Lucy didn't recognize the voice. She glanced over her shoulder. Her yelp of shock turned to helpless laughter at the sight of three cheap plastic Halloween masks. The kids had turned themselves into, of all things, the Powerpuff Girls, a trio of huge-eyed TV cartoon superchicks. They were all there: Buttercup, the brunette; Blossom, the redhead; and Bubbles, the blue-eyed blonde.

God, how she loathed the Powerpuff Girls. Diana, her five-year-old niece, forced her to watch the show every time their paths crossed. Had Lucy ever mentioned her aversion to John? She must have.

"Very nice," she told her son, "but you're about six months late for Halloween."

No, wait, Buttercup wasn't John. This guy had a more solid build. The neck was thicker, the shoulders wider under the hooded gray sweatshirt. She looked at Blossom, somewhere between six five and the stratosphere, his maple-colored hair pulled back in a long braid. And Bubbles was blond for real. John had inherited Lucy's hair, dark as espresso and utterly straight.

Lucy stood, letting the quilt slide to the floor. A crawly sensation tightened her scalp.

Buttercup produced a pistol and a roll of silver duct tape. "Don't fight and you won't get hurt."

"*What?*"

They came at her. She fought like hell. Adrenaline surged with every dunk-shot bang of her heart. She writhed out of their grasp. Her fists and feet flew. Popcorn scattered. The CD rack toppled. The framed baby picture of Lucy and her sister crashed onto the hardwood floor, along with one of Frank's giraffes, the eighteen-inch bronze. She lunged for the sculpture and got a two-fisted grip on its neck, holding it at the ready like a baseball bat.

Blossom, the giant, whooped. "A feisty one, God be praised!"

"Take whatever you want," she said. "Take it and leave."

Buttercup pocketed the gun and tore a strip of duct tape off the roll.

Lucy backed up a step. "I've got money." She nodded toward the antique rolltop desk. "In there."

They didn't so much as glance at the desk. Bubbles, the blond one, made his move. She swung the giraffe. He ducked under it and body-slammed her against a bookcase. Pain exploded in her back as first editions went flying. She thought she heard Buttercup bark, "Easy!" as Bubbles wrenched the giraffe from her.

Inkblots crowded her vision. She blinked them away and saw Buttercup looming over her. He said, "You okay?"

Stupidly she nodded.

"Good." He slapped the tape over her mouth and spun her toward the other two, who held her still while he taped her wrists together behind her back.

The instant they released her, Lucy sprinted toward the multipaned French doors. She was thinking of the inky expanse of woods that lay beyond her manicured back lawn. If she could just make it past the pool and gardens to the tree line . . .

She threw her weight at the locked doors. Shards of pain lanced her shoulder.

Blossom cackled in appreciation. He tilted his mask and drained the glass of bourbon.

Bubbles muttered, "Jesus, the bitch never gives up."

Buttercup bent to retrieve the baby picture. He studied the pair of dark-haired one-year-olds through the cracked glass.

Lucy balanced herself on one bare foot and took aim at a windowpane with the other.

"Whoa!" Buttercup dropped the picture and launched himself at her, yanking her back an instant before her foot would have made contact. He wrapped his arms around her from behind. "All right, that's enough," he said when she continued to struggle. "We're all very impressed."

Bubbles swaggered up to them. "I think the lady needs a lesson in who's in charge." He sounded younger than the other two. "I think I'm looking forward to teaching that lesson."

Using Buttercup's bear hug for leverage, Lucy torqued her hips up and punched the heel of her foot into Bubbles' thin plastic mask.

He screamed like a steam whistle and ripped off the mask. *"Fug!"* He held his nose. Blood seeped between his fingers. He gaped at Lucy. "Whud the fug didja do thad for?"

Lucy had guessed right. Bubbles was young, early to mid twenties. Not much older than John.

Blossom laughed and handed him a couple of tissues. "I had a feelin' about this job." His baritone voice was flavored by the Emerald Isle. He wagged a finger at Buttercup. "You didn't want to listen."

"Yeah, you're perceptive as hell. Help me get her into the car."

"I'b *bleedeeg*." Bubbles pressed the tissues to his crooked snout. "By *doze* is broken."

"Payback for that offside tackle," Buttercup said. "Quit bitching." He and Blossom clamped their fingers around Lucy's arms and marched her out of the library. Bubbles trailed behind, bleating like a lost lamb.

Her assailants didn't seem to care that she'd gotten a good look at one of them and presumably could pick him out of a lineup. This did not bode well for her longevity.

The little group proceeded through the greatroom into the kitchen, where Lucy heard, for the second time that night, the side door unlock.

John. Who else could it be?

Buttercup said, "Shit."

Lucy pleaded with her eyes. She shook her head and mewled shamelessly under the tape. *Don't hurt him. Oh God, don't hurt my boy.*

Blossom murmured, "This is where it gets messy, lads," as the door swung open.

Two men crossed the threshold. Neither was Lucy's son. She felt confident of that even though both wore black ski masks that exposed only their eyes. The masks were a piquant accompaniment to their all-black ensembles: silk turtleneck, wool slacks, and lambskin bomber jacket for the portly, dark-eyed man; jeans and a windbreaker for the compact fellow with the aqua-by-Acuvue eyes.

"Who the fug are you?" Bubbles demanded.

The newcomers appeared just as bewildered. The big guy looked at the little guy. Buttercup looked at Blossom. All five of them looked at Lucy.

Don't look at me!

"Okay, there's been some kinda misunderstanding here." The big guy spread his hands in a conciliatory gesture. He sounded more than a little New Yawk. "My associate and I have been retained for this particular undertaking."

Lucy was an *undertaking*?

"You know anything about this?" Blossom asked Buttercup, who leveled a threatening look at Lucy, right through his mask's perky, round-eyed grin.

She glowered back.

"This bij is *bad dews*." Bubbles was busy cramming strips of paper towel in his nostrils. His hands and face were smeared with blood. "Led these dickwads hab her. Good fugeeg riddance."

"Shut up." Buttercup turned to the pair in black. "Get lost."

The second man tugged on his friend's sleeve. "Come on, Wesley, let's go. We didn't bargain on this."

Wesley took a step toward Buttercup. "This is our show, my friend. We have a deposit."

"Debosid *dis*, lard-ass." Bubbles went for Wesley, but the big Irishman was quicker. He shoved the young hothead against Lucy's Viking range, with a command to "get a fekkin' grip."

"We were here first." Buttercup tightened his grip on Lucy's arm. "End of story."

Wesley dipped into his breast pocket and produced a knife which Lucy instantly identified as a six-inch Wüsthof boning knife. Seventy-two bucks at Zabar's. She herself was a Henckel gal. She gazed longingly at her beloved eight-piece set in its countertop knife block right there in full view—and within arm's reach of Lucy herself, if only she had use of those arms. She'd put a fresh edge on those blades just yesterday.

Buttercup displayed the pistol. "Go away."

"Oh my God." The smaller guy's eyes widened. "Wesley, he's got a gun."

"Ha!" Bubbles crowed. "Broughd a dife to a gudfight, ya fugeeg abateurs."

"This is bullshit," Wesley said. "We have an *agreement*."

"He's got a *gun*, Wesley. It's not worth it."

His partner wheeled on him. "Why don't you say my name *again*? *That's* incredibly helpful."

"You can stay and get yourself killed. I'm leaving." Wesley's pal slammed out of the house.

The strange assemblage stood staring at one another. Blossom turned to Buttercup. "Well, lad, what are we goin' to do with this pesky fella?"

Buttercup shrugged. He raised the gun. "Shoot him."

Lucy squeezed her eyes shut. Instead of a gunshot, she heard the door slam. Bubbles hooted in delight. He trilled, "Rud, Wesley, rud!" The squeal of car tires, then silence.

"That was interesting." Blossom scratched his chin under the mask. "Let's get her out of here before someone else shows up."

Buttercup glanced around, looking for something. He turned to Lucy. "Where's your purse?"

That was more like it. As a motivating factor for this freak show, filthy lucre beat out all other choices hands down. Lucy might walk away from this thing alive after all. She nodded toward the menu desk in the breakfast nook. Bubbles located her Coach shoulder bag and strolled back, pawing through it. Buttercup grabbed it from him, spilled the contents on the floor, and kicked the mess around with the toe of his running shoe. Her lipstick rolled across the antique French granite floor tiles and came to rest against Frank's new under-counter wine cellar.

He faced her again, with an impatient sigh. "Where are they?"

Her frown asked, *Where are what?*

"Your birth control pills, Mrs. Narby?"

Astonishment popped her eyes.

Buttercup yanked the tape off Lucy's mouth in one swift tear. She screamed.

"Don't make me ask again," he warned.

"Master bathroom. Top vanity drawer. That *hurt.*"

Buttercup slapped the tape back over her mouth. A minute later Bubbles had returned with her monthly pill compact, which Buttercup pocketed.

Her birth control pills. Lucy couldn't begin to figure that one out. Granted, these creeps seemed less than enthusiastic about plundering, which left that raping thing kind of front and center, but *birth control pills?*

Buttercup propelled her toward the door.

It was chilly outside—mid to high forties. Downright arctic by Lucy's admittedly wimpy standards, especially since the only thing between her pampered hide and the elements was a pair of mismatched flannel jammies.

A nearly full moon provided the only illumination. Her five-acre property was isolated from her nearest neighbors by dense woods and a quarter-mile cobblestone driveway. She'd always appreciated the solitude. Until tonight.

The tender soles of her feet found every sharp pebble as Buttercup and Blossom half dragged her toward a dark sedan parked out of sight of the house. Bubbles jogged ahead to pop the trunk.

She screamed beneath her gag as the men hoisted her and dumped her on top of a tire iron and a set of jumper cables. The trunk also held a coil of rope. Buttercup hogtied her with practiced efficiency, lashing her ankles and tethering them to her wrists by a short length of rope behind her bowed back.

Bubbles leaned into the trunk to taunt her, now that those lethal feet were safely restrained. His nose was a pomegranate. The moonlight turned all that blood to black warpaint. "I'b gudda hab sub fud wid you, bij. Just you wait."

The other two exchanged a look. Buttercup elbowed Bubbles aside to blindfold Lucy with an oily rag.

The trunk lid slammed shut. She heard car doors open and close. The vehicle rocked and settled. The engine rumbled to life, turning the trunk into a vibration chamber.

Trussed as she was, Lucy couldn't keep herself from pitching to and fro as the car started rolling. Her stomach lurched. *Oh yeah*, she thought, *that's just what I need right now.* A geyser of ice cream, popcorn, and bourbon, with only her nostrils for an exit.

She forced herself to take slow, deep breaths, forced her mind to function. Why would anyone want to kidnap her? Correction: Why would *two* anyones want to kidnap her, these trick-or-treat maniacs and whoever hired those two whiny chuckleheads who came late to the party?

When had it become open season on Lucy Narby?

She had to keep her head, no matter what happened. It was her only chance.

Don't panic, Lucy commanded herself, right before something small and furry crawled up her pajama leg.

2

WILL KITCHEN DIDN'T have long to wait. The racket in the trunk commenced before he was halfway down the drive.

"Josephine didn't waste any time." Fergus removed his Blossom mask. He tossed it and Will's Buttercup mask into the backseat, where Mick sat nursing his busted beak.

"It probably smells the popcorn on her." Will pushed the sweatshirt hood off his head.

"Think she'll be okay?"

"Josie or Lucy?" He turned onto the two-lane that wound through this affluent community on Long Island's North Shore.

"Wee thing's apt to get squashed." Fergus cocked his head, listening to the commotion.

"I can always swing by a pet store later." Will shrugged. "One white mouse is as good as another."

Mick snickered. "I'b telleeg Tob."

Tom was Will's son, and Josephine the Mouse belonged to him. Josie was an exceptionally sociable beast who'd been trained to scamper over the hulking bipeds who populated her simple world and exhume treats tucked into the odd pocket or cuff. Will had borrowed the animal earlier in the day and put her on half rations, wanting her hungry when she met his captive, who was scared to death of rodents. Lucy, of course, had no way of knowing the varmint terrorizing her was in fact a child's harmless pet on the prowl for a Cheez Doodle or Reese's Piece, but willing to settle for some of the popcorn she smelled.

He hoped Lucy didn't flatten the thing in her frenzy to escape it, because he'd never get away with pulling a switcheroo on the boy. No freshly minted pet-store mouse could hope to pass for fat and friendly Josephine.

A fresh bongo riff from the trunk prompted Mick to pound his feet on the floorboard. He hollered, "Watch out, Lucy. That rat's gudda bite your tit off," followed by that braying laugh of his. "Tell it to leeb sub for be."

Fergus glanced at Mick, then at Will, meaningfully.

Mick Jagger Drinkwater was Will's nephew, being the noisome spawn of Will's half sister Judith, who'd taken time off after graduating from Emerson twenty-five years earlier to embrace the groupie lifestyle and thereby "find herself." She found herself pregnant by a third-rate guitarist with profound pharmaceutical issues. With only a handful of evasive maternal hints to go on, Mick had convinced himself he'd been sired by Keith Richards.

If anything, the frantic thumping in back was getting worse. Maybe Will should have padded the trunk.

"The lass is a firecracker." Fergus wagged his bushy eyebrows. "Gave us some kind of workout, she did."

"Can't say we weren't warned."

"No, can't say that. It was fun," Fergus said, "till Mutt and Jeff showed up."

"It would seem our client hired two teams."

"That's how it looks. But why?"

"I intend to find out." Will glanced at his nephew in the rearview. "Clean yourself up, Mick. Get that blood off your face."

"Later."

"Now," Will said. "We could get stopped. I've had enough nasty surprises for one night."

"What about her?" Fergus asked. "Slammin' around back there. I mean, I know we can handle it if some cop pulls us over, but who needs that?"

Will said, "She'll run out of steam."

"Hope not," Mick snickered. "Not till I'b had my fud."

"Listen, lad." Fergus glowered over his shoulder. "I don't know what you think is goin' on here—"

"Fug you." Mick spat on a dish towel he'd swiped from Lucy's kitchen and scrubbed his face. "Loog what the bij did to me. I'b entitled."

Fergus sent Will another look, a look that expressed more eloquently than words ever could just how ticked off Fergus was, what a bratty loose cannon Will's nephew had proven to be, and what the hell was Will going to do about it.

Will didn't leave him in suspense. He met Mick's gaze in the rearview. "Your part in this is over."

Mick stopped scrubbing. "What?"

"You'll still get paid."

"No way." Mick grabbed Will's seatback, got in his face. "I bid id on this thig from day one. You can't kick me out now that the fud part's starteeg."

"Back off. You're bleeding on the upholstery."

"Goddabbit, I'b id on this. I'b a natural."

Mick was a natural *something*. Maximum-security guest of the state, something along those lines. So much for doing Judith a favor. No more nepotism. Next time Will would write a check to one of his sister's charities.

"This is not negotiable," Will said. "I'm dropping you at your mom's place. You've got to get that nose fixed up. She'll take you to the ER."

Mick pounded the back of Will's seat. "You habit heard the ed of this."

THERE IT WAS AGAIN. That scream. Reflexively Lucy turned her head toward the sound, though she was still blindfolded, still gagged with tape, and still securely bound, now tied hand and foot to a hard wooden chair.

She'd heard the scream a handful of times since her arrival here— wherever *here* was—about an hour and a half earlier. It was muted, as if from several rooms away, and at first she'd thought it was part of the background music she was being subjected to. Christina Aguilera at the moment, whining about being underappreciated, at about 150 decibels. Or was that Britney? Funny, Lucy wouldn't have pegged Buttercup and his crew as fans of timeworn peroxide pop. Misogynist rap, perhaps. Heavy metal, for sure. Either one of which Lucy would gladly choose over this loathsome crap. Only, how could she forget it when it was blaring in her ears nonstop?

She ached all over from her struggle in the house, not to mention the one inside the car trunk, where she'd tried without success to evade that rat or whatever the horrid thing was. How had it even found its way inside the car? At least she'd left it behind when they'd hauled her inside.

There it was again. Another short, hoarse scream. What were they doing to that poor woman? It definitely sounded like a woman, and she was obviously suffering terribly. Lucy swallowed hard, wondering if the same agony was in store for her.

The ride from her house had taken over an hour, with one stop along the way. She'd heard a car door open, then slam with some force. A voice outside the vehicle had spat, "Fug you, man. Fug you and that bij. You'll be sorry, both of you." Bubbles. He'd punched the lid of the trunk as the car backed up and turned onto the road.

They'd ejected Bubbles. One small mercy in a terrifying ordeal.

At least she was finally warm, though she had yet to stop shivering.

Lucy had been doing some thinking. Her abductors had possessed her house alarm code and presumably a copy of her key. They knew about her birth control pills, her only regular medication if you didn't count Cherry Garcia. None of which was public knowledge, and all of which pointed to your basic inside job. Unless her son, John, had gone completely batshit, that left his father. She didn't want to consider that Frank might be behind this, but who else could it be?

Yet why would he do such a thing? It was true that twenty years of marriage entitled her to a hefty settlement, but she'd never known her husband to be either tight-fisted—with her at least—or vindictive. And if, for the sake of argument, he preferred widowhood to divorce, wouldn't he simply have hired someone to do the deed right there in her home? Make it look like the proverbial robbery gone bad?

Lucy had married too young as an act of rebellion against her hippy-dippy upbringing, exchanging "I do's" with the first buttoned-up, golf-playing, proper-fork-using, upwardly mobile M.B.A. she could strong-arm down the aisle. By the end of their four-week Italian honeymoon, she knew she'd made The Biggest Mistake of Her Life. Problem was, somewhere between the Colosseum and the Bridge of Sighs, her young bridegroom had planted his hardy seed, and hadn't Lucy sworn she'd never subject any child of hers to the kind of undisciplined, anything-goes single-parent household she and her sister, Ethel, had endured?

Add to that the fact that her mother, Savannah Moss, a.k.a. Savannah Banana, an unreconstructed peace-and-love throwback, had actively lobbied against the marriage—well, against marriage in general. Savannah would have been smug as hell if Lucy came crawling back after less than a month of wedded bliss.

So she'd stuck it out, and as the years piled up and one decade slid into the next, she'd settled into a kind of passive dependence. Her existence was safe and comfortable, if not particularly stimulating. When Frank's business travel increased to the point that he was away more than he was home, she found she didn't resent it as most wives would. In fact, she looked forward to the respites from having to pretend theirs was a healthy, satisfying marriage.

The dissatisfaction was purely one-sided. Frank would happily have gone on forever the way they were. He didn't deserve to be hurt. He might not be the most exciting husband, but aside from a few irksome personality quirks, he possessed nothing she could point to as a fatal flaw. He was attentive, honest, and neat. Not to mention an outstanding provider. He'd never raised his hand to her in anger. In fact, they never argued. Frank was a good father, and not the type to cheat on her. He respected—one might even say revered—the institution of marriage.

And yet their relationship had been flawed from day one. She'd hoped they would grow closer over the years, that this pleasant young man she'd chosen to share her life would, in time, become her soul mate. But that deep attachment never materialized. She'd sensed a polite distance between them from the beginning, as if some crucial part of him were destined to remain hidden from her. For the longest time Lucy assumed it was her fault, that she was deficient as a wife. She bent over backward to apply corrective measures. Romantic vacations. Shared hobbies. Couples therapy. She even took a massage class, hoping to literally pound some closeness into their marriage. All in vain. Over the years, the polite distance widened into a gaping chasm.

She told herself she was simply asking too much, her expectations warped by Hollywood and her own girlish fantasies. But as time passed and she witnessed the emotional intimacy other couples enjoyed, she could no longer delude herself. Her marriage was sick. And no, it wasn't her fault, though it took her twenty years to realize it.

Telling Frank she wanted a divorce was the most painful thing she'd ever had to do. She'd waited until he returned from yet another extended trip to KrunchWorks' Midwest distribution facility in Chicago, then broke it to him as gently as she could. He'd been stunned, dumbfounded. He'd never seen it coming. Lucy regretted the misery she was causing him, but now that she'd taken the long-overdue first step, she was damned if she'd back down. Forty wasn't too old to start over, to see what her life could have been, could still be.

As for John, now that he was in college, the whole broken-family thing was less of an issue. That wouldn't have been the case if she'd succumbed to Frank's desire for a big family. In a rare display of assertiveness, she'd drawn the line at one child, despite his constant cajoling those first few years to fill their big house with little Narbys. She'd denied her husband the brood he'd always wanted: something else to feel guilty about.

Frank had moved into a studio apartment in Queens close to KrunchWorks company headquarters. He called her every day, the consummate sales professional using all the powers of persuasion at his disposal.

Was it possible? Could her husband of twenty years—the father of her child—be behind her abduction? What could he gain by bringing her here, except perhaps to keep the bloodstains off the antique Ispahan carpet?

Lucy forced herself to put aside these questions for the moment and concentrate on her first priority, which was, simply, survival. Second on the list was escape. She would cooperate and appease and, just maybe, get away from this horrorfest with her hide intact.

A door banged open. Lucy yelped beneath her gag. Footfalls—two sets of them—approached her. Then silence. They were in the room with her. What were they doing? Why didn't they say something? Do something?

No, that's okay, she thought. *Don't do a damn thing.* Whatever these creeps had in mind, she'd just as soon never find out.

A voice inches away made her jerk. "What was that all about back there,

Lucy?" It was Buttercup. The man in the gray hoodie. The Grand High Poobah of this operation.

A perplexed grunt made it past the tape sealing Lucy's mouth. He ripped it off. She managed not to scream this time, but only through force of will. Did people really have their *crotches* waxed?

"What kind of game are you playing?" he demanded.

"What? I—I don't know what you're talking about." Lucy's heart banged painfully.

"What did I tell you, lad?" It was the big Irishman. "She's a stubborn one, all right."

"I asked you a question," Buttercup said. He was behind her now. "Don't play stupid."

"I'm not, I swear." She craned her neck to face him, despite the blindfold. "I—I really have no idea what you're talking about. What do you mean, 'game'?"

Two big hands slammed onto the chairback and tipped it backward. She cried out. His voice was a low growl near her ear. "Like they say in the movies—we can do this the easy way or we can do it the hard way."

He let the chair drop forward. The front legs hit the floor with a thump. If Lucy hadn't been tied to it, she would have sprawled onto the floor. Couldn't they give her a hint, for God's sake? How did they expect her to *think* with some perky bimbo warbling about losing her cherry at head-throbbing volume?

"The lass is trying," Blossom said, from farther away now.

"I don't think she is," Buttercup said, still behind her. "I don't think she's trying at all. I think she needs a little incentive."

"Oh, lad." Blossom sounded dismayed, even a tad alarmed. "Not that. There's no call."

"What?" Lucy cried. "Don't! Please. I really am trying—"

Something dropped onto her head. Something small and solid and warm, with tiny feet that scampered down her hair and under her collar.

"*No!* Get that thing off me!" She jerked wildly, arching her back. Only Buttercup's grip on the chairback kept her from pitching face-first onto the floor.

"Get it off! Get it off of me!" The little beast was perched on her left nipple.

"If you insist." Buttercup started to slip his hand into her pj's.

"Don't you dare!"

The animal, excited by the commotion, ran down her torso and leg. Lucy heard one of them intercept it. Not to squash it or trap it, but to cuddle and coo to the damn thing.

"Did that great loud harpy frighten you?" Blossom's gruff Irish brogue turned syrupy. "Poor wee beastie. Here you go, Josie. A little treat I swiped from Quint. I won't tell if you won't."

"You sick bastards." Lucy couldn't stop herself. "What was that for? Just to terrorize me?"

What was that thing anyway, a gerbil? Some harmless hamster? It made little difference. Lucy was pathologically terrified of rodents. Mickey Mouse or plague-ridden rat, it was all the same to her. Her captors had no way of knowing that, of course. Lucky guess on their part.

The source of her phobia was no mystery. It could be traced back to the winter of her tenth year and the foul Gladsome Farm, one of a series of die-hard hippy communes Savannah had drifted into and out of during her daughters' impressionable years. The specific middle-of-the-night incident involved a sleeping pallet placed amid disintegrating barrels of flour and oats, and about eighty million voracious field mice.

"I expect answers when I return." Buttercup leaned in close. His warm breath tickled her ear. "Josephine has friends."

Lucy heard them moving toward the door. "Wait! Why are you doing this? What do you want?" No response. "Did you call my sister? My mother? I'll give you their numbers. They'll pay!"

The peroxide pop climbed a few decibels, right before the door slammed.

3

FRANK NARBY WAS dreaming about the packaging concept for KrunchWorks' New, Reduced-Fat Tac-O's, Original Flavor and Picante Gigante, when something interrupted his sleep. He blinked at the unfamiliar shadows and reached for a soft, feminine body that wasn't there. A seasoned traveler, he didn't succumb to panic but groped for the bedside lamp as a fresh burst of pounding brought him fully awake.

Light flooded the Lilliputian studio apartment he'd moved into five weeks ago when Lucy asked him to move out.

Oh yeah. This rat hole.

Frank shuffled to the door, a mere ten feet from his futon. Scratching his balls through his Ralph Lauren glen plaid boxers, he peered through the peephole. He turned the deadbolt and threw open the door. "What are you doing here? You didn't leave her alone, did you?"

Wesley McIntyre shoved Frank in the chest, making him stumble backward. "What the hell are you trying to pull, Narby?"

"Shh. Hold it down, will you, Wesley? I've got neighbors. It's—" He glanced at the bedside clock. "Christ, it's almost five in the morning. It was supposed to be done by now."

"It was done. Don't worry." Wesley stalked into the kitchenette and began throwing open cabinets. "Your cartoon cuties got there ahead of me. Where do you keep the booze?" He looked under the sink.

"What are you talking about? Did you grab her or not?"

"You gotta have a bottle of something around here."

"There's a Coors Light in the fridge."

From the look on Wesley's plug-ugly face, you'd think he'd been offered a bucket of horse piss.

"Answer me," Frank said. "Who's watching Lucy?"

Wesley grabbed a half-full bag of KrunchWorks Ched'r Wheelz With X-treme Cheese! off the counter and heaved his bulk onto a rickety folding chair. "I trusted you to play straight with me, Narby. Not that this asinine scheme of yours isn't the stupidest thing I've seen in all my years as a PI, but still. We had an agreement, my friend."

"Yeah, and we still do. What's your problem?"

"Who'd you figure as the backup team, that's what I wanna know. Me and Joe or those other yahoos?"

"What other yahoos?" Frank ducked the handful of Ched'r Wheelz Wesley hurled at him.

"The freaks in the kiddie masks, who the hell do you think I mean? The ones that snatched your wife before I could get to her."

"The ones . . ." A dizzy rush threatened Frank's balance. "Are you telling me someone else kidnapped Lucy?"

Wesley paused with a handful of Ched'r Wheelz at his mouth, studying him. "You're shittin' me, right?"

"Oh Christ."

"You didn't send those guys?"

"Oh Christ." Frank groped behind him for a chair, lowered himself into it. "Oh Christ."

"Answer me, Narby. Did you send 'em or not?"

"No!" Frank's head began to throb. "No, I did not send any goddamn freaks in any goddamn kiddie masks. I sent *you*. What happened?"

A long sigh fluttered out of Wesley, like a beach ball deflating.

"Who?" Frank demanded. "Who were these guys?"

"How the hell do I know? Me and Joe, we let ourselves in with the key you gave me, and there they were, three men in Halloween masks hightailing it out of there with your wife."

"Was she hurt?"

"Nah, she looked okay. Tied up is all."

"Tied up. Oh Christ." Frank scrubbed a hand over his bristly jaw.

"Well, that's what I woulda done if I'd gotten to her first."

"Yeah, but just for show," Frank said. "So she'd *think* it was real."

The plan was to have Wesley grab her out of her bed, cart her off to an abandoned cider mill out east, and let her sweat for a day or two until her devoted husband tracked her down, vanquished her fiendish kidnapper, and rescued her.

She'd see how much he loved her, realize how much she still loved him, offer her tearful apologies, and beg him to come home. Frank figured his scheme would ensure the happily ever after he had every right to expect, made happier still with the addition of a few grateful blow jobs.

"Who would've taken her?" Frank asked. "And why?"

"Ransom, why else? As for who . . ." Wesley shrugged. "Someone who's seen your fancy digs in Crystal Harbor, the yacht club, your precious vintage 'Vette."

Frank jumped up. "I'm calling the police."

"Yeah? What are you gonna tell 'em?" Wesley mimed holding the receiver. "Yes, Officer, she was snatched just before three a.m. The way I know, the guys I hired to grab her, they saw the whole thing go down."

"You don't need a witness to report something like this. She's *gone*, isn't she?"

"The cops won't care. A grown woman, practically divorced—"

"Temporarily separated."

"Until you hear from the kidnappers, the cop'll figure she's at Club Med playing grab-ass with the towel boys. No ransom demand?" Wesley shrugged. "Could be days before they'll even talk to you."

"*Days?*" Frank raked his fingers through his hair. "Anything could be happening to her. You were there. Didn't you try to stop them?"

Wesley drew himself up. "What do you think, I gave up without a fight?"

Frank looked him up and down. "You don't look like you've been in any fight."

"What I thought at the time, you blabbed to these fellas, maybe trying to get it done cheaper—which, excuse me, but is just the kind of dumb-ass stunt you'd pull—and these other guys never got the message it wasn't their gig. Either that or you hired all of us, kind of like a Team A and a Team B, just to make sure the job got done. Another brilliant move I wouldn't put past you."

"So you *did* give up without a fight."

"You kidding? One of these fellas, you should see his nose. But you gotta understand, there were *three* of 'em. Big fuckers. Plus they were armed."

"*They* were armed. What about you? Weren't you packing?"

"If you're asking was I carrying a concealed weapon, the answer is yes. I brought a knife to wave in your wife's face if she gave us any trouble."

"That's all?" Frank demanded. "A knife?"

"You know what? I wish to God I never went along with this loony plan of yours in the first place. If me and Joe didn't need the money so bad, I would've told you to shove it."

"Who's this Joe? You're the one bringing other people into this thing—"

"Don't worry about Joe," Wesley said. "We can trust him. He's my partner."

"I thought you worked alone."

"I do. Not that kind of partner." Wesley crumpled the empty Ched'r Wheelz bag. "You got any Doritos?"

"*Doritos?* You ask the national sales manager of KrunchWorks if he's got Doritos? What does that mean, not that kind of partner?"

"You just hop off the Way-Back Machine or what? My *partner*, Einstein. Who lives with me? As in king-size Beautyrest? His and his bath towels?"

"Christ, you're kidding. *You?*"

Wesley answered with an amiable, openhanded gesture: *li'l old me*. He uncrumpled the bag and rooted for crumbs.

"Huh," Frank said. "You don't look like a, uh . . . I mean . . ."

"Fag?"

"I wouldn't put it that way."

"Sure you would," Wesley said. "You called your wife's dentist a fag the first time I met you. She can't be getting it on with Dr. Dwyer, you said. He's a fag."

"Well, you had me fooled, that's all I'm saying."

"Gosh, that's a relief. The macho lessons must be working. You owe me money, my friend."

"What, for letting some psycho creeps snatch my wife?" Frank said.

"Way I see it, you owe me the deposit back. A thousand bucks."

"Right. That'll happen."

"You stand by with your thumb up your ass while my wife gets—"

"I know where they took her."

Frank stared at him. "You followed them?"

Wesley shrugged. "It's what I do."

"Where is she?"

"Eight grand." Wesley wagged eight thick fingers.

"Eight!"

"You wanna rescue the little missus, you wanna play big-dick hero? Here's your chance, my friend."

Here was his chance to get himself killed, was more like it. Going up against real, honest-to-God kidnappers was not part of the game plan. He should leave it to the cops. Still, it might not be such a crazy idea. He had the element of surprise on his side. But he chafed at the money.

"Two grand," Frank said. "For shadowing them. That's more than fair."

"'Shadowing.'" Wesley chuckled. "Listen to you."

"All right, all right. Four. What we agreed on."

"You cheap prick. What, you think I don't know what you're worth? I make it my *business* to know stuff like that. Eight grand is chump change to a man like you. You telling me it's not worth eight grand to find out where these sick fucking perverts have taken your wife?"

"Six. But for that you have to help me do this thing."

"No way, my friend." Wesley put up his hands. "My part in this is over. *Finito.* You are on your own."

"Three against one?"

"Actually, you only got two to deal with. They let one guy out along the way. See? The odds are improving. Besides, I gotta go out of town today. Might not get back till tomorrow."

"Come on, Wesley. You're a pro. You used to be a cop. You know how to do stuff like this."

"There you go, mistaking me for Magnum, P.I. I get that a lot, on account of I look so much like Tom Selleck. What I know is how to sneak around and take dirty pictures of people cheating on their spouses. Which is what you hired me for."

"Initially," Frank agreed. Only, in Lucy's case, there'd been no dirty pictures. Almost from the moment she'd given Frank the boot, he'd had Wesley McIntyre following her, observing her every move. She hadn't so much as shaken another man's hand. She'd let no one in the house except her mother and sister, her little niece, and a couple of female friends. Oh, and the handyman, but George Fuller was about eighty and suffered from a severe case of plumber's crack. Frank had been thrilled that his darkest suspicions had not borne fruit. His only problem then had been convincing Lucy to take him back.

Now things had gotten a bit more complicated.

"Can you get me a gun at least?" Frank asked.

"You don't want a gun. Guns are dangerous."

"These men are *armed*, you said. I need *something*."

Wesley frowned. "You really gonna do this?"

"They won't be expecting me. I'll get the drop on them."

"Yeah, well, while you're 'getting the drop' on 'em, try not to shoot your dick off."

"So you'll get me a piece?"

Wesley sighed. "When I get my eight grand, you get your 'piece.'"

"Seven."

Wesley brushed greasy crumbs from his leather-covered paunch and started for the door.

Frank said, "You're a goddamn thief, you know that?" *And a fat, ugly, over-the-hill fag,* he thought, but didn't say it. The PI had four inches and about eighty pounds on him, and it wasn't all flab.

Wesley turned back to him. "For your information, I have expenses. Me and Joe are getting married."

Frank failed to squelch a snort of derision.

"A real church wedding—none of this 'commitment ceremony' shit. Black tie. Real, live clergy. Our picture in the *New York Times* Vows section." Wesley got in Frank's face. "You got something to say about that, my friend?"

"Tell me where the bride is registered, I'll buy him a frickin' crock pot, *my friend.* You'll get your eight grand when the bank opens. Now, tell me where my wife is."

4

AL LYNCH FOUND the old road through the woods as if he'd driven it just yesterday. Whoever owned this section of the mountain liked to hunt, and he ignored the posted trespass notice today just as he had twenty-five years before. It hadn't been deer season then and it wasn't now.

This isolated corner of the Catskills was only about two hundred miles from Attica, New York, where Hal had spent those twenty-five years as a guest of the state, but it might as well have been on the moon. Not an hour had gone by that he hadn't thought about this negligible patch of land and what he'd stashed here in the middle of a rainy March night all those years ago. At the time, he figured he'd be back for it within days—a few weeks at most if he had to lie low for a while. But fate had something else in store for him.

Fate had had a little help putting him behind bars. Judith was his next stop.

Hal kept a keen eye on his surroundings as he maneuvered the borrowed rattletrap along the rutted dirt road. His spine felt every tree root and rock. Early morning sunlight spilled through the budding foliage; it was just past dawn. The road widened near a small hunting cabin. That hadn't been here back then. No matter. The place he was headed for would have remained undisturbed. He hadn't told a soul about this place.

As he neared the spot where he'd parked the bus back then, he peered through the trees. There it was: the tooth. Hal smiled. He set the parking brake and retrieved the shovel from the trunk. Time to perform a little gum surgery.

The ground wasn't half-frozen as it had been back then, which was a blessing. He was no longer a young man, no matter how much iron he'd driven on the inside. It was slow work. Hal paused to strip off his light pullover sweater and toss it onto the tooth—in actuality a boulder nearly his height shaped like a chipped molar. He knew the exact spot; he'd pictured it in his mind's eye a million times during the intervening years. Periodically he paused to wipe his sweaty palms on his jeans or take a pull from the plastic bottle he'd brought along. He turned the bottle to examine the label. From the springs of Maine. He shook his head in disbelief. Back when he went away, you never could have convinced him he'd pay cash money for a bottle of water.

When Hal had gotten down to about two and a half, three feet with no trace of a plastic-wrapped suitcase, he didn't worry. The ground settles. By the time he'd gone almost another two fruitless feet, he was sweating from more than the exercise. He peeled off his damp undershirt and mopped his face with it.

This was the spot. This was the damn spot. Right here under the chip in the molar. He studied the ground on either side of the hole he'd made. Okay. Soil shifts over time, right? He picked up the shovel and started in on the patch of ground to the right of the hole.

The sun had passed its zenith when Hal tossed the shovel out of the moat he'd excavated, six feet deep and completely encircling the molar. Every muscle in his body throbbed; his back was on fire. His palms were a mass of bloody, chewed-up blisters. He scrambled out of the hole. He leaned on the nearest tree and took deep, calming breaths until his heartbeat slowed.

Another man might have cursed and raged at the top of his lungs, but that would accomplish nothing. *Okay, think.*

He hadn't told anyone, and no one could have simply stumbled onto the site. Only Judith knew he'd even parked the bus in these woods, but she didn't know the two million bucks had stayed here. She thought it was sitting in five separate safe-deposit boxes. That was what he'd told her.

The kid, then. Somehow he'd seen something. It was the only explanation.

Ricky Baines's freckled grin flashed across his mind's eye, the way he'd seen it hundreds, probably thousands of times during the past two and a half decades on the inside. His fellow cons couldn't get enough of that stupid sitcom. Some snarling gangbanger was always surfing channels in the dayroom, searching for his *In No Time* fix. And finding it, more often than not; with cable, the damn show was always on the air somewhere. If Hal had a buck for every time he'd heard that parrot squawk, *"I'm having conniptions!"* he wouldn't need the two million.

He grabbed the shovel, reached across the moat with it to pluck his sweater and undershirt off the boulder, and headed for the car.

Good thing he'd never let the kid see his face.

"EES BREAKFAST."

The accent was French, the pitch decidedly feminine. But Lucy, still blindfolded, had not needed to hear the voice to know a woman had entered the room. The overpowering stench of Joy perfume preceded her.

"But first," Frenchie said, "you need the W.C., I think, *oui?*"

Oui oui was more like it. Lucy was absurdly grateful for the offer, having dreaded the prospect of waiting for one of the Powerpuff guys to reappear and then begging for a potty break.

The woman worked at the rope securing Lucy's left ankle to the chair leg, picking at the knots, her long fingernails grazing Lucy's skin. *"Merde,"* she muttered. "That Will, he always makes the knots too tight."

Will. That must be the leader. The one in the gray hoodie. At least she could stop thinking of him as Buttercup.

His name is Will, she would tell the police if she ever got away from here. *About six feet tall. No telling hair color, not with that hoodie, but his eyes are blue.* She'd made them out standing so close to him in her kitchen.

"Voilà!"

Lucy felt the rope go slack. She sat still like a good little captive while Frenchie released the other ankle and her hands.

"Ah, you are steef. The circulation, eet suffers when one sits for so long."

Gee, I'll try to remember that. This woman didn't seem too menacing.

Lucy was tempted to ask her to turn off the music, if one could call it that, but decided not to push her luck.

"You will behave yourself, *oui?* You will not take off the blindfold. You will not try to get away. Eef you try anything, I will shoot you." Her tone was amiable. She could have been swapping recipes with a girlfriend. "Ah. You do not believe I have a gun."

"Sure I do."

"Will calls it a SIG-Sauer. Such an ugly name. Eet is real. I show you."

"That's not—" Lucy gasped as something cold and metallic kissed the side of her neck.

"You are thinking thees is not a gun," the woman said. "You are thinking eet is something else. A lipstick perhaps."

"No. No, I believe you. It's a gun. I'll behave."

"*Bon.* Come now." Frenchie prodded Lucy with the weapon. "Thees way." She directed her through the open doorway and down some sort of hallway. They pushed past a swinging door. The floor under Lucy's bare feet changed from smooth linoleum to a gridwork of cold porcelain tiles. The acoustics of the place told her where she was even before Frenchie steered her into a stall.

Lucy groped for the door latch and fumbled blindly with her jammies, not daring to dislodge the blindfold. What was this place, a school? If so, they couldn't be too far from civilization. She could be in the middle of a town. This building could be on a major road, although she doubted it. She'd listened hard since her arrival, straining for hints as to her location. At one point she'd heard a far-off police siren and briefly entertained a fantasy of the entire Nassau County Police Department rushing to her rescue. During lulls in the music, she'd made out birdsong, but muted.

"You are lucky to be a woman, madame. The men . . ." Frenchie lowered her voice to a conspiratorial whisper. "Sometimes they make them use a coffee can. *Barbare.* Ah. But I say too much. Will is always telling me I say too much. He says that is why my name suits me."

And that would be what? Chatty Kathy? Lucy flushed the john and, with Frenchie's assistance, found a sink and soap dispenser. She tilted her head in Frenchie's direction. "You seem like a . . . a nice person. Can I ask you something?"

"*Certainement*, madame."

Lucy leaned in close. She whispered, "Why was I kidnapped? Who's behind this? What are they planning to do to me?"

Her companion laughed delightedly. "You are a naughty one. And so *convaincante*."

While Lucy struggled to recall her high-school French, she heard it again. That pitiful, far-off shriek. Frenchie appeared not to notice.

Back in the room, the woman removed Lucy's blindfold. Lucy blinked at her austere surroundings. She was in a black box of a room, about twenty by twenty feet. The walls, door—even the acoustic ceiling tiles and the plywood nailed over the windows—were painted flat black.

A lone wooden chair occupied the center of the room—her butt was on intimate terms with that hard seat—and a thin, bare mattress lay in one corner. That was it in the way of furnishings, if you didn't count the pair of speakers mounted near the ceiling—dispensing Britney now, with her profound, soul-searching admission that *oops!* she did it again. About a dozen iron rings, some with chains attached, studded the floor and the cinder-block walls.

Signs of wear marred the walls and hardware, telling Lucy she wasn't the first resident of this dingy little torture chamber. What kind of operation were the Powerpuff guys running here, to require this kind of setup? Was this some sort of kidnapping mill? Did they advertise in the yellow pages or was it all word of mouth?

Frenchie was still behind her. "Oh! Where is my head? Don't turn around yet." Lucy heard her fumbling with something. "Eet is the details that are important. Will is always telling me this. I must keep in mind the details. All right, madame. You may turn around now."

She did, and saw a woman with big, frosted hair adjusting the blond Bubbles mask, crumpled now where Lucy's heel had made contact last night.

Frenchie wasn't a young woman. The mask concealed her face, but the crepey, sun-damaged skin and flabby muscle tone—what Savannah called "underarm dingle-dangle"—were revealing. Lucy was thinking mid-fifties. Late forties at the very least. The legs, on display below a body-hugging minidress, were Rockette-perfect.

No, I didn't see her face, Officer, but she's French and she wears the costliest perfume in the world and it wouldn't kill her to do a few triceps presses.

"Are you hungry?" Frenchie asked.

"I guess." Being kidnapped and terrorized always piqued her appetite.

Lucy didn't notice the food tray near the door until Frenchie gestured toward it with the pistol, the same ugly gray-black semiautomatic Will had brandished last night. "Breakfast, madame." She swung the gun in an expansive gesture, her finger on the trigger the whole time. Lucy had to remind herself to keep breathing. She looked at the tray. She saw her birth control pills and . . . Was that what she thought it was?

Frenchie said, "You have here wheatgrass juice and bulgur mush. Very nutritious, *oui?* Very cleansing to the system."

Lucy was well acquainted with wheatgrass juice and bulgur mush. As a child, she'd known nothing but this kind of macrobiotic crap; Taco Bell and Pizza Hut may as well have been in the next galaxy. She'd been as much a captive back then, to Savannah's loopy counterculture lifestyle, as she was now to her abductors. She hadn't tasted real food until she'd lit off on her own at age seventeen.

If Lucy were home, she'd be tucking into a Western omelet with nice oily home fries and about a half pound of bacon right about now. Or maybe she'd have gone out to Wafflemania for a Belgian waffle à la mode and a heap of sausage links. Either way, there'd be about a gallon of hot black coffee on the side. Her stomach whined like a spanked pup.

"Is something wrong, madame?"

"No. No, of course not. It looks—" *prechewed* "—very nutritious."

"You must finish all of it, of course." Frenchie wagged the gun at Lucy, whose heart squirmed into her throat, presumably to make itself a smaller target. "Every bite. You understand?"

"Yes. Fine." *I'll make all gone with the bulgur slop, you silly tart.*

"Bon appétit." Frenchie disappeared through the doorway. The lock turned with a decisive click.

THE DOOR TO 1602 Jefferson Court swung open, revealing a tall woman in her mid-thirties with curly chestnut hair. She was about seven months pregnant. A toddler clung to her leg, begging to be picked up.

Wesley McIntyre offered a disarming smile and a passable Latino accent. "Mrs. . . . ." He pretended to consult his clipboard. "Narby? Anne Marie Narby?"

"Yes?" The woman crouched and lifted the whining child with a grunt, settling her on her hip. She reached into a pocket of her maternity tunic for a tissue to scoop twin ropes of green mucus off the girl's flushed face.

"I've got one about that age," Wesley said, winking at the tyke, who hid her face in her mother's shoulder, then peeked out again and rubbed her eye. "What is she, two? Two and a half?"

"Nineteen months." Anne Marie Narby shifted her burden. "This one's a moose. What's this about?"

"Mrs. Narby, my name is Carl Ramirez. I'm with the volunteer fire department here in Egerton." Wesley tapped his pen on the generic fire department patch he'd sewn onto the left breast of his navy baseball jacket. Egerton was a middle-class suburb of Chicago.

"We gave."

"I know that, and the department is grateful for the support of community residents like yourself. Reason I'm here, every family that makes a donation, we offer a free inspection of all their smoke detectors and fire extinguishers."

"Thanks, but we don't need anything like that." She was already backing up.

Wesley halted the door's swing with a meaty hand. "Is Mr. Narby home?"

"No. He's working."

"Your husband works weekends? Hey, I know what that's like."

"He travels to New York a lot. For business."

"Well . . ." Wesley gnawed his lip, studying his clipboard. From inside the house came a burst of rancorous noise—kids squabbling over a video game, by the sound of it. "See, it was Mr. Narby that scheduled the inspection. He was worried some of your equipment is obsolete."

"He was?"

"Can you tell me this, Mrs. Narby? Is your kitchen fire extinguisher the ABC multipurpose type?"

Mrs. Narby frowned. The child fussed to be let down, and her mother wearily complied.

"I'll be in and out in a jiffy," Wesley said. "Two, three minutes, tops."

"Mom," a boy called from the depths of the house. "Where are the Ched'r Wheelz?"

"There's a case in the basement," Mrs. Narby called. "Don't make me run the stairs."

"Kid's got good taste." Wesley patted his paunch, chuckling. "Those things are my downfall."

The little girl rubbed her face on her mother's pants leg, smearing snot. She raised her chubby arms again, whining. Stepping past the threshold, Wesley went to lift her. "Ya mind?"

"She's got a cold," Mrs. Narby warned.

"I should be worried? After all the bugs my kids've brought home?" He swung the tot into his arms. She detonated a big, juicy sneeze right in his face. He laughed. "Bulls-eye."

Forty-five minutes later, Wesley waved goodbye from the front porch, gingerly so as not to drop any of the dozen bags of Ched'r Wheelz Anne Marie Narby had pressed on him. He found the nearest Burger King drive-thru, parked, and dug out his cell phone.

"What are you eating?" Joe demanded.

"Grilled chicken sandwich. No mayo. Side salad." Wesley licked Whopper residue off his fingers and hammered home the last of the fries.

Joe wasn't buying it. "They're going to have to let out your tux, you know that, don't you? You won't be able to squeeze into it by December. And there's that little matter of your *cholesterol?* Are you drinking plenty of water at least?"

"Uh-huh." Wesley pried the lid from his thick shake and sucked down a wad.

"When will you be home?"

"Can't get a flight out of O'Hare till morning." Bad luck. He'd hoped to get back to New York in time to derail Frank Narby's rescue mission; he'd had no luck getting through to him by phone. In light of what he'd just learned, he didn't want the idiot getting himself killed just yet.

"Last-minute flights. Hotel. This has turned into an expensive trip." Joe made that little fretting noise Wesley had always found both endearing and exasperating. "We shouldn't talk long. These are roaming minutes," Joe said. "Chicago's out of your calling area."

"Don't worry about that. It's an investment. This one's gonna pay for the wedding, Joe."

The line was silent a moment. "Are you serious?"

Wesley laughed. "It's just like I figured."

"I do not believe it. That weasely son of a bitch. What's that slurping sound?" Joe was on full alert now. "You got a thick shake, didn't you? Grilled chicken my ass."

"Okay, I'll get off now."

"No!" Joe said. "Tell me everything."

"I don't have all the juicy details yet, but it seems old Frankie tied the knot with the second Mrs. Narby twelve years ago. Big Italian wedding. I saw the album. Only—whoops!—he forgot to divorce the first Mrs. N."

"How embarrassing."

"I love it when you giggle," Wesley said.

"Shut up. That was a manly chortle."

"Frank and Anne Marie didn't waste any time. They've got five cookie snatchers, age one and a half to eleven, with number six on the way."

"Oh my God, that poor woman," Joe said.

"She's raising them in a crappy little split-level with a postage-stamp yard." Wesley tore open a bag of Ched'r Wheelz. "It's Dogpatch, Joe—a free-range kiddie farm. You could fit Anne Marie's whole house into Lucy's greatroom, practically. Guess there wasn't much bread left for family number two."

"So he, what, commutes halfway across the country from one family to the other?"

"Basically. Company headquarters and East Coast distribution are in Queens. Midwest facility is out here in Chicago. Guess where he's been spending more and more of his time."

"And Lucy doesn't suspect a thing?"

"Nope, and neither does Anne Marie," Wesley said. "If Narby had half a brain, he'd let Lucy cut him loose like she wants and thank the god of bigamous fools she never found out. But he's determined to keep them both, and that's good news for me and you. Next time you talk to the caterer?"

"Yeah?"

"Cancel the Korbel. Tell him to lay in Dom Perignon."

5

"**S**HE LIKES YOU," Will said.

Lucy jerked her head away as her captor, still in the ridiculous mask and gray hoodie, brought the fat white mouse close to her face. She would have jumped up on the chair, but seeing as she was shackled hand and foot to the rough black wall, that wasn't an option.

Somewhere between the bulgur gruel and the wheatgrass chaser, she'd decided there was something fishy about this whole operation. This latest scenario was a case in point. If Lucy were to kidnap someone, she'd refrain from turning her victim into a living depiction of every corny dungeon cartoon she'd ever seen, the ones with bearded, bedraggled prisoners exchanging bon mots while dangling by their wrists.

Not that she was actually dangling. Her arms were stretched over her head, secured to iron rings; her feet, similarly restrained, were nevertheless on solid ground. Will had carefully calibrated the length of chain and degree of slack. It was as if he wanted her uncomfortable, but not too uncomfortable. Dungeon Lite.

It was just Will this time; the big Irishman was absent. The background "music" still blared, the same vacuous lyrics in the same jailbait voices, the same synthesized rhythms assaulting her over and over and over. At least Will had dropped that bizarre "What kind of game are you playing?" business, though if Lucy had her druthers, she'd take the interrogation over the rodent any day.

Will let the little varmint crawl on his hand. A shudder racked Lucy.

Josephine, they called the thing. Someone's twisted idea of a pet. Hadn't these sick creeps heard of dogs and cats? Lucy would sooner cuddle up to a rattlesnake than willingly touch something like that.

He moved the animal so close, its twitching whiskers brushed her cheek. She choked out a sob. She looked into the beast's pink eyes and felt her nutritious, cleansing breakfast begin to rise.

"Please . . ." she pleaded in a tiny voice. "I can't . . . can't breathe."

"Aw, don't be like that. Here, she wants to give you a kiss."

Lucy's panic bubbled over. She screamed and thrashed, pulling hard against the iron shackles.

"All right, take it easy." Will backed up a step. "You're going to hurt yourself." He brought his left hand up to seize the mouse as it moseyed up his right forearm, and that was when she saw it.

He was missing a finger. Specifically, the pinky of his left hand.

A change seemed to come over him. She sensed him mentally switching gears as he deposited Josephine on the bare mattress. He reached into the pocket of his sweatshirt and tossed the mouse a handful of KrunchWorks O-Zings, onion-flavored extruded potato rings—Lucy recognized them instantly—which Josie pounced on with unalloyed ardor. Lucy shuddered and averted her eyes.

Will pulled a key ring from the pocket of his jeans and unlocked a small metal panel set in the wall, revealing several electrical switches and knobs. He flipped one and the music died, right in the middle of Britney's breathy confession that she's a slave for you. The abrupt silence, after about eight hours of warbling bimbos, was such a relief, Lucy practically wept with the sheer visceral pleasure of it.

Will planted a palm on the wall next to her head. He leaned in, just a little. "Better?"

"Yes." She took a deep breath. "Thank you."

He tucked back a strand of dark hair that had fallen over her face. His smoky voice got smokier. "You know, things don't have to be so hard for you here."

"Oh." Her voice was barely audible. "No?"

"Your stay could be much more enjoyable." He trailed a fingertip down her throat and idly traced the vee collar of her pajama top. His eyes locked on hers through the mask's twin holes. "For both of us."

Lucy's throat constricted as he moved closer still. He smelled good, dangerously seductive. Like a man-flavored birthday cake. He dipped his head to her temple and slid the mask up. She couldn't see his face, but she felt his humid breath stirring the short strands along her hairline.

He smoothed back her hair and pressed a delicate kiss to the tip of her ear. She emitted a little gasp. "You like being in control," he whispered, "out there."

Since when had she ever been in control of anything? she wondered, but then he brushed his lips along her jawline. It felt good, and that was bad. Their chests touched. She tried to squirm away, but the chains and Will's hand on her waist kept her pinned.

"But you're not out there," he said. "In here, I call the shots." He nibbled the base of Lucy's neck. The ripple of pleasure shocked her. His hands moved on her body, lightly fondling, his touch sensual but not overtly intimate. Her eyes drifted closed.

They flew open when she heard the scream—the same hoarse, agonized cry as before, louder now that the music was off.

The sound had the effect of a fire hose at full throttle. What on earth was she doing, responding to this maniac? If this was the Stockholm syndrome, it sure as hell hadn't taken her long. Eight hours had to be some kind of world record for getting hot for one's captor.

Will continued to nuzzle and caress her.

"Don't," she said.

His voice was a husky murmur against her throat. "Am I going to have to gag you again?"

"Please." Her voice quavered. "Stop. This is . . . I don't want this."

"I think you do." He kissed her collarbone, while toying with the top button of her pj's. "I think you want it hard and fast against this wall."

"No." Tears of panic clogged her throat. "Please. Don't do this."

Will lowered his mask and straightened away from her. He studied her for a long moment. Lucy was shaking so hard, only her restraints kept her upright. Slowly, deliberately, he pressed his palm to the center of her chest. Her heart was a battering ram. She couldn't fill her lungs.

"Lucy." He dropped his hand. "You know how to put on the brakes. Did you forget?"

She could make no sense of his words. "Just . . . just stop. Please."

He sighed in exasperation, a sentiment echoed by his body language. "That's not how it works. You know that."

"I don't . . . how what works?"

He tossed up his hands. "I never thought I'd hear myself say this, but Mick was right. I should've pulled the plug back in your kitchen when Tweedle Dee and Tweedle Dum showed up."

He stalked to the mattress and scooped up the corpulent mouse, now snoozing amid O-Zing crumbs. He started to tuck Josie into his sweatshirt pocket, then glanced at Lucy and set the beast on the floor near her shackled feet. "Wouldn't want you to get lonely." Then he flipped two switches in the electrical panel, turning on the music full blast and turning off the overhead fluorescents.

"No!" she cried as the room was plunged into impenetrable blackness. "Wait!"

The door swung open, turning Will into a shadowy silhouette. "We're going to have an interesting chat when this is all over, Mrs. Narby."

WILL STEPPED OUTSIDE into dazzling sunshine and shirtsleeve temperatures: a taste of summer in early April. The building at his back was a long, low-slung stretch of pale tan bricks set well back from the road, the very essence of spare postwar architecture. The first time he'd set eyes on this Stalinesque pile, he'd dubbed it the Gulag—a prescient name, all things considered, and long since shortened to "the Goo."

Lucy's screams were audible even through the boarded-up windows, but Will never looked back as he ambled a hundred yards to the sprawling Queen Anne Victorian he called home. The house, once a proud painted lady, had already begun showing her age back in the 1950s when a Presbyterian congregation held its first services there. The church eventually erected the Goo, which housed a sanctuary, classrooms, commercial kitchen, and social hall. Will had purchased the three-acre property in the early nineties when the growing congregation pulled up stakes and moved to larger digs.

He'd been eighteen at the time, his TV days long over. Still, the enduring popularity of *In No Time* translated into a respectable annual income for the former child star. Respectable, not bottomless as some seemed to think. The princely sum that had secured this property came from an altogether different source—a sudden, secret windfall that only two other people knew about.

In No Time had teetered on the brink of cancellation for two and a half seasons in the early eighties until Will's abrupt departure sealed the show's doom. Ironically, the notorious details of that departure immediately elevated *In No Time* from forgettable sitcom to cult classic, ensuring syndicated reruns in perpetuity. The show's signature catchphrase *"I'm having conniptions!"* had long ago been absorbed into the popular lexicon, taking its place alongside such venerable chestnuts as *"What you talkin' 'bout, Willis?"* and *"He's dead, Jim."*

Likewise, the show's tragic young star had become a household name. Thankfully, people rarely made the connection between cute, carrot-topped Ricky Baines and thirty-four-year-old Will Kitchen, currently playing the part of a grown-up.

He was halfway to the house when the sound of car tires on gravel brought his head around. He watched the dark green Acura roll up the long driveway at the far side of the property and disappear behind the Goo. There was a little parking lot back there, a weed-choked strip of asphalt that hadn't been replaced or even resurfaced since the church days. Will wasn't what you'd call handy. The list of needed repairs just kept growing.

He retraced his steps and met his half sister, Judith, as she strolled around the near side of the building. She pushed up her Ray-Bans to hold back her chin-length blond hair, and the two exchanged cheek-pecks. As they started toward the house, she squinted at the action on the big wraparound porch. "What's Fergus doing to Cuba?" By the next breath, she'd figured it out. "That screwy old crackpot."

"Fergus isn't so old. Fifty-four," Will said. "Only seven years older than you. I can't argue with screwy or crackpot."

She grimaced. "He's going to make the poor girl look even more ridiculous."

"Ridiculous" wasn't how Will would describe the fifteen-year-old runaway. "Complicated," maybe. He served as unofficial guardian to Cuba Johnson, a discarded child trying to hide her emotional neediness beneath a fragile veneer of don't-give-a-shit. Will could identify with the girl's pain all too well.

Of course, Judith was referring to Cuba's physical appearance: the lank hair, dyed shoe-polish black, and the grungy boy's clothing she insisted on wearing, mostly vintage thrift-shop finds, including the patch-bedecked Boy Scout shirt she threw on over her T-shirt most days. The shirt was from the eighties, Will figured, and several times too large for her slender frame.

Cuba was one of Will's "strays," as Judith called them, one of the handful of permanent houseguests who'd drifted into his life and home over the years, and stayed. They'd become his family in a way.

Tom was on the porch, too. The nine-year-old lifted Cuba's brown and white lop-eared rabbit, Hasenpfeffer, off her lap. He held it awkwardly against his chest, squeezing it tighter when its hind legs jerked, whispering something close to its head. A balloon expanded in Will's chest. This was his son, his precious boy. He loved him so much, it scared him sometimes. He'd do anything to keep his child safe.

As he and Judith climbed the porch steps, Will confronted Gabrielle Fonteneau, stretched out on the bench swing, reading *In Style* magazine. "Gabby, how can you just sit there and watch that big, dumb Irishman maim this poor child's head?"

Cuba sat in another rocker, her narrow shoulders draped with a towel, the rabbit once more on her lap. Fergus stood behind her, using Gabby's pinking shears to turn the girl's chin-length black hair into freaky little spikes. All three of them cast disdainful glances at Will.

Gabby looked up from her magazine. "Eet is very fashionable, this cut. *C'est le dernier mode.* And Cuba is perfect for it, the dainty head, the big eyes. Fergus knows what he is doing."

"Why, thank you, Gabby, for that vote of confidence." Fergus's shaggy eyebrows arched, twin chinchillas facing off over smiling eyes the color of Irish whiskey. "As a show of gratitude, you're next in this chair. A free trim."

"*Certainement.* So long as you understand, you cut my hair, I cut yours."

Fergus was vain about his long, light brown hair. When he wore it loose, like now, it came practically to his waist. "Maybe I'll sneak up on you," he told Gabby, and snapped the shears menacingly.

"You do that." She flipped the page of her magazine. "Then I will take those things and I will snip off something of yours, something you will miss perhaps a bit more than I will miss my hair, *oui?*"

"Ha!" Cuba hooted. In her lap, the bunny flinched.

He chewed back a grin. "I wouldn't put it past you."

Judith stared pointedly at Fergus's blue and gray plaid kilt, which he'd paired with a Wile E. Coyote T-shirt. "Well, that thing should provide easy access to her target. If it's true what they say about what one wears—or doesn't wear—under a kilt."

"Maybe it's true and maybe it isn't," he said, as another chunk of Cuba's hair dropped to the plank floor of the porch. "But I tell you what, Mrs. Drinkwater, you're welcome to find out. Just reach one of those dainty hands under there and have a pull."

"You don't get an offer like that every day, Jude," Will said. "Better hurry or he'll change his mind." He leaned against the wooden balustrade, which squeaked under his weight and began to list toward the shrubbery. He jumped back. Okay. Something else to add to the repair list.

"What are Fergus and Aunt Judy talking about?" Tom stood by Cuba and petted Hasenpfeffer.

"Never mind, *chéri.*" Gabby wore a mysterious little smile as she rubbed a scented perfume ad on her wrist. In French she told him, "They are just being silly, those two." Tom rolled his eyes theatrically and answered, in the same language, "They're *always* being silly."

Idly Judith lifted the fur-covered pouch hanging on the front of Fergus's kilt. "You know, I hate to break it to you, but only Scots can get away with this getup. You're Irish in case you haven't noticed."

"I'll thank ye not to be fondlin' me sporran, Mrs. Drinkwater."

She frowned. "Why do you call me that?"

"Why, it's your name, is it not? A little more off the sides, lass?" he asked Cuba, who lifted a hand mirror and examined her shorn head from various angles.

"Yeah, okay. But don't cut off the scraggly stuff. I like that."

"My name is Judith." She scowled at Fergus. "You call me Mrs. Drinkwater just to make some kind of stupid point. You've been doing it for years, and I don't like it."

"Why, I just mean to show respect."

"You just mean to show insolence," she said. "You're just trying to aggravate me."

"Not that it ever works," Will observed.

Fergus was all wide-eyed innocence. "Since when is it insolent to address a fine, respectable widow lady by her proper title?" *Snip, snip.*

Judith planted her hands on her hips. "Since when is it gentlemanly to bait a 'fine, respectable widow lady' just to see her lose her cool?"

"Well now, there I must plead guilty, Mrs. Drinkwater. The way you're lookin' now, with those bonny eyes spittin' blue fire, your color all high like you've just been—" He cut his eyes toward Tom "—tickled good and proper—"

"Oh, for the love of—"

"Why, I just can't help myself, that's all there is to it. I plead guilty as charged." *Snip, snip.*

She stabbed a manicured nail close to his nose. "What you're *guilty* of is a failure to mature. You are a *child* and you always will be. You know why? Because you *like* it that way."

"Will you two get a room?" Cuba cried.

"I could turn the hose on them," Will offered.

"What is *wrong* with you people?" Judith said. "This is not about *sex.*"

"Uh-oh." Tom clapped his hands over his ears, giggling.

"If you two aren't engaged in some tediously protracted mating ritual," Will asked her, "why does Fergus's accent become pronounced only when you're around?"

"That's not true." She glanced at Gabby for confirmation. The Frenchwoman shrugged, the mysterious smile still in place.

"It's true, Aunt Judy," Cuba said. "You two should totally hook up and put the rest of us out of your misery."

"He always sounds like that." Judith turned to Fergus. "You always sound like that."

In a thick Yiddish accent he said, "Like vhat? You think I pay attention to how I sound? Feh!"

"Has it occurred to you," Cuba asked Judith, "that Fergus has been in this country, like, forty years? He cranks that accent up and down. It's his babe magnet."

"Impudent brat," Fergus said. "Show some respect for your elders."

Cuba flipped him the bird. He pretended to close the pinking shears' snaggleteeth around the upraised middle finger.

"Cuba," Judith said, "do you really think that's an appropriate gesture to teach Tom?"

"I knew it already," Tom said. "Aunt Judy, do you want Fergus to be your boyfriend?"

"Of course not, honey. We're just friends."

In a brogue as thick as Mulligan stew, Fergus said, "To be sure, a refined lady like your aunt Judy would never *dream* of consortin' with a great Irish brute like meself. I'm too far beneath her, don't ye know? Sure and doesn't she have that *fine* Dr. Milton payin' her court in style like she deserves."

"Oh, I give up." To Will she said, "He's worse than you are. Neither of you will ever grow up."

Will grabbed a beer. "Growing up is overrated."

Not that he expected Judith to agree. Mick's birth twenty-four years ago had marked an abrupt turning point in her life. No more multi-city rock tours. No more screwing her way through the bus, from lead singer to lowliest roadie. No more hazmats eagerly filtered through lung tissue, nasal passages, and stomach lining. Once the blessed event was imminent, the former Groupie of the Year settled into single motherhood and a series of dead-end jobs with flexible hours that allowed her to raise her son but not to claw her way out of the ranks of the working poor. Richard Baines, Sr., expressed his disappointment in her lifestyle choices by snapping shut his checkbook and refusing all contact with his daughter and grandson.

In his more forgiving moments, Will almost pitied the old prick. His two children had managed, themselves, to produce only bastards—not one legitimate heir between them. So much for visions of dynastic glory.

Eventually Judith had married Donald Drinkwater, urologist and deacon. She got all church lady, devoting her life to doing good works and posting bail for her no-account son. By then, she'd given up any hope of a reconciliation with their father. Deacon Donald succumbed to a triple-bogey heart attack on their country club's golf course last year, leaving Judith a comfortably well off widow. Recently she'd begun dating Roger Milton, the president of the club, whose wife had passed on several months earlier. The two couples used to socialize regularly, so her pairing off with Roger struck everyone in their social circle as both natural and sensible.

"There you go, lass." Fergus whipped the towel off Cuba with a flourish. She tentatively fingered her new do.

"Gabby, I've got a little job for you." Will jerked his head toward the Goo.

"Let me!" Cuba jumped up, clutching the rabbit to her chest.

Will held up his hand to forestall the girl's latest plea. "I told you before—"

"Not fair. Everyone gets to participate but me."

"I don't," Tom said.

"Duh. You're nine. Come on, Will." Cuba tugged on his sleeve. "I can do anything Gabby can do. I can, what, tie someone up, get in their face." She screwed up her delicate features and mimed holding a gun, a less-than-convincing display considering she cradled a bunny rabbit in the other arm. "Up against the wall, motherfucker."

Judith rolled her eyes. "Could you *please* watch your language in front of Tom?"

"We'll talk about it when you're eighteen," Will said. "This is nonnegotiable."

"I probably won't even be here when I'm eighteen," she muttered. "If my fucking parents decide—"

"Cuba!" Judith said.

"Aunt Judy, I've *heard* those words *before*," Tom said. "It's not gonna make me say 'em."

Fergus agreed. "That's right, Mrs. Drinkwater. Just because Cuba chooses to be a potty-mouth doesn't mean the rest of us have to lower ourselves to her level."

Outwardly Cuba fretted that her mother and stepfather would force her to return home. Inwardly she had to know what had been clear to Will and the rest of them from the get-go, that her folks wanted nothing to do with their troubled daughter and were counting the days until their legal obligation ended. Her bluster was a coping mechanism, he knew, an effort to convince the world, and herself, that she was wanted.

Gabby had come across the young runaway while Christmas shopping in Manhattan last December. Cuba was just fourteen at the time, panhandling in the East Village with no coat while the wind chill pushed the temperature into the single digits. There were several ways this Dickensian scenario could end if the girl remained on the streets, none of them good. So Gabby brought her home.

Will allowed Cuba to stay indefinitely on the condition he clear the arrangement with her parents. Denise Johnson Tauber and her husband, Len, readily agreed, though they didn't know thing one about Will. Their indifference stunned him. He could have been a sexual predator for all they knew. A pimp or worse. During their meeting at the couple's Jersey City home, Will sensed an undercurrent of jealousy and possessiveness: Denise considered her pubescent daughter a sexual rival.

Will kept the Taubers informed, but it was a one-way communication. Never once had they called to check up on their daughter.

"I will pay our Lucy a visit." Gabby set aside her magazine and teetered on her high-heeled mules down the porch steps. "Is there anything I should know?"

Aside from the fact we've got a take-no-prisoners control freak on our hands? Lucy Narby had stood there in her jammies, chained to a wall, utterly helpless in every respect, yet had managed to get him so twisted around he no longer knew who was calling the shots.

She'd even had him half hoping that little psychosexual scene back there would play itself out, that she wouldn't cut it short and neither would he. A major breach of his own rules, of course, but once the fantasy had sunk its teeth in, there was no shaking it.

I think you want it hard and fast against this wall.

Will should have been prepared for her manipulations; it wasn't as if he hadn't been warned. He needed time to shore up his defenses before facing her again. "She's had enough for now," he told Gabby. "You'll see what I mean when you go in there. Give her a break, and bring her some more of that health-food glop she hates so much."

Cuba made a face. "Oh, *that's* what that shit was. I saw it sitting on the counter. I thought Hasenpfeffer puked up his bunny chow or something."

Judith was brushing Cuba's hair off the porch with the discarded towel. Will plucked it from her fingers. "We need to talk," he murmured, and steered her around the corner to the far end of the porch.

She sighed. It was the unhappy little sigh she reserved for conversations about her son. "What happened with Mick last night?" she asked when they'd settled on Adirondack chairs out of earshot of the others.

"He was out of control, Jude." Will's tone was gentle, but he refused to mince words.

"How did he get the broken nose?"

"He got too rough. She responded in kind."

Judith said nothing; he let her imagination fill in the blanks as she extracted a pack of smokes from her bag and lit up.

"This kind of work takes self-discipline," he said. "Mick doesn't have it."

She turned away to exhale a stream of smoke. "No." After a moment she added, "I shouldn't have asked you to take him on. Thanks for trying."

He shrugged. There was nothing more to say. "So how are things going with Roger?"

"It's a little awkward. I always feel like Donald and Barbara are hovering over our shoulders." It was her turn to shrug. "But we always have a nice time together."

Will arched an eyebrow. "You sure you can handle all that excitement?"

"For your information, Roger and I are going to Bermuda tomorrow, for a week. It's a last-minute thing. Very impulsive. Doesn't *that* qualify as exciting?"

"You two going to share a room?" he asked.

"Yes."

"How many beds?"

Judith's gaze slid away. "I'm not ready. He's okay with it."

"The soul of chivalry, our Roger. Which brings us to Bachelor Number Two." Will propped his crossed ankles on the railing. "When are you and Fergus going to stop dancing around and get down to it?"

She groaned. "Don't you start."

"You used to like the wild men."

"That was another life. Some of us mature with age."

"Oh, I don't know." He cocked his head. "Some tastes, one never outgrows. Grandpa Will ate Jiffy Pop for breakfast every morning of his life."

"Fergus isn't Jiffy Pop. He's . . ." She reached over the railing to tap the ash off her cigarette. "He's Jell-O shots. Seems like a fun idea at the time, but then there you are, hugging the bowl, promising yourself, never again."

"What's Roger?" He answered his own question. "Oatmeal. Not too exciting, but you know what you're getting."

"I like oatmeal."

"You tolerate oatmeal. But deep down, you're a Jell-O shots kind of gal."

"Just for the record," she said, "I would never consider getting involved with a man who's as secretive about his background as Fergus Dowd is. I half expect to see his mug shot every time I turn on *America's Most Wanted*."

"That's called a mysterious past. It's supposed to drive the girls wild."

"He was either a mobster or a spy, I can never quite decide." She shot him a look. "You can tell me. It won't go any further."

"What makes you think I know?"

"Okay, play it coy. I don't care."

"Let me ask you this," he said. "If you were to find out all about him, and it turned out to be something not quite kosher, where would your priorities lie?"

"You mean would I turn him in?"

"Fergus being your good friend and all." He smirked. "Like you told Tom."

"That's not a fair question. We could be talking, I don't know, double agent or something."

"What, like selling classified information? To who?"

"It was just an example." But there was a speculative gleam in her eye.

"Well, you know . . ." He lowered his voice and leaned toward her. "I did meet him shortly after the collapse of the Soviet Union. That probably put a lot of spooks out of work."

She narrowed her eyes, trying to decide how full of shit he was.

He shrugged. Spread his hands. "I'm just saying."

"You have a vivid imagination," she drawled, but her color was high, and unless his eyes deceived him, she was breathing a tad faster.

"Jell-O shots," he said. "You never forget your first one."

6

LUCY SAT CROSS-LEGGED on the mattress, valiantly choking down her steamed tofu and carrot juice, when the lock turned and the door creaked open. Probably Frenchie again, demanding to know why Lucy hadn't finished her meal yet. Or perhaps the big Irishman was putting in another appearance. Maybe this was the boss man himself, back for more of whatever that was he'd treated her to a few hours earlier. Seduction? Sexual intimidation? If simple ravishment were his aim, she'd be a ravished woman by now.

The music still blared, but at least Frenchie had turned on the lights and let her down from the wall. Most important, she'd removed Josephine from the premises. Lucy had hovered on the brink of gibbering, tongue-swallowing panic the entire time she'd stood there chained up in the dark. *They're going to forget I'm in here*, her inner voice had sniveled. *I've lost feeling in my arms.* Whenever she'd managed to get a tentative grip on her composure, that disgusting beast licked a toe or scurried over her instep. Lucy's throat was sore from screaming.

To her surprise, a kid slipped into the room, a skinny boy in his early to mid teens, by the looks of him, but since that crumpled Powerpuff mask covered his face, it was impossible to tell for sure. He wore baggy jeans and a baggier Boy Scout shirt, and his black hair stuck up in artfully unruly clumps. He shut the door quickly and stood with his ear pressed to it for several seconds before slipping the key ring into his jeans pocket and pulling out the now familiar SIG-Sauer.

What was an underage kid doing here? Was this someone's idea of a swell after-school job? *Gee, should I go with McDonald's or the kidnapping ring?*

"I'm not finished," Lucy said. The kid seemed confused, so she indicated the magnificent repast before her. "Frenchie—uh, the lady said I have to eat it all, but she just brought it a little while ago, so . . ." She forked another chunk of gelatinous bean curd into her mouth and washed it down with carrot squeezings.

The boy started to nod at the reasonableness of this statement, then seemed to catch himself. His body language got all movie-villain tough. He gesticulated with the gun. "You better eat all that health-food shit or I'll put one right between your eyes."

Lucy gaped. "You're a g—" She bit her lip.

The kid stood frozen for a second, then whipped off the mask. "Of course I'm a girl. What did you think?"

"I . . . um . . . It was hard to tell, you know . . ." *Please don't shoot me.*

The girl glanced down at her own droopy gangsta pants and shapeless Scout shirt, liberally sprinkled with what appeared to be cat hair. Her fingers drifted to her short hair, the roots several shades lighter than the inky tips. She had a cute little face, now that Lucy could see it.

"I like the hair," Lucy said.

"Yeah?" She looked heartbreakingly insecure in that instant. "Fergus cut it."

"Fergus?"

"Big guy?" The girl reached up to indicate height. "Way long hair? Irish?"

"Oh. Yes, of course. Fergus. A man of surprising talents." Lucy kept her tone casual. "So what's your name?"

"Cuba," she said without hesitation, and speared the audio speakers with a malignant glare. Britney was *oops*ing again, at maximum volume. "Do we *have* to listen to this shit?"

"Um . . . not if you want it off." Cuba didn't seem to know how to accomplish that, so Lucy pointed to the electrical panel. "The switches are in there. One of those keys you have opens it."

"Cool." Cuba chattered as she located the right key and flipped switches until the music stopped. "So Will asks me to make a Britney-

Christina mix album, and I'm, like, what the fuck? Can't be for him—he's all about jazz, classic rock. Some bluegrass. Some Motown. So these tunes are for you, huh? Did you, like, special-order 'em? No offense, but you're kinda old for Britney."

Did I *special-order* this music? Lucy wondered if she'd heard right. Clearly this girl had missed a few company memos.

Lucy scooped the last wad of tofu into her mouth and bullied it down her gullet. She tilted the empty bowl to show Cuba, who shuddered in revulsion. "That other woman," Lucy said, "with the French accent. What's her name again?"

"Gabby."

The Frenchwoman's words came back to Lucy. *Will is always telling me I say too much. He says that is why my name suits me.*

She had all their names now, first names anyway, and she'd seen a couple of faces. It was a start.

"Those are cool." Cuba indicated Lucy's pj bottoms, white with little pastel telephones printed on them. They didn't match her top, anthropomorphized vegetables on a field of yellow. "Where'd you get 'em?"

"Don't do that."

"Don't do what?" Cuba was scratching behind her ear with the barrel of the gun, her finger firmly on the trigger. Lucy almost threw up. "Oh." The girl shrugged and pointed the pistol at Lucy. Big improvement.

"Okay, so . . ." Cuba glanced around, considering. She gestured with the gun. "Stand over there."

Lucy rose and moved to the middle of the room.

"Now, uh . . . sit on the chair."

Lucy did.

Cuba thought some more. "I know—I'll tie you up. Where's the rope?"

"Well, I'm not sure where they keep—"

"Shh." The girl pressed a finger to her lips. She stood still, listening, and Lucy heard it, too. Footfalls. Someone passing in the hallway. The sound receded, and Cuba released a sigh.

Lucy said, "You're not supposed to be in here, are you?"

The big blue eyes got bigger. "Don't narc me out."

I do not believe this.

"It's not fair," Cuba whined. "Will thinks I'm, like, this little kid. He won't let me do anything. I just wanted to show him I can."

"You showed him. You did good."

"Yeah?"

"Sure. A real pro."

"Thanks." Cuba's smile faded. "But don't say anything, okay?"

Lucy mimed zipping her lip. Lord knew she had plenty of practice not saying what needed to be said.

Cuba crept to the door and listened. She wagged farewell with the gun, slipped it into her pocket, cracked open the door and peeked into the hallway. Then she was gone.

Lucy listened to the girl's sneakered feet sprint down the hall. She sat on the chair, staring at the closed door.

The door Cuba had forgotten to lock.

HAL DROVE SLOWLY along Argyle Court, peering at house numbers. Ritzy neighborhood. Judith had done pretty well for herself, but that was no surprise. She'd been merely playing at being the rebel, way back when. He'd known it even then, known it was only a matter of time before she realized being the play toy of a raunchy band like the Puny Earthlings might not be the swiftest career track for a girl whose black-tie sweet-sixteen party at the Waldorf Astoria had been attended by three Kennedy cousins and a Partridge.

So Hal wasn't exactly shocked at the breathtaking speed with which the band's trashiest skank had morphed into Martha Stewart. Not that he'd been at liberty to observe the miraculous transformation firsthand, but buddies on the outside had done a little checking up for him. He'd learned that during the past twenty-five years, Judith had married a solid citizen, squirted out a brat, and lent her good name to the boards of several charitable foundations. Big-bellied babies. Save Bambi. Stuff like that.

Hal didn't hold any of that against her. Hell, it would've been stupid to keep on like she was doing back then, considering her options. Judith might have been mixed up, but she was never stupid. So she'd done a one-eighty, reverted to type. But as for the rest of it . . .

Well, she was going to have to answer for the rest of it. Then they'd talk about her brother.

He rolled to a stop in front of 1530 Argyle. A dark green Acura sat next to a big redbrick colonial on a half acre of knife-edged, mower-striped broadloom. It was dusk. He wished he'd waited for full dark, when his eleven-year-old Hyundai, dented and duct-taped, wouldn't have stood out in this slick neighborhood like the proverbial turd in the punch bowl. Not that it was his car, exactly. It belonged to Karen Schultz.

There were groupies and then there were groupies. Judith had been the conventional type, excited by the proximity to fame and the allure of the forbidden. Sex, drugs, and rock and roll: bringing horny musicians and slutty fans together for half a century. Karen was an altogether different breed, the kind who got her ya-yas by cuddling up to very bad men. She'd started by writing to Hal at Attica—soulful morale boosters that soon gave way to cheesecake photos and dirty letters. Then she was making the seven-hour drive every month. Then twice a month. Then every weekend.

Karen was by no means the first. Hal had spent two and a half decades behind bars. Precisely half his life. He'd learned early on there was no shortage of murder groupies, particularly if the murderer in question possessed all his teeth and was yoked up. But Karen was different for two reasons. She'd latched on to him less than a year before his first parole hearing, and she lived on Long Island—only twenty minutes, as it turned out, from Judith Drinkwater's place in Port Adams. If he believed in God, he would have called it a sign from above.

Hal checked himself out in the rearview. It had been a long time, but he had no doubt Judith would recognize him. His eyes were the same piercing silver-gray, fringed by thick black lashes. Those eyes had served him well. By his fifteenth birthday he'd perfected a sexy, hooded stare that netted him more pussy than he knew what to do with. The angles of his face were sharper now, and a few fine lines had settled around the eyes and mouth, but there were worse things for a guy's looks than a hint of cragginess.

His hair was very short, in contrast to his Puny Earthling days when he'd worn it long. In prison he'd shaved his head, even before it was fashionable, letting the other cons speculate on how he got that wicked scar behind his right ear. He'd let it grow out a bit before his parole hearing, just long enough to conceal the jagged pink ridge. He wasn't as blond as he used to be, and it was coming in gray around the temples, but summer was around the corner. A few days on the beach would restore that golden-boy glimmer. He'd be able to walk into any dimly lit bar and be mistaken for Sting.

He let himself out of the car, strode up the flagstone path to the front door, and stabbed the doorbell. No answer. He rang it twice more, straining his ears for sounds from inside.

Hal glanced around: no one out and about in the immediate vicinity. Casually he strolled around the house. Nothing to see in the windows, most of which were covered with drapes or blinds. But the lights were on. The big backyard was as meticulously landscaped as the front, bordered by flowering shrubs and studded with shade trees, just now coming into bud. He spotted a little garden sitting area in the far corner, and what appeared to be a koi pond, of all things.

Hal thought of the Judith Baines he used to know. He thought about her on the floor of that seedy motel room in Atlanta, bent over a mirror streaked with lines of coke, and him behind her pulling her panties down. A koi pond. He had to smile.

He crossed the fancy multilevel deck to the sliding glass doors. Wouldn't hurt to try, though no one who could afford a spread like this would forget to lock—

The door slid open on a whisper of sound. He found himself in some kind of family room leading into a kitchen that looked like it belonged to one of those TV chefs. The decor was cool, pale elegance, except for the Chinese takeout containers littering the coffee table in front of the giant flat-screen TV. The place smelled like potpourri and lo mein. Somewhere upstairs, "Sympathy for the Devil" was playing. Hal's smile broadened. She always did have a thing for Jagger.

He took the carpeted stairs two at a time.

LUCY HAD BEEN staring at the doorknob so long, her eyes burned. She knew what would happen if she walked over to the door and turned that knob. It would open.

Then what?

It had been a couple of hours since Cuba had slipped out. During that time Lucy had listened, waiting for a lull in activity outside the room. Every time she'd wiped her sweaty palms on her pj's and crept toward the door, she heard someone pass by. Then for a long while they'd all seemed to congregate somewhere down the corridor to the left. The sounds of lively conversation had drifted to her, as well as the mouthwatering aroma of lasagna. Maybe baked ziti. No bulgur slop for her captors, no siree. Their dinner had ended about twenty minutes ago. The place had settled down. All was quiet.

This was it. She'd prayed all day for a chance to escape, and her prayers had been answered, thanks to a careless, preoccupied teenager with a big goddamn gun. Someone was bound to come for Lucy soon, to dispense yet another round of bizarre torment. She couldn't wimp out now. She forced her feet to move, one in front of the other. She stood by the closed door, shaking, hugging herself.

Lucy reached out and wrapped her icy fingers around the brass doorknob. She turned it, held her breath, pulled the door open a fraction of an inch.

And shut it.

I can't do this. They'll kill me. How could she hope to escape this place with all these people coming and going and kissing her ear and—

Lucy grabbed the sides of her head to rein in her swirling thoughts. She told herself not to be rash. Will and his crew hadn't hurt her, not really. If they intended to kill her, she'd probably be dead by now. She should just sit tight, continue to cooperate, and sooner or later this thing would blow over and she'd be back home, with her gourmet coffee beans and her hot, hot shower and the brand-new locks and security system she'd have installed first thing. Who knew? Maybe she'd even meet her deadline for *Johnny Sherlock and the Painted Poodle.*

She nodded. She was comfortable with this decision; it felt natural. It was what she always did, after all, let events unfold on their own, take the path of least resistance.

Well, almost always. She hadn't taken the path of least resistance back at the house. When those three masked maniacs had come at her, she'd fought like a rabid wolverine. She'd acted on raw instinct and thrown everything she had into it. It hadn't been enough, but at least she'd tried. The difference between then and now was that now she had time to think, time to talk herself out of it, as she'd talked herself out of almost every self-assertive action she might have taken during her entire adult life.

The real Lucy, she decided, was the one who'd fought like hell back at the house, the one who'd been willing to slice open her foot on the slim chance she could crash through the French door and lose her attackers in the woods. The one who'd kicked in that insolent bastard's face because *somebody* had to do it.

It was that Lucy who resolutely crossed the room and pressed her ear to the door. Not a sound. She filled her lungs and slowly let the air out. She eased the door open a couple of inches, listened again, and peeked out. The corridor extended farther right than left from where she stood, and was vacant in both directions. The two doors on the right side of the hallway probably led to other rooms like the one she occupied. Men's and women's rest rooms were on the opposite side. She took the shorter route left, willing an exit to appear.

Straight ahead, she saw that the corridor opened into a large space decorated with floor plants and wall hangings; a rowing machine and some other exercise equipment came into view. She hugged the wall as she approached the room and spied, near the entrance, a plate-glass door leading to the outside. Every muscle in her body tensed for the sprint to freedom. She started to cross the threshold, only to spring back and flatten herself against the wall.

In a split-second glance she'd recognized the girl Cuba, sitting at a long dining table huddled over a spiral-bound notebook and some loose papers, her back to the doorway.

Lucy retraced her steps, padding as silently as she could toward the other end of the corridor. As she did, she noticed that the door of the room where she was being held was labeled "C." She tried the knob on door B; it was locked. She hoped to come across something she could use as a weapon.

She expected door A to be locked as well. To her surprise, it swung open and she stood staring at a skinny, youngish man clad only in white Jockey shorts, hanging upside-down in the center of the room. His spindly forearms were duct-taped together behind his back. His face appeared parboiled.

She scooted inside and pulled the door closed behind her. "Oh my God. I've got to get you down from there."

The man frowned in confusion. The speakers in this room dispensed a song she recognized from *The Sound of Music*: Julie Andrews *do-re-mi*'ing her little heart out.

Lucy peered at the chain-and-hook arrangement connecting his leather ankle cuffs to the ceiling. "How long have you been like this?"

"Who are you?"

"Never mind that. We don't have much time." She spotted a straight chair identical to the one in her room. She dragged it close to the man and hopped up on it.

"You can't do that," he said. "He promised me longer."

Had the torture begun to warp the poor guy's mind? "Who promised you?" Straining against his weight, she tried to lift the chain so the hook would slip out of the ring in the ceiling. It didn't move so much as a millimeter.

"Your boss," he said. "The one in the George W. mask."

George W. Bush? What happened to the Powerpuff Girls?

"You really shouldn't be doing this," he said.

"Let me worry about that." Lucy gave another mighty heave. She hadn't made noises like these since she was in labor. Whatever the scrawny twerp weighed, it was too much for her.

"You're not here to rough me up?"

"Don't worry, there'll be no more of that."

"You know what I liked? All that screaming a while ago. Sounded like it was coming from right next door. It was *blood-curdling*. Was that you?"

"'Fraid so."

"Nice touch. I'll tell you who I *really* like, though—that mademoiselle in the Mary Poppins getup." His eyebrows wagged. "I need my spoonful of sugar."

"Let me guess." She gave the chain one more grunting, vein-popping, pushing-the-head-out try. "You despise Julie Andrews and you vote Democrat."

"Why don't you send Mary Poppins back in here? Tell her to bring her umbrella. You ever get smacked with a closed umbrella?"

"Okay, you know what?" Lucy jumped down from the chair and started tearing at the duct tape binding his arms. "I'm going to undo your hands and push this chair under you. Then you're going to do kind of like a handstand to raise yourself up so I can—"

"I get it." He squirmed like an eel with an itch, making it impossible for her to grip the tape. "You're gonna make me *work* for it."

Those strange vibes Lucy had gotten earlier, the nagging sense that something about this operation didn't compute, were back with a vengeance. She couldn't waste any more time here; someone could walk in any second. "Listen." She bent over to look the fellow in the eye. "You just hang in there. I mean . . . you know what I mean. I'm going to come back with help."

"Hey, why aren't you wearing a mask?"

After a quick listen at the door, Lucy slunk out of the room. Great. Now she'd never get do-re-bloody-mi out of her head. At the end of the corridor was a vestibule—and another door to the outside. She sprang for it.

Locked, and the key was nowhere in sight. Through the plate glass she viewed a massive expanse of lawn and trees in the twilit gloom, reinforcing her sense that this place was off the beaten path.

She gave the door another futile tug and quickly scanned her surroundings. A table against the wall held three identical boom boxes. The machines were labeled A, B, and C. Wires snaking from them had been bundled and stapled up the wall to where it met the ceiling. Down the corridor, the wires split into the three classrooms, where they were no doubt connected to the speakers and electrical panels. No sound came from the machines themselves.

Boom box A was on. A stack of CD cases sat next to it, the top one featuring a picture of Julie Andrews belting it out on an Alp. The others were soundtracks from *Mary Poppins* and the stage versions of *My Fair Lady* and *Camelot.* Lucy pushed the Off button. From inside his room, she heard her upside-down pal shout, "Hey! Where'd Julie go?"

She turned her attention to machine C, popping it open to find a recordable CD on which someone had scrawled "Spears/Aguilera for L. Narby." The mix album Cuba had made. Using the table for leverage, Lucy snapped it in two. So there.

The other side of the vestibule had clearly served as a coat room in another life. A mélange of garments hung from three steel rods arranged in a U shape against the walls. They included army camos, police uniforms, nuns' habits, priests' cassocks, a full-body yellow Big Bird costume, a leather Hell's Angels jacket, an intricately detailed gladiator getup, an SS uniform, several head-to-toe burkas, a doctor's white lab coat, and a short-skirted nurse's uniform. Not to mention a whole mess of clown outfits that looked like they'd been purchased at Big and Tall Bozos. A laundry basket sat at one end of the coat rack, piled high with coordinating hats, wigs, and props—everything from a rubber gasmask to a German spiked helmet.

Of more immediate interest were the objects on the wire shelves above the rods. Chains. Ropes. Handcuffs. Shackles. Stacks of blank CDs. About thirty rolls of duct tape; Will must get a volume discount. A stack of empty coffee cans. A pile of knit ski masks. She looked inside a shoe box and saw sticks and tubes of makeup in white and primary colors—the kind of makeup she'd used one Halloween to turn John, then age six, into a clown.

Then there were the masks: a couple of dozen plastic Halloween masks neatly stacked on the shelves. Buttercup, Blossom, and bashed-in Bubbles had been set aside, as had Dubya and Mary Poppins. The presidential pantheon included everyone from Nixon through Obama, the single exception being Gerald Ford. Maybe no one hated him enough. The usual superheroes were present and accounted for, as were various monsters, from Frankenstein to Freddy Krueger, in pliable, full-head latex.

A cardboard carton sat on the shelf. Still on the lookout for a weapon, Lucy reached up and shook it. All that clanking and rattling sounded promising. She started to haul the box down when her gaze lit on an item that had been tucked behind it.

The SIG-Sauer. Just sitting there. She snatched it up. She'd never held a gun. It was heavier than she'd expected. This was the only firearm she'd seen during her ordeal. With any luck, it was the only one in the whole place.

Lucy was debating the wisdom of returning to Cuba, of forcing the girl at gunpoint to free her, when that familiar hoarse shriek split the silence. She jumped. It was louder than before, less muted. It came from behind the closed pocket door that led off the vestibule. How many people were in there? She wondered yet again what they were doing to their poor captive. Those screams were practically inhuman. She pressed her ear to the door and made out voices. She looked at the weapon in her hand.

Lucy knew if she hesitated, she'd just talk herself out of it. As it was, her galloping heartbeat threatened to choke her. She gripped the gun in both hands. Her index finger teased the trigger. She said a quick prayer, yanked open the door, leapt across the threshold . . .

And found herself in a large space outfitted as a living room, with mismatched furniture, lamps, and area rugs clustered into discrete seating areas. Eclectic artwork, including children's drawings, adorned the walls. The voices she'd heard emanated from a gigantic flat-screen television tuned to a shopping channel. If Lucy had ever craved a cubic zirconia butterfly broach with a cunning loop from which to dangle reading glasses, here was her chance. Only $39.95, plus $5.95 shipping. An elderly Asian woman dozed in a recliner not three feet from the blaring TV. A gold AmEx card and cordless phone rested on her afghan-draped lap.

The long wall opposite was interrupted by two sets of double doors, both closed. Creeping to the nearest one, she detected activity behind it— real, honest-to-God human activity this time, by the sound of it. This had to be where the poor woman was being held. Lucy's fingers were so slick with sweat, she barely kept her grip on the gun as she took a deep breath and pushed through the door.

IN JUDITH'S HOUSE, Hal followed the music up the carpeted stairs and down the hall to an open doorway, where he saw two young people on a king-size bed, copulating to the lively beat of "Sympathy for the Devil." A blond guy was on top of a slim girl with blue-tipped platinum hair, her ankles hooked over his shoulders, her tiny tits rocking, her sharp gasps keeping time to Jagger's irreverent lyrics.

It was a pretty good show and Hal watched for a while until the girl looked over and screamed. Romeo didn't even slow his rhythm as he demanded, "What the fuck is this?" He'd gotten his nose broken recently; it was bruised and swollen.

"Don't rush on my account." Hal leaned on the doorframe, arms crossed. "I'll wait."

The stud would have kept going, but his girl kicked up a fuss and knocked him off her. If anything, the smoky black makeup rimming her eyes only emphasized her youth; this little girl wouldn't be legal for three more years at least. She made no effort to cover up but simply glared at both men, snatched up a pack of smokes by the bed, and stalked into the adjoining master bathroom. The door slammed as the next song started: "I Can't Get No Satisfaction."

The kid spread his arms in a gesture that said, *You happy?* He glanced around and grabbed a pair of jeans off the floor. "I don't know who you are, but if you're still here when I zip up, I'm gonna toss your ass down the stairs."

"Aren't you a little old for a stunt like this?" Hal asked. "Leaving wet spots on Mommy and Daddy's bed?"

With barely one leg in his pants, the kid charged like a pit bull on crack. The heel of Hal's hand shot out and tapped the purple nose. The guy flew backward as if on a string, shrieking and grabbing at his face as fresh blood gushed forth. If he expected his girl to investigate the commotion, he was to be disappointed. The bathroom door remained shut.

The kid sat blubbering on the floor, his back against the bed, legs tangled in the jeans. Hal tossed him the bed sheet. "Get a grip, you pathetic little shit. What's your name?"

"Fuck you."

Hal crossed to the bathroom door and rapped on it. "Hey. What's your boyfriend's name?"

"Juan Carlos."

Hal regarded the sandy-haired fool spitting blood onto his mother's fine linen sheet. "No, this guy here."

"Oh. Mick."

"Thanks, honey."

A cream-colored dressing table and matching chair sat against one wall. Hal hauled the chair in front of the kid and planted himself on it. "I'm going to ask you this just once, Mick. Where are your folks?" Mick started to speak. Hal flipped open his switchblade. "Do yourself a favor, my man. Don't say 'fuck you.'"

"My stepdad's dead."

"Mom?"

"On a date." Still sitting, Mick started to struggle into his jeans.

"When's she getting home?"

Mick shrugged.

"Stepdad, huh?" Hal studied Mick's eyes, the shape of his face. "How old are you?"

"What is this, a fucking job interview?"

"Let me guess," Hal said. "You're twenty-four. Your birthday's . . . sometime in the fall."

Mick's eyes narrowed. "November seventeenth. So what?"

"So Judith has even more to answer for now, that's what."

Mick sopped up blood with the sheet. "If this is about my mom, go bother her and leave me the hell alone."

"Nice to see you're so protective. What did she tell you about your real dad?"

The bathroom door opened and the girl came out. "Take me home, Mick." She plucked her undies off the floor. At some point during Hal's enforced sabbatical, females had started shaving their pussies, a little or a lot. This one had gone for a lightning-bolt design. He still wasn't sure what he thought of the trend. Hot, yeah, but where was the mystery?

"He's a little preoccupied," Hal told her. "If you can wait a bit, I'll give you a lift. What's your name, honey?"

Her gaze flicked over him. An interested smile tugged at her mouth as she wriggled into a sheer black thong. "Winnie."

"Wait for me downstairs, Winnie. Mick and I have to talk."

She gathered her things and started out of the room.

"What, are you nuts?" Mick asked her. "This guy broke into my house. You're gonna get in his car?"

"It's okay," Hal told her. "I'm Mick's dad."

Mick snorted, then choked on a fresh gout of blood. Winnie turned at the doorway and glanced from one man to the other. "Oh yeah, I see it now. Hey." She scowled at Mick. "This jerk-off told me his dad is Keith Richards."

"It worked, didn't it?" Hal asked, and he and Winnie laughed.

"My dad *is* Keith Richards," Mick insisted. Winnie rolled her eyes and sauntered out. "Why'd this dickwad have to ask you my name," he called after her, "if he's my dad? Huh? Dumb bitch."

"You're one smooth operator," Hal said. "I can see why you need that line about Richards."

"You don't know what you're talking about."

"Check it out, sonny." Hal pointed to his own face with the tip of his switchblade. "Look familiar?"

"So you got gray eyes, too," Mick sneered. "So what? You fucked my mom way back when? You back for more? Be my guest. The ice queen could use a good corn-holing—dislodge that stick up her butt."

"You talk about your mother that way?"

Hal never raised his voice. He didn't have to. The quiet menace in his tone drew Mick's gaze to his face, to those eyes so like his own. Mick opened his mouth to speak, then thought better of it. He was learning.

"I don't know what Judith told you about your real father," Hal said, "but here's the deal. I knew your mother twenty-five years ago. We were together the first part of the year till the middle of March. She wasn't with anyone else during that time." Hal had kept her on a short leash—he didn't like to share, and the other guys knew better than to come sniffing around behind his back. "How good are you at arithmetic?" Hal asked. "Can you count back nine months from your birthday?"

"Why should I believe you?" Mick got to his feet and buttoned his fly.

"Richards and I are both guitarists, but the similarity ends there, at least since I got off the dope." Hal gave him a dubious look. "You *want* to look like him? You should've picked Clapton. More of a resemblance *and* he's the better guitarist. For looks alone, Cobain—but he was too young."

Mick had gone still. "You're a guitarist?"

"Used to be."

Mick frowned, studying Hal's face as he pulled on his T-shirt. "Mom said my dad was a guitarist."

Hal stood, pocketed his switchblade, and spun the kid toward the dressing table mirror. He gripped his neck and made him look at the two of them standing side by side. "We can do a DNA test if you want, my man. Or you can open your eyes."

Hot color crawled into Mick's face as he took in the truth. He jerked out of Hal's grasp and faced him. Hal recognized the kid's malignant glower; he'd seen it in the mirror often enough.

Mick's hands balled into fists at his sides. "Get out of here."

"Not yet." Hal settled back on the chair. He folded his arms over his chest. "We have business to discuss."

"Business! You couldn't be bothered sticking around when I was little. What makes you think I wanna have anything to do with you now?" Mick snatched a wad of tissues out of the decorative holder on his mother's dressing table and pressed them to his nose.

"I can't say whether I'd have stuck around or not," Hal said, "but I wasn't given the choice. Your mother didn't tell me about you. Even if she had, I wouldn't have had much quality time with you. I've been in the joint your whole life, Mick. Got paroled last month."

"Bullshit." Mick kept staring at Hal's face. Hal saw the instant he realized it was true. "Jesus. For real? What were you in for?"

"Second-degree murder. Twenty-five to life."

"No shit. Did you do it?"

"Yes."

Mick blinked. A little gust of laughter escaped him. "Jesus," he repeated, with none of the alarm a sensible person might exhibit in similar circumstances.

"Your mother sent me to Attica," Hal said, and Mick's smile faded. "She fed the cops information that got me convicted."

Mick was shaking his head. "Why would she do that? If you two were, you know, tight."

That question had cost Hal a lot of sleep. It couldn't be simple greed; Judith had no clue where he'd stashed the money. Now that he'd made the acquaintance of his son, though, her betrayal was beginning to make sense. "I thought she and I might have a little chat about that," Hal said. "Among other things. But now you're here, and she's not, and I'm thinking it's better this way. There's something I could use your help with. *Son.*" Hal put his arm around the kid's shoulders.

"Yeah, right." Mick eyed him suspiciously. "Like I'd help you with anything. Tell you what—I'll help you find your way outta here, how's that, *Dad?* You're on parole? You're not supposed to have a weapon? Maybe I'll *help* you by not telling the cops about that switchblade in your pocket."

"Two. Million. Bucks." Hal smiled, watching his son. "Yeah, I *thought* that'd get your attention."

"Who's got two mil? Not you."

"I will." He squeezed Mick's shoulder and released it. "We both will."

"What, you want me to help you rob a bank or something?"

Hal shook his head. "We're talking about money I had. Money I stashed away for safekeeping, where no one could possibly stumble across it. All those years inside, that cash was all I thought about. Counting and recounting it in my head. Spending it nine hundred different ways. It's all that kept me sane, that two mil."

"Yeah? So?"

From downstairs Winnie called, "Sometime today, Pops?"

"Did she call me *Pops?*"

"So?" Mick persisted. "The money?"

"So I finally get out and what do you know—the money's not there."

"Like it ever was." Mick tossed the bloody tissues on the carpet and grabbed another handful. "You show up here after all this time like Father Fucking Knows Best and tell me you stuffed two million bucks in a piggybank somewhere, but oops! it walked away. Tell me another one."

"Do you know what happened to your uncle Ricky when he was a kid?"

"I don't have any uncle Ricky," Mick said. "Are you talking about Ricky Baines? My mom's half brother? Used to be on that old TV show *In No Time?*"

"That's the one."

"He changed his name—to Will Kitchen. It was my great-grandpa's name. I don't remember him, but the two of them were kinda close until the old man croaked, like, twenty years ago. What's this got to do with two million bucks?"

"Answer me. Do you know about what happened to your uncle?" Hal asked. "When he was nine?"

"Sure. Everyone knows. He was kidnapped. Held for ransom. Fucker chopped off his finger. So what?"

"So I'm the fucker who chopped off his finger."

LUCY'S DRAMATIC ENTRANCE went unnoticed by the two men playing Foosball in a cavernous room that appeared to be some kind of private amusement arcade. The modernistic stained-glass windows along one wall were an intriguing touch. The men's attention was riveted to the game, their bodies tense as they hovered over their respective sides of the table, wrists jerking on the handles that made the tiny painted soccer players kick the little white ball toward the end goals. *Thwack. Thwack. Thwackthwackthwack.*

Here were her captors, unmasked at last. There was no mistaking Fergus, he of the lofty stature and flowing locks. Fergus exuded a kind of manic idiosyncrasy that made the kilt he wore seem like the most natural thing to throw on.

But the other man. Lucy could only stare. She knew it was Will, though she'd never before seen him without the mask and sweatshirt hood. She'd come to know those intense blue eyes. Those beefy shoulders. But who would have guessed the man was a *redhead!* His hair was a pleasing dark copper hue, not some garish orange, but still. Not at all what she'd imagined.

Get a grip, Lucy commanded herself. *What difference does it make what color his hair is?* She raised the gun in two quaking hands. Will and Fergus had yet to glance her way. She cleared her throat loudly.

The little ball slid past Will's defense into the goal pocket. Fergus roared in triumph.

"Next time," Will grumbled, "don't spin the rods."

Something about Will was disturbingly familiar, but Lucy couldn't put her finger on it.

"Cheer up, lad," Fergus said. "Nobody likes a sore loser."

"Hey," Lucy croaked. She eased a little farther into the room. She raised her voice. "Hey."

"What?" Will said distractedly, never taking his eyes from the Foosball table as he served the next ball.

"Dad, who's that lady?"

The child's voice startled Lucy. She swung the gun toward the far corner, where a young boy and a well-padded old Asian man sat at a hobby table, wielding tiny paintbrushes on what appeared to be a miniature water tower. They'd paused in their work to stare at her.

It took her a moment to realize she was pointing a gun at a child. Shaken, she pivoted once more, taking aim at Will, who'd noticed her at last. He did not share Fergus's gleeful chuckle.

"This lady is one of our guests, son," Will informed the boy.

The gun wobbled in Lucy's two-fisted grip. "This guest has enjoyed as much of your hospitality as she can stand." She jerked her head toward the doorway. "Get the keys. You're letting us out of here. Now."

"Us?"

"Me, that guy hanging upside-down, and the other woman."

The men looked at each other. Fergus asked, "What other woman, lass?"

Lucy glanced around the huge space. She saw commercial pinball and video games, a Ping-Pong table, an inlaid game table set with chess pieces in the shapes of *Simpsons* characters, a sprawling model train layout, shelves crammed with books and board games, and—elevated altarlike on some sort of platform at the far end of the room—a Ping-Pong table. But no keening torture victim.

Will gave her a long, assessing look. "How did you get out of that room?"

"Who cares?" Ridiculously, she didn't want to squeal on Cuba. She gestured with the gun. "Let's go. The rest of you, stay here." She was about to warn them she'd shoot Will if they attempted to intervene, but she couldn't bring herself to utter the threat in front of his son.

Not that any of them appeared concerned. Clearly Fergus was enjoying the show. The boy and old man watched her curiously but without alarm.

From directly behind her came an earsplitting scream. She screamed, too. Whirling around, she spied the source of the noise.

A parrot. All green, except for red tail feathers and a splash of yellow on the back of the neck. It was about the size of a pigeon, a gorgeous animal, its only flaw a misshapen left wing. It perched on the limb of a small bare tree rising from a wooden platform, some sort of avian jungle gym adorned with birdie play-pretties: a length of braided rope, a string of chew toys, assorted shiny objects. The bird paced back and forth on its perch and, with faultless diction, announced, *"You'll put your eye out!"* It underscored this dire warning with another hair-raising shriek.

Lucy's jaw sagged. *This* was what she'd been hearing since she'd arrived. It was this stupid parrot all along, screaming itself silly, not some fellow captive being treated to a bamboo manicure. The parrot bobbed its empty little head. She could almost hear it thinking, *Gotcha!*

Will took advantage of her dumbfounded stupor to pluck the gun from her hands. She roused long enough to put up a brief struggle and pull the trigger.

Click.

The gun had been unloaded all along. No doubt the others had all known that.

The parrot stood on one foot and wagged the other—like a toddler demanding attention. Fergus offered his arm. "Well done, Quint. You foiled the vixen's dastardly plans." Not content with the forearm, the bird tugged at Fergus's sleeve with beak and talons until he let him relocate to the shoulder. "He likes to be the tallest one in the room. You happy now?"

Quint settled himself with a satisfied fluff of the feathers and squawked, *"I'm having conniptions!"*

Will pocketed the pistol. With a long-suffering sigh he asked again, "How did you get out of the room, Lucy?"

A little gasp drew her gaze to the doorway. Cuba stood there, her eyes wide with the realization that she'd neglected to lock Lucy's door. She looked so vulnerable, the mother in Lucy couldn't bring herself to narc out the poor kid.

"I picked the lock," Lucy said.

Will stared at her a long moment. He didn't buy it. Good. He scowled at each of the others in turn, a mute interrogation that yielded no confessions. Cuba had managed to school her expression. Fergus must have caught on, though. Lucy caught him giving the girl a conspiratorial wink. She suspected not much got past the big Irishman.

"I hope you enjoyed your little adventure." Will's fingers circled Lucy's upper arm like an iron band. "Because you're about to pay for it."

The boy's eyes lit up. "Whatcha gonna do to her, Dad?"

Good grief, even the kid was in on it.

Will refrained from answering his son, which Lucy considered an inauspicious sign.

So. Her captor was a daddy. Did Cuba belong to him, too? Could Gabby be their mother? The Frenchwoman was a good deal older than Will, but she wasn't *that* old. A mom-and-pop kidnapping ring. How positively quaint.

The Asian guy addressed Lucy. "Did you really break Mick's nose?"

Mick. One more name to add to her growing roster of ne'er-do-wells. Not that she had any use for it. Lucy doubted she'd get a second chance at escape.

"You broke his *nose*?" the boy asked. "What did it look like? When you punched him. Was there lots of blood?"

"She didn't punch him, lad," Fergus said, "she kicked him. See, the thing we didn't know goin' in, this lady's a kung fu grandmaster. Ninth-degree black belt. Took all three of us to truss her up."

"Wow!" The kid jumped out of his seat and tried a couple of experimental jabs and kicks. He turned to Lucy. "Can you teach me?"

"Sorry, son." Will started to march Lucy out of the room. "The grandmaster will be otherwise occupied for the foreseeable future."

Cuba slid her a surreptitious look: *Sorry.*

For what? Leaving the cookie jar within reach? Lucy was the one who'd opened the lid and taken a great big bite of double-stuff Now I've Done It.

She couldn't bring herself to regret it, though. Whatever happened to her from this point forward, at least she hadn't given up without a fight.

Still perched on Fergus's shoulder, Quint busied himself with the feathers under his bad wing, pausing in his grooming just long enough to squawk out a little melody.

Deep in the recesses of Lucy's brain, a mental switch flipped. She knew that tune. She stopped in her tracks, even as Will tried to bully her out of the room. The bird returned her goggle-eyed stare. What had it said earlier? *You'll put your eye out. I'm having conniptions.* She'd seen this parrot before. She'd heard it spout those same mommy's-had-it-up-to-here phrases. She used to hum that same catchy theme song as a kid.

Savannah had rejected all trappings of modern industrialized society— except for television. Lucy's mother was hooked on the reruns of the shows that had been her favorites as a child. She'd hauled their geriatric thirteen-inch black-and-white RCA from commune to commune all during Lucy's youth.

"I hope you're not planning to beg for mercy." Will yanked on her arm. "I'm not in a particularly merciful mood."

She gaped at him. No wonder he looked familiar. It came back in a rush. All those adolescent Wednesday evenings planted in front of the tube, watching a time-traveling, carrot-topped kid and his loquacious parrot in a goofy sitcom called *In No Time.*

"Oh my God," she said, "I've been kidnapped by Ricky Baines!"

7

WESLEY HAD GIVEN Frank directions to the place where he said they were keeping Lucy. It was a sizable spread with a couple of buildings—a massive relic of a house and a one-story tan-brick structure. Fairly isolated for this part of the Island. Frank drove slowly past the place, scoping it out. He continued about two hundred yards before parking his Mercedes S500 off the deserted road. He was so jazzed on adrenaline, he was practically vibrating.

That morning Wesley had given him a .38 and shown him how to point and fire the thing. Frank had wanted a semiautomatic—he savored a mental image of himself aiming a 9-millimeter in that cool sideways slant like he'd seen in the movies—but that fat fag had insisted on a revolver. A simpler mechanism, he'd said; less chance of it jamming. Frank had pleaded his case, but Wesley refused to budge.

The guy owned a mini arsenal, as it turned out, at least a dozen assorted guns, some registered, others sans pedigree, like this well-worn Smith & Wesson. If the police found it on Frank, it couldn't be traced back to the PI. For a man who didn't like to carry a weapon, Wesley sure had a lot of them. At least give me a silencer for this thing, Frank had said, I may have to shoot out some locks. Turns out you can't silence a revolver. Who knew?

Frank had again tried to get Wesley to accompany him, but the PI had to go out of town that day. Tracking someone down for one of his matrimonial cases, he'd said. Well, a fellow had to make a living. And anyway, Lucy would be a lot more impressed when Frank rescued her all by his lonesome.

It was close to three a.m. Frank cursed the bright full moon. Not that he'd be that easy to spot. He'd found a military surplus store with a back room that catered to demanding customers with deep pockets. He was dressed in green and black night camos, head to toe. He flipped open the little camo face paint kit and smeared matching greasepaint onto his cheeks and chin.

Next came the night-vision goggles. He adjusted the straps, turned them on, and saw his surroundings materialize in shades of luminescent green, almost as clear as day. He could have gotten ordinary NVGs for a couple of hundred bucks; instead he'd shelled out five grand for a state-of-the-art fourth-generation model. Hey, wasn't his Lucy worth it? Plus, these things were just so cool; he'd always wanted an excuse to buy a pair.

In addition to the .38, Frank carried a big-ass British army pig-sticker knife. The final touch was a night camo helmet.

He imagined Lucy's reaction when he came for her, the weepy gratitude, the awe and excitement she'd be helpless to conceal. Hell, *look* at him. He was goddamn Rambo.

Frank started back toward the kidnappers' lair, slinking through the woods, keeping out of sight of the road. The air was frosty, but he was too wound up to feel the cold. The buildings came into view. His heart banged. Which one was she in? Security lights illuminated the two entrances to the tan building. He'd be too exposed. The house was dark except for a lone porch light. He'd start there.

He darted from tree to tree, commando style. Wesley had firmly instructed him to keep the gun in his pocket. Don't take it out unless you're forced to, he'd said. And if you do, keep your finger off the trigger. He showed him how to hold it the "safe" way. Frank didn't see the point to all that. Cops and soldiers didn't keep their weapons tucked in their pockets. They remained alert and ready to respond, and so would he. This was a kind of police action, after all. He was a one-man SWAT team.

Frank relinquished the shelter of the last tree and sprinted low toward the side of the house. He flattened himself against the brickwork and listened hard for sounds of movement from inside. Nothing, just the trill of insects. He scooted to the nearest window. It was locked, with curtains drawn.

He made his way to the back of the house, where there was a screened porch. Part of the large backyard had been turned into a vegetable garden, not yet planted this early in the season. In the distance was a fenced playground. An elevated wood-and-wire animal hutch sat closer to the house. Frank peered through the wire mesh and saw a lop-eared bunny. The thing thumped its hind legs and gave him a spooky green-eyed stare.

What if they had dogs? he thought. A surly rabbit was one thing. All he needed was a couple of snarling Dobermans lunging for his jugular. Take it easy, he told himself. If there were dogs on the premises, they'd have made their presence known by now.

Then he remembered: He was armed. *Release the hounds!* He could dispatch the beasts swiftly enough with the help of his faithful friends, Mr. Smith and Mr. Wesson.

Lights were on in the back room. He took a careful peek. It was the kitchen; no one was in there. He slunk to the porch door. It squealed slightly when he opened it, and he paused, listening, before crossing to the kitchen door and trying it. Locked. The door had glass panes in it, though. He supposed he could try to gain entry by breaking one, but it would make a lot of noise, and he hadn't thought to bring tape and a glass cutter. Wasn't that how they did it in the movies?

Frank slipped around the other side of the house, hoping to find a window that had been left open. No such luck, and the side door was also locked. His best bet was that kitchen door. He retraced his steps, rounding the back of the house, and came face-to-face with a fat old Chinese woman in a zippered fleece bathrobe.

She raised a humongous meat cleaver over her head. "You go away."

Frank jumped back. "Holy shit!"

"Go away, schmuck." She advanced on him, wagging the cleaver. "You go rob someone else. *Irving!*" she cried.

Frank backed up, hands raised placatingly. Nervous tension tightened his trigger finger, and the gun erupted with a kick, firing a round into the night sky. "Christ!" He dropped the .38.

"Irving!" the woman screeched. *"Irving!"* Lights came on all over the house. A window slid open on the third floor and a man's grumpy voice called, *"What?"*

Frank took off running in the direction of his car. He tore through the woods, tripping on tree roots and snagging his new camos on thorny limbs. He was almost at the road when a hand shot out from behind a tree and seized the back of his collar, bringing him up short.

The hand belonged to a giant clown with a parrot on his shoulder. Frank's bladder nearly let go. The clown's white face paint glowed night-vision chartreuse. A tiny bowler sat at a jaunty angle atop his frizzy wig. Above the waist he was regulation clown, complete with undersized tuxedo jacket and oversized polka-dotted bow tie. Below the waist he wore a plaid kilt.

The parrot screeched, *"You're grounded, buster!"*

"THAT'S PERFECT." Will read the name on their visitor's driver's license. "Francis Asa Narby. The husband. Utterly goddamn perfect." He tossed the license onto the table next to the man's wallet and car keys, his .38, now emptied of bullets, his helmet and goggles, and that preposterous knife.

Francis Asa Narby said, "I go by Frank."

They were in the kitchen of the old house. Will and Fergus stood over Frank, who occupied one of the ladder-back dining chairs. Quint had been returned to his spacious cage in the foyer. Gabby had gone back to bed once the commotion had died down. Will had had a tougher time getting Cuba and Tom to stop playing with the night-vision goggles, but finally they, too, had trudged off to their rooms.

Yawning, Irving Hung tugged on the sleeve of his wife's robe. "Will has this under control, honey." He added a few words in Mandarin.

Strips of Scotch tape crisscrossed Ming-hua's hair, protecting her iron-gray perm from the ravages of sleep. She maintained her death grip on the cleaver. "I call nine-one-one."

"Not necessary," Will said. "We know who he is."

Her eyes narrowed in her doughy face. "This schmuck friend of yours?" Ming-hua's accent was much more pronounced than her husband's.

"Not exactly." Fergus's grin cracked his clown makeup. "But we're about to get better acquainted, aren't we, Frankie?"

"It's Frank." Lucy's husband eyed Ming-hua's cleaver warily. "Where's my wife?"

Will addressed the old couple. "Take Irving back to bed, Ming-hua. He needs his beauty sleep."

Ming-hua gave Frank one last malignant glare, then handed Fergus the cleaver and shuffled out of the room with her husband.

Fergus was scary to behold even without the weapon. His clown makeup was meticulous if a tad intense, with that painted rictus of a grin and the satanically arched eyebrows. His outfit was in the best clown tradition, at least until you got to the kilt. The whole package, including Fergus's height and irrepressible Fergusy attitude, was, well, just plain scary.

No wonder the pediatric staff at the local hospital had asked him not to come around anymore, with his weird balloon animals and plinky ukulele and scolding parrot. Volunteer clowns are supposed to be members of an approved organization, they'd explained, like the Shriners. But that wasn't the real reason. Simply put, Fergus scared the snot out of the grownups. Their young patients, on the other hand, got a kick out of him. Oh sure, there were always one or two who burst into tears at the sight of the big, grotesque clown, but most of the kids were bored silly in their hospital beds and welcomed the diversion. So Fergus ignored the nervous nurses and continued his good works. Tonight he and Quint had stayed late at the hospital, helping to distract a six-year-old hit-and-run victim. He'd just gotten home and was still in costume when Frank commenced his clumsy reconnaissance.

"Where is she?" Frank demanded again. "Where's Lucy?"

Will leaned back against a cabinet; he folded his arms over his bare chest. "We don't discuss ongoing jobs with outsiders. That includes spouses."

"Well, this 'ongoing job' is my wife!" Frank stabbed a finger at his chest. "You kidnapped her, you son of a bitch. I want to make sure she's okay. Once I get to see her, speak with her, then we can talk ransom."

Will and Fergus exchanged a look.

"I expected to hear from you before now, but hey." Frank tossed up his hands. "I'm here. I'll pay. So let's just do this thing and get it over with."

Will scrubbed a hand over his bristly jaw, trying to decide whether this chucklehead was for real. He probably was. If anyone was playing games here, it was the little missus. "How did you find us, Frank? How did you know where she was?"

Frank hesitated. "I have my resources."

"Cut the bullshit," Will said. "We were followed."

"By those two in the ski masks," Fergus put in, but Will had already figured that out.

"How do you know Wesley and his pal?" Will asked Frank, whose shifty gaze prompted him to add, menacingly, "Do not lie to me."

Frank sighed gustily. "Okay. What the hell. I hired them. Well, I hired Wesley. He brought along the other one."

"Jay-sus!" Fergus the Clown advanced on Frank, who shrank back in his chair. "Your own wife. What did you tell them to do, leave her in a ditch somewhere? Haven't you heard of divorce, you miserable piece o' shite?"

Will's expression never changed, even as he fought the urge to commandeer that cleaver and start carving Lucy's significant other into eensy teensy pieces. *Thank God I got to her first.*

"It's not like that," Frank bleated. "*She* wants to divorce *me*. She kicked me out of the house. I can't let her go through with it. I had to do *something*."

Fergus settled a big hand on Frank's shoulder. "Okay, now I'm going to hurt you."

"I was just going to *scare* her," Frank cried. "Make her *think* she'd been kidnapped."

Fergus tightened his grip. Frank grimaced in pain. "Why would you do that, Frankie?"

Will answered for him. "So he could rescue her. Right, Frank? You wanted to show her what a brave, devoted fellow she'd be giving up if she left you."

"It would've worked too," Frank said, "if you guys hadn't beaten me to it."

"Do you really believe that?" Fergus gave the shoulder one last, punishing squeeze and released it.

"I haven't known your wife that long," Will said, "but I'd bet real money she's not dense enough to fall for a lame stunt like that. Then again, she stayed married to *you* for . . . how long was it?"

"Twenty years." Frank rubbed his shoulder. "And counting. We have a solid marriage. Lucy's just feeling a little at loose ends. Empty-nest syndrome and all that. She just needs to know I still care."

"Nothing says you're special like being terrorized by strange armed men wearing ski masks," Will said.

"Marriage is a sacred institution." Frank straightened his spine. "There's never been a divorce in the Narby family."

Lucy had married Frank for the same reasons Tom's mother had tried to corral Will. Of that, he had no doubt. They were the same reasons his own mother, his pediatric stepmother, and even his half sister, Judith, rehabilitated wild child that she was, had chosen their mates: a life of queenly sloth and a reserved parking space at the country club. Divorce would almost certainly impact Lucy's standard of living, and not in a good way, no matter how brilliant her lawyer was. Perhaps the prospect of another three or four decades with Francis Asa Narby was simply more than she could stomach.

"I hate to break the news to you," Will told Frank, "but you don't know the little lady as well as you think you do."

"What's that supposed to mean?"

"Only that she's having a lot of fun at your expense," Will said. "Ours too."

"Being kidnapped is *fun*?" Frank sneered.

"It can be. When you've hired your own kidnapper."

Frank stared at him in befuddlement. "Say again?"

"It's what I do for a living," Will said. "People pay me to abduct them and hold them prisoner, for anywhere from a few hours to a few days."

"Wait." Frank held up a hand. "You expect me to believe there are people who actually want to be tied up, dragged from their houses, held against their will?"

Will shrugged. "It takes all kinds. I don't judge. I simply accommodate them. For a price."

"Who would do something like that?"

"Someone who craves a little adventure without any real risk," Will said. "It's a safe thrill. Some folks just want to see how much mental and physical abuse they can take. I've got this fellow over there now, an aspiring poet who doesn't think he's *suffered* enough to write serious poetry. By the time we're done with him, he'll be Henry Wadsworth Longfellow. Sometimes the client has a phobia he wants to confront. We get a lot of control freaks who want to abandon control for once in their life. That's how your missus described herself."

"Now I know you're bullshitting me," Frank said. "*Lucy*, a control freak?"

This man had no clue about his own wife. "She met with us last week. We discussed what kind of custom kidnapping experience she wanted. I watched her sign on the dotted line. Either she felt no need to inform her estranged husband about it or she's getting off on the thought of you freaking out and running to the rescue. My money's on the second thing."

"No way." Frank waved away the notion. "No frickin' way would my Lucy go in for some kind of sick custom-kidnapping thing. You made all that up. She never asked to be snatched. If this isn't about ransom, what *do* you want?"

Fergus said, "There's only one thing to do, lad."

"On your feet, Soldier." Will hauled Lucy's husband out of his chair.

LUCY HAD LONG ago lost feeling in her butt, but that was nothing compared to what was happening above her shoulders. She'd been tied to this hard chair for hours, forced to watch back-to-back episodes of *The Powerpuff Girls*. Will had rolled a TV/DVD unit into her black box of a room and popped in a long-running disc of her niece's favorite show. Couldn't they have just clubbed her to death and gotten it over with? This was worse than Britney and Christina, worse than the bulgur gruel. Even Josephine the mouse was preferable to hour after hour of the animated kiddie show.

It was the middle of the night. Lucy hadn't slept in twenty-four hours. Her exhaustion, combined with the endless antics of Buttercup, Blossom, and Bubbles on the small screen, had fried her brain all nice and crisp. Thus when the door swung open and she saw Frank standing there looking like G.I. Joe with a hundred-dollar haircut, she assumed she'd begun hallucinating. Until he opened his mouth.

"Holy shit, Lucy, what've they done to you?"

She would have liked to tell him, but her mouth had again been sealed with duct tape, possibly to deprive the upside-down man next door of those blood-curdling screams he so relished.

Frank was accompanied by Will and a giant zombie clown wearing Fergus's kilt. Maybe she was hallucinating. Will wore only thin pajama bottoms and a scowl. He clicked off the show and said, "Your knight in shining armor here seems to be suffering under a misapprehension, Lucy. He thinks you've been abducted against your will. You're going to set him straight."

Excuse me? She said it with her eyes.

"I'm in no mood for more of your nonsense," Will warned. "Just tell him you hired me and that everything's hunky-dory." He ripped the tape off her mouth.

"Help me, Frank!" she cried. "Pay them whatever they want. Just get me out of here."

Fergus let out a big, jolly clown laugh.

Will cursed. He leaned down and got in her face. "Very funny, Lucy. Frank thinks you were really kidnapped. You understand? You've had your fun, we're all tickled as hell. Now let your husband in on the joke."

At least Lucy now knew that Frank had nothing to do with her abduction. "I don't know what he's talking about, Frank. Please," she beseeched him. "I can't take any more. Do whatever you have to, but *get me out of here!*"

"What have you done to my wife?" Frank demanded.

Fergus turned to Will. "Maybe it's time to call this one quits."

"No." Will's expression was mulish. "Only *she* can call it quits before the four days are up. I know you remember the signals," he told Lucy.

Frank said, "Signals?"

"A 'safe word,'" Fergus explained. "A sort of password we all agreed to ahead of time. She says that word and we stop whatever we're currently doing, or even let her go if that's what she wants."

Will said, "There's also a gesture she can make even if she's gagged and tied up. Lucy knows how to put an end to all this. She came up with the signals herself when we met with her last week. You don't think your wife's a control freak?" He glowered at her. "Who do you think is pulling the strings right now?"

"Why are you doing this?" she asked Will. "We'll give you money. We won't go to the police, I swear."

"Speakin' of which." Fergus jerked his head toward Frank. "What do we do with this fella? If we let him walk out of here thinking his wife's been honest-to-God kidnapped, the cops'll be breaking down our door before sunup."

"I know." Will looked thoroughly disgusted.

"This one was fun," Fergus said, "but it's gotten a wee bit messy. Let her go."

"Not a chance. The lady paid for four days of abuse and I aim to see she gets her money's worth." Will stared down at Lucy. "Unless she decides to play by the rules and signal me to stop."

"I don't know about any damn signals." She strained against her bindings. "You're sick. Demented. He's Ricky Baines," she informed Frank. "Did you know that?"

Frank frowned in bafflement. "Who?"

"The child star? Didn't you watch *In No Time*? He calls himself Will, but it's really him. It's Ricky Baines. Oh yeah. Ask him."

"Calm down, Lucy," Frank said. "This is a bad time to get hysterical."

Let your husband in on the joke, Will had said. If anyone was enjoying a joke here, it sure as hell wasn't her.

A joke. Lucy's head snapped up. A joke! Of course!

Will claimed Lucy had met with him last week. There was only one person who could have pulled that one off. Why hadn't she thought of it sooner?

Because their practical jokes had never risen to these outrageous heights before, that was why.

"I know what's going on!" she cried. "I've figured it out."

"So happy to hear it," Will said, even as he started to replace the strip of duct tape over her mouth.

"No! Wait!" She tried to twist away, but his long fingers held her head like a vise. "The woman who hired you. It was—" The rest was lost in grunts from behind the tape.

—my twin sister, Ethel.

8

ETHEL VANDERMEER WATCHED the big Irish fellow set up a camcorder on a tripod. "What's that for?" she asked his boss.

"We always record the initial interview on videotape." Will Kitchen settled in a leather-upholstered armchair facing her and opened his spiral notebook to a blank page. "It's helpful in preventing misunderstandings."

"Otherwise known as lawsuits."

He tipped his head to confirm her interpretation. "Between the video and the detailed, signed contract, the client can't come back later and claim we did something he, or she, didn't ask for."

"Covering your ass," Ethel said. "Makes sense in your business, I suppose."

Will glanced around Lucy's greatroom, a high-ceilinged space done up in earth tones with navy and sage accents. "Nice place you have here, Mrs. Narby."

"Please." Ethel smiled. "Call me Lucy." The décor in this room, as in the five thousand square feet of house surrounding it, was refined yet comfortable, and boring as hell. Typical of her sister's decorating style, not to mention her taste in husbands.

It was time to shake up Lucy's world.

Ethel knew they wouldn't be interrupted. Her brother-in-law, Frank, had moved to an apartment in Queens weeks ago, her nephew John was in the middle of his second semester at Cornell, and her sister Lucy would be out of the house most of the day. Lucy had driven to a bookstore in New Jersey to sign copies of her latest children's mystery, *Johnny Sherlock and the Cracked Clock.* She wouldn't be back until four at the earliest. That gave Ethel more than enough time to let herself into the house with the keys and alarm code Lucy had given her in case of emergency and to meet here with Will Kitchen and his assistant, Fergus Dowd.

Ethel had chosen a typical Lucy outfit: dark red blouse, cropped khaki slacks, and cordovan flats. That morning she'd let her hairdresser cut her hair in long layers just past the shoulder, the way Lucy wore it. She also got a dye job to cover her highlights and restore her natural dark brown color. Drastic measures, to be sure, but it would be worth it. Ethel only wished she could see the look on Lucy's face when it happened.

The twins had traded practical jokes their entire lives. It had started when they were three and little Ethel decided it would be great fun to hide Lucy's favorite baby doll. Lucy retaliated by hiding Ethel's security blanket—in the compost pile. As time passed, the girls' pranks became more sophisticated: gluing dishes to the table, filling shoes with shaving cream. By the time they were teenagers, it was everything from plastic wrap stretched over the toilet bowl to red Kool-Aid powder in the shower head to a birthday cake with chopped-liver frosting.

As adults, they strove to outdo each other. When Ethel poured a bottle of detergent in Lucy's toilet tank, Lucy filled Ethel's car with Styrofoam peanuts. Ethel got her revenge by hiding a whole bluefish under a wheel cover of Lucy's car—in August—whereupon Lucy had Ethel's bedroom furniture relocated to the roof of her garage. During the holiday shopping season last winter, Ethel sewed department-store antitheft strips into the lining of Lucy's coat. Lucy's response was to plant a metal cutout of a gun in Ethel's carryon baggage. The security staff at JFK were not amused.

Every time Ethel got in a good one, her sister always managed to outdo her. But a *kidnapping*. Let Lucy try to one-up her this time.

Fergus looked up from the camcorder's little LCD screen. "We're rolling."

Will uncapped his pen. "Lucy, I think you told me on the phone that you found me through my Web site, is that right?"

"Yep," Ethel said. "I was surfing the Net one night and I just stumbled onto your site. I was intrigued."

She noticed Will was missing a finger—the left pinky. He noticed her noticing. "I wrestle crocodiles on the side," he explained. She responded with a polite chuckle, but couldn't help wondering how it had really happened.

Will got back to business. "What is it about the idea of custom kidnapping that appeals to you?"

"Well, it's just such a complete loss of control, isn't it? Scary, but not too scary. Not actually dangerous, right? I mean, you don't really hurt people."

"No more than they want to be hurt," Will said. "And if someone wants to be hurt a lot, a red flag goes up. We turn those people away."

Ethel gave him an impish smile. "So if it's S-and-M action they want, they've got the wrong man?"

Will nodded. "We also attract our share of mental cases, people who think they deserve to be punished, that kind of thing. That's part of the purpose of these interviews. To weed out the masochists and nut jobs."

"But about sex," she said. "As long as we're on the subject."

"Yes?"

Ethel let out a nervous laugh. She felt herself blush, which surprised her. She considered herself fairly sophisticated; there wasn't much that rattled her. But it rattled her to ask this good-looking, well-built young man whether he was planning to sex her up. And with that Fergus character videotaping the whole thing, no less. She said, "Um, how far does it go? I mean, I guess what I'm asking is—"

"There's no sex," Will said. "I assume you're talking about intercourse."

"Yeah. So you never, uh, do that."

"Never with a client." His placid expression remained unchanged. *He* didn't blush, damn him. "So if that's part of the fantasy you've constructed—"

"No." She raised a hand. "It's okay. I mean, that's not what I want, not what I'm looking for." Ethel was relieved. It was one thing to engineer her sister's fake abduction, but there had to be limits. If Will had said sure, of course we're going to get it on, that's part of the thrill, she'd have booted his tight little buns out the door.

He leaned back, rested the notebook on his lap. He looked her straight in the eye. "What *are* you looking for, Lucy?"

Good grief, this man was sexy. Was Ethel really going to sic him on her poor, unsuspecting sister?

She bit back a grin. Damn right she was.

Ethel leaned back, too. She steepled her fingers. "Well, I guess you could say I have some issues related to power. To being in charge. Making decisions."

"Are you a control freak?"

He asked it so matter-of-factly, all she could say was "Yes." In truth, no one who knew the real Lucy Narby would ever describe her that way. Far from being a controller, she was the controlled. Especially when it came to her pathetic excuse for a marriage. Ethel had been thrilled when Lucy announced she was finally leaving Frank. If Ethel had stayed with her own tedious bore of a first husband for two decades, she never would have made it to husband number three, the keeper. She never would have had her wonderful daughter, Diana.

Will said, "So you'd like your kidnapping experience to be about . . ." He gestured for her to fill in the blanks.

Ethel shrugged. "Well, about losing control. About being dominated. Not like we were talking about—I mean, not in a, you know, sexual way."

"I know I said there's no actual sex, but there is a psychosexual component to this kind of experience, Lucy. It's unavoidable. Our sexual impulses are bound up in a kind of primal stew with the rest of our emotional baggage—our fears, our frustrations, our desires." He looked directly at her. "Our control issues."

Ethel squirmed in her chair. "Okay."

"So what I need to know is, do you want that part of it, the psychosexual part, to stay up here?" He tapped his head. "Or would you like a little acting out?"

"Short of actual sex."

"Short of actual sex. This part is up to the client. I'll work within your comfort level—or to be more precise, your *dis*comfort level." Will held his pen poised over the notebook. He could have been her broker discussing municipal bonds versus midcap mutual funds.

"Well, I guess . . ." Ethel thought not of her sister, but of how she herself would respond if a man this hot spirited her away and held her captive for four days. Her face burned. "I guess I want some, um, acting out. Nothing *too* intense."

"No problem." He made a note. "Now I'm going to ask you to choose a word and a gesture, Lucy. You use either one, it puts an immediate halt to all action. Make it a word you won't forget, and a gesture you can manage even if your hands are immobilized."

"A word . . ." Ethel thought for a moment. She smiled a secret smile. "Smarg."

"That's the word?"

"That's the word." She spelled it. "S-m-a-r-g."

"I'm not going to ask what it means," he said, jotting in his notebook, "as long as you're sure you'll remember it."

"Don't worry. She—I will." Ethel had heard that some identical twins develop a special language only they share. She and Lucy had always made do with standard English, but in a moment of inspired silliness when they were eight years old they made up a word: *smarg*. Use of this word by either of them invariably sent the girls into peals of giggles and sent grownups sprinting for the nearest dictionary. Only Ethel and Lucy knew they'd just uttered "the worst curse word in the world." From then on, whenever one of them bested the other with a practical joke, the jokee would utter a disgusted "smarg" or one of its manifold variations, such as "I don't smarging believe this," "I've been royally smarged," and "Just you wait, you smarging bitch."

Fergus glanced up from the camcorder. "I've got a funny feelin' about this one, lad."

"I know, I know," Will said distractedly, "you and your sixth sense."

"What?" Ethel looked from one to the other.

"Fergus thinks you're going to be trouble," Will said. "Are you going to be trouble, Lucy?"

"Who, me? I'm just looking for a little fun." She indicated their staid surroundings. "I mean, the most exciting thing I have to look forward to around here is flirting with the landscapers." Which Ethel's sister would never in a million years do, but how were these guys to know?

"That's good enough for me," Will said.

"So listen." She had to ask. "This 'acting out' thing. The sexy stuff. I thought you said on the phone that most of your clients are men."

He smiled at the unspoken question. "I have a female associate who works with me."

"Ah."

"Choose a gesture, Lucy. We're talking head or foot."

"Okay," she said, "what if I wiggle my toes."

"Make it the whole right foot, and make sure it's more than a little twitch so we'll notice it."

Naturally, Lucy would have no way of knowing she could end her ordeal simply by wagging her foot or by uttering "the worst curse word in the world."

Next came a discussion of food. Ethel informed him that she, meaning Lucy, adored junk food and couldn't stomach so-called health food, having been raised on the stuff. He asked about her fears and pet peeves. She was deathly afraid of rodents, not so crazy about the dark, and felt the cold keenly; Lucy was definitely a warm-weather person. She couldn't bear the vacuous songs churned out by those ditzy girl singers. And Ethel remembered how much Lucy hated it when five-year-old Diana made her watch *The Powerpuff Girls*. She added that to the list of things Lucy wished would drop off the planet.

She'd be with him and his associates for four days, he reminded her. Did she own any animals that needed looking after? Not since Frank left, she said. Any chronic medical problems? Medications she needed to take? Ethel assured him she was healthy. Then she remembered.

"I do take birth control pills every day." Lucy took them to regulate her cycle. With Frank out of town so much, she probably didn't have enough sex to worry about contraception.

"That's it?" Will asked, writing. "No other meds? Nothing we should know about?"

"That's it."

"Keep the pills in your purse," Will said, "so no matter where we grab you, you'll have them."

"Uh, okay." That might be a problem. Ethel had no idea where Lucy kept her birth control pills. She decided not to worry about it. "So I won't have any idea where you'll come for me? It could be any place?"

"It could be any place—the beauty parlor, the supermarket. It could be right here in your own home. Speaking of which, I'll need the keys and alarm code."

She handed them over. "What'll you do if I go out somewhere? Follow me?"

"Just go about your normal routine," Will said. "You'll never see it coming, so don't bother looking over your shoulder."

A shiver of excitement raced up Ethel's spine. She almost wished she were the one being abducted, and not Lucy. "It could happen anytime, right?" she asked. "Day or night?"

"That's right."

"I have one request. Let's call it a requirement. I want it to happen on my birthday."

"Which is . . . ?"

"Next Saturday," Ethel said. "See, this whole kidnapping thing is my birthday present to myself. I'm turning forty." She waited for a statement of incredulity. Forty? No way. You don't look a day over thirty. To her annoyance, Will simply plowed ahead with the next item of business.

"I need the name and phone number of someone who'll be willing to come and get you," he said.

"Come and get me?"

"When the four days are up, we'll call this person and tell him where to find you. You mentioned that you and your husband are separated, so he's probably out."

"Frank does *not* get to be a part of this. Call my sister. Here." Ethel reached for his notebook. "I'll give you her number."

Will examined the page when she handed it back. "Ethel Vandermeer." A smile tugged at his mouth. "Her name is Ethel?"

She sighed. *Here it comes.*

Fergus wore the most irksome grin. "Your parents named their daughters Lucy and Ethel?"

"As in . . ." Will hummed the jaunty theme song. The two men snickered.

"Don't mind me, guys." She gestured for them to yuk it up. "Go ahead. Get it out of your system."

"I never could stand that show," Fergus said. "Must be an American thing."

"Well, my mom couldn't get enough of it," Ethel said. "She grew up watching *I Love Lucy*. Never missed an episode. Started a fan club and the whole bit."

"Hey, it could've been worse," Will said. "Lucy's an okay name. You could have been the one saddled with *Ethel*."

Ethel bullied her lips into something approaching a smile. "Every day I thank my lucky stars."

"Well, I think that covers everything." Will handed her the contract and his pen.

"Just so you know." Ethel scrawled her sister's name. "I intend to really throw myself into this kidnapping thing. As if it were totally unexpected."

"That's the idea," Will said.

"No, I mean I'm going to act like it's real. I mean, *really* act like it's real. I'll probably be, you know, pretty enthusiastic."

"We like enthusiasm, don't we, Fergus?"

"I'm still getting' that feelin', Will."

"Take an Alka-Seltzer."

"And later?" Ethel said. "During the whole four days? I'm going to be, um, staying in character, you might say."

"I hope so." Will slipped the contract into his notebook. "Otherwise, what's the point?"

9

FRANK VOICE-DIALED HIS home in Egerton, Illinois, as he drove away from the place where Lucy was being held. Anne Marie picked up on the fourth ring. "Hello?" Her voice was scratchy from sleep and held a hint of alarm.

"Oh gee, I completely forgot what time it is." The car's hands-free Bluetooth permitted him to simultaneously drive, scrounge tissues to wipe off the camo makeup, and talk to his wife. The dashboard clock read 5:07 a.m.

She said, "Frank. Is something wrong?"

He heard the rustle of bedcovers and pictured her propping herself on an elbow. "No, no, I'm sorry, sweet pea. I should've waited to call. I wasn't thinking."

"You sound odd. Are you sure everything's okay?"

"I just had to tell you, I love you so much. *So much*, Anne Marie. I don't think I realized how much until tonight."

"Well, I love you, too, Frank. But it's not *tonight* anymore. It's four in the morning."

"And here I am waking you up, and you probably won't be able to get back to sleep. I'm a selfish bastard."

"Ah . . ." Her voice softened. "Amy'll be up soon anyway."

"How's her cold?"

"Worse. She had a hundred and two last night. And she gave it to Matthew and Theresa."

"Can your mom come over to help out?" he asked.

"She's at Cindy and Gary's watching their kids. Cindy's water broke last night."

"Really? That's great. Call me as soon as you hear anything."

"Sure, sure. Listen, as long as I have you." She yawned. "The man from the fire department came by to check the smoke detectors and all that."

"Who?"

"He said you asked for an inspection. Everything checks out, by the way. Nice fellow."

Frank must be losing his memory; he couldn't recall asking for any inspection.

"So that's all you called for?" she said. "To tell me you love me? You big dope, you're such a romantic."

He loved the sound of Anne Marie's laughter. She had this sexy, throaty chuckle. It was one of the first things that had attracted him to her that fateful night thirteen years ago when he'd rushed to a Chicago ER with chest pains that turned out to be nothing more serious than a giant burrito with double refried beans. She was so young and fresh in her nurse's scrubs and white sneakers, with strands of curly, cinnamon-colored hair springing loose from a big tortoiseshell clip. She was gentle and compassionate, but strong, too, a take-charge professional who brooked no nonsense from either patients or doctors. That was his Anne Marie, tender and tough. The Amazon warrior with a heart of gold. He fell that night, and fell hard.

When he met her he couldn't help wondering if there really was such a thing as the seven-year itch. That was how long he'd been married to Lucy at that point, seven years, and in all that time he'd never cheated on her. Was that all this was, he wondered, boredom and hormones? But soon enough he realized his feelings for Anne Marie Ciccone were the real deal. True love. Just like with Lucy. He didn't love Lucy less just because he had Anne Marie in his life. Besides, marriage was forever. End of story. Frank wasn't going to be the first Narby to shame the family with a divorce. What would Mother and Father say?

And it wasn't as if he couldn't keep both parts of his life separate. He could afford to maintain two households, though he'd had to scale back a little—okay, more than a little—when he bought the house in Egerton;

there wasn't *that* much money. Frank insisted on handling all bills and investments himself, forestalling any awkward questions about where, precisely, the cash was going.

As far as Lucy was concerned, he lived on Long Island and took business trips to Chicago. Anne Marie thought it was the other way around. Lucy never expressed interest in accompanying him on any of his Midwest trips. Anne Marie had made noises in the beginning about wanting to see New York, but she got pregnant within days of the wedding, and from then on she was always tied down, with one in diapers and another on the way. Just the kind of big, sprawling, raucous passel of kids Frank had always dreamt of—and that Lucy had refused to give him.

As much as he loved Lucy, he couldn't deny it had hurt him deeply when she'd drawn the line at one child. By the time he met Anne Marie, John was six, an only child and destined to remain so. Anne Marie was from a big family and wanted to make another big family with Frank. He couldn't have been more thrilled. This sweet twenty-three-year-old beauty desired nothing more from life than to be with him and make his babies. But there was that other side to her personality, too—the decisive, pragmatic side he found equally appealing.

After tonight, he'd have to add *possessive* to the list of Anne Marie's character traits. Not that he minded. On the contrary, he was immensely flattered. Never in his life had he imagined a woman would go to such lengths to keep him all to herself.

"I also wanted to tell you," Frank said, "that from now on, there won't be any secrets between us."

The line was silent a moment. "What do you mean, from now on?"

"I know you were behind this whole thing with Lucy. I tracked her down." A wry chuckle escaped him as he opened the driver's-side window and tossed out the used tissues. "It's just like you to carry out a bold plan like this—scaring off the competition, staking your claim. You have no idea how that turns me on."

"Who's Lucy?"

"There's no need to keep pretending, sweet pea. I know you hired that guy Will. Lucy figured it out too. She tried to say your name, but he gagged her before she could blurt it out. I realized it could only be you, though, especially with no ransom demand. I didn't tell Will I knew. See, he made up this cockamamie story about Lucy hiring him herself—for kicks, can you believe it? Guess that's all he could come up with on the spur of the moment. Still, you gotta give the man credit. He never mentioned your name, not once. I wish I could instill that kind of loyalty in my employees. Anyway, I just let him think I bought his story and eventually he had to let me go. I mean, what was he going to do, keep *me* prisoner too?" He thought he heard Anne Marie sit up in bed.

"Frank, have you been drinking?"

"Sweet pea, if I'm drunk, it's on love. I'm awed—*awed*—by the devotion you have demonstrated with this act."

"All right," she said, "back up. This Lucy—"

"At first I couldn't figure out how you two found out about each other." He merged into the sparse traffic on the Southern State Parkway. "Then it came to me. She hired a PI, just like I did. I should've anticipated that."

"You hired a private investigator?" Anne Marie sounded wide-awake now.

"Lucy's PI must've found out about you and reported back to her," he said. "She called you, just to make sure you're for real, and that's how *you* find out about *her*. You'd think I would've seen that one coming. Hope it didn't upset you too much—in your condition and all."

Her voice was hard. "Frank, are you trying to tell me you're having an—"

"I know why you had her snatched," he said. "To shake her up, rattle her cage, scare her into giving me up without reporting me to the authorities."

"*Reporting* you?"

"It's a solid plan, sweet pea. I think it's going to work. There's just one thing I need you to understand. I'm not going to divorce Lucy."

"*What!*"

"Now, hear me out. My life with her is over, as of tonight. She and I will never again live together as man and wife. You're so much better for me, Anne Marie. You're my soul mate. The ironic part? Which if you'd known it, you might've thought twice about the kidnapping? Lucy wants to divorce *me*. She kicked me out weeks ago. I don't know," he said, shaking his head. "You spend twenty years with someone and they call it quits, just like that."

"Twenty years," Anne Marie groaned. "Jesus, Mary, and Joseph."

"I know, I was shocked, too. But you know me—I refuse to put asunder what God has brought together. Plus John doesn't deserve to have his family broken up. So I'm going to stay married to her, but in name only. The rest of your plan is good, sweet pea. You should've seen her, all trussed up in this bare cell, scared out of her wits, talking crazy. She won't give us any trouble, not after this. I can't see her reporting me for bigamy."

Anne Marie didn't respond. All Frank heard were these strange gurgling noises. Poor thing. The morning sickness never stopped with her. He'd better let her go.

"Kiss the kids for me, sweet pea. I'll be home before you know it." Frank gave her a loud, smacking air kiss and broke the connection.

"YOUR WHITE KNIGHT couldn't wait to flee the premises," Will said. He leaned indolently against the closed door, arms crossed over that broad bare chest.

It was just the two of them now, both in their jammies—which might have lent the scene a cozy intimacy if Lucy weren't tied to a wooden chair, her mouth sealed with duct tape. *Just take the tape off*, she silently urged him. *Let me speak. Then this will all be over.*

"Frank changed his tune at the end," he said. "He pretended to buy my explanation about how you hired me. I don't think he believed it for a minute, but I had to let him go. My only other option was unlawful imprisonment. You might be a master manipulator, Lucy, but even you can't make me kidnap someone for real. He could still go to the police—I can deal with that if I have to—but I'm betting he won't. He did a one-eighty after seeing you. The guy was downright gleeful by the time he left. What was that about, do you think?"

Lucy jerked her chin and made noises behind the tape, pleading with Will to remove it.

"You've got three more days with me, Lucy, and I guarantee they'll be three days you won't soon forget." Will pushed off the door and came to stand directly over her. His smile held more than a hint of malicious anticipation. "You want a little excitement, you said? You want to lose control, be dominated? There's an old expression—you might've heard it. 'Be careful what you wish for.'"

Her grunts became more vociferous. She rocked the chair in her desperation to be heard. *Take the goddamn tape off my mouth.* A fraction of a second was all she needed.

"Oh, I almost forgot," he said. "Just so you know what your loving spouse has been up to. Seems he couldn't bear the thought of you leaving him—so much so that *he* hired those other two yahoos who tried to grab you last night. Not for any nefarious purposes," he added in response to her poleaxed expression. "Those guys were supposed to carry you off so Frank could come to your rescue and save you from the evil abductors. At which point you would realize the error of your ways and beg your husband's forgiveness for even thinking about divorcing him. What do you have to say to that?" He ripped the tape off her mouth in one savage, eye-watering pull.

"Smarg."

10

HAL FINE-TUNED THE binoculars, bringing Ricky Baines's house into sharp focus. Only, Ricky wasn't calling himself Ricky anymore. Best not to forget that. A tree limb obscured his view, so he shifted his stance to peer around the trunk. "Who's the kid?"

"Kid?" Mick leaned against a nearby tree, ostentatiously bored. It was close to noon. The two of them had skulked into the woods adjacent to Will's spread so Hal could case the place and get some idea of how best to proceed. "Must be Tom."

"Tom, huh?" Hal handed Mick the binoculars. "I don't think so, sonny."

"I told you not to call me that." Mick grabbed the binoculars and scanned the front lawn. "Oh, baby. Didn't know there were actual titties under that Boy Scout shirt."

"Barely. Who is she?"

"Her name's Cuba."

"How old?" Hal squinted toward the distant figure chasing a lop-eared rabbit across the grass. It was another warm day, and the girl wore a snug white undershirt and stretchy athletic pants.

"Uh . . . fourteen? fifteen? Something like that," Mick said. "The fuck she do to her hair?"

"Give me those." Hal tapped Mick's arm.

"Just a minute." Mick giggled. "No bra—we got a little jiggle goin' on. Hey, sweet thing." He grabbed his crotch. "Cousin Micky's got something for you."

"She's your cousin?" Hal snatched the binoculars from his son and trained them on the house. Shadows moved behind the windows.

"Not really. Cuba's a runaway. Will took her in last winter."

"Is he banging her?"

"Who knows? Maybe they're into three-ways—him, Cuba, and Gabby. That, I'd pay money to see."

A scraping noise drew Hal's attention. "Knock that off." His genius son was etching his initials into the tree bark with a key.

"How long we gonna be here?"

"Till I decide I've seen enough," Hal said, as Mick continued to gouge the bark. "I said quit that."

Mick's dismissive sneer faded as Hal treated him to the scary dead-eye stare that had served him so well inside. Mick punished the tree with one last jab and pocketed his keys.

"It's not like that between him and Gabby, is it?" Hal asked. "I mean, the woman changed his diapers."

"The fuck should I know? She's old but—whaddayacallit—well preserved."

Hal trained the binoculars on the house, then on the other building— what Mick had called the Goo—before scanning the lawn once more. The girl, Cuba, sprawled on the grass, cuddling the rabbit.

"I cannot believe my mom, man." Mick's eyes shone with mixed incredulity and pride. "She never said word one about all this. I mean, I know about the groupie thing, the drugs and all that. She figured if she was up front about that stuff, if she 'kept the lines of communication open,' it'd keep me from making the same mistakes."

The strategy appeared to have failed, Hal mused.

"But kidnapping her own brother." Mick giggled again.

"Half brother." Hal set the binoculars in the crotch of the tree. "Judith detested him."

"They're pretty tight now."

"Yeah, well, back then it was a different story. Her mom and dad split when she was a kid, and she got caught in the middle of this big battle. Custody, money. He was balling his secretary. The usual crap."

"Yeah, I know all that. When Grandpa married Will's mom is when she really started 'acting out,' the way she puts it. Getting high all the time, cutting school, staying out all night with guys."

"Ricky was treated like a little prince," Hal said. "The heir apparent. I'd listen to Judith bitch about him for hours. Star of his own TV show. So adorable, with the freckles and all. He could do no wrong. Even her own mother, wife number one, fawned all over the kid once he was on TV. His manager got him a sweet deal. Everyone figured him for the next Jay North."

"Who?"

"Judith got shunted to the side—at least that's the way she saw it."

"So she wanted to get back at her brother," Mick said.

"That wasn't it. She was afraid of being disinherited. She'd been the bad girl for so long, even when she was in college. Barely managed to graduate. And then when she did graduate, Daddy's checks stopped coming. He told her it was time for her to start supporting herself. She convinced herself he was fixing to alter his will, to cut her out and leave the whole shebang to the little prince and his mother. The ransom money was supposed to be her insurance."

"Oh, like so at least she'd walk away with a piece of the pie."

"That was the idea." Hal peered toward the house. The lawn was deserted. Cuba must have gone inside. "There'd be just enough ransom money, after my cut, to keep her in coke and Cristal till she could decide what to do with her life."

"Aside from blowing second-rate rockers."

Hal calmly advanced on Mick, who flinched and backed against the tree. Hal got in the kid's face. "If my old man ever heard me talk that way about my mother, he'd have beat me within an inch of my life."

"What?" Mick blustered, while avoiding Hal's flat gaze. "Everyone knows about her. It's not like I'm making it up." Hal waited. "All right, all right, my mom was a virgin on her wedding night. She found me under a fucking cabbage leaf. You happy?"

Who did this little cockroach think he was? Hal had spent the past two and a half decades butting heads with men who wouldn't have hesitated to gut him like a trout for looking at them the wrong way. One of these days he was going to have to take this insolent pup down a peg or two.

"I'll tell you what Mom *didn't* find," Mick said. "She didn't find any two-million-dollar ransom, if that's what you're thinking. She was working as a diner hostess when she hooked up with my dad. I mean, you know, my stepdad. Anyway, until then, we were staying in this crummy apartment in someone's basement. We couldn't afford steak. It was spaghetti on a hotplate four, five nights a week. I was only seven when we moved out of that two-room shit-hole, but I'll never forget it. I can tell you one thing—Mom never dug up any two million bucks."

"If I thought Judith had the money, why would you and I be here right now, scoping out Ricky Baines's place?"

"The fuck should I know? It's your big fucking secret."

"Because you have a big fucking mouth, *sonny*."

"There he is." Mick pointed, and Hal quickly trained the binoculars on the man now descending the house's porch steps and loping toward the Goo. He was youngish, mid-thirties, on the tall side and fit. He had red hair.

Ricky Baines. Looking far different from the last time Hal had seen him, when the nine-year-old had been practically catatonic from terror and pain, pale as death with his left hand swathed in a filthy, blood-encrusted bandage.

The man he'd grown into moved with an air of confidence and self-assurance. *Do you think about it?* Hal silently asked Will Kitchen, watching as he disappeared behind the Goo.

A minute later a dark sedan—a Camry, it looked like—emerged from behind the far end of the Goo and stopped about halfway down the driveway. Will got out and waved to someone. Hal swung the binoculars back toward the house and saw a woman on the porch, wearing pajamas and plastic flip-flops. "Who's this, a girlfriend?"

Mick glanced toward the house and was instantly galvanized. "That's the bitch that smashed my nose. Lucy Narby."

"A *woman* did that?" Hal's long-lost son was making him prouder by the minute.

"Why's she walking around free?" Mick cried. "She should be hanging by her tits for what she did to me."

Hal hauled Mick back behind the tree. "Keep your voice down. And stay out of sight." Mick had described Will's bizarre kidnapping business on the way there. This Lucy must be one of his weirdo clients.

"The doctor says my nose'll never be the same," Mick griped. "He says it'll always be a little crooked from now on."

"A tragedy," Hal muttered. Someone might see that nose and mistake the whiny weasel for a real man. "Let's stick to the business at hand."

"She *is* the business at hand." Mists of spittle punctuated Mick's rant. He stabbed his finger toward Lucy, now crossing the lawn to the car. "She's totally the business at hand. You need my help? Fine. I help you, you help me."

"Help you what?"

"Get back at that miserable cunt, that's what."

Will met Lucy near the sprawling, thick-trunked tree in the middle of the lawn and escorted her to the car. His hand rested briefly on the small of her back. A young boy bounded out of the house and raced to catch up to them. He tried to wheedle his way into the car. Will turned him away.

He wanted to be alone with her. Interesting. "Get back at her how?" he asked.

"However I feel like," Mick said. "What's it to you? That's the deal. Take it or leave it."

What did Hal care, as long as Mick played his part? "Fine," he said. "But all that stuff comes after. If you do what you're supposed to and my thing goes as planned, Lucy Narby will be the next item of business. I promise."

WESLEY'S KNEES THROBBED. Shafts of pain speared his left butt cheek and right shoulder. He was perched ten feet up a tree overlooking the property where those Powerpuff goons had brought Lucy Narby on Friday night. Wesley had taken up position just inside the woods with his high-powered mini scope, only to have to scramble up the branches like a squirrel at the sound of someone else approaching through the woods. Two someones, as it turned out.

Gingerly he shifted his weight. This was misery. Wesley had assumed his tree-climbing days were long over. He still worked out, still had the power to haul himself up the branches. Only thing, nowadays he was hauling a hell of a lot more of himself than he used to. He'd chosen a stout limb to support his bulk; he hoped to God it held.

Joe was right. He had to get a grip on this flab. Maybe he'd give that Atkins thing a try again. Joe made a mean bacon-wrapped filet mignon. Wash down a few of those with some heavy cream and you'd never miss the potato.

Wesley had gone there to scope out the situation, to see if Frank had, by some miracle, managed to rescue his wife—which, he was less than shocked to discover, he had not. Of course, he could simply have asked his client, but Narby was not what you'd call forthcoming. So he'd decided to check it out firsthand before paying Frank another surprise visit. With that in mind, he'd gotten an early flight from Chicago, retrieved his car from JFK's long-term parking, and driven straight there.

The property belonged to one Wilbur Kitchen. The name meant nothing to Wesley, though he suspected if he ran it past some of the contacts he'd made during his fourteen years with the NYPD, he just might hit pay dirt. The house where the kidnappers had jettisoned that young loudmouth Friday night was owned by a Judith Drinkwater. No bells had rung there either.

With his scope, he had no trouble watching the two men, some twenty yards away. They had binoculars and were doing what Wesley himself had gone there to do: spy on Wilbur Kitchen's place. One of them was the hothead from Friday. Wesley didn't recognize the other one, who looked like an older, harder version of the kid. Father? Uncle?

Wesley was too far away to hear their conversation, though their body language came through loud and clear. The older one wasn't taking any shit from the kid, who tried to act tough but was hopelessly outclassed.

Wesley tried yet again to rearrange his weight on the limb, to ease the pressure on his knees, with no luck. The tree bark was scraping the hell out of his new, seven-hundred-dollar lambskin jacket.

Forget the jacket, he commanded himself. If this thing with Narby paid off, he'd buy the damn jacket in every color—after paying off the hall, caterers, band, florist, printer, tailor, and all the rest. Plus something nice for Joe. Maybe that new bedroom set he'd been jonesing for.

When Wesley and Joe had made up their minds to get married, they'd agreed on a simple, inexpensive affair. A handful of close friends for a morning service, followed by an omelet brunch. Two, three grand, tops. Then Joe started listening to his stepmother and sisters, to his thousand and one gal pals, and before Wesley knew what was happening, their modest little wedding had morphed into something better suited to Westminster Cathedral.

Joe had been in hog heaven planning this extravaganza. Wesley didn't have the heart to deny him. Naturally, finding a way to pay for it was *his* headache.

He wondered how hard he'd have to lean on that bigamous schmuck Narby to squeeze out a healthy chunk of hush money. Probably not all that hard. The man was obviously determined to maintain the status quo, to hold on to both the East Coast wife and the Midwest wife. KrunchWorks was set to expand to the West Coast in a couple of years. The national sales manager could find himself the sultan of a far-flung harem.

Meanwhile, if Lucy and Anne Marie ever found out about each other, Narby's life would be in the toilet faster than you could say, "Next on Eyewitness News: Shocking Bigamy Scandal!" How much would the man be willing to pay to keep his multi-family lifestyle out of the headlines?

Through the lacework of early spring foliage he was just able to make out the action at Kitchen's place. The redheaded man with Lucy Narby had to be one of the three who'd grabbed her on Friday night—the coolheaded one in the hoodie. That dark blue Camry was the same one he'd followed. He figured this was Wilbur Kitchen.

There was definitely something hinky going on here, Wesley thought as he watched the victim smile and chat with her kidnapper. The two settled into the car, and the boy sprinted back to the house.

Wesley focused his scope on the duo conducting their own little recon. He didn't dare abandon his perch while they were nearby. Fortunately they began to retrace their path as soon as the vehicle drove out of sight.

Snippets of conversation drifted to him as the two men neared him. He sat as still as a corpse, despite the big-ass spider that chose that moment to crawl onto his right hand, the one holding the scope.

". . . bitch . . ." Wesley heard in that whiny voice he remembered from Friday, and ". . . payback . . ." The older one counseled patience. Then he asked the younger one something.

The kid said, "That dickwad Will's on my shit list, too, Hal. One way or another, I'll get you in there."

They were a few feet from Wesley's tree now. The spider paused on his knuckle and assumed a contemplative pose, as if pondering whether to indulge in a venomous bite. The damn thing tickled.

"Don't get cocky, Mick," Hal said. "Something tells me your uncle's no dummy."

So. This little turd was Wilbur Kitchen's nephew.

"Yeah, well, he's not as smart as he thinks he is," Mick said. He stopped in his tracks, smack-dab under Wesley's tree. Wesley stopped breathing.

The spider's head moved. Wesley bit the inside of his cheek, braced himself for the bite, and almost stroked out when a buzzing tingle shot through his left nipple.

His cell phone. It was set to vibrate when a call came in. Correction: It was set to vibrate for a few moments and then play the *Flintstones* theme song at maximum volume. Joe, probably, asking him to pick up eggs on his way home.

Bzzz.

Directly below him, Mick scratched his ass and glanced around. "Did we come this way?"

Wesley kept one eye on Mick and Hal, and one eye on the spider. He struggled to maintain his precarious balance as his left hand relinquished its death grip on the nearest branch and tugged on his jacket's brass zipper pull. The ratchety whisper of metal on metal sounded unnaturally loud in the stillness of the woods. Thankfully, Mick and Hal didn't seem to notice.

Bzzz.

How long did the damn phone vibrate before the tune kicked in? Five seconds? Eight? Droplets of sweat congregated on Wesley's upper lip as his left hand contorted itself to grope under the left side of his jacket where the cell phone was jammed deep in the breast pocket.

Hal turned to Mick. "What do you mean, did we come this way? Weren't you ever a Boy Scout?"

So not the father, Wesley thought, if he had to ask. Plus, Mick called him by his first name.

Bzzz.

"Yeah, I was," Mick said. "Well, a Cub Scout. Till they kicked me out. What of it?"

Wesley's fingertips teased open the pocket. He braced himself for *"Flintstones! Meet the Flintstones!"* His fingers burrowed deeper. Where was that goddamn phone?

He watched the spider execute a languid turn and make its way up the outstretched middle finger of his right hand. *Yeah, screw you, too, my friend.*

"Just remember," Hal said, "we're talking about two million bucks. Don't jump the gun on this business with the Narby woman."

Wesley's nape prickled. Lucy Narby. In that instant one lone fingertip made contact with the smooth case of his cell phone.

Bzzz.

He'd been hoping to extract maybe twenty thou from Narby for keeping mum about the missus and the missus. Now here was this yahoo mentioning Lucy Narby and two million dollars in the same breath.

Wesley's damp fingers snagged the phone at last. He hauled it out of his pocket and pressed the disconnect button just as the first note of *"Flintstones!"* began to chirp. Fortunately, Hal's voice drowned it out.

"What's your number?" Hal flipped open his own cell. Mick recited seven digits, which Wesley punched into the keypad of his phone, storing the number in the phone's memory as Hal did the same. Meanwhile the spider had reversed course and was preparing to crawl under the cuff of Wesley's jacket sleeve.

"That's my mobile," Mick said. "The house number—"

"Forget the house number." Hal stowed his phone. "That's all I need, is to get your mother on the line."

"Relax," Mick said. "She won't be back from Bermuda till next week. What's your number?"

"*I'll* call *you*. The road's that way. Come on."

Wesley waited until the two men were out of earshot, then flicked the spider onto the tree trunk and smeared it under his mini scope. He clambered down the tree as fast as his stiff knees would allow and trailed Hal and Mick at a discreet distance.

The visit to Narby could wait.

11

25 years earlier

WAS HE ON a boat? That was what it smelled like, that diesel smell like when Grandpa Will took him deep-sea fishing. Also a sour tang, like mildew and stale beer. But there was no movement. If Ricky were on a boat, he'd feel some rocking, wouldn't he, even if the boat was docked. And not a whiff of fish. A truck maybe? Trucks ran on diesel. But what truck was carpeted? He felt matted shag under his butt, which did nothing to cushion the hard floor he'd been sitting on for over two days now.

And the shivering. It would stop for a second or two, then start up again, worse than before. He'd never known your whole body could ache just from shaking so much. It was from fear, but it was from cold, too, a damp March cold that penetrated the air, the floor, his entire body. Wherever he was, it was unheated, and all Ricky had on was jeans, sneakers, and a thin Rugby shirt.

The jeans had taken forever to dry. He was so scared at first, he'd wet himself, to his immense shame. Where he was now, there was a toilet a few steps away in a tiny bathroom. That, too, reminded him of a boat. The "head," he called it in his mind. Twice a day the man unlocked the chain around Ricky's waist and let him use the head, still blindfolded. Until then, he had to hold it, and he did. Ricky refused to pee himself again, no matter how scared he got.

The man had hit Gabby on the head with his gun. She collapsed against the vending machine where they'd gone for snacks during a break in shooting the show. There was so much blood, Ricky knew she had to be dead. Gabby was more than a nanny to him, she was like another mother. He'd known her for nine years, his whole life. He tried not to think about what the kidnapper did to her.

Or what he almost did to his co-star Quint as the bird lay wounded next to Gabby, screeching at full volume, struggling to right himself with one wing bent at a crazy angle. The man pointed his gun at Quint, and Ricky knew he was going to shoot him, he could see it in his face. He knew from the movies that the chunky thing on the barrel was a silencer. Even unmuffled, a gunshot would make less noise than Quint.

So he begged. He blubbered like a little kid, pleading with him not to kill Quint, promising he'd do whatever the man wanted. What he wanted was for Ricky to go with him. Numbly, he had.

Ricky tried to shift his weight; his tailbone hurt worst of all. When he wasn't thinking about Gabby, he thought about his parents, especially his father, Richard Baines, Sr. Ricky had always been afraid of his dad, though he'd never admitted that to anyone, not even Gabby. He had a feeling she knew, though.

Had his kidnapper called his parents? It had been more than two days. He must have gotten in touch with them by now, right? He'd want money. They always wanted money when they kidnapped someone in the movies. Sometimes in the movies, the family paid the money and the kidnapper killed the person anyway. Something else Ricky tried not to think about.

His dad had a lot of money. Ricky hoped it would be that simple. The man names a price, his dad pays it, Ricky goes home.

One good thing: The man hadn't molested him. Not yet, anyway. Ricky knew stuff like that happened, though he was hazy on the particulars.

He felt, more than heard, a distant door opening. The floor quaked with the man's footfalls as he came toward him. Ricky's shivering got worse. What was his kidnapper doing here? His next bathroom break was several hours away. And the remains of his last meal—another peanut butter sandwich and a plastic cup of water, same as always—still littered the floor in front of him. It was hard to eat and drink with his wrists taped together. He could have reached up and pulled the blindfold off anytime, but he never knew when he was being watched. And anyway, he was pretty sure he didn't want to look into the man's eyes.

Ricky flinched as something fell onto the carpeting right in front of him, something small, by the sound of it. The man didn't say anything, but that was nothing new. He hadn't spoken since he'd tossed Ricky into that van. Ricky smelled mild BO as his kidnapper yanked off the blindfold. Ricky squeezed his eyes shut, but a slap across the cheek snapped them open.

A plastic mask loomed over him, a smiling dark-haired princess mask with a crown, the kind a girl might wear to go trick-or-treating. The man had blond hair pulled back in a messy ponytail. There was a large bandage behind his ear. Ricky realized he must have been wearing a dark wig when he pretended to be a security guard at the studio. This was the same man; he had no doubt about that. The mustache had probably been fake, too. He stared now at that princess mask, eerily lit by a lone utility lamp dangling over their heads. The only part of the man's face he could see was the one he didn't want to: a pair of pale gray eyes, partially visible through the little eye holes.

The BO smell got stronger as the man shoved him onto his back and pinned him to the floor with his knees. He picked up what he'd dropped before: a wood-handled hunting knife, the kind Grandpa Will used to gut bluefish.

The man slammed Ricky's bound wrists onto a scarred plank of wood. He clamped his fingers around all of Ricky's, except for the pinky finger of Ricky's left hand, which he pressed to the plank. He positioned the knife and waited, watching, as Ricky screamed and sobbed and pleaded, bucking under the man's unyielding weight. Ricky's face was drenched in tears and snot, his body bathed in icy sweat.

The princess mask turned from Ricky's face to the plank. The man reared up. His knees dug in harder. Ricky squeezed his eyes shut. Pain exploded in his finger. His head filled with a pulsing energy he only dimly recognized as his own screams. Wet warmth flooded his pants. Dark spots obscured his vision.

It wasn't over. The man examined his handiwork, muttered a curse, and put his weight into the task. The dark spots spread and coalesced, and Ricky let the blackness take him away.

12

"**H**OW DID YOU end up with Quint?" Lucy asked. "That *has* to be the same parrot from the show. He's got all the lines down."

Will changed lanes as the exit sign for Crystal Harbor came into view. "He and I hit it off on the set. I really enjoyed working with him, and I didn't have any pets at home. My dad wouldn't allow an animal in the house. Anyway, Quint's broken wing ended his TV career, so when my mom offered a generous sum for him, he became mine."

She hesitated before asking, "That happened when you were kidnapped, right? His broken wing? I remember that from the news stories." The kidnapping of Ricky Baines had dominated the news for days.

"Quint got KO'd," he said, "but not before taking a chunk out of the guy's scalp. The two of them tried to protect me, Quint and Gabby. She got pistol-whipped."

Lucy winced. Will had already explained that his parents had hired Gabby as a teenage au pair shortly after his birth; the two of them had always been close. "So your dad finally said okay to a pet?"

"No." His smile was grim. "It was one of the few times Mom stood up to him. Her child was hurting and she was determined to soothe that hurt any way she could. Plus the old prick had shown his true colors by then."

"What do you mean?"

"When the ransom demand came, he refused to pay."

"What?" Her eyes widened. "Why? He had the money, didn't he?" That was another detail she recalled from the news coverage back then. The young star's folks were loaded.

"Pride. He had no intention of forking over a million bucks to some punk just because he snatched his kid. Even the authorities advised him to pay, but he thought he knew better, thought he could bully and threaten the kidnapper into giving me up." Will shrugged. "Bullying and threatening had worked pretty well for him up till then."

"But the kidnapper didn't give you up." Lucy's gaze strayed to his left hand.

"When the package arrived at the house—" he wiggled the stump of his pinky "—my mom went berserk. That's what I've been told. They had to pull her off my dad. She demanded he pay—threatened to hold a news conference, tell the world what a self-involved, penny-pinching bastard he was, reveal all his shady business dealings. By then, the ransom demand had doubled. It was understood that every finger my parents received would cost them another million."

Lucy's hand drifted to her mouth. Will's tone was dry, a matter-of-fact recounting of events. She took a deep breath. "So your father paid the ransom."

"Yeah, he paid it—with my money, my earnings from the show. A million three." He turned onto Lucy's long driveway. "The old man had to dip into his own funds to bring it up to two mil. Never forgave me for costing him so much."

"Wait a minute. I thought he was a millionaire."

Will nodded. "Many times over. Made his fortune with a chain of gyms. Empire State Athletic Club."

"So . . . he could've paid the entire ransom out of petty cash and never felt the pinch," she said.

"Hey, you don't stay rich by giving it away, right?"

Something else Lucy remembered from the news stories back then: The man who'd kidnapped and maimed little Ricky Baines was never caught. He was still at large, after all this time. She stared at Will's profile, wondering about his decision to reinvent himself as a designer kidnapper.

He slowed at the top of the drive. "Is that your husband's?"

She followed his gaze. Her stomach sank. "What's he doing here?"

Will pulled in next to the gold Mercedes. The two of them silently stared at the third vehicle sharing the parking area at the side of the house: a yellow box truck with *Trout Bros. Moving Co.* stenciled on the side.

Will killed the engine. "I'm coming in with you."

"Don't be silly. It's just Frank. Though I have to say, I'm surprised. He promised to respect my privacy when we separated. It's not like him to just pop in like this."

"With a moving van," Will said. "Looks like he's done a one-eighty on the divorce issue."

Lucy now wished she'd asked Frank to relinquish his house keys. She started to thank Will for the ride, but he was already letting himself out of the car. She got out too. "Really, Will, maybe it's better if you don't—"

"Frank was acting weird last night, Lucy." Will followed her to the truck. "And he admitted siccing those two pseudo-kidnappers on you."

"Well, that was a boneheaded move, but—"

"It was beyond boneheaded, it was dangerous. You could've gotten hurt trying to fend off what you thought were real kidnappers."

She gave him a *You don't say* look. "Imagine that—being accosted in your own home and not knowing it's all a charade."

Lucy braced herself as the open rear of the moving truck came into view, expecting to see her antique dining room set, her hand-forged iron bedstead, possibly even—please God, no—her Isamu Noguchi glass-and-wood coffee table, one of the originals from the 1940s. But the truck held only a few tall wardrobe cartons, Frank's golf clubs, and several boxes marked: *FRAGILE.* his collection of giraffe sculptures, no doubt. She sighed in relief. "Looks like I got here in time."

Will accompanied her to the side door. He placed a finger on her lips when she started to protest. "I'm coming in. This is nonnegotiable."

The corners of her mouth twitched as he tried the door and found it unlocked. "You're off the clock, Buttercup. Nobody's paying you to boss me around."

In the kitchen Lucy's gaze homed in on the bare counter space previously occupied by the old-fashioned milk-shake machine and the enormous commercial cappuccino maker. Well, that was okay. They were Frank's toys, after all. She didn't even like cappuccino. She wondered if he planned to rip out his beloved under-counter wine cellar.

They found Frank in the library, directing three moving men as they secured padded quilts around the pigskin chair and a half. "Take it through here." He unlocked the French doors.

All three movers wore eyeglasses, ponytails, and forearm tattoos depicting spotted fish. One even wore a Phish concert T-shirt. *I get it,* Lucy thought. The Trout brothers.

The biggest Trout unwrapped a pink nugget of bubble gum. "What happened in here?" His gaze took in the overturned furniture, the scattered popcorn and broken picture glass. "You guys get robbed?"

"Something like that." Frank turned then and spotted his wife and her kidnapper. She saw the gears turning behind his hazel eyes. "Oh. Right." He addressed Will. "Makes sense she'd tell you to let Lucy go."

"You know about that?" Lucy and Will exchanged a dubious look. When did Frank find out about Ethel's practical joke?

"You didn't have a clue last night," Will reminded him.

"That's what I wanted you to think. Hey, be careful!" Frank said as the Trouts wrestled his beloved chair through the French doors. "That's a custom-crafted piece."

Lucy and Will followed Frank outside, where he clucked over the men as they horsed the chair into the truck. "I mean, who else *could've* been behind it, right?" Frank asked his wife. "I called her after I left you guys."

It irked Lucy that Frank had deduced Ethel's role in the kidnapping before she had. She lowered her voice. "You told me you wouldn't do this." She indicated the truck. "Raiding the house when I'm not here. What happened to keeping this divorce civilized?"

Her husband made a face. "If civility means me rolling over and letting you walk away with the whole shebang, think again. The last couple of days must've taught you *something.*"

Lucy frowned. "What does that have to do with . . . ? I know you sent those two idiots in the ski masks. Am I supposed to be *impressed* by that warped stunt?"

Frank returned to the house. She stalked after him. Will trailed behind, a silent but comforting presence. "Am I supposed to swoon with delight because my husband hired a couple of goons to *terrorize* me? What the hell is wrong with you?"

Frank stared at her, clearly taken aback. In twenty years she'd never spoken to him like that. It had always been so much easier to take the path of least resistance. What had she imagined would happen if she stood up for herself?

They were both about to find out.

Her husband drew himself up. "Guess what I found in the kitchen garbage."

"You went through my *garbage*?"

"It was lying right on top. An empty Fritos bag. *Fritos!*"

This was the final betrayal, Lucy knew, the ultimate act of defiance for a tediously loyal KrunchWorks wife. "If you'd dug a little farther, you'd have found a Pringles can."

He flushed a furious brick red. "Are you trying to kill me?"

"Get out, Frank."

"Like hell."

Lucy turned to Will. "This is between me and Frank. Do me a favor and wait outs—"

"No." Will scooped a few stray kernels of popcorn off the mantelpiece and tossed them into his mouth.

"Oh, for heaven's sake." She turned back to her husband. "You promised to respect my space, Frank, to wait for a fair, negotiated settle—"

"Things have changed, in case you haven't noticed," he said. "You don't call the shots anymore."

There was that admonition again, for the second time in less than twenty-four hours. The only time she'd ever "called the shots" was when she'd finally kicked Frank out of the house. And apparently she hadn't even done *that* right.

"Take your clothes, take your cappuccino maker." She was nearly shouting. "Take your giraffes and your golf clubs and Babe."

"Who?"

She flung her hand toward the vacant space recently occupied by his chair and a half. "That ugly pigskin . . . *thing* that cost us more than our first car. Take it and leave. You're not making off with anything else. Not now. Not this way. We're going to do this thing right."

"Meaning what? That I'm supposed to roll over and wait for your lawyer to rob me blind?"

"I don't have a lawyer." A mistake, putting off that inevitable, painful step. "Yet."

"So you say," he sneered.

"When have I ever lied to you? What's gotten into you, Frank?"

"If you did hire a lawyer," he said, "*un*hire him. There's not going to be any divorce."

She groaned. "Oh, don't start that—"

"I'll let you keep living here," Frank continued, "provided you cooperate."

Lucy's jaw dropped. "*Excuse* me? You'll let me *live* in my own home?"

"Who holds the title?" Frank's cold smile said, *Didn't think of that, did you?*

"That's irrelevant and you know it," Lucy said. "The court will divide the marital assets equitably."

"You're not listening." Frank got in her face. "No lawyers. No divorce court. You and I remain married—on paper anyway. I'll be moving permanently to Egerton."

"Where?"

Frank smirked. "Like you have no clue what I'm talking about. Like you've never heard of Egerton, Illinois. This isn't the way I'd have chosen for it to come out, but now that it has, I've gotta tell you, it's a relief."

Lucy looked to Will, silently asking if he had a clue what Frank was babbling about. Will shrugged.

"You're a good man, Will. Loyal to the end." Frank slapped him on the back. "But listen, you can drop the hush-hush stuff now, okay? Lucy knows about her, she knows that Lucy knows, everyone knows everything. We're all on the same page here."

Same page? Lucy thought. She wasn't even in the same book.

The Trout brothers returned, and Frank fretted over the antique rolltop desk as they prepared to move it. It embarrassed Lucy to watch her husband fuss over their possessions like that. Auntie Frank. Had he always been so prissy and officious? Looking back, she had to admit that yes, this lovely trait had always been part of his personality. She'd been blind to his faults, willfully so, determined as she was to keep the family together for the sake of their son.

Lucy turned to the movers. "Stop what you're doing." Her own strong, authoritative voice surprised her. The Trouts snapped to, awaiting further instructions. She straightened the sleeves of her jammies. "You are not to touch anything else in this house."

"Don't listen to her." Frank sounded bored. "This is my house. This is my stuff. Get that desk out to the truck."

"It is not his house. This is a divorce situation," Lucy informed the Trouts, whose heads whipped around on the word "divorce." "The contents of this house are not my husband's to dispose of. If you remove anything else—"

"Hey, *no problemo*," The biggest Trout said. All three brothers showed their palms and took one giant step back. Big Trout turned to Frank. "We'll settle up now."

"No," Frank said. "Why are you listening to her? *I* hired you, and I'm telling you to—"

"We don't get in the middle of divorces." Big Trout blew a gum bubble and popped it.

"There is no divorce," Frank said. "She's mistaken." The Trouts' eyebrows rose in unison. "I mean, she's lying. It's a trick."

The littlest Trout scratched his cranium stubble. "You two aren't splitting up?"

"No! That's what I'm trying to tell you."

"So then why're you moving stuff outta here?" asked the medium-sized Trout.

Frank tossed his hands in frustration. "Why do you care? I pay you, you move stuff. You don't need to know why."

Lucy folded her arms across her chest. She addressed the moving men. "We split up over a month ago. He's just trying to steal everything in the place. If you let him use you to do it, my lawyer will—"

"Yeah, yeah." Big Trout waved away the threat. He jerked his head toward the French doors and the moving truck beyond. "You got a problem with him swiping the stuff we already loaded?"

"I'm not 'swiping' anything!" Frank shouted.

"No problemo." Lucy smiled at the Trouts. She nodded toward her husband. "I'd demand cash if I were you."

Big Trout popped another bubble and winked at her. He was actually kind of cute. He handed her a business card. "Gimme a call when you get it all sorted out."

13

JUDITH SLATHERED SPF 45 on her pallid arms and upper chest. She leaned forward on the poolside chaise to squirt the stuff on her legs, and hesitated. Would it kill her to get a little color? If she returned to New York as pale as she'd left, no one would even believe she'd been to Bermuda.

She sighed. If she allowed even the trace of a tan, she'd have to hear about it from Roger, the dermatologist. She started to squeeze the bottle, only to have it snatched away by a big, masculine hand.

A Gaelic-inflected voice said, "You missed a spot."

Judith's heart did a back flip. She squinted into the brilliant morning sun, blinking as the man's lofty shadow fell over her and his features materialized. It *was* him! "What the hell are you doing here?"

Fergus Dowd perched next to her on the padded teak chaise, hip-butting her to make room. "Helping you to maintain a corpselike pallor." He evened out the lotion on her chest, his fingers straying dangerously close to the modest scoop neck of her forest green one-piece.

She slapped his hand away. "Answer me. Why are you in Bermuda? And make it good."

A woman several chairs away looked up from her newspaper. The pool area was sparsely populated this morning, the temperature only in the seventies. April wasn't August, even in Bermuda.

"Dr. Milton is shirkin' his duties." Fergus upended the bottle of sunscreen and glopped some onto her bare thigh. She tried to jerk her leg away, but he moved like a cobra, seizing her calf with one hand and spreading lotion with the other. "He's out there on the fairway knockin' a little ball around when he should be here protecting his woman from the lethal rays of the sun."

And from wild Irishmen with intriguing pasts and magic hands. She restrained a groan of pleasure as his long, slick fingers kneaded the muscles of her thigh. "How do you know Roger's on the golf course? No, don't tell me." She arched one eyebrow, taking in Fergus's antiquated sporting costume, complete with knickers, argyle sweater, goofy hat, and golf shoes with spikes. "You just came from there."

"Your fella has a decent swing, but he doesn't seem to know what that darlin' wee hole is for." A suggestive grin accompanied this comment, and Judith bit back another groan.

One year, four months, and thirteen days. That was how long it had been. Even when Donald was among the living, their sex life barely had a pulse.

Judith bought batteries by the case.

She tried to dislodge Fergus's hand, now loitering at the lower edge of her suit. She may as well try to dislodge the Blarney Stone. "How did you know we were staying here?" she asked. "Have you been spying on us?"

His luxuriant brows twitched. "A scurrilous accusation like that from such a refined lady as yourself? I am shocked, Mrs. Drinkwater, and that's the truth."

Judith imagined Fergus skulking around the resort—to the extent a long-haired Irish giant with outlandish taste in clothes can skulk—waiting patiently for Roger to make himself scarce so he could get her alone.

That notion settled where all good notions do, making her squirm. "I don't know what you think you're doing here, Fergus, but you're wasting your time. Go home."

"Has Dr. Milton been mistreatin' you, Mrs. Drinkwater?" He squirted more sunscreen and tenderly smoothed it up her inner thigh. "Is that why you're so prickly?"

"Dr. Mil—Roger treats me just fine, he's a gentleman, and if you don't want me to be so damn *prickly*, you could try taking lessons from him. Stop that." She grabbed his wrist. "I'm not going to sunburn *there*."

"Oh, I don't think I'll be takin' lessons from Dr. Milton anytime soon. I know what that darlin' wee hole is for."

Her eyes narrowed. "Have you been talking to my brother? Has Will been blabbing to you about my personal life?"

"You mean did he tell me you have yet to receive a thorough examination from the good doctor?"

"That bastard!" She jerked upright, heedless of the stares of those around her.

"No, he didn't, but thanks for verifyin' my suspicions, lass. Flip over now so I can do your back." He squeezed more lotion onto his palm.

Judith could have refused. She could have continued to spar with Fergus as she always did—which never failed to give him the upper hand. This man was a master at keeping her off balance. It was time to turn the tables.

She shifted onto her stomach and folded her arms under her head. "Your powers of deduction are impressive, Fergus. That you could guess that about me and Roger."

"Guesswork had nothin' to do with it, Mrs. Drinkwater."

"Oh yes, I forgot. You're trained in that sort of thing."

His fingers stroked between her shoulder blades. "Meaning what?"

"Will told me all about you. Oh." Judith tossed a disingenuous look over her shoulder. "Was he not supposed to?"

"Told you what precisely?"

"You know." She twitched her shoulders in a little shrug. "Your past. It's okay, Fergus. My lips are sealed. But I am curious as to what it was like. How you, you know, got into that line of work."

Fergus shifted his attention to the back of her thigh. His hand felt huge and strong and deliciously rough. Somehow she managed not to wriggle.

One year, four months, and thirteen days. God help her.

"How I got into that line of work?" He repeated her question. "Oh, by the usual routes, I suppose."

"It sounds fascinating, Fergus. I'd love to hear about it."

"That part of my life is over," he said. "It wasn't nearly as exciting as you make it out."

"Oh, I find that hard to believe. All right, just tell me this. Did you ever have to . . . terminate anyone?"

"Ah, lass, I'd really rather not get into—"

"You did, didn't you?" Judith twisted around to look him in the eye. She felt a flush of heat that had nothing to do with the sun. "How many?"

Fergus smoothed sunscreen down her calf and massaged it into her ankle. "It's not somethin' I like to speak of."

"Yes, but . . ." But she was dying to know. Judith slumped onto her stomach. She pictured it in her mind's eye. Fergus Dowd, double agent, extracting secrets from a Russian spy. And then poisoning the man's martini. Or maybe it's an American spy. A beautiful American spy whom he first seduces to gain her trust—before receiving the order to terminate her, which he obeys, regretfully but without hesitation.

Maybe his past had nothing to do with the Cold War. There was always the Irish Republican Army. Of course, it was entirely possible he hadn't been a spy at all. She'd imagined him as a "made man." Some sort of Mafia kingpin. Was there an Irish Mafia?

Judith found the notion of Fergus Dowd, master criminal, even more stimulating than Fergus Dowd, master spy.

She sighed. "You're not going to tell me anything, are you?"

"I'm afraid not, lass. My first career involved secrets which I am not at liberty to share. You understand." He lifted her foot and began to massage it with the slippery lotion.

"You don't have to do that. I doubt I'll burn on the bottoms of my—" She broke off with a moan of pleasure.

"Better safe than sorry." His sinewy fingers found every pressure point. He fondled the arches, the toes, and between them.

Judith knew she should stop him—this kind of fondling had nothing whatsoever to do with sun safety—yet she couldn't find the will to do it. Her eyes fluttered shut. When was the last time she'd had a foot rub? Not from Roger, certainly, and Donald hadn't been the touchy-feely type.

It had to have been Hal, she realized. He'd definitely been the touchy-feely type—that is, until he'd become the Jekyll-Hyde type. He used to rub her feet, brush her hair, and . . . well, the man had just the most talented mouth. Hal Lynch had without a doubt been the most physical, sensual, just plain sexual man she'd ever been with.

Of course, that level of intensity wasn't restricted to his libido. He'd been possessive to the point of obsession, a circumstance she'd found flattering until even her platonic male pals were afraid to stop by for a beer or a few puffs on the bong. And she'd been afraid to let them.

"You're frowning." Fergus's voice was low and intimate. "Am I doin' it wrong?"

She allowed herself a snort of amusement. They both knew what he was doing, and he was doing it just right—damn him. "I was just thinking of someone I used to know."

"And I remind you of this cad?" He switched to the other foot.

"No, it's just . . . he used to do that. Rub my feet."

"Did your husband know about this foot-rubbing bloke?"

"This was before Donald. Before I cleaned up my act." She sighed. "I'm sure Will has filled you in on my 'before.' All the gory details."

"I know some of it. No one but you knows the whole of it, lass, not even your brother, I'd wager."

"Thank God for that," Judith whispered into the cradle of her arms. She hadn't meant to say it aloud.

He was quiet a few moments, kneading her heel with his slick thumbs.

"Don't mind me." She forced a light tone. "Sunshine brings out my maudlin side."

"Tell me more about this foot-rubbin' fella," Fergus said. "Does he still come sniffin' around?"

"He couldn't if he wanted to. He's locked up for life." Judith's stomach did that little twist it did whenever she thought about where Hal was—and that she was the one who'd put him there. Not that she regretted it for an instant. But fear and secrecy were a sickening combination. "The sentence was twenty-five to life, actually, but there's no way that psycho's getting out."

Only Judith knew who had kidnapped her brother from the studio in Astoria. And only she knew the man wasn't running around free. Harold Stuart Lynch would never run around free again. He'd told her the ransom money was stashed in five different bank vaults. No doubt he'd been paying rental fees on the safe-deposit boxes all these years, in the pitiful hope that some parole board might suffer collective insanity and decide to release him.

Judith didn't even want to know which banks he'd chosen. She wanted nothing to do with that blood money, not since she'd seen what Hal had done to her brother to get it.

As far at the rest of the world was concerned, the kidnapper was never caught. In fact, he was caught, but for an unrelated crime. Will must have spent the past twenty-five years looking over his shoulder. Judith had spent the past twenty-five years wishing she could tell him not to worry. He'd never lay eyes on that monster again.

"Sounds like a complicated bloke, this foot rubber," Fergus said.

"You *would* describe him that way. But actually, yes, he was—still is, I guess—a complicated bloke."

"Who did he kill?"

"How do you know it was murder?"

"They don't give life sentences for jaywalkin'."

"He killed a drug dealer—the guy who supplied his coke. I don't know the specifics, except that he slit his throat. After he'd had a little fun with his knife." She paused, remembering. "He liked knives."

"And you were tight with this fella?"

"Like I said—complicated." She glared at him over her shoulder. "I'm sure you must know someone like that."

She expected to see Fergus's trademark impish grin. Instead he said, "The world is filled with men who fall somewhere between your sociopath and your urologist."

"Roger's a dermatologist. Donald was the urologist."

"Good policy, sticking with the M.D.s." Fergus nodded sagely. "A stable, high-earnin' breed. You don't have to choose between one extreme and the other, is what I'm sayin'."

"I don't suppose you have someone in mind?" Her tone was dry. "Who falls somewhere in the middle?" Perhaps a bit closer to the sociopathic end of the spectrum.

That was why she was attracted to Fergus, she knew. She'd always had a weakness for the wild men, and look where it had gotten her. She'd been forced to snitch on her lover—the father of her unborn child. To send him to prison for the rest of his life.

And if she hadn't? Judith would never forget that final beating, which had spurred her to action at last. She could have lost the baby. Hal hadn't known she was pregnant; she'd avoided telling him. He was so volatile, and she was terrified of him by that point.

Judith reached under the chaise for her cigarettes and lighter. "On second thought, don't answer that." She turned over and raised the back of the chaise so she could sit up. She tossed her towel to Fergus to wipe his hands. He studied her closely as he did so.

He said, "You don't have to keep it all inside, you know."

That was the only safe place for it. No one knew about Hal, or that he was Mick's father. No one knew about her role in Will's kidnapping, and no one ever would. It was her biggest secret and her greatest shame. It had been the proverbial albatross around her neck for the past quarter century, and it would be so until she took her dying breath. Lord knew she deserved worse. She'd give anything if she could go back in time and undo it.

"No offense, Fergus, but my personal life is none of your business."

"Have you ever talked to a professional?"

"You mean a shrink?" She tapped her cigarette on a small ceramic ashtray decorated with the resort's logo. "You think I've gone over the deep end?"

"I think something's been eatin' at you for a long time, lass, and it wouldn't hurt to have a chat with someone who could help you sort it out."

"Thanks for the advice, *Doctor* Dowd."

"I am at your service as always, Mrs. Drinkwater." There it was, the impish grin. "Make another appointment on your way out."

14

WILL BUTTONED HIS charcoal gray suit jacket while scanning the bar of the elegant Adriane restaurant in midtown Manhattan. The place was crowded for a Monday night. His gaze settled on a couple flirting over martinis, seemingly oblivious to everything but each other.

Will lingered on the periphery of the customers thronging the bar, watching the couple. After a minute, the woman surreptitiously checked her wristwatch. She glanced around and locked eyes with Will.

Gabby looked eminently pick-upable in a short-skirted, pimento-colored suit. She wore no blouse under the jacket's gaping neckline, just a sheer silk scarf tucked with enough artful carelessness to turn self-possessed professional men into gibbering simps. Her companion's gaze shifted south every time she leaned toward him, which she did far more often than necessary.

The man was middle-aged and reasonably attractive if ear-to-ear comb-overs were your thing. Gabby whispered something to him. He grinned, tossed back the remainder of his drink, and slapped some money on the bar. Gabby led the way toward the door, only to stop short when Will stepped in her path.

She gasped and dropped the man's hand. "Steve!"

Will's outraged scowl shifted from Gabby to his client, who had yet to recognize him from their one meeting several weeks earlier. The martinis and the bar's dim lighting helped, as did Will's wig and fake goatee.

Ben Porter puffed himself up. "Who's this?"

"My husband," she said.

"Shit." Porter raised his palms and tried to melt back into the throng of customers. "I didn't mean anything."

Will advanced on him. "Who do you think you are, messing with my wife?" Heads turned in their direction.

"I didn't know she was married. I swear."

"Yeah, I can see how you might miss *this*." Will grabbed Gabby's left hand and shoved it in Porter's face. The ring finger bore a thick wedding band and a four-carat faux diamond. A few customers snickered. The bartender, a pretty brunette, politely asked the gentlemen and lady to take their conversation outside. Will grabbed Porter, crushing the collar of his three-thousand-dollar suit.

"Steve, don't hurt this one!" Gabby screamed.

"Shut up, Monique."

"*Outside*, please." The bartender displayed the handpiece of the bar phone, a warning.

"No problem." Will propelled Porter toward the doorway. The crowd parted before them. One or two refined male voices offered unrefined suggestions for how to deal with the cuckolding SOB. Gabby tottered along in her four-inch heels, flapping her hands and squealing her dismay in the language of her birth.

Several bar patrons followed them into the damp night air, eager for a show. Will's Camry was parked at the curb. When he beeped it open and started to cram Porter into the front passenger seat, the man finally found his backbone.

Until Gabby discreetly shoved the SIG in his ribs. Porter's eyes bulged. "Get in, Benny," she murmured, pure steel beneath that sweet Gabby smile.

Benny Porter obeyed, and Will saw the instant his client got it, the instant he realized this outraged husband was in fact the designer kidnapper he'd hired to deliver the thrill of a lifetime. Gabby settled into the backseat as Will slipped behind the wheel.

Porter's voice shook. "I—I've got to call my wi—"

"You're not calling anyone." Will watched for an opening and pulled into late-night traffic on Fifty-Second Street.

Gabby leaned forward, pressing the pistol into Porter's side. "I have a few ideas what to do with this one. Oh, but we are going to have so much fun."

Will pulled off the hairpieces as he headed for the Fifty-Ninth Street Bridge. He and Gabby kept in menacing character during the hour-long ride, reminding their client he'd signed up for a realistic abduction experience, not Club Med without the bar beads. Once they were on less-busy back roads, Gabby handcuffed Porter and blindfolded him with her scarf, which reeked of her perfume.

They started up the long drive to the Goo a little after midnight, only to find their way blocked by Mick's red Mustang convertible. Will muttered a curse. He hadn't seen his troublesome nephew since he'd ejected him from the car Friday night.

"What do you think he wants?" Gabby asked.

Will shrugged. He'd sent Mick a check for services rendered, via Judith. He'd been more than generous, all things considered.

"What's going on?" Porter asked.

"Shut him up, Monique," Will said, and Gabby obligingly crammed Porter's own monogrammed hankie into his mouth.

Mick strolled across the lawn toward them as they led Porter to the Goo. He had someone with him, a man Will didn't recognize.

Now it was Gabby's turn to curse. In French she said, "He knows better than that." There was nothing illegal about Will's business, but letting uninitiated strangers hang around and observe was verboten, and Mick knew it. Peering more closely at the man, she murmured, "He looks like Sting."

"Need some help?" Mick asked, falling into step with them.

"Not from you. Who's he?"

"Aw, will you forget about the other night?" Mick whined. He tapped his nose, still bruised and lumpy. "I got the shit end of it anyway, in case you didn't notice."

"I said, who is he?"

The stranger answered. "I'm Keith Kitchen."

Will's head snapped around on the last name.

"Long-lost cousin." Mick grinned. "Pretty cool, huh?"

Keith held the door open for Will as he thrust his docile client over the threshold and marched him toward the room recently vacated by Lucy. "I never heard of any cousin named Keith."

"He's like a fifth cousin, three times removed," Mick said. "Something like that. Right, Keith?"

"Nothing like that."

Their visitors followed along as Will and Gabby ushered Porter into the room. "It's crowded in here," Will said. "You two wait in the hall." He pulled the gag out of Porter's mouth, a gesture the blindfolded man took as a signal to go apeshit.

"You'll never hold me, fuckers!" He launched himself away from Will, tripped over the edge of the mattress, and executed a spectacular front roll, ripping the seat of that nice suit in the process. His undershorts were navy silk. He was up like a shot, zigzagging across the room, his lacquered comb-over flopping around like a wounded grackle. Will managed to grab him by the collar and haul him back. The man swung around and landed a punishing kick to his shin.

Will cursed and stumbled. Mick could have stopped Porter's blind rush for the boarded-up windows; instead he stood giggling at the spectacle. Will wished like hell Fergus were there. He *should* have been there. Instead he'd left a Post-it with a terse message: *Later, lad.* No hint of where he'd gone off to, but Will could guess.

Cousin Keith lunged past Mick and tackled Porter before the man managed to kill himself. It was like watching a lion bring down a gazelle, except that this lion made a conspicuous effort to keep his prey from cracking his head open.

"Settle down!" Keith barked. He knelt on Porter's back, exerting just enough pressure to immobilize him.

Porter never stopped ranting. "Lemme go, you sons o' bitches!"

Mick gleefully advanced on Will's client, now that the man was helpless. Will shoved his nephew into the hallway.

"Where do you want him?" Keith stood, pulling Porter up with him. Will's cousin was no spring chicken—probably around Fergus's age—but clearly he was fit.

"*Merci*, Keith," Gabby said. "We will take it from here." She shoved the handkerchief back in Porter's mouth while dodging the man's flailing feet.

Her neck scarf still did double duty as a blindfold, affording the men an unobstructed view of her black-and-silver push-up bra.

"Yeah, thanks." Will cast a speculative eye over the various chains and shackles adorning the room.

"You folks got any rope?" Keith asked. "Looks like we've got us a kicker here."

"Do *we* have rope?"

In no time Keith had Porter hog-tied hand to foot, sweating through his suit and issuing garbled threats around the wadded-up hankie.

Will admired his cousin's Marlboro Man efficiency. "You've done this before."

A funny look flashed across Keith's face, until he saw Will's lopsided grin. "Only on the Thanksgiving turkey."

Will treated his client to the requisite dark threats and flicked on the TV/DVD player. Episode One of *Friends* flickered to life. Porter howled through his gag. Will cranked up the volume and led the way out of the room, locking his client in with Rachel and Ross.

"Now that that's out of the way." In the corridor, Will pumped Keith's hand. "Nice to meet you, Cuz. You handled yourself like a pro in there. If you ever need a job, give me a call."

Mick slouched against the wall, reaming out his ear canal with a finger. Will's words brought him to life. "Funny you should mention—"

Keith silenced the kid with a look.

"What?" Will asked his cousin. "You looking for work?"

"Let's just say I'm between jobs. Which has nothing to do with my looking you folks up," he added quickly.

Gabby jabbed her elbow into Will's ribs. "Introduce me, *gosse*. You were brought up better than that."

"Ow. Keith, this *sorcière* is Gabrielle Fonteneau. An old friend of the family and one of my most valuable associates. You can call her Gabby." Will knew better than to add that Gabby had raised him. Judging by the way she was looking at Keith, she wouldn't appreciate the reference to her age.

Gabby smiled prettily and extended an elegant hand, which Cousin Keith held a tad longer than necessary, while treating her to the full power of his amber-colored gaze. This fellow must have been some lady-killer in his youth, Will thought. Probably still was. He confirmed the impression by asking how Will got any work done in the presence of such beauty. Gabby didn't simper or blush. To her, such compliments were simple statements of fact.

"Where are you from originally?" Keith asked her.

"Nice."

"Ah, the magical Côte d'Azur."

She brightened. "You've been there?"

"Sadly, no. But I've always wanted to go."

Gabby's smile broadened, and Will could almost see the itinerary begin to take shape: a romantic getaway for two to the South of France. She clapped her hands. "A family reunion means champagne."

To Gabby, a day without a natural disaster of biblical proportions meant champagne. Will followed meekly with the others as she led the way to the Goo's big commercial kitchen, where she poured four generous flutes of Veuve Clicquot. Mick tossed back his drink and went for a refill as Will, Keith, and Gabby raised their glasses in a toast.

"To long-lost cousins," Will pronounced, and they sipped in unison. He studied Keith Kitchen over the rim of his glass. There was a family resemblance, no doubt about it—not to Will himself necessarily, but certainly to his nephew. Even the shape of their eyes was the same. The color was different, though. Mick's eyes were gray, Keith's the color of whiskey.

"So how are we related?" Will asked. "And where have you been holed up that we haven't run across each other before now?"

Mick started to answer but wilted under a quelling look from Keith. He'd just met the kid and already seemed to have his number. Perceptive chap, this cousin of theirs.

"Your grandpa Will had three younger sisters," Keith said.

"Rose, Lilly, and Marguerite."

"French for 'daisy.'" Keith gave Gabby an intimate smile as she topped off his glass. Now she did blush, and a couple of drops landed on the tile floor.

"Rose and Lilly are widowed," Will said. "They share an apartment in the city."

"Central Park West," Gabby added. *Très chic.*

"Marguerite was the youngest. The family lost touch with her." Will served almond biscotti from a ceramic cookie jar shaped like the Bates Motel. "Didn't she move to the other coast?"

"Seattle." Keith handed Gabby a cookie, then took one for himself. "That's where she met my father. It didn't last. She had to sue him for child support, so she refused to give me his name."

"That's how come he's named Kitchen," Mick added, helpfully.

"So not a fifth cousin after all," Will said. "More like, uh . . ."

Gabby held up a finger. "First cousin, once removed."

Will shrugged. "Sounds good to me."

Keith's smile was just for her. *"Vous êtes beau* et *intelligent, mademoiselle."*

Good grief, there she went again, blushing like a schoolgirl.

"Why haven't we crossed paths before?" Will said. "Did my grandfather know about you?"

"No one knew about me. Mom didn't want to face the family's condemnation for having a child out of wedlock."

"Grandpa Will wouldn't have condemned her."

"No, she knew that," Keith said. "But everyone else would have, so she stayed out there and severed herself from her old life."

"What made you look us up now?"

"Mom died in February. I decided it was time for a change of scenery, and time to . . . to find the rest of my family." Keith's voice cracked. "I only wish I'd done it when Uncle Will was still alive."

Will watched the most unsentimental woman he knew blink back tears of emotion. Even he had to clear his throat before he said, "He was quite a guy, Grandpa Will. You would've liked him."

Keith responded with a bittersweet smile.

As always, Mick could be counted on to annihilate the mood. "So how about giving the cuz a break, huh, Will? Like he said, he's out of—"

"Listen, man." Keith faced Mick, who flinched under the older man's direct gaze. "I appreciate it, but I can speak for myself." He turned back to Will. "I'm new to the area, is all. Just getting my feet under me. I'll find something, no problem."

"What do you do?"

"I'm a personal trainer."

"I figured it was something like that. Something physical, anyway." Will indicated his cousin's impressive musculature.

Gabby agreed enthusiastically, squeezing his biceps for emphasis. "I am thinking he is a lumberjohn, this one. So *musculaire.*"

Mick grimaced. "A what?"

"I think you mean lumber*jack.*" Keith smiled at Gabby as if she were the only other person in existence, certainly the only female person. "You're in excellent shape yourself, Gabby. I noticed a lot of iron in the other room. I'd love to work with you one-on-one. Gratis, *naturellement.*"

She responded with a giggle and a long string of incomprehensible Franglish, a display Will's cousin clearly found charming.

Will set down his glass. "I can't offer you the kind of work you're used to—"

Keith held up his palms, clearly embarrassed. "Listen, man, Mick shouldn't have said anything. I don't expect—"

"Now, hold on. I'm shorthanded at the moment." Will glanced at the last family member he'd tried to hire; Mick was shaking the champagne bottle over his flute to dislodge every last drop. "My number-two man is out of town for who knows how long, and I could use someone with your skills." Keith's physical prowess was only part of the picture; more important, the guy had a level head. Even so, Will wouldn't have been so quick to make the offer if there hadn't been such a strong family resemblance.

Keith appeared uncertain.

"I can offer you temporary work until Fergus returns." Privately Will predicted he'd end up offering Keith a permanent position. And it was Mick, of all people, who'd discovered him. Go figure. "How does two hundred bucks a day sound?"

Keith smiled knowingly. "It sounds overly generous, Cuz."

"You have a place to stay?" Before Keith could answer, Will added, "We've got plenty of room in the house." He stuck out his hand.

After a moment, and with a nod of gratitude, Keith clasped it. "I don't know what to say, man. Thanks."

"Hey, way I figure it, I'm getting a bargain. Taking advantage of family."

"*Très bien*. It is settled." Gabby hauled another bottle of champagne out of the fridge. "We will celebrate."

15

S HE SHOULD'VE CALLED ahead. Lucy stared through the driver's-side window at Will Kitchen's big old Victorian home, looking like a Christmas card through the veil of a light snowfall. The T-shirt temperatures of the past few days had given way to dismal skies and snot-freezing cold. And now it had started snowing, of all things. What had happened to spring? Why couldn't April just be *April*?

And why *hadn't* she called ahead? He might not even be home.

So? Lucy chided herself. She wasn't there to see him. What did it matter if he wasn't home? Or if no one at all was home? There was always the mailbox she'd just passed, standing sentry at the curb. She could leave the gift in there with a little note.

A week ago she would have done just that, crammed her offering in the mailbox without hesitation and burned rubber out of there. But the past few days had taught her something about the real Lucy, the proactive Lucy, the Lucy who'd been grinding down her molars for twenty years watching the Stepford Lucy fluff pillows and perfect her handmade ravioli stuffed with lobster and ricotta in a brandy cream sauce. Frank's favorite dish.

Squinting through the flurries, she spied threads of smoke curling from two of the house's four chimneys. Someone was home.

She pulled her Volvo in to the driveway, parked behind the Goo between a purple Viper and Will's Camry, and tramped toward the house. Her toes had barely brushed the first porch step when she remembered her reason for going there—or her *excuse* for going there if she was being honest with herself. Now, there was a worthy goal for the new, improved Lucy: self-honesty. By the time she'd retraced her steps and trudged back to the house with the gift, Will was waiting for her in the open doorway, wearing a thick cable-knit sweater and faded jeans, his fingers wrapped around a steaming stoneware mug.

"You look like a Maxwell House ad," she said.

"It's not coffee." He offered the mug and she took it. Hot cocoa.

A sexy man offering her chocolate. That was worth an hour and a half behind the wheel any day.

He said, "To what do we owe this—"

She held up the autographed copy of *Johnny Sherlock and the Cracked Clock*. She'd gotten to know his son, Tom, before returning home last Sunday, and discovered the boy was a fan of the Johnny Sherlock series. That had been three days ago. Between lawyering up for the divorce, compiling the necessary financial documents, and struggling to meet her writing deadline for *Painted Poodle*—which, miracle of miracles, she'd manage to accomplish—those three days had passed in about forty-seven minutes.

A surge of welcome warmth greeted Lucy as she stepped over the threshold, carrying with it the humid perfume of simmering soup—chicken, if her nose could be trusted—along with hot chocolate and woodsmoke, and the merest hint of birdcage: Quint's lavishly furnished abode dominated the foyer. It was a gargantuan aviary from another century, a marvel of delicate Victorian ironwork. Quint was perched on the domed top, running feathers through his blue-gray beak.

The interior of Will's house existed in the same time warp as the exterior. From the solid mahogany door to the elaborate crown molding kissing the high, high ceiling, the century-old woodwork appeared intact if a tad exhausted. The clang of cooking utensils drifted from the rear of the house. A stereo somewhere belted out high-energy jazz dominated by fancy piano work.

Quint paused in his preening to offer Lucy a greeting—*"I'm having conniptions!"*—followed by one of his signature hair-raising screams. Will draped her snow-flecked coat and scarf over the monolithic newel post.

From the kitchen Ming-hua screeched, "Irving!" Quint answered for him: *"What!"* The old woman started cussing the bird in Mandarin.

Will called to her, "Irving and Gabby are upstairs, Ming-hua. They're playing Texas Hold 'Em."

Lucy had also met Irving and Ming-hua Hung last Sunday. The couple had been live-in gardener and cook for Will's parents for thirty-three years until age and arthritis began to slow them down. That was when Richard Baines, Sr., gave them the boot—and Will promptly took them in.

The door to the large front room stood open, and Lucy stole a glance inside. The space had probably begun life as a formal parlor but now served as a bedroom: Will's room, judging by the clothing thrown around. She spied dark, antique furnishings, including a high, unmade four-poster bed strewn with the various sections of the *New York Times.* Lucy's antique rolltop desk would look right at home in here.

Whoa there, girlfriend. Lucy crammed the errant notion back into her sex-starved id and commanded herself to *not even think about it.*

"Tom's in his room." Will knocked on the next door and opened it. His son sat with a middle-aged man on a multicolored shag rug, concentrating on the project before them: a two-foot-high model of the Addams Family haunted house constructed entirely of tiny Lego blocks. The structure was astonishing in its accuracy of detail.

Tom greeted her and, when prompted by his father, introduced the fellow with him, a cousin as it turned out. She shook Keith Kitchen's hand and praised his skill with the Legos.

"Tell that to Tom," Keith said. "He constructed this beauty. I'm only helping with the finishing touches."

"You're kidding." She turned to Will. "How old is Tom again? I can't believe a nine-year-old could do this."

"I'm nine years and eight months old," the boy said, "so I'm really almost ten."

"Well, I have to tell you, Tom, this is just amazing. Do you want to be an architect when you grow up?"

He shook his head. "I'm going to be a biomedical engineer. I'm going to invent nanoscale implants to help paralyzed people walk again."

Lucy didn't chuckle indulgently or send his father a conspiratorial wink, not after seeing this haunted house he'd constructed, complete with spooky turret and a high ledge from which to decant cauldrons of boiling oil. If this kid said he was going to get quadriplegics on their feet again, who was she to doubt?

She bent to examine the structure more closely. "You have a thing for small-scale stuff, don't you? I'm thinking of that model railroad layout I saw you working on in the game room the other day. That was pretty impressive, too."

Tom beamed with pride. Keith ruffled his young cousin's hair. "This kid is hard to keep up with. Makes me feel like a dolt."

"Yeah, right," Will said. "When it comes to construction, Keith's no dolt. He's been doing all the repairs around here I kept putting off."

"I saw the new lumber in the porch railing out there," Lucy said.

"And the basement door that was off its hinges." Will ticked off the completed tasks on his fingers. "And the loose bathroom tiles. And the buckling kitchen floor. And he's been here, what, two days."

"And my desk drawer," Tom said. "He fixed that, too."

"Plus helping to terrorize our client over there." Will nodded toward the Goo. "Cousin Keith can be one scary dude when he puts his mind to it."

"Sounds like just the fellow you need around here," Lucy said. "Fergus better watch his back." Keith was a good-looking man a bit older than she, though he was in excellent shape. The sleeves of his navy vee-neck sweater were pushed up, revealing forearms ropy with muscle.

Tom spied the book in Lucy's hand. "Is that the new Johnny Sherlock? Can I see it?"

"Yes and yes." She handed it over. "It's yours."

"Cool. Thanks, Lucy!" He launched himself at her, nearly knocking her off balance.

Tom's bear hug took her back a decade to when her own son was this age, that magical interlude between innocent young childhood and the fraught teen years. Tom was so sweet, all naked enthusiasm, his slender arms surprisingly strong.

"You're very welcome, honey." She squeezed him tight, breathed in the boy-scent of laundry soap and peanut butter. She kissed his smooth cheek. "Enjoy it."

"She wrote this," Tom told Keith. He opened the book's cover and showed him her photo. "See? That's Lucy."

Keith made a show of comparing the photo with the real live Lucy. "So it is. But the picture doesn't do her justice. She's much prettier in person."

Lucy's cheeks warmed under his admiring gaze. Quite the silver-tongued rascal, this Cousin Keith.

He turned to Will. "Speaking of books, Tom and Cuba want me to take them to the library. That okay with you?"

"No, I prefer the kids spend their spring break getting drunk and boosting cars. Think you can handle that?" He ruffled his son's hair.

"I'll get right on it, Dad."

Lucy and Will left the two to their construction project. He told her he had to check on a client and invited her to tag along. Once inside the Goo, he led the way down the corridor to the costume rack, where he hung up their coats and began riffling through the assorted outfits. "So. You're really going through with the divorce."

"Was there any doubt?"

"After last Sunday? That scene at your place?" Will selected an old-fashioned dress, grandma style, brown with tiny white dots, and slung it over his shoulder. "I guess not. Have you thought about all you'll be giving up?"

"You mean like Frank's small-mindedness, Frank's self-indulgence, Frank's inability to—"

"I was thinking more along material lines. Your children's books are a blast, Lucy, but something tells me the royalties don't come close to what Frank pulls down."

"Of course they don't, but I won't be walking away from my marriage empty-handed."

"Yeah, but still . . ." He rummaged in the laundry basket full of headgear for a few moments, finally settling on a gray woman's wig. "Forget it. It's not important. Hold this."

She took the wig from him, automatically smoothing its severe salt-and-pepper bun. "Do you think I'd stay in a rotten marriage just to maintain my standard of living?"

"Isn't that what you've been doing all these years?" He reached into a carton on the shelf and shoved a wooden ruler into his back pants pocket.

"For your information, no, it is not."

"Come on, Lucy. I'm not judging you." He started back down the hall, leaving her to stalk after him.

"Sure you are."

"Okay, I'm judging you, if you want to call it that." Will stopped at the door to the room Lucy had occupied last weekend. He lowered his voice. "Look, Lucy, I'm a realist. I know a lot of women marry for practical reasons. You weren't the first, you won't be the last. I don't particularly like it, but hey, as long as it doesn't affect me directly, no skin off my nose. Judging isn't the same thing as condemning."

"That's big of you, but I'm not one of those 'practical' women. I'm certainly not like Tom's mother. I know that's what you're thinking."

Last Sunday he'd told her about how he'd come to be a single dad, about his four-month fling with a young schemer named Hope Paulsen. Determined to marry into money, Hope had become pregnant. "Accidentally on purpose" was the phrase Will had used. When he'd refused to marry her, she'd scheduled an abortion. That was when he'd offered to support her in style for ten years—provided she relinquish custody of the child.

That was Will's version of events. Lucy wondered what Hope would have to say about it. She wasn't likely to find out. Tom's mother lived in Arizona. The last time she'd seen her son was when she'd handed him over in the hospital.

Will persisted. "So in other words, Frank Narby's bank account played no part in your decision to marry him."

Lucy wanted to flatly deny it. She wished she could. "He wasn't so well off then."

"He was on his way, though, and you knew it. The hungry little hippie girl yearning for middle-class respectability and Ched'r Wheelz."

She was struggling to formulate a response when Will slipped the baggy dress over her head. "What are you doing?"

He pulled her arms through the sleeves and zipped the back; the ugly thing hung like a sack over her own clothes. "You're Miss Schiemann." He folded her fingers around the ruler and tucked her hair under the wig.

"Who?"

"Benny's third-grade teacher."

"Who's Benny?"

But Will had already opened the door and propelled her inside the room. A middle-aged man sat jammed into one of those little student desk/chair combos, the kind used in elementary schools. Heavy chains secured his torso and ankles. Metal handcuffs encircled his wrists; the cuffs were bolted to the desktop but left enough freedom of movement for him to scribble on a child's lined penmanship pad with a crayon. Sheets of paper had been torn out of the pad and lay scattered across the desk.

She turned back to Will. "Now, wait a minute—"

He swung her back around and pushed her toward the man, who scowled at them, crayon in hand. "Look who's come to visit, Benny," Will said. "It's Miss Schiemann, your third-grade teacher. She's not very happy with you—are you, Miss Schiemann?" In her ear he confided, "The two of them didn't get along."

"Oh, for crying out loud. I did not sign up for this, Will."

Lucy's wig listed to the side. Will straightened it. "He's not crazy, just bored," he murmured in her ear. The warmth of his breath, the yummy scent of him, made it hard to concentrate on his words. "Have fun with it, Lucy. You'll make the guy's day." He gave her one final shove so she was standing over the poor schlub, ruler in hand.

"Uh . . ." She gave the ruler a feeble wag. "Have you been a bad boy, Benny?"

Benny yawned.

Will took her aside. "Listen, you're the old bitch who used to wash his mouth with Brillo, you're not Santa Claus, okay? A little method acting here?"

She cleared her throat, layered a few decades and some menace onto her voice. "What have you been doing, you naughty boy?"

"Fuck you," Benny snarled.

Lucy was shocked. What third grader spoke like that to his teacher? She glanced at the scribblings in front of him and, even upside down, was able to determine he'd been very naughty indeed. She snatched the pad of paper and shook it at him. "Where on earth did you learn such words?"

It looked like a deranged squirrel had made a nest of Benny's sparse hair. His white dress shirt was rumpled and pit-stained; he smelled a little ripe. Lucy deduced he'd been there a couple of days. A Chock Full O' Nuts can sat in the corner of the room, and she recalled what Gabby had told her that first day when she'd escorted her to the ladies' room.

Ewww . . .

Benny sneered. "Shove it up your ass, *Machine Gun*."

I get it, she thought. Miss Schiemann, Machine Gun. The height of third-grade wit.

"Now, you listen here, young man." She took a step closer. "You do not speak to your teacher in that fashion. There are consequences for behavior like that."

He stuck out his tongue and treated her to a sloppy raspberry.

"I think Benny's just begging for a little corporal punishment, Miss Schiemann." Will tapped the ruler in her hand.

"Is that legal?"

Benny faked a lunge toward her, making her leap back. Thank goodness the desk was bolted to the floor. "You don't have the balls to do it, do you, *Machine Gun*?" He dropped the crayon and saluted her with his middle finger.

Lucy's ruler hand itched. This man was so *rude*.

Will singsonged in her ear, "He's *wayyy-ting*." It was true. Benny sat there drumming his fingers, a smug smile on his unshaven face.

She whispered back, "Maybe I could just make him write a hundred times, 'I will not curse at Miss Shiemann.'"

Will sighed. "I thought you'd get a kick out of this, Lucy. My mistake." He held the door open for her.

Lucy looked into those blue, blue eyes and knew what he was seeing: Stepford Lucy in a gray wig and grandma dress. "Wait, I didn't say—"

"Go!" Benny hollered. He was rocking the desk so hard, the bolts actually began to loosen. "Go on, get out of here, you fascist cow. *Moo-ooooo!*"

Lucy caught herself wondering where a third grader would have learned the word "fascist," before giving herself a mental shake.

"Moo-ooo-ooo!" Benny ripped pages out of his pad, flinging them as far

as the handcuffs would allow. "Machine Gun's a big old fascist cow. Moo moo moo moo moo!"

Lucy swung on him, gesticulating with the ruler. "You stop that this instant."

"Make me."

She got in his face. "Don't tempt me, mister."

He crammed the last piece of paper in his mouth and chewed vigorously, both middle fingers now at full attention. He paused to display the saliva-soaked wad to her, then continued chewing.

"Uh, Lucy?" Will said. "You'd better—"

"Not now." She turned back to Benny. "You need help, you know that? I mean real, honest-to-God head-shrinking, not this—"

Benny drew himself up and launched the wad of paper, now a giant spitball, at Lucy. He would have hit her square in the kisser if Will hadn't yanked her aside at the last second.

"He *spat* at me!" Lucy was bug-eyed with outrage.

"You telling me you didn't see that one coming?"

"I will not be spat at!" She *thwacked* Benny's knuckles with the ruler.

"Ow!" Benny examined his unmarked flesh. He glowered at her. "That hurt. I'm gonna tell my parents."

Lucy was momentarily paralyzed. *What am I doing?* She started to back up. Will blocked her with his body.

"Was that so hard?" He patted her shoulder. To Benny he said, "Miss Schiemann's going to come back if you don't behave. Are you going to behave?"

Benny's eyes narrowed. They had their answer.

Will unlocked a cabinet and produced a fresh pad of penmanship paper. He slapped it in front of his client. "Your assignment, Miss Schiemann?" He looked at Lucy expectantly.

She said, "Benny, you will write five hundred times, 'When I get out of here, I will find a healthy hobby.'"

WILL AND LUCY returned to a quiet house. The kids had gone to the library with Keith. Irving and Gabby were upstairs playing poker. Even Ming-hua—Will craned his head toward the kitchen—was nowhere to be seen. No doubt she'd followed her husband up to their apartment to hover and cluck and ensure the penny-ante game didn't get out of hand. Quint was in his cage, wooing his mirror reflection with a string of Mandarin swear words. Will shucked his leather-trimmed barn jacket.

"Well, I should be going." Lucy tucked her scarf under her coat collar. She slung her purse strap over her shoulder. "I just wanted to bring that book by for Tom."

"Yeah, that was nice of you. Thanks."

"No problem."

He shoved her against the newel post and locked his mouth onto hers. She hauled him against her hard enough to knock the air from his lungs. They remained glued together, a two-headed beast, as they shuffled and groped and lurched their way past Will's bedroom door, which he kicked shut with enough force to elicit a startled scream from Quint.

They tumbled onto the unmade bed. He was hyperaware of her heat, her pliant curves, the heady, womanly scent of her. Also the fact that the two of them made a comfortable fit, horizontally speaking. That kind of observation, once acknowledged, was impossible to ignore, and sure enough, no part of him managed to ignore it, particularly the part pressed against her thigh.

Beyond the closed door, Quint began ringing his little bell and running through his repertoire of gripes: *"You'll put your eye out"* and *"I'll wash your mouth with soap"* and *"Because I said so!"*

"Why's he carrying on like that?" Lucy's breath was chocolate-scented.

"Because I never taught him to say, 'Hey, you guys, whatcha doin' in there? Come out here and pay some attention to *me!*'" Will tossed her scarf to the floor. Her coat followed.

He was now thoroughly and uncomfortably aroused. He hadn't gotten so hard so quickly since he was a teenager. Her eyes were glazed, her face flushed. He wondered how long they had till the kids came home. He should get up and lock the door.

"Take out the garbage!" Quint was really jangling that bell now. *"Were you raised in a barn? You're grounded, buster!"*

Where was his duct tape when he needed it?

Their hands got busy, and eventually they had to break off the kiss just to suck in oxygen. Lucy's shirt was half-unbuttoned. Will's sweater and undershirt were hiked to his armpits.

She rolled on top of him, and he flicked her last few shirt buttons free. Her lacy beige bra might not have been the most alluring undergarment Will had ever seen, but tell that to the little head. She stroked her hands up his rib cage and proceeded to do things with her fingernails that were probably illegal in the red states. "Has it occurred to you—" she pinned his wrists near his ears "—that *you* might be the one with some major control issues?"

"Yes," he said. "Yes, I have major control issues. What are you going to do about it?"

She grinned. "I'm serious. Well, half serious." Still holding his wrists, she snaked her body down his, then nudged the sweater aside with her nose to get at his nipple. Will's spine arched off the sheets as he tried to hold on to the top of his head.

"Who's that?" she murmured against his chest.

"That's Mr. Happy." He thrust his hips upward.

"No, I mean . . ." She lifted her head. "Who's at the door?"

He heard it then: the front door knocker. *Clunk. Clunk.*

Quint screamed, *"Door!"*

"Forget it." He tugged her head back down. "If someone's selling Girl Scout cookies, they'll come back."

She cocked her head, listening intently. "Did you lock the house when we came in?" God bless Lucy: the mature adult who thought of everything.

From the porch, a man's voice called, "Hello? Mr. Kitchen? It's Archie Esterhaus. We—" A violent sneeze interrupted him. "We spoke on the phone?"

"Oh God." Will scrubbed a hand over his face. "I forgot he was coming over."

Lucy sprang off the bed and drove her arms into her shirtsleeves in one elegant movement. "Who is it?" she asked, buttoning up.

"This guy who called . . ." He waved his hand as if he could wave away Archie Esterhaus.

Lucy grabbed hold of his arms and hauled him to a sitting position. She tugged his sweater down.

Clunk. Clunk. Clunk.

"Door!"

Will tried to pull her onto his lap; she was having none of it. He stage-whispered, "We don't have to let him in." He heard the front door creak open. The floorboards in the foyer groaned. Too late. The man had let himself in.

"Did I get the time wrong? Hello?"

"Did he?" Lucy finger-combed her hair as she crossed to the door. "Get the time wrong?"

"Shhh . . ." Will pressed a finger to her lips. "He'll go away."

"If you made an appointment with this man, you can't just *not* be here." She turned the knob. "Get out there, Will."

16

WESLEY STOOD IN the foyer of Will Kitchen's house, wiping his runny nose and eyeing a green parrot in a fancy cage the size of Joe's potting shed. The bird scooted along its perch and clung to the ironwork, getting as close to Wesley as it could manage. It cocked its head and gave him the stink eye. Then it spoke.

"Wipe your feet!"

He couldn't have heard right.

"Were you raised in a barn?"

Wesley looked around; he didn't even *see* a doormat. The parrot chose that moment to emit the loudest, most piercing scream he'd ever heard—and during fourteen years in the NYPD followed by eight as a PI, he'd heard more than his share. He clutched his heart, only to be startled anew, this time by the pillowy numbness of his chest. Oh. Right. The damn fat suit.

He wanted to avoid any chance of being recognized from last Friday night and his part in Frank Narby's misbegotten kidnap scheme. Sure, he'd had on that ski mask, but you could never be too careful. So part of his disguise today was, of all things for *him* to don, a fat suit. Hell, if someone invented a *thin* suit, he'd live in the thing. But barring such a miracle, he'd had no choice but to go in the other direction. His only problem had been finding a fat suit fat enough to fit his fat ass and make it even fatter. He'd finally tracked one down at a theatrical supply house.

So this was what he'd look like, and feel like, if he packed on another hundred pounds or so. Belly folds, man-tits, the works. The suit was as heavy as real flesh, otherwise the fake flab wouldn't jiggle right.

Maybe that South Beach thing was worth a try. Were people still doing that? A string of sneezes racked him as he foraged in his pocket for more tissues.

"Mr. Esterhaus?" It was Lucy. Frank would blow a blood vessel if he saw Mrs. Narby the First emerging, flushed and tousled, from what appeared to be the master bedroom.

"That's me." Wesley knew she wouldn't recognize his voice, thanks to the killer cold he'd caught from Anne Marie's little girl. He stuck out his hand. "Call me Archie. You must be Mrs. Kitchen."

"Uh, no. I'm just a friend. Lucy."

A friend, huh? This was the woman Kitchen had abducted by force last Friday—or rather, pretended to abduct. That was one of the things Wesley had learned in the past couple of days, that this Will Kitchen ran some freaky fake-kidnapping racket. All on the up-and-up supposedly, but then how to explain the two mil Kitchen's nephew Mick and his pal Hal had yapped about? While Kitchen could have made that kind of bread legitimately, Wesley tended to trust his cop's instinct—that precious "blue sense"—and right now it was screaming that there were two million dirty bucks floating around here somewhere.

If so, Wesley wanted them. But only if they were dirty and untraceable. If it turned out the money was legit, he'd back off and revert to Plan A: squeezing Frank Narby for a generous early wedding gift.

"Listen," Wesley said, "I apologize for letting myself in like that. I thought maybe no one heard me knock."

"Think nothing of it."

Will shuffled into the foyer. One look at his mussed appearance and baleful countenance confirmed Wesley's suspicions. These two had been about to do the deed before he'd interrupted them. He grabbed Will's hand and worked it like a pump handle. "You must be Wilbur. Archie Esterhaus. I really appreciate this, Wilbur. Mind if I call you Wilbur?"

"It's Will. I forgot you were coming." He waved his arm. "Go ahead and look around, Archie. Be my guest."

Lucy turned to Will. "Are you selling the place?"

"No, Archie just wants the two-cent tour. He used to live here when he was a kid."

"Really?"

"Yeah, see, I've been living out in St. Louis for twenty-something years now," Wesley said. "Turned out I hadda go back to New York on business—" He sneezed again; his nose felt like it had been sandpapered. "The International Beauty Show. I'm in hair products. And I'm thinking, jeez, long as I'm in the Big Apple, why don't I try to get out and see the old place again. So I call Will here out of the blue. He doesn't know me from Adam, but he's as nice as can be. Tells me I can come by and have a look around."

"You lived here with your family?" she asked.

"Yeah, on the top floor." Wesley pointed toward the ceiling. "There was this little apartment."

"It's still there." Will Kitchen made an obvious effort to act welcoming, but his crossed arms and stolid countenance spoke volumes on the subject of nookie interruptus. "An elderly couple live in it now."

Wesley nodded. "Good size for two people, that place." He was sweating like a son of a bitch in the padded suit. He loosened his necktie and pushed the costume eyeglasses up his nose. "Kinda cramped for a family of four, which is what we were, you know—me, my sister Nancy Lynn, she lives in Rochester now, and our folks. Plus a shepherd mix named Sidney." Wesley had done his homework, in case Kitchen actually knew a thing or two about the former residents, or in case he was careful enough to have done his own homework before opening the door to a stranger. "He was a good dog, Sidney. Long gone now, of course. Jeez, but he used to love running around that big yard."

"Archie's dad was the church custodian for many years," Will told Lucy. "Most of this house was used for classrooms and offices back then."

"That's right." Wesley gazed reverentially at his surroundings. "This old place sure holds memories for me. So the church, it got, what, declassified?"

"Decommissioned, yeah," Will said, "Listen, Archie, *mi casa es su casa* and all that. Snoop around to your heart's content."

"Well, I know you want to *show* him the place." Lucy sent Will a pointed look, less concerned, Wesley thought, with possible theft than with the lapse in hospitality.

The parrot rattled the door of its cage. *"I'm having conniptions! You're grounded, buster!"*

Lucy turned to Wesley. "Would you like some coffee? Or hot cocoa?" She politely ignored the rivulets of sweat streaming down his face. That was nothing compared to what was going on under the fat suit. "Unless you'd prefer something cold?"

Gratefully he accepted a tumbler of ice water and insisted he didn't need an escort, and besides, he'd been kinda looking forward to reacquainting himself with the house at his own pace, if that was all right. No problem, Will said, as he opened the parrot's cage and let it walk onto his arm. His housemates were expecting Archie. Most of them were out of the house at the moment anyway.

How fortuitous. "Nice-looking bird," Wesley said. "What's its name?"

"Quint." The parrot dipped its head for a neck scratch, and Will obliged him. "Named for the shark hunter in *Jaws*. He was born the year the movie came out. 'Seventy-five."

"Yeah? That's right, these guys live a long time, don't they?" He stepped closer to get a better look at the bird. "Hey there, fella. Polly want a cracker?"

"Take out the garbage!"

"Bossy thing, aren't ya? Say, what happened to its wing? It's crooked."

"Skiing accident."

Wesley forced a chuckle. "Stick to the bunny slopes, Quint." Outwardly he was nonchalant. Under the layers of latex and foam, his heart skipped a few beats. *Quint.* How many parrots could there be with that precise coloring, and that precise name, *and* a busted wing?

The bird was perched on Will's left arm. Surreptitiously Wesley glanced at the hand attached to the arm, knowing now what he'd find there. One thumb, three intact fingers, and a stub where the pinky should be. He hadn't noticed the missing digit during that standoff in Lucy's kitchen.

Wesley had always assumed Ricky Baines had moved far away. God knew if Wesley had endured what that kid had, the Australian Outback wouldn't be far enough to escape the memories. Though he could see how quietly changing your name and shunning the public eye as Ricky Baines had done might achieve the same objective.

Ricky's unsolved kidnapping had been the most frustrating episode of Wesley's tenure with the NYPD. He'd been a young cop back then, not quite a rookie, but not far from it. Still idealistic, still thinking he could do some good. Not yet outed and persecuted by his brothers in blue. All that would come later.

The Baines case had been a high-profile "red ball," meriting an all-out effort by law enforcement and engaging every big swinging dick in the department and Bureau. Wesley had fought hard to remain on the case, having been first on the scene when the call came in about an assault and kidnapping at the Astoria Studios.

The nanny had been clocked pretty bad. Once she'd been stabilized, Wesley had turned his attention to the injured parrot, flopping around the floor on its broken wing. Its handler was nowhere to be found, and the civilians were as crazed as the bird. Relying on common sense, Wesley snatched a towel off a makeup chair and swaddled Quint's wings close to his body. He'd proceeded to secure the site with the parrot tucked under his arm football-style.

The ransom the kidnapper eventually had made off with? Two million bucks.

Some coincidence, Wesley told himself. His special instinct responded, *Coincidence my fat blue ass. It's the same two mil.* But that didn't make sense. What would Ricky Baines be doing with the ransom money from his own kidnapping? Ransom money the perp had disappeared with twenty-five years ago? And what, if anything, did that money have to do with Lucy Narby?

Wesley had heard Mick assure Hal he'd get him "in there." They could only have been talking about this place, the property they'd been spying on. He wondered if Hal had made contact with these people yet.

"Does he bite?" Wesley extended his hand toward the bird, wondering how long parrots' memories were.

"He's pretty well behaved as long as you don't rile him," Will said, then added, "He likes anything shiny," as Quint mouthed the metal band of Wesley's wristwatch. Its beak felt about how you'd expect a beak to feel, but its black tongue was a surprise, supple and warm and absolutely dry as it probed the watchband.

Lucy yelped and leapt behind Will. The men followed her gaze to the floor, where a white mouse waddled along the molding. Darn thing looked like it was wearing its own little fat suit.

"I'll get it." Wesley snatched a *Scientific American* off a nearby console table, rolled it up, and advanced on the creature.

Will beat him to it, scooping the mouse off the floor. "Did Tom leave your cage open again? This is Josephine," he told Wesley. "She belongs to my son."

"Whoa. You got anything else running around here I should be on the lookout for?" Wesley asked. "A family of slugs? Pet cockroach or two?"

"Just a flop-eared bunny," Will said. "You'll need a bigger magazine."

THE SNOW HAD tapered off to a few random flakes by the time Hal parked Gabby's car behind the Goo. Lucy's silver Volvo was still there, as well as a white Maxima he'd never seen before, which triggered his early-warning radar.

As expected, their little excursion to the library had gone without a hitch. Hal had taken pains to fit in with Will Kitchen's little band and secure the trust of everyone in the household, to cultivate just the right long-lost-kin persona: responsible and capable, yet needy enough to be taken under his more affluent "cousin's" wing.

Will was generous and welcoming, if less gullible than Hal had hoped. He'd found himself deflecting some probing questions—questions about Marguerite, about Seattle. Some of them he'd been prepared for, and some of them he'd bullshitted his way through. Will seemed to buy his story. If Hal could manage to keep his swaggering loser of a son from unwittingly sabotaging this little fact-finding mission, he might just discover what became of his old-age fund—and get it back, with interest.

He figured he had until Sunday, four days from now, when Judith was scheduled to return from Bermuda. Meanwhile, if she phoned here and her brother mentioned newfound cousin Keith, she'd more likely exhibit pleasant surprise than suspicion. As far as he knew, Judith had no idea he'd gated out, and he intended to keep her in ignorance—for the time being.

When she did find out, it would be on his terms. That promised to be one interesting, long-overdue meeting.

Hal lifted an armful of books out of the car trunk. "Did you guys leave any books in the library?" Tom was hooked on science books and kids' mystery novels. For Cuba, it was graphic novels, funky craft books, books on music and film, and sweet, old-fashioned romance novels, of all things. These last she tried to hide under a thick coffee-table book about body piercings. Hal found it kind of endearing, the bad-ass chick with a secret taste for hearts and flowers; crunchy on the outside, soft and gooey on the inside. She was a good kid.

They were both good kids. He'd had some decent conversations with them during the past few days, and more than decent conversations with Gabby, who was sexy in a confident, seasoned way. She'd been just as confident, though less seasoned, twenty-five years ago when he'd known her as the Baineses' pretty French au pair. He and Gabby had flirted every time their paths crossed at the Astoria Studios, where *In No Time* was shot— right up until the moment he'd pulled his gun. He'd been in full disguise back then: the uniform, makeup to darken his complexion, mouth inserts to fill out his face, a fake mustache, and a short, dark wig, which he'd almost lost at the scene when that bird had attacked him.

Hal had bided his time at the studio, studying the child star's movements, anticipating when he'd be in that deserted corridor with the vending machines. And with no one but his nanny to defend him; Gabby rarely left his side. He couldn't recall what, precisely, he and Gabby had discussed in the days leading up to the kidnapping, but it certainly hadn't been his plans for her precious charge or where he intended to bury the ransom money.

No matter what angle he examined it from, he kept coming back to Ricky himself. The kid had been blindfolded, paralyzed with terror, and doped to the gills, once he'd lost his finger. Besides which, the windows of the bus—the Puny Earthlings' decrepit tour bus, a shooting gallery on wheels—had been sealed with blackout shades. How could Ricky have seen what his abductor did with the ransom money? And if by some miracle he did, wouldn't he have informed his folks? Yet in all the news reports that followed, there was no hint of the money having turned up. Everyone assumed the bad guy had lit out for some tropical paradise where two million of Daddy Baines's unmarked bucks would buy plenty of pink drinks with tiny umbrellas, and just as many bikini-clad honeys to share them with.

Maybe Daddy didn't get the money back. Maybe Will didn't have it either, but he knew who did. Hal wasn't concerned about Will recognizing him. It was raining like hell the day Hal hauled that shrink-wrapped suitcase and the shovel out to the boulder; he wore a dark green rain poncho, the hood pulled low over his forehead.

Judith was the one who doped up the kid after the finger thing, with injectable morphine she'd scrounged from who knew where. She flipped out when she saw that bloody little stump, went completely off the wall, even tossed her cookies. Hal had to knock her around pretty good just to get her settled down. That was all he needed, Ricky Baines recognizing his half sister's voice and telling the cops about it later. She'd give Hal up in a heartbeat.

Either you shut your yap or I'll shut *him* up for good, Hal warned her. That got her attention faster even than his fists, which he wielded with cool deliberation. Hal wasn't stupid; he was careful to leave no marks where they'd be visible and cause Daddy Baines to ask all sorts of inconvenient questions.

Snuffing the brat hadn't been on the menu when he'd cooked up the kidnapping idea. All Judith had wanted was money, assurance she wouldn't be shut out of the family fortune. Treating her coddled prince of a half brother to an all-expense-paid trip to the woods had seemed an acceptable way to accomplish that. It was Hal who'd come up with the scheme, but he couldn't have done it without someone on the inside. He'd convinced Judith it would be a lark, a prank—one that would pay off handsomely. By the time he'd finished with her, the silly girl had thought it was her own idea, thought she was in charge of the operation and could call him off with one flick of her queenly little hand. That had been her first mistake.

Tom chattered nonstop as the three of them lugged their haul of books toward the house—about his next science experiment, about his next Lego project, about some trick he was teaching Josephine. It wasn't hard for Hal to hold up his end of the conversation. A well-timed grunt here, a "Yeah?"

or "Cool!" there, proved sufficient. Cuba acted ostentatiously bored with Tom's prattle, but when the overburdened boy started to trip on his way up the porch steps, she sprang to his rescue, catching him and keeping him from tumbling after his books.

By the time they'd brushed the snow off the books and trudged up to the porch, the front door had swung open. Gabby stood framed in the doorway, looking like a tarted-up yoga instructor in a stretchy top, flared white leggings, and the ever-present high heels.

"You make so much noise, I heard you all the way across the lawn," she complained, but she was smiling. Hal figured she'd been keeping an ear cocked, waiting for his return. She'd freshened her makeup, he noticed, and marinated herself in more of that perfume she always wore.

He scooted past her through the doorway with his pile of books, deliberately brushing against her with a silky smile of his own. He murmured, "Oops." She quietly scolded him in French even as she pressed a little closer.

That was as physical as their flirtation had gotten. As much as he wanted to jump her bones, she didn't seem inclined to take it further than this teasing byplay, at least for the time being. Hal could deal with that. He'd already taken out a quarter century of sexual frustration on murder groupie Karen Schultz. Not that Karen had objected, even when it meant she couldn't sit without wincing.

Cuba, coming up behind him, witnessed the entire exchange. Without a word she tucked her pile of books under one arm, shook out a couple of smokes from a pack of Kools, and offered them to the grown-ups.

"*Très drôle,*" Gabby said, as she snatched the contraband pack from the girl and crumpled it.

"That's dumb," Tom told Cuba as he scooted past the three of them and headed for his room. "They don't smoke."

Hal had been concentrating on how hot Gabby looked and thus failed to prepare himself for Quint's inevitable reaction to his presence. "God Almighty," he muttered, as the bird let loose a brain-rattling scream. "I will never get used to that thing."

At least Quint was confined inside his cage at the moment—which didn't keep him from screeching and hissing as he punished the antique ironwork with his beak, struggling to open the door and get at his old adversary.

Will's voice sang out from up on the third floor, "Something tells me the cuz is home."

"The Keith alarm," Hal's housemates called Quint's berserk reaction to him. He'd been startled to see the TV parrot again after all these years; he'd had no idea Ricky Baines had adopted it. The scar behind Hal's ear throbbed every time he laid eyes on the damn thing.

Gee, that's odd, Will had said that first night. *Quint likes everyone. Why's he going on like that?* Thinking fast, Hal had convinced his housemates he had a phobia about birds. Outwardly he managed to act calm, he'd explained, but birds always sensed his fear and always went off the wall like that. They'd bought the explanation, and Quint's performance around Hal had turned into a household joke.

Hal stared into the bird's orange eyes, the pupils shrunken to pinpoints, and sent a silent promise: *Next time it won't be just the wing.*

Cuba started up the stairs with her load of books. "Yeah, he's happy to see you, too, Quint. Hey," she greeted the stranger lumbering down the steps.

The man was immensely fat and sweating profusely. He barely managed to squeeze past the girl as she flattened herself to the banister. "'Scuse me, dear," he mumbled. "Sorry."

"Ah. Archie," Gabby said. "Did you see the old club-foot tub? You must remember it, no? It is the original."

Archie clung to the newel post at the base of the stairs, huffing like a locomotive. "Club-foot? Oh, claw-foot. Yes, yes, I took many a bath in that old tub." He sneezed into a wad of tissues as Gabby introduced him to Hal before excusing herself to re-join the poker game upstairs, which apparently had expanded to include Will and Lucy. She invited the two men to accompany her. Archie said thanks anyway, he had to go, and Hal said he'd promised to sand and oil Ming-hua's butcher block.

"What's with him?" Archie pointed to the parrot, still screaming, still trying to get at Hal. "He was happy as a clam before."

"I can't stay in here with this racket." Hal went back out onto the porch. Archie followed him.

"And the heat. Jeez, is it hot in there or is it me?" Archie opened his suit coat to the cold breeze. He mopped his face with more tissues. "Maybe it's me. I bet I have a fever."

"Lousy cold, huh?" Hal pushed on the wooden railing, testing his repair.

"You got that one right. So you're Will's cousin."

"That's right." Something about this man didn't ring true. Nothing more than an ex-con's paranoia, maybe, but he couldn't shake the feeling.

Archie settled his bulk on the porch swing, which creaked alarmingly. "Nice, having relatives nearby."

Watching him, Hal realized what it was. He didn't move like a guy that size should move. Most men that big developed a kind of grace, a way of carrying themselves, of moving past and around obstacles. Hal had spent the past two and a half decades honing his people-reading skills in an environment where the slightest misstep could mean a shiv between the ribs. Archie was waiting for a response. Hal said, "I guess."

"Gabby told me about you," Archie said. "Your mom taking off like that all those years ago. Then one day you just show up on Will's doorstep, the long-lost cousin. Didn't know things like that really happened." He honked into some tissues. "So. You thinking of settling around here?"

"Maybe."

"Yeah, well, this place is nice and secluded." Archie gazed around the sprawling property, fringed with woods. "Most of the Island's more built up now. What would you do, move in here with your cousin? Like permanently?"

"I don't know about that. For now, yeah, it's a job and a place to crash. At least till I get on my feet. Will's a generous fellow."

Archie glanced at the closed front door. He lowered his voice. "Yeah, well, there's generous and there's, like, being a sucker. No offense. I'm not talking about you, you're a relative. But those others? You can't tell me they're earning their keep. And this place. Jeez, it must cost a fortune to keep up. The property taxes alone." He shook his head. "And don't even get me started about the heating oil. For both these buildings? I know, trust me. I used to help my dad maintain the furnaces."

"It's gas."

"Huh?"

"Natural gas heat. Not oil. Both buildings." Hal watched the other man closely, watched as his mind braked for this mental speed bump where moments before there had been nothing but smooth macadam.

Archie said, "You sure?"

Hal nodded. His hunch had paid off: The man's snooping hadn't taken him as far as the heating plants. "So that's kinda funny, you remembering oil-burning units."

Archie waved away the discrepancy. "They must've converted to gas at some point—you know, with the cost of oil so high."

"Not according to Will. This place went straight from coal to gas the same year the new church building went up." Hal nodded toward the Goo. "I'm thinking that'd likely have been before you were born."

Archie cogitated on this. "You know, I think you're right? What threw me, we had oil in the place we moved after. I remember 'em now, the gas heating systems they've got here. So, Keith. Tell me." Archie leaned forward as much as his ponderous gut would permit. He paused for a sneezing fit, then asked, "Where does your cousin get the bread for all this?"

"Why don't you ask him?"

"Forget I said anything." Archie raised his palms as he slumped back onto the bench swing. "I'm too curious about things that are none of my beeswax. It's the salesman in me, I guess. Always schmoozing with the accounts, trying to boost the assortment."

If this character was a salesman in town for a trade show, then Hal really was the Baineses' long-lost cuz. Whoever Archie really was, there was a more pressing question: What did he want? Maybe he was some kind of tabloid hack sniffing around for mud to sling at a former child star. Could it be that simple? That relatively benign? In Hal's experience, complications were rarely simple and never benign. This man was after something, as in some *thing*, and Hal couldn't discount the possibility it was the same thing—or two million things—he'd set his own sights on.

So far he'd had no luck in tracking down his money. He'd spent every free moment doing what Archie had doubtless spent the past couple of hours doing: searching for money, evidence of money, documents about money, oblique references to money, the faintest, most ephemeral whiff of money. For a guy who was basically a slob, Will Kitchen was careful about not leaving the important stuff lying around.

Or maybe Gabby was the careful one. Hal figured Will's surrogate mom still picked up after him, or at least squirreled away financial records where they couldn't be violated by prying eyes. One thing Hal *had* been able to ascertain during the past couple of days was that Gabby paid the bills. Not out of her own pocket, of course, but she doled out Will's dough to the butcher, the baker, and the purveyor of chains and duct tape. So at the very least, she knew how much there was and where it was. If he was lucky, she was also authorized to make withdrawals. Wiping-out-the-account-type withdrawals. Which would make Hal's mission that much easier.

All this was assuming Ricky Baines had managed to come into possession of his own ransom payment, the cash his old man had finally coughed up. Until a likelier candidate emerged, Hal would follow the only lead he had.

And nobody, this nosy son of a bitch included, was going to beat him to it.

"Well . . ." It took three tries, but Archie finally succeeded in grunting himself out of the swing. "Gotta head back to the city—I'm taking a buyer to dinner." He looked at his watch. "Jeez, hope the traffic's not too bad."

Hal asked, "Where'd you get the Maxima?"

"What?" Archie pressed a snot-rag to his dripping nose.

"Your wheels have New York plates, not Missouri. And they're not rental plates. It's the weakest part of your scam."

Archie met Hal's hard gaze without flinching. "Listen, my friend, I don't know what your problem is."

"I'm hoping I don't have a problem, Archie. At least where you're concerned. What's your real name, by the way?"

Archie shook his head as if to clear it. "This conversation's getting too weird for me." He began to shamble down the snow-dusted porch steps. "Tell Will thanks and I'm sorry I had to run. And for the record," he tossed over his shoulder, "the car belongs to a buddy of mine that works in the showroom."

Hal rattled off a series of three letters and four numbers. Archie stopped halfway down the steps.

"Old habit of mine," Hal said, "memorizing license plates. You never know when it'll come in handy."

Archie turned and faced him squarely. Neither of them stated what they both knew, that a resourceful person could trace the vehicle's owner with that one piece of information.

Hal stared down at the man from the top step. "And *for the record*, your first guess was on the money. This place uses oil heat and always has. I'm curious. How much of that is padding and how much is you?" He couldn't resist rubbing it in. "Score—the Cuz two, Fat Fraud zero."

"I wouldn't be so cocky, Hal."

The sound of his real name was a fist to Hal's solar plexus. He glanced quickly behind him at the closed front door, then descended the steps to join Archie, who ticked off a point on an imaginary scoreboard. "Score one for the Fat Fraud."

Hal was hyperaware of the switchblade in his back pocket. He recognized the itch, respected it, but had no intention of succumbing to it. The ability to exercise restraint, to delay gratification, was one of the traits that had separated him from the lower life-forms at Attica.

It had to have been Mick, that loudmouth loser. He was the only person who knew who Hal really was. Kid probably got drunk and ran his mouth about all this bread he was going to split with his old man, leaving Hal to mop up after him. How many others were going to come poking around?

"So. What now?" Hal spread his hands. "Do we march inside and bust each other? What'll that accomplish?"

"Two million dollars is a lot of money," Archie said.

"Not split three ways." Hal folded his arms across his chest. "Even assuming the principal is intact."

"'The principal.'" Archie shook his head, amused. "Listen to you, the investment banker. How much *principal* could there still be after twenty-five years?"

"The whole wad plus some, I figure." He peeked over his shoulder at the house again. "Kitchen has his TV money, too, don't forget. He's got expenses, no doubt about it, but these people don't eat caviar. They don't drive Bentleys." He tossed his arm toward his own recent repair of the railing. "They don't even put that much into the place."

"Yeah, but just *buying* a spread like this coulda wiped out the whole two mil. And how exactly do you figure the ransom money ended up here? With the *victim*?"

"We'll talk about that." Hal had questions of his own. Such as: How much did Archie know? Had Mick bragged to him about his dad's role in the kidnapping? Hal needed to find out, and fast. As for the location of the two million, the fact was, that money might be here, there, or nowhere. It might be sunk into real estate, like Archie said. The both of them might be on your basic wild-goose chase. He said, "You better split or they're gonna start wondering."

"I'll be in touch." Archie produced his cell phone. "What's your number?"

"I'll call *you*. What's yours?"

"That's okay." Archie pocketed the phone and began to shuffle toward the parking area. "I've got our boy Mick on speed-dial."

Of course you do, Hal silently fumed. *That witless cocksucker.* "Hey. Who are you for real?"

"Name's Joe Silver." The man never broke stride. "I'm a middle-school guidance counselor."

17

“I APPRECIATE YOU fitting me in like this, Dr. Sullivan.” Frank fidgeted with the tilt of the leather recliner. He couldn't get comfortable. He never seemed able to get *comfortable* anymore. “I couldn't wait till Monday. I could not wait.”

“You sounded quite anxious on the phone.” Dr. Sullivan jotted a note on the legal pad perched on his knee. “Has something happened?”

“Oh, you could say that.” Frank yanked on the chair's control lever; the chair jerked him upright. “You oughta get this frickin' thing fixed. Or replace it with a couch. What happened to couches? Why don't shrinks have those anymore?”

“Did something happen with Anne Marie? With Lucy?”

“Try something happened with Anne Marie *and* with Lucy. Last week I had two wives. Two families. Today I've got nothing. Zip. Zilch. Zero.” Frank slammed his head against the headrest. The chair collapsed into its flattest position. “Christ!”

“Did one of them find out about the other?”

“Bravo, Sigmund. You just earned your three hundred bucks.”

“I know you're stressed, Frank, but sarcasm is not prod—”

“Then tell me what is productive.” Frank struggled to sit up. “Tell me how to get my wives back. Anne Marie has changed the locks. *Changed the locks!* I sent roses. I sent chocolates. Godiva. She tossed them in the yard for the squirrels. *Godiva!*”

Dr. Sullivan's pen scritched across the pad. “How did she find out about Lucy?”

"I told her."

Dr. Sullivan looked up.

"I didn't mean to. I thought she knew. I thought she—thought she knew and hired this guy to kidnap Lucy and scare the piss out of her and get her to give me up."

Dr. Sullivan's eyes widened. "Someone kidnapped Lucy?"

"Do you mind?" Frank poked his chest. "We're talking about *my* problems here?"

Dr. Sullivan tapped his cheek. Frank hated it when he did that. But it *really* bothered him now. "We'll get back to that. You're looking a little . . . well, you're usually so well put together, Frank. A sudden lapse in grooming can be a sign of emotional distress."

"You think? Or try this." Frank groped for purchase, trying to lean toward the man. "My wife kicked me out of the house. *Both* my wives kicked me out of the house. I'm living in a frickin' *motel*, all right? With ants in the carpet and dirty movies on the TV. This is what my life has come to."

"We discussed just this eventuality, if you'll recall. We discussed how your present situation—a wife in every port, so to speak—could not last forever."

"*You* discussed it." Frank stabbed his finger toward the shrink. "There was no reason it couldn't last forever. I had everything in control. Then *Lucy* had to get herself *kidnapped.*"

Dr. Sullivan rested the pad on his knee. "Yes, to get back to that—"

"And I tried to do the right thing. I tried to *rescue* her. And what do I get for my troubles? I'll tell you what I get. I get ants in the carpet and dirty movies on the TV, that's what I get."

The door to the waiting room swung open. Dr. Sullivan turned toward the intruder. "I'm with a patient. Please wait in—"

"It's okay, we're family." Frank's brother-in-law Richie sauntered into the room, followed by Anne Marie's two other brothers, Gary and Nick, and her sisters' husbands, Murray and Lee.

"Shit." Frank tried to shrink into the recliner as his wife's burly menfolk surrounded it.

Dr. Sullivan looked stern. "I'll have to ask you gentlemen to leave."

"Don't worry, we're going." Nick pulled on Frank's arm. "Come on, bro, we have some things to discuss."

"Don't let them take me!" Frank clawed at the recliner's armrests as the men hauled him off of it. "Call nine-one-one!" he shrieked at Dr. Sullivan, who was now on his feet and looking thoroughly panicked. "I'm being kidnapped!"

"Take it easy." Gary clamped a hand around Frank's left arm and helped propel him through the waiting room, down a short flight of stairs, and onto the sidewalk outside the Egerton Medical Building, where an icy drizzle now fell. "We ain't kidnapping you, Frank."

"Then let me go."

"We'll let you go, bro." Nick, the thirty-year-old baby of the family, shoved Frank's coat at him. "After we've had our little talk."

They quick-marched him down the street, past the startled gazes of window-shoppers and moms pushing strollers. "Where are you taking me?" Frank bleated.

"We're just going for a little drink." Lee, who had hold of the right arm, patted Frank's shoulder. "A little chat with your bros over drinks. What's so scary about that?"

"I don't want a drink." Frank's feet barely touched the pavement. Someone's fist was crushing the back of his suit jacket.

"How can you not want to share a pitcher with your bros, bro?" The suit-crusher was Murray Saperstein, husband of Anne Marie's sister Cookie and onetime pro wrestler: the Murminator, a.k.a. The Hebrew Hulk. Murray was the biggest and scariest of Frank's big, scary in-laws. "Hey, what time is it?" the Murminator demanded. "Is it four yet? Happy hour, four to six at Shay's. Five-dollar pitchers. Free nachos on Tuesdays."

"It's Wednesday," Richie said.

"Bullshit." The Murminator gave Frank a hard shove through the door of Shay's Lounge. "It's Tuesday."

"Richie's right," Gary said. "it's Wednesday."

The brothers greeted the only other patron in the place, a regular named Jeff, who abandoned his stool and moved to the end of the bar so the brothers could sit together.

Only two of them, Gary and Lee, actually took seats, positioning themselves on either side of Frank after more or less mashing him onto a barstool. The other three closed ranks behind him.

"Whaddaya say, Frank?" Gary asked. "Is today Tuesday or Wednesday?"

Glumly Frank regarded their reflections in the mirror behind the bar. "Wednesday."

"Bull! Shit!" The Murminator thumped the heel of his hand between Frank's shoulder blades, knocking the air from his lungs.

"Hey, Danny," Nick called to the bartender, who was filling a pitcher with beer. "What's today, Tuesday or Wednesday?"

"Wednesday." Danny shoved the pitcher across the bar, along with six glasses. "Chicken wings."

"All right, all right, whatever," the Murminator groused, as the others jeered this evidence of senility.

"I suppose you're wondering why I brought you all together," Richie said. Everyone laughed except Frank. Nick poured the beer.

They seemed to be in a decent mood, Frank thought. A few beers might help that along. In Frank's experience, the drunker these guys got, the jollier they got. Of course, under the circumstances, their collective mood could go south at any moment.

"Listen." Frank tried to put starch in his quaking voice. "We have to talk."

"That's what we been saying." Lee thumped him on the back. "Here, drink up."

Obediently Frank took a sip. "I don't know how much Anne Marie has told you . . ." He waited. No one seemed eager to fill him in. "I love your sister with all my heart. You guys know that."

"Of course we do, Frank." Gary patted his back. "We're kinda fond of her ourselves."

"Terrific girl, Anne Marie, am I right?" The Murminator raised his glass, and all followed suit.

Richie placed a beefy hand on Frank's shoulder. He leaned in close. "That's why we're all a little confused about how something like this could happen."

Frank nodded vigorously. He cleared his throat. "Yeah, it's crazy, isn't it? There are times I can hardly believe it myself." He tried to smile, but his reflection in the bar mirror could more accurately be described as a rictus of terror.

"Twenty years, Anne Marie said." Nick sounded impressed. "Twenty years you been married to someone else."

"Holy crap." Danny looked over from the snack bowls he was filling. Jeff, at the end of the bar, simply *tsk*ed into his whiskey.

"Lucy," the Murminator said, and all agreed, yes, that was the name their sister had mentioned. "She nice, this Lucy?"

Frank swallowed hard. "She's okay."

"Just okay?" Lee emitted a bark of laughter. "That all you got to say after twenty years?"

"You two have a kid, right?" Richie said. "How old is he?"

"Uh, nineteen."

"Nineteen. Almost grown. Does he know he's got five brothers and sisters? And number six on the way?"

Frank shook his head.

Nick shook his head, too. "That ain't right." No, the others solemnly agreed, that ain't right at all. "In the end, family's all you got."

"That's it. That's it exactly." Frank grasped at this straw. "It's all about family. Keeping the family intact. You all know how important that is to me."

"Gee, Frank." Gary sounded sad and perplexed. "We thought we knew. Now we ain't so sure."

"When I met Anne Marie, I was blown away," Frank said. "It was love at first sight. I thought, here's my soul mate. Here's the girl I waited my whole life for."

"Except you were already married," the Murminator pointed out. "For . . ." His face scrunched as he struggled with the numbers.

"Seven years," Danny, the math whiz, offered.

"So why didn't ya get a divorce?" Richie asked. "That's what people do when they meet their soul mate and they already got a wife."

"That's what *I* did," Lee said. "I divorced Jean, *then* I married Terry. In that order."

A couple of the brothers gestured toward Lee as if to say, *See? That's the way you're supposed to do it.* Frank mumbled his response. They pressed in around him. "What's that, Frank?"

"I said, I don't believe in divorce."

The brothers nodded gravely. They could respect that. "We ain't crazy about it, either," Gary said.

Lee raised his hand. "Even me."

"Thing is . . ." The Murminator wrapped one gigantic hand around the back of Frank's neck. And squeezed, in a friendly sort of way. "We like bigamy even less. That means having two wives at the same time," he added helpfully.

"It's illegal." Nick was also being helpful.

"I know that, I know." Frank nodded his head, now drooping between his shoulders.

"You got a picture of your Lucy?" Richie asked.

"Sure." Frank slid a snapshot out of his wallet.

The brothers crowded in for a closer look. They handed the photo to Danny, who passed it to Jeff, nursing his double whiskey at the end of the bar. All expressed polite approval of Frank's pretty first wife. Richie slipped the photo into his own pocket. What he needed the picture for, Frank chose not to contemplate. Likewise, when his brother-in-law asked where on Long Island Lucy lived, Frank rattled off the address without hesitation.

Gary asked, "Does Lucy know about Anne Marie?"

"Yes. No, I guess . . . Oh hell, I don't know anymore." He cradled his head in his hands.

"You know what you gotta do, bro." Gary slid a comradely arm around his shoulders. "You gotta choose."

"I have chosen." He lifted his head and attempted to make eye contact with each brother in turn in the bar mirror. "I need to be with Anne Marie. There's no question about that. If she'll still have me."

"And not Lucy." Richie felt the need to put a fine point on it.

"And definitely not Lucy," Frank agreed, meaning it. "No way."

Lee riffled through his wallet and produced a business card. "I got a great divorce lawyer."

"Divorce . . ." Frank groaned.

"Oh, now, don't start that again." The Murminator gave the back of

Frank's head a jocular tap. It felt like a wrecking ball.

"What will Mother and Father say?"

"Your priorities seem to be a little off base, Frank." Richie squeezed his shoulder. "Your biggest worry right now ain't Mommy and Daddy."

No, the brothers agreed. Heads shook all around.

Richie's genial tone never faltered. "You divorce Lucy pronto or we'll kill you, bro."

Frank whipped his head around, seeking help from Danny, who never paused in his lime-cutting as he said, "Count me in."

Jeff, his nose in his whiskey, raised his hand in a me-too gesture.

"You're—you're threatening my life!" Frank spluttered.

"We'll make sure it hurts, too," Nick added, and the others nodded as if to say, *Nice touch*.

Lee slapped the lawyer's business card and his cell phone on the bar in front of Frank. "No time like the present."

18

I'VE *GONE TOO far this time.*

Ethel was supposed to have been contacted Wednesday morning— over thirty hours ago. That was when the fake kidnapper was going to release Lucy, assuming she hadn't sprung herself early by saying the magic word. Ethel rehashed all this in her mind as she steered her PT Cruiser up Lucy's driveway. She'd waited all day yesterday for Will Kitchen's call telling her where to find her sister. Nothing. And no response to her increasingly anxious phone messages and e-mails to both of them.

She braked at a sloppy angle in the parking area at the side of the house. Lucy's Volvo was nowhere to be seen. Well, it could be in the garage. She hurried toward the door to the kitchen.

She'd definitely gone too far this time. She'd turned over her sister— her flesh and blood, her identical twin, *her genetic clone!*—to a complete stranger. Why? Because he had an intriguing Web site.

What had she done? And how would she explain it to the police?

Forget the police. How would she explain it to Lucy's son?

Be home, Ethel silently pleaded with her sister. *Please, please be home.* Privately she vowed to abandon the practical jokes, even to concede defeat in this decades-old competition of theirs, if she could just get out of this without having screwed up in some horrible, irreversible way.

She started rummaging in her shoulder bag for the key to Lucy's house before remembering she'd given it to Will Kitchen during her client interview. She'd just bang on the door, then. If Lucy wasn't home, she'd camp out on the stoop and wait for her.

"I've been having a look around."

Ethel stifled a yelp of surprise. The unfamiliar voice belonged to a tall, youngish woman with wavy chestnut hair, now strolling into view from behind the house. She stopped a few feet from Ethel and pressed a hand to the small of her back. Her plump belly strained the buttons of a wool maternity coat that looked like it had seen better days.

"Can I help you?" Ethel asked.

"Will you look at this place?" The woman shook her head, as if she couldn't believe her eyes.

Ethel glanced over her shoulder at the glossy shrine to conspicuous consumption she liked to call "Barbie's Dream House," just to tweak her sister. Not that Lucy had had much to do with purchasing this nouveau riche manse; that had been Frank's decision. Ethel's brother-in-law kept a tenacious grip on the purse strings. "It's something, isn't it?" she agreed.

The other woman didn't share her wry smile. Her expression couldn't even be called cordial. At first Ethel had assumed this was some friend or neighbor of her sister's, but now she wasn't so sure. The visitor's hard gaze lingered on the house before settling on Ethel. "How much does a house like this go for around here, with all this land? Close to a million, I bet."

Try three million. Before she could decide how to respond, the woman continued, "My kids'd never believe one family could have a pool like that." She nodded toward the back of the property, still not cracking a smile. "They're always after me to take them to the rec center."

"Excuse me," Ethel said, "I don't believe we've met."

"You want to know what's funny?" The woman moved closer, her eyes glittering with a dangerous mixture of betrayal, rage, and incredulity. Ethel resisted the urge to back up. "My house? My house is a dump. A lousy dump, only I didn't *know* it was a lousy dump until I set eyes on this place."

"Are you, uh, looking for the Realtor's open house?" Ethel gestured vaguely westward. "Because I think that's the next property over."

"'It's the biggest place we can afford, sweet pea.' That's what he said, and I believed him. I thought, he's got such a good job, such an important job, how come he's not making more? But I didn't say anything. Why? Because I trusted him. Because I didn't want to embarrass him. Is that funny or what?"

"Okay, I have to go." Ethel produced her keys, but the other woman planted herself between Ethel and her car.

She searched Ethel's face. "You don't know who I am, do you?"

Sure I do, Ethel thought. *You're some wacko who lives in a dump.*

"I'm Anne Marie."

"Pleased to meet you, Anne Marie." Ethel tried in vain to edge around her. "I have to go now."

"He told me about you. He didn't mean to, he thought I already knew. He thought you knew about me, too."

Ethel didn't like the way Anne Marie was looking at her. "Listen, I don't know who you are or why you're here, but this conversation is over."

"It hasn't even begun." Anne Marie took hold of Ethel's arm; she was surprisingly strong. "Into the house, Lucy. We have some things to discuss."

"Ohhh!" Ethel brightened. "You think I'm Lucy. I'm Lucy's sister. I don't think she's home right now, but I'll tell her you stopped by."

"Cut the crap." Anne Marie drew a wallet-size photo from her purse and showed it to Ethel, who recognized a shot of her sister taken during the Narbys' last New Year's Day open house. "I know it's you."

"We're *twins*," Ethel insisted. "Identical. My name is Ethel."

"Now I know you're lying." Anne Marie half-dragged her to the side door. "Like anyone would name their kids Lucy and Ethel." She produced a small black pistol from her coat pocket.

"Oh my God. Is that thing real?"

"I am not going to tell you again to unlock that door."

"I don't have the key."

"To your own house?" She aimed the gun at Ethel's heart.

"Listen. Just tell me what you want to talk to my sis—what you want to talk about. Maybe I can, you know, clear up some misunderstanding."

Very slowly and clearly Anne Marie said, "Your husband, Frank Narby, is a bigamist. He's married to both of us."

Okay, the woman was certifiable. She must be one of those delusional stalkers, only instead of latching on to a movie star, she fantasized about being married to the national sales manager of a major snack-foods company.

Anne Marie's lips thinned. "You don't believe me."

"I didn't say that." Ethel kept a wary eye on the gun.

"I don't know much," Anne Marie said, "except you decided to divorce him after twenty years, and he's determined to stay legally married to you. Well, to both of us, but to you in name only. That's why I'm here, to make sure you go through with the divorce, no matter what he thinks he wants."

"Let me see if I have this straight," Ethel said. "You want to make sure I . . ."

"Divorce my husband. Plus, you keep your mouth shut about all this. Not one peep. Not to the cops, not to the media, not to KrunchWorks. No one. Frank may have made a mistake, but there's no better dad. We have five kids." She patted her belly. "Six in July. He loves them and they love him, and I'm not about to let anything or anyone mess with my family. You listening, Lucy?" She poked Ethel with the barrel of the gun.

"I'm listening, I'm listening. No better dad. No messing with your family."

"You know, I wasn't so sure you'd be here. Because of something else Frank told me." Anne Marie cocked her head. "He said you were *kidnapped?*"

Ethel's heart kicked so hard, she nearly toppled.

"By someone named Will?" Anne Marie continued. "Frank seems to think I had something to do with it."

Ethel's mind reeled. How could this random stranger, this nut job, know about Will Kitchen and the fake kidnapping Ethel had arranged for her sister? That stupid practical joke.

Practical joke. Ethel looked at Anne Marie with a fresh eye. *Wait just a goldarned minute.*

"I get it." Ethel raised her palms, chuckling. "I get it, Anne Marie. Is that your real name? This was good. *You* were good." She pointed an admiring finger at the other woman. "Really. I want you to know that. It would've worked. That last bit, though, about the kidnapping, that was the giveaway. You can put away the gun now."

Anne Marie gave her a flat stare. "What the hell are you talking about?"

A giddy laugh erupted from Ethel. She clapped her hands together. "You really are very good. Are you a professional actress? Are you really preggers?" She patted the hard belly under the wool coat. "Nice touch. Six kids! Like anyone's careless enough to squirt out *six kids* in this day and age."

Anne Marie gawked as if the tables had turned and she were doubting Ethel's sanity. This woman really was totally believable. No wonder Ethel fell for it.

She was on a roll. "Like that limp dick Frank could even *father* six kids. Have you *met* the guy? I sometimes wonder where John came from, and that's the truth."

They heard it at the same time, the sound of car tires on cobblestones, a whisper that turned to a silken moan as Lucy's silver Volvo came into view.

Yes! Now Ethel could rub it in while it was still fresh. *I win! You tried to get your revenge and you failed. Miserably. I win! I win! I win!* The self-flagellation to which she'd subjected herself just minutes ago might never have happened, so swelled with glee was Ethel at the prospect of lording it over her sister.

"Whoever that is—" Anne Marie slipped her gun hand into her coat pocket "—get rid of them."

LUCY PULLED IN next to Ethel's car. She wasn't surprised to see her sister, whose increasingly frantic calls she'd been dodging since yesterday morning. Let her sweat. But who was her friend? The woman stared in slack-jawed astonishment as Lucy stepped onto the cobblestones and greeted them.

Far from frantic now, Ethel appeared elated; she was practically dancing a jig. "I keep telling her she can drop the act, sis. I caught on right away." She draped her arm around the other woman's shoulders. "No fault of Anne Marie's, though. I want you to know that. She was awesome."

Ethel only called her "sis" when she was feeling particularly pleased with herself, usually when she'd bested Lucy in the practical-joke department. Which, of course, she'd just done with that custom kidnapping, but what was this about an act?

Lucy rested her shoulder bag and the grocery sack from King Kullen on the hood of her car. "Anne Marie, is it?" She stuck out her hand and introduced herself.

"You're . . ." Anne Marie didn't shake her hand; she was pale as wax. "You're Lucy."

Ethel's grin faded as she looked from Anne Marie to Lucy and back again. "This is part of the act, right, Anne Marie?" The other woman didn't respond. *"Right?"*

Lucy asked, "What's going on?"

"Oh my God," Ethel said. "Oh my God, Lucy, I think she's for real."

Anne Marie pressed a hand to her stomach; she took shallow breaths. To Ethel she said, "I guess you were telling the truth about the twin thing."

Ethel nodded robotically. "And you . . .? The . . . and the . . . all of it?"

"Of course." Anne Marie was turning an unbecoming shade of green. "Who'd make up a thing like that?"

Ethel covered her mouth and stared dumbfounded at Lucy.

Anne Marie covered her mouth, too, but only to hold back the tide as she lurched across the cobblestones and vomited into a bed of tulips just pushing their tender shoots toward the sun. She groped in her coat pocket, pulled out a shiny black gun, and stuck the barrel in her mouth.

"No!" Ethel launched herself at the woman. "No man is worth it. Think of your baby."

She failed to reach her in time. The sisters braced themselves as Anne Marie pulled the trigger, swished, spat, and took a second hit off the water pistol.

When Lucy could speak again, she said, "Morning sickness?"

"If it was just the morning, I'd be thrilled." Anne Marie wiped her mouth with a tissue and pocketed the toy. Her color began to return.

"Come on inside." Lucy grabbed her things and started for the door. "I think I can scrounge up some saltines and a cup of tea."

"Uh, you might want to hold off on the hospitality." Ethel gave Lucy a significant look. "Until you find out what brought Anne Marie here."

"Oh, please, Ethel. Don't you think we've had enough drama for one day?" Lucy slid her key in the lock and ushered her visitors into the kitchen, where Anne Marie gaped at the room's luxurious size and appointments. "Tea and crackers for Anne Marie, and something stronger for *moi* to restart my heart. Pomegranate martini for you, Ethel?" Lucy's sister was fond of girlie drinks. "No?"

Anne Marie proceeded to make herself at home, shucking off her coat and easing her gravid self onto a barstool at the cook island. "Do you have any decaf tea?"

"You know, I think I do." Lucy handed her the box of saltines. She filled the electric kettle and riffled through her canister of tea bags while Ethel paced the granite floor tiles and gnawed her nails. Something had her rattled. Good. After what Lucy had recently endured in the name of practical jokesterism, the perpetrator could just stew awhile.

"Okay, okay," Ethel groaned. "A pomtini. A small one." She shot a glance at Anne Marie, now peering at Frank's under-counter wine cellar as if it were the space shuttle. "Make it a double."

Lucy arranged everything on a lacquer tray and ushered the small group into the greatroom. The way Anne Marie craned her neck to take in the expanse of vaulted ceiling put Lucy in mind of tourists from the heartland ogling Manhattan skyscrapers.

By the time they'd gotten themselves settled around the Noguchi coffee table, Ethel had decimated a brand-new set of acrylic tips. She gulped down half her pomtini before Lucy had taken one sip of her bourbon.

Anne Marie held her teacup with pinky extended. She wore a faded denim jumper over a ruffled cotton blouse: a Wal-Mart version of the sort of maternity outfits Lucy had worn back when tentlike smocks ruled.

Lucy looked from one woman to the other. "Someone gonna tell me who died?"

Anne Marie sipped her tea. Ethel jumped up and resumed her pacing.

"I was kidding." Lucy sat forward. "Did someone die?"

"Not yet." Ethel had her back to her, staring at the original framed Miró over the mantel. "When you find out what Frank's been up to, that may change."

"Oh, for heaven's sake. I'm *divorcing* the man. His escapades are no longer my concern. Do you know what that idiot did, Ethel? Excuse me." She smiled at Anne Marie. "You don't know my husband—soon-to-be *ex-*husband. I don't use the term 'idiot' lightly."

Anne Marie pursed her lips and reached for another cracker.

"He showed up at Will's place. In, like, SWAT gear. He tried to *rescue* me. Do you believe that?"

Ethel turned to face her. "How did he even know you'd been snatched? I never told him a thing. *I* didn't even know where you were."

"The fake kidnappers *Frank* hired followed us to Will's place and reported back to him." Lucy enjoyed watching her sister's jaw sag in astonishment.

"This fake-kidnapping thing," Anne Marie said. "Is it the latest craze or what?"

"I didn't think so." Ethel folded her arms across her chest. "I thought it was real cutting edge or I wouldn't have done it."

"Well, thanks so much for making me a trendsetter," Lucy said.

"So *you*—" Anne Marie pointed at Ethel "—hired someone to kidnap *you*." The finger shifted to Lucy.

"And paid a pretty penny for the service," Lucy snickered. "Too bad you didn't get your money's worth—I was there for less than twenty-four hours when I *smarg*ed my way out of it."

"Frank thought I was the one that did it." Anne Marie set her cup and saucer on the coffee table.

Lucy blinked in surprise. "You know my husband?"

"Okay, I'm going for a little walk." Ethel hightailed it across the room.

"Oh no you don't," Anne Marie called to her retreating back. "I went through this once when I thought you were her. It's your turn to explain, Ethel."

Ethel stood framed in the arched doorway, hands raised as if to ward off whatever was coming next. "This is none of my concern. It's between you two. And Frank."

"Get back in here," Anne Marie intoned, with all the authority of a seasoned mom. Ethel slunk back into the greatroom. "Sit." Ethel sat, avoiding Lucy's gaze.

"This is going to be horrible, isn't it?" Lucy's hands had gone clammy.

Anne Marie grabbed a cracker. "Your sister's waiting, Ethel."

Ethel sighed. She took a deep breath. "Okay." Another deep breath. "Okay, it's about Frank."

The suspense was feasting on Lucy's stomach lining. "Get to the horrible part."

"He got married," Ethel choked out.

"That *is* pretty horrible, but I'm trying to remedy the situation."

Ethel dropped her head in her hands. "You're making this so hard."

Anne Marie gave Ethel a disappointed look. She turned to Lucy. "Our husband is a bigamist." She waited for that to settle in.

Our. She said *our.* A word that definitely did not belong before *husband.* Which was why Lucy was having a little trouble processing the information.

On another level, it made all the sense in the world.

"Here." Anne Marie hauled her purse into her lap. She dug around in it and produced a compact photo album with the words "Mommy's Brag Book" embossed on the front. She offered it to Lucy, who watched her own hand reach out and take the thing.

Numbly she opened the little book. The first plastic sleeve held a picture of a little girl, surrounded by other kids, blowing out candles on a birthday cake. It was a home party with balloons and paper hats. Anne Marie stood bending over the girl, but her beaming face was lifted to the person behind the camera.

Anne Marie craned her neck to see. "That was Christina's fifth birthday, in January." She made a gesture like flipping pages, and Lucy obeyed. The next shot was Pin the Tail on the Donkey. This one showed a man's back as he spun a blindfolded boy holding a paper donkey tail. The man wore the shirt John had given Frank last Father's Day. The back of his head looked all too familiar. On the facing page was a photo of the kids chowing down on pizza. The same man stood at the table, holding a squirming toddler in one arm and sliding slices out of the box with the other. His head was cut off.

Lucy looked up. Anne Marie made that flipping gesture again while Ethel sat hugging herself and staring into middle distance. *Do not go catatonic on me now,* Lucy silently commanded.

She flipped to the next picture. There he was, her husband, Frank Narby, holding the birthday girl on his lap and laughing as she tried to feed him cake and only succeeded in smearing icing on his face. The rest of the shots were similar. Frank collecting crumpled wrapping paper and ribbon as Christina tore open her presents. Frank attaching training wheels to his daughter's new bike, with the help of two young boys. A sledgehammer walloped Lucy's ribs. It seemed like yesterday he was doing the same thing for John. She turned the page. Frank and Anne Marie holding slices of birthday cake on paper plates, sharing a mom-and-dad kiss under birthday balloons. Lucy closed the book.

She swallowed hard, but the knot in her throat refused to budge. Anne Marie stared at her, awaiting a reaction. Lucy opened her mouth to refute the evidence. No words would come. She tried to laugh off the absurd, impossible notion that her husband of twenty years, her dependable, honest husband, had another family. Another life. All that came out was a strangled whimper.

Her eyes dropped to the crystal glass on the table in front of her. Ice cubes melting in a splash of amber liquid. She watched her hand carefully reach for the glass, lift it, bring it to her mouth and upend it. The bourbon settled in her stomach like jet fuel. She watched the glass touch down on the coaster, a hard landing.

With immense effort she raised her eyes to Anne Marie. "You live out there. In Chicago."

Anne Marie nodded. "A suburb called Egerton."

Lucy's gaze dropped to Anne Marie's belly. "Frank's baby."

Ethel managed to croak, "Number six."

Lucy couldn't have heard right. She looked to Anne Marie for confirmation.

"That's right." Anne Marie patted the mound under her jumper, causing the diamond solitaire on her left ring finger to spark with light. "We have three girls and two boys at home. This little man will make it a fair fight. Andrew James."

The jet fuel smoldered in Lucy's stomach. She refused to lose her lunch. Not here, in her own greatroom, in front of this . . . this *wife* of Frank's.

"I never suspected." Anne Marie cocked her head at Lucy. "Did you?"

Lucy shook her head. She should have, though. The signs were there. The increasingly lengthy stays in Chicago, the difficulty getting in touch with him there, the lame excuses. The emotional distance for which she'd accepted blame for so many years. And the *money*. Lucy felt sick recalling how readily she'd stepped back and allowed her husband free reign over their finances. Less work for her, she'd reasoned. And it wasn't as if she'd wanted for anything.

"You've been married for twelve years," she informed her husband's other wife.

Anne Marie's eyebrows rose. "You *did* suspect."

"Not then." She took a shaky breath. "You know what they say about hindsight. John was born nine months after the wedding, and Frank had been after me ever since to have more children. For *years*. Then one day he drops the subject. Just like that. I was relieved. I thought, he accepts the size of our family, at last. I should've known better." She tried to smile. "Frank has never been very good at depriving himself."

Anne Marie said nothing. Perhaps she noticed Lucy's chin quiver.

"I don't know why I should care." Lucy's voice wobbled as her eyes welled over. "I don't *want* him, I'm *divorcing* him. I haven't *loved* him for . . ." She shrugged helplessly. Her tears galvanized Ethel out of her stupor; she rushed to her side and wrapped her arms around her. Lucy's conflicted grief wracked her, threatened to devour her. "What kind of wife was I?" she choked out between sobs. "What kind of wife was I to make him go and do something like this?"

"Oh honey." Ethel squeezed her tighter. "You're asking the wrong question."

Vaguely, in the far recesses of Lucy's mind, she knew her sister was right. She was reverting to the old Lucy, the Stepford Lucy who questioned her worth as a spouse every day of her life.

But it *hurt*. Frank's betrayal was a giant fist twisting her insides, condemning her. She clung to Ethel, bawling shamelessly, not even caring that the better wife sat there watching. Finally the tears wound down. A hand appeared, holding a wad of tissues. Lucy looked up. It was Anne Marie, standing before her.

"It was a shitty thing he did," Anne Marie said. "To both of us. No way to sugarcoat it. But I've had some time to think about it, and I love him anyway."

"You're welcome to him." Lucy honked into the tissues. "But that man is *not* getting off scot-free."

"I have a few ideas about that." Anne Marie settled back into her chair. "You go first."

19

THE BERMUDA FARMERS MARKET was a riot of colors and scents, sprawling across a parking lot off Canal Road. The bustling bazaar was, ironically, a balm for Judith's nerves, which had been stretched to the snapping point during what was supposed to have been a romantic, relaxing getaway with her significant other. She and Roger would have a week to really get to know each other, she'd assumed, a week to nurture their relationship and find the passion. After all, how could two people spend seven days together in this balmy paradise and not find romance and passion?

How? The key lay in that *together* part. Every morning after breakfast, Roger gave her a peck on the lips and took off for one of the island's fabled golf courses, hauling his obscenely expensive Honma clubs and the ever-present jug of sunblock. Judith was welcome to accompany him, of course, but they were in *Bermuda*, for crying out loud. Land of pink-sand beaches and men in necktie and bare knees. She had not come all this way to do what she and Roger could, and did, do with tedious regularity at their country club back home: namely, whack a little ball around the grass. So during daylight hours, she opted to find her own amusements.

Roger always reappeared by dinnertime. Invariably they dined at the hotel restaurant where they were staying. The best porterhouse on the island, according to Roger's unimpeachable sources. Why go anywhere else? After dinner they adjourned to the hotel's lounge for cabaret-style entertainment and the obligatory rum swizzle, and were in bed—correction, *beds*—by eleven.

The Farmers Market comprised dozens of display tables, shielded from the sun by large, colorful umbrellas. Judith happily blended in with the horde of locals and tourists scrutinizing farm produce, seedlings, fresh-caught fish, and locally made preserves and handicrafts. She'd already purchased several jars of honey and jam, three sand-molded candles, and a quart of mixed berries to share with Roger later. Perhaps in their room, with a frosty bottle of champagne?

She struggled to forge the mental image: their hotel room, romantically lit, redolent with the mingled perfumes of candles, fruit, and fine champagne; her, reclining on one of the two queen-size beds in the black silk teddy she'd crammed into the bottom of her garment bag, *just in case*; Roger, overcome by the sights and smells of seduction, tossing aside his golf bag and tearing out of his Crayola-hued polo shirt and pants as he succumbed to the raging lust he could no longer hold in check.

Lust? Roger? This was the man who'd packed eight sets of crisp Brooks Brothers pajamas for this trip, one for each night plus an extra: *his* version of just in case. The man who'd accepted, without the slightest moue of disappointment, her assertion that she wasn't ready for intimacy. The man with whom Judith had shared a room for seven days and still didn't know whether he wore boxers or briefs.

Maybe she'd eat the berries during the bus ride back to the hotel.

As she strolled and shopped, she found herself scanning her surroundings, wondering when—not *if*—Fergus would make his appearance. Every day since last Monday when he'd materialized by the pool, he'd just happened to show up wherever she was, to join in whatever she was doing. Horseback riding. Cave exploring. Kayaking. At first she'd been disconcerted, even indignant. How dare he follow her, *stalk* her. If he didn't leave her alone, she'd tell Roger. To his credit, Fergus managed not to laugh at the ludicrous threat. She couldn't even imagine Roger Milton, M.D., five feet seven and a half inches of slope-shouldered tapioca, mixing it up with the sinewy Irish giant.

She peered down the row of vendor stalls, straining her eyes for any hint of said giant—and spun with a squeak of surprise when a familiar hand settled on her shoulder. "I wish you'd stop doing that," she said.

It was a lie, and his lopsided smile said he knew it was a lie. Today Fergus had secured his hair in a braid that hung down his back. He was dressed as close to civilized as she'd ever seen him, in a short-sleeved ivory guayabera shirt, wrinkled cargo shorts, and leather sandals. She turned her attention to the plastic grocery sacks dangling from his fingers. "What did you buy?"

He held the bags open, revealing a dozen eggs, an assortment of fresh veggies, and something wrapped in white butcher paper. It would appear he had access to a kitchen. She'd never asked where he was staying on the island. Obviously a simple hotel room was too prosaic for the likes of Fergus Dowd, Man of Mystery.

He poked his nose into her sacks, expressed approval of her purchases, and gallantly took possession of them. Together they strolled the market with the homey familiarity of an old married couple. Fergus paused at a table laden with fragrant baked goods, where he flirted shamelessly with the proprietress, a sturdy, coffee-colored woman with gray dreads tied back with bakery twine. He purchased a half dozen scones and a crusty baguette. Also a chocolate-filled croissant, which he handed to Judith. It was obscenely delicious.

She couldn't deny it was exciting to be, well, *pursued* by this sexy, determined, possibly dangerous male. Make that decidedly dangerous—and not because of his shadowy past. If she lowered her guard even for an instant, if this canny, insightful man managed to worm his way inside her head and find out about her role in Will's kidnapping, she could forget about keeping it from his boss and bestest buddy. Then what?

Then Will would be lost to her forever. Tom would no longer have an aunt Judy. He'd grow up knowing the terrible thing she'd done to his dad. Despising her.

Fergus was studying her. "Why so quiet?"

She shrugged. "Just wishing I didn't have to go back home tomorrow."

"Who says you have to?"

"This is a one-week trip. Roger and I are flying home tomorrow."

"Flights can be changed," he said.

Judith stopped walking. She looked him square in the eye. "What are you saying, Fergus?"

"Stay here with me." Just like that.

Judith opened her mouth to speak. She wanted to tell him he was being absurd. She wanted to tell him she was here in Bermuda with another man and that he had no business making such an offer.

She wanted to say those things and mean them, but she couldn't, so she didn't.

She started walking again and he joined her, taking one long-legged stride for every two or three of her dainty, womanish ones. She asked, "How can you even suggest something like that?"

"I wasn't tryin' to rile you, lass."

"I'm not a lass—will you stop calling me that? Good grief, Fergus, I'm forty-seven years old. Forty-seven. What do you think, that I'm going to just, just dump Roger at the airport, forget about my obligations back home, and, and *shack up* with you here?"

"That's more or less what I had in mind." His eyes crinkled. "Lass."

"Give me that." Judith started rooting through the pastry bag.

"Do you always turn to food when you're conflicted?"

"What are you, my *shrink* now?" she groused around a mouthful of scone. "Make up your mind, shrink or lover. You can't be both."

"Oh, lover, definitely. If I must choose."

The way Fergus said "lover," in that Gaelic-flavored baritone, made Judith stuff half the scone in her mouth. They'd reached the parking area before she realized that was where he was leading her.

She tried to get her bearings. "Where does the bus stop? A pink bus will take us to Hamilton—"

"We're not takin' a bus." He kept walking, leaving her no choice but to scurry after him; he had the bags with her purchases.

"Well, I'm not getting on any damn moped." Tourists weren't permitted to rent cars in Bermuda.

"You're right about that," he said, stopping next to a full-size motorcycle. He stowed their sacks in the saddlebags and managed to get his and Judith's helmets secured, despite her attempts to bat his hands away and retrieve her purchases.

Within minutes they were on the coast road, going well above the posted speed limit *on the wrong side of the road.* Rationally she knew they weren't on the wrong side of the road. Here, you were *supposed* to drive on the left. But still. Fergus accelerated to pass a Citroen which was itself speeding. Bubble-gum-colored homes were visible beyond exotic vegetation that smelled spicy-sweet, like unburnt incense. He shouted something at her over the roar of the engine, something about cutting off the blood supply to his liver. Only then did she realize how hard she was squeezing his waist. That was the other thing that had her discombobulated, being coerced into close physical proximity with this man she should by all rights avoid like polyester.

His body was hard and hot under the fluttering guayabera shirt; she felt every twitch of muscle as he negotiated the bike along the winding road. Mostly she felt the motor's vibrating heat between her legs, a pornographic sensation that spun her back in time to those dangerous, wasted years when she'd followed the band and done every self-destructive thing she could snort, steal, or hump to get Daddy to notice her.

When he stopped at a light, he placed one of his hands over hers in a gesture of reassurance, whether about the ride or the two of them, Judith couldn't say. Unaccountably, her eyes stung under the helmet's clear shield. Whatever Fergus Dowd was—and she'd probably never get a straight answer on that one—what he *wasn't* was the kind of sophomoric, self-fixated "wild man" to whom she'd once been fatally addicted. She didn't bother to ask where he was taking her. Somehow she knew it would be okay.

As it happened, it was more than okay. "How on earth did you find this place?" She stared awestruck at the secluded cove, a private haven of shrimp-colored sand, turquoise water, and azure skies tucked into a cluster of craggy rock formations. The only sound was the lazy snore of the surf.

Fergus leaned the motorcycle against a rock wall. "I've been doin' a bit of exploring."

She wondered when he'd done this exploring, considering all the time they'd spent together during the past few days. He withdrew a silver pint flask from one of the bike's saddlebags, along with a lightweight blanket, which he shook out and spread on a shady spot close to the rocks.

Judith laughed. "Real smooth, Casanova." All the elements for seduction present and accounted for.

He kicked off his sandals, stretched out on the blanket, and offered her the flask. She took a tentative sip, then a sturdier belt, of the silkiest cognac she'd ever tasted. She sat cross-legged next to Fergus and they passed the flask back and forth.

"Okay, I have to ask," she said. "What are you going to do with those groceries you bought?"

"Make you dinner."

She paused with the flask at her lips. "Where? No, you can't. I mean, I can't. I have to have dinner with Roger."

"Do you want to have dinner with Roger?"

"That's not the issue and you know it."

"You're a grown woman, Judith. When are you going to give yourself permission to do what you want to do?" He took the flask from her.

"I *do* do what I want," she said. "What I *don't* want is to hurt a person I care for, a person who thought enough of me to take me to Bermuda."

"Will Roger even notice if you're not sittin' across from him at the table? The man seems more interested in his porterhouse and his Scotch and soda."

"That's ginger ale." So Fergus had spied on them in the hotel dining room. Why was she not surprised? By habit she groped inside her purse. Then she remembered and emitted a whine of frustration.

"What?"

"I gave them up." She snapped her bag closed. "Cigarettes."

"You quit? When did that happen? You lit up yesterday after we went kayakin'."

"I did indeed, even though I was winded from the exercise. Which I wouldn't have been if I didn't smoke in the first place." She made a face, as if struggling to follow her own warped logic. "Anyway, the thing is, Tom has finally stopped asking me to quit. So that's it. I threw away my last couple of packs last night."

"Because he *stopped* asking you."

"He gave up on me." She shrugged. "Figured Aunt Judy's a lost cause. I know it makes him sad. This time it has to stick."

"Canny little man."

"Listen. Fergus." Judith dragged in a deep, shaky breath. "Can we just have sex now and get it over with?"

He peered at her from under those heavy eyebrows.

"Because we both know where all this is leading, okay?" she said. "We're both grownups, we don't have to dance around the thing, let's just do it."

"Get it over with."

"Right."

"Then we'll never have to do it again." Just the hint of a smile.

"Come on, Fergus, the suspense is killing me. It's been killing me for, for I don't know how long."

"See, that just illustrates how different we are." He cocked his head. "Me, I fancy the suspense. Not bein' quite sure *if* it'll happen, much less *when*. Keeps the excitement alive."

"If the excitement were any more alive, it'd have fangs and claws. The suspense part is over. *Finis*. It's time for the other part."

"The part where this—" his hand churned the air as he groped for words "—this pesky sex thing that's been festerin' between us can finally come to a head and erupt in a white-hot shower of . . ." Still churning. "Help me out here."

"No, the exploding-zit analogy works for me." She rolled her eyes.

"Once the pressure is released, the healing can begin, is that right? No more inconvenient passion. No more cravin' those bad boys." His arms thrust heavenward. "Hallelujah, I've been cured!"

"Oh, for crying out loud."

"Isn't that what we're talking about?" he asked. "Takin' the cure?"

Of course it is, she thought. "Of course it isn't," she said. "Is there some reason you can never take me seriously?"

"We'll get all this sex stuff out of our systems and become respectable middle-aged folks who spend whole Sunday afternoons rockin' on your brother's porch, never even *thinkin'* about each other's naughty parts." He nodded in mock approval. "By God, I think it'll work."

"Why are we *talking* about it? Jesus, all this *talking!*" She didn't know her voice could get so shrill. "You are analyzing the hell out of something that should be a simple and straightforward . . . *act*. Just fuck me, Fergus. Could you just fucking *fuck* me already?"

Her words brought a beatific smile to his face. "Ah . . . romance."

"That's it." She jumped up and stalked to the motorcycle. "Your window of opportunity has officially slammed shut. Take me to my hotel."

"Come here." He patted the blanket. "Let's talk about this."

Judith's howl of frustration reverberated off the rock formations and freaked out the gulls, who took off in a flurry of flapping wings. She clomped back to the blanket and jammed her sandy feet into her shoes. "I mean it, Fergus. Take me back. Right this instant, or I swear to God I'll . . ."

He waited patiently for her to finish the thought.

"You are such a dick. All this . . ." She spread her arms, encompassing the blanket, the cognac, the romantic setting. "The purpose of all this was to lower my defenses. To humiliate me. You don't *want* me, you just want to know you can *have* me. The big man. The *stud*. I've known too many men like you—I can't believe I fell for your horseshit." She shocked herself by kicking sand on Fergus. So much for the mature forty-seven-year-old.

He sat up and shook off the grains of sand as if they were random raindrops, the work of a benign higher power: God or Mother Nature, not some shrill, sex-starved harpy who'd gotten her little feelings hurt. "What did he do to you, Judith?"

"What? Who?"

"The foot rubber. The bloke doin' life for murder."

Judith's heart did a dunk shot. She slammed her hands onto her hips and scowled down at him, masking her alarm under a veneer of perplexed indignation. "How did Hal come into this conversation? This has nothing to do with him."

"You're the one who brought up the men in your past." He shrugged. "I'm just tryin' to hold up my end of the conversation."

"What difference does it make what, if anything, the man may have done to *me* twenty-five years ago? He's in Attica because of what he did to that coke dealer. All that matters is that he take his last breath in a maximum-security lockup."

"You've got yourself pretty worked up over a twenty-five-year-old drug murder."

"Would you like me to tell you what, precisely, he did with that blade of his before he finally let the man die?" Judith couldn't believe they were discussing the crime that put Hal Lynch away for life. She diligently avoided thinking about it, much less talking about it. "I know you've been asking yourself what made me take up with a monster like that in the first place."

"Not really." One shoulder lifted in a lazy shrug. "We all do things we're not proud of when we're young and stupid."

"Cute." Judith banded her arms around her middle. "Try young and *criminally* stupid. Is that still cute? When people get hurt?"

"I wasn't referring to your foot-rubbin' monster."

"Neither was I."

He said nothing, just sat gazing at the waves rolling onto the sand. Judith hugged herself tighter and told herself to shut up. Told herself there was nothing to be gained, and everything to be lost, by pursuing this particular conversational thread.

But she was tired. Good Lord, she was so tired, her secret a lead-filled backpack she hauled with her everywhere. And it only got heavier with time, a burden she could share with no one. She closed her eyes and fought for composure. *So go spill your guts to a shrink,* she told herself for the hundredth time. Psychiatrists were legally bound to keep their patients' secrets, weren't they? She could heave that lead pack off her back, let someone else support some of the weight for a change.

She couldn't say why she'd never made an appointment. Perhaps because she'd grown accustomed to the weight of the guilt and to the psychic exhaustion that went hand-in-hand with it. Perhaps because, when it came right down to it, the guilt and exhaustion were scant punishment for the terrible thing she'd done, and she didn't deserve to talk-therapy her way out of one iota of that punishment.

She opened her eyes to find Fergus still gazing at the water. Discreetly she swiped moisture from the corners of her eyes. She cleared her throat and asked, "What's so fascinating out there?"

He reached for her hand, and she let him take it. She let him pull her down, let him tuck her into the cradle of his bent legs, both of them facing out to sea now, his arms encircling her.

Judith searched the horizon for whatever had captured his attention.

She saw nothing, no ship, no sailboat, just turquoise water stretching without end. Her chin lowered. She squeezed her eyes shut, but the tears came anyway, hot and silent. Fergus said nothing, only continued to hold her. Her lapse in control didn't last long. Within seconds she was wiping her face and mumbling a lame apology.

He brought his mouth close to her ear. His arms tightened around her. "I'm going to tell you something, Judith. I'll not be sayin' this but once, so mind my words. You are a fine, strong woman."

She groaned. "Shut up." He placed a big palm over her mouth, lightly. She pulled it away. "I mean it, Fergus. I know you're just trying to cheer—"

"Something's crushin' you from the inside, and has been for a long time, I'll wager. It's destroying you. You don't have to let it."

Judith patted his arm, soothingly. "It's not your problem."

"There you're wrong, lass. The problems of the people I care about are my problems."

A little smile tugged at Judith's mouth. Just being included in that rarefied class of humanity—the people Fergus Dowd cared about—made that lead backpack just a tad lighter.

"I would never betray your confidence," he added, and she didn't doubt he believed that. If she were to confess to, well, to almost anything, he would keep his word. But as much as he professed to care for her, his first priority would be to his best friend and employer.

He read her mind. "What we talk about here is between you, me, and the seagulls. Unless your brother grew wings and a beak, he's not part of this conversation."

She failed to restrain a mirthless chuckle. Will couldn't be more a part of this conversation.

Fergus gave her a comforting pat on the arm. "It's all right, you don't have to tell me." Judith started to sigh with relief until he added, "I'll find out on my own."

20

HAL CINCHED THE last restraining strap, stood back, and appraised the young genius who'd paid dearly to be trussed up à la *The Silence of the Lambs*, complete with blue coveralls, straitjacket, and leather-and-steel faceguard. A case of too much bread and too little imagination.

He moved behind the man-sized handcart, tipped it back—a little gasp from beneath the faceguard—and wheeled his conveniently mobile client, a physics grad student named Justin Wornak, into a corner, facing solid black walls. It was late Sunday morning, nearly noon. Judith's flight was due in at three-forty, and Hal had made zero progress in sniffing out his two mil. More than once during the past week he'd questioned his sanity for willingly placing himself in close proximity to people who could, if he slipped up by one iota, send him straight back to prison. Hal knew if those big gates clanged shut on him again—a possibility not to be discounted, there being no statute of limitations on first-degree kidnapping in New York—he'd likely die behind bars.

He'd launched conversational feelers during the past few days, trying to determine if Will had managed to sneak a peak through the tour-bus windows at just the right moment, but his "cousin" made it clear that the subject of his long-ago kidnapping was off limits.

It was true, what he'd told Mick. Not a day had gone by during his long incarceration that he hadn't pictured those trim stacks of C-notes in their subterranean hidey-hole, mentally counted and re-counted them, always coming up with the same figure. He'd fixated on that buried suitcase, secure in the knowledge it would be waiting for him when he got out.

That cash had preserved his sanity, kept him impersonating a damn choirboy for the past two and a half decades. He'd sucked up to the COs, shunned the Aryan Brotherhood, racked up the college credits, and welcomed Jesus into his heart. Every action, every word, had been geared toward acing his first parole hearing. Besides turning himself into the model reformed felon, Hal had cultivated contacts outside the joint, anyone and everyone with the juice to influence the three individuals who would one day interview him, examine the pertinent reports, and say yea or nay to early release. And it had worked.

Bottom line: As implausible as this lead was, it was the only one he had. One way or the other, he was going to walk away from this place with two million dollars. Failure was unacceptable.

Justin called out from the corner, "Yo. How long you planning to keep me in this thing?" Hal ignored him. He unlocked the cabinet set into one wall and hurriedly began searching the top shelf, tossing aside CDs, DVDs, restraining hardware—the accumulated detritus of all the fake unlawful imprisonments that had taken place in this room. He pulled out a rubber chicken dressed in doll clothes. He pondered it for a while, then decided he didn't want to know. Ditto for the set of dental instruments.

Flashlight. Deflated exercise ball. Spray bottle. Earplugs. Three-year-old issue of *The Economist* magazine. A snake's nest of neckties. It all sailed to the floor. Hal knew he was getting careless—he paused for a moment and listened for movement outside the closed door—but the clock was ticking and every second counted.

He'd had high hopes for Gabby at first. Who better to pump for info than the onetime nanny? Not only had she been solidly in the picture back then, but her role in Will Kitchen's strange little universe had expanded to include employee, business manager, and confidante, not to mention surrogate mother and French tutor to Will's son and to his ward, if that was what Cuba could rightly be called. If anyone had knowledge of a sudden infusion of cash, it would be Gabrielle Fonteneau. Plus she was an irrepressible blabbermouth, and female to boot. Hal was an expert at manipulating the ladies, a skill he'd only refined during those long years inside, thanks to the murder groupies. Early on, he'd ID'd Gabby as the weak link in Will's inner circle, and as a result had wasted far too much time chatting her up.

The nanny freely and cheerfully blabbed about everything *except* money. Apparently she'd been raised with a strict code of ethics regarding thrift, savings, and keeping mum about one's financial affairs. A search of her room, as well as everyone else's, had turned up nothing.

Hal had—he glanced at his watch—just under four hours to see what tidbits he could unearth before the wheels of Judith's jet kissed the tarmac at JFK. Once she was around, the long-lost cousin would have to get lost for good. She'd recognize him in an instant.

The cabinet was deep. Stretching to reach the far end, he pulled out the last few items: a ball gag, a catcher's mitt, and a can of WD-40.

"Yo. Didja hear me?" Justin strained to look over his shoulder. "I think I've had enough of this thing. Get me out of it."

Hal had conducted two thorough inspections of both the Goo and the house, including the basement, which he knew belonged to Will's pal Fergus Dowd. He'd never met this Fergus, but after an exhaustive inspection of the bizarrely appointed warren of rooms the man called home, he had to admit to a certain curiosity about him.

Hal had returned to Will's office on the second floor of the house repeatedly, usually in the middle of the night, flashlight in hand. He'd jimmied the locks on the desk and filing cabinet so many times, he could probably do it faster with a pick than with a key. He'd turned up client records, personal correspondence and memorabilia, your basic little black address book, issues of *Model Railroader* that stretched back fifteen years, and a lot of other crap he couldn't care less about.

He'd tried to get into Will's laptop computer, but it was password-protected, and Hacking 101 hadn't been on the list of courses available at Attica. Tom and Cuba shared another laptop, unsecured, but that contained only the kinds of files you'd expect for kids of their ages and interests.

There was actually a big, old-fashioned floor safe in Will's office, probably original to the house, and that had been the toughest to get into. It contained property deeds, passports, a gold watch inscribed with the initials *WSK*, Grandpa Will's handwritten diary, a box of ammo for the SIG, and a thick string-tie envelope, the sight of which boosted Hal's spirits until he shook out the contents: a dozen snapshots. All were taken in Will's bedroom, and all featured the same woman, a blonde cutie with full, high tits and—he aimed the flashlight and brought one of the pictures close to his nose—a tawny landing strip down there. More topiary pubeage. Hal figured if he was ever going to fondle a full bush again, he'd have to plant an azalea.

So Will didn't keep his cash or bank records or investment statements or any of that in the most logical places, which left Hal no choice but to explore the least logical places. He'd started outside with the garage and tool shed, and even given the bunny hutch a cursory inspection, before moving on to the laundry and furnace rooms, kitchen pantry, and crawl spaces. He'd given the same treatment to every corner of the Goo: game room, kitchen, supply closets, everything. He'd already checked the cabinets in the two unoccupied client rooms. What was left after this—digging up the yard?

Hal turned his attention to the cabinet's next shelf, set below eye level. He swept items off it with manic intensity until something blocked his way, something large and boxy. Bending slightly, he peered inside, then jerked upright, struggling to process what he'd just seen.

"I know you're there." Justin was growing impatient. "Get me out of this thing, man. Let's go."

Hal's heart leapt so hard and so suddenly, he wondered if he'd given himself a coronary. It wasn't until Justin demanded he speak up that he realized he'd been whispering a string of incredulous curses. He bent again and took a second, longer look. The suitcase he'd buried the money in had been constructed of olive green vinyl embossed with a paisley design. He'd swiped it from his mother's attic twenty-five years earlier, stripped it of all identifying tags, and crammed it full of stacks of hundreds. The money had barely fit.

He reached inside with both hands and pulled out the suitcase. It was heavy, just as heavy as it had been that rain-soaked day in the woods. This was the same piece of luggage, no doubts on that score. It was worn in the exact same places. There was the corner that had split and been restitched by the shoe-repair man. The last time he'd seen this thing, it had been triple-sealed in trash bags and strapping tape, and he'd been tossing dirt onto it in the pouring rain. He heaved the case onto the bare mattress and squatted in front of it.

Even if the lock hadn't been busted, he'd have had no trouble getting into the suitcase. The combination was burned into his memory: three, zero, and eight, representing Mom's most lucrative night at Holy Resurrection, where she spent every Thursday evening playing twenty cards at a time without a bingo marker, surrounded by her cheering section of lucky troll dolls.

God Almighty, his fingers were shaking. The cheap latches flipped open with a satisfying snap.

"What was that?" Justin demanded from his corner. "What are you going to do to me? *Why won't you say anything?*"

Hal lifted the lid of the suitcase. It took a moment to register the fact that he wasn't looking at stacks of hundreds.

"Yo, Keith, whatcha up to?"

Hal slammed the lid shut. Cuba stood in the doorway, frowning in puzzlement as she took in the mess. The contents of the cabinet were strewn everywhere.

"I . . ." He gave a short laugh, thinking fast. "I was looking for something."

She came into the room. Glanced at the empty cabinet. Looked at the rubber chicken in its cute little outfit. "Looking for what?"

"Who's that?" Justin demanded. "Clarice? Is that you?"

Cuba didn't spare their client so much as a glance; she was staring at the closed suitcase. Hal came to his feet, feeling the joint-popping burden of his fifty years for the first time. He gave her a disarming smile and lowered his voice to a whisper. "Not so sure myself what I hoped to find. Something to make his stay with us a little more memorable." He nodded toward Justin.

Cuba didn't return his smile. There was too much going on behind those big blue eyes. Whatever problems this kid had, stupidity wasn't among them.

"Guess I got kind of carried away." He nudged a Chinese folding fan with the toe of his work boot. "Maybe I'll make Hannibal there pick it up."

"Hannibal?"

Still whispering, Hal said, "Guy thinks he's Hannibal Lechter. You know, from the movie?"

"That's, like, pitiful."

"I *heard* that," Justin chanted. "You're not Clarice. Where is she?"

"Who's gonna do Clarice?" Cuba asked, sotto voce.

"Who do you think?"

"Gabby's too old. I mean, no offense, but Clarice is supposed to be, like, in her twenties. And she's not French."

"Nice try, but you know what Will says. When you're eighteen."

She hissed, "That is such bullshit and you know it. I could do Clarice. I could do her a lot better than Gabby."

Cuba's color was high, her eyes bright. Her attention had shifted from Hal's obvious snooping, and he wanted to keep it from shifting back. He scratched his chin. "Well . . ."

"What the fuck happened here?" Mick sauntered into the room, surveying the clutter.

At the sound of his voice, Cuba pulled a longsuffering face.

He sidled up to her. "What are you looking for? Your vibrator?" He grabbed his crotch. "I think I found it."

"What's that about a vibrator?" Justin's voice was tight. "I did not agree to anything weird."

Cuba gave the client a withering look. "I'm sure." Her voice oozed the kind of corrosive sarcasm only a teenage girl could master. "He only paid, like, a million bucks to get tied to a handcart. So about Clarice." She shoved Mick's hand off her shoulder and turned back to Hal. "You're here. It's not like I'll be alone with the client or anything."

Hal made a show of puffing his cheeks, mulling it over. "You sure you can handle it?"

Her little face lit up. "I've seen the movie, like, a dozen times. I can *so* do Clarice. Where's the costume? With the others?" She was already halfway out the door.

Hal shook his head with a little smile, as if she'd worn him down. "Remember, this is between us."

Cuba emitted an earsplitting squeal and rushed back in to give him a bear hug. "You are *so cool,* Keith. I'll be, like, two minutes."

Mick watched her sprint out of the room. "Wish she'd grope me like that."

"Pick up all this stuff." Hal kicked the pile of clutter.

"Why me? I didn't do it."

"And make it fast." Lowering his voice again as he closed the door, he added, "I don't want your uncle to start asking questions."

Mick tried to stare him down, but in the end he averted his gaze and began tossing items helter-skelter back into the cabinet. "I've been outta the loop a few days. You fuck her yet?"

Hal shook his head. "She's playing hard to get. Anyway, that turned into a dead end. If she knows about the money, she's not sharing." The suitcase lay right there in full view, but he had no intention of mentioning its significance.

Mick made a face. "I wasn't talking about Gabby."

"I don't fuck kids, Mick. Keep your voice down."

"You make it sound like she's in diapers." Mick spun the DVDs like Frisbees toward the back of the cabinet. "She's fourteen."

Cuba was fifteen. Hal didn't correct him.

"You telling me you never fucked a fourteen-year-old?" Mick sneered. "You are so full of shit."

"I like grown-up women who know the score."

"What, you think Cuba's some kinda innocent young thing? She was living on the streets when Gabby found her." He offered a leering grin. "*On the streets,* Hal. What do you think she was doing to feed herself, huh? Selling flowers? And you know, once they've gotten popped, they gotta have more, I don't care how young they are. It's like this addiction."

Hal's boneheaded son was lecturing him about the fairer sex. He didn't know whether to laugh or cry.

"Don't kid yourself," Mick said, "she wants it."

"Yeah, I can tell."

"The young ones are nice. You don't know what you're missing. And tight?" Mick pumped his closed fist. "Like a milking machine, I swear. I'm talking twelve, thirteen years old."

Justin spoke up from his corner. "That's messed up, man."

Mick laughed. "You know what they say, 'Old enough to bleed, old enough to breed.' I'll have to introduce you to some fresh meat, old man." He found himself slammed against the wall before he could draw his next breath. "What? What?"

"You don't call me that." Hal's voice was a controlled growl.

"Don't call you what? Lemme go."

"I'm not old and I'm not interested in being anyone's old man, especially yours." Hal tightened his grip. "You got that?"

"Yeah. I got it. Fuck."

Hal released him. Mick tried to shrug off the humiliating encounter. His expression and his little cough of laughter said, *What's his problem?* He avoided Hal's gaze as he hurled the last of the mess into the cabinet. "What about that?" Mick nodded toward the suitcase on the mattress.

"Nothing. Junk. Put it with the rest."

Mick kicked open the lid of the suitcase. "What's all this shit?" He plucked a newspaper clipping that was lying on top. "'Ricky Baines Recovering in Hospital. Acting Community Expresses Relief.' *The New York Times*." He peered more closely at the faded newsprint. "The network put up a reward for information leading to the conviction, blah blah blah. A hundred grand. Sweet." He dropped the clipping and lifted another, this one featuring a full-page headline. "'Ricky Maimed! Parents Receive Grisly Present.'" Mick cackled. "*The Daily News*."

"Close that thing."

"Check it out. It's all stuff about the kidnapping." Mick picked up a supermarket tabloid. "'The Severed Finger! Exclusive Photos!'" He flipped to the next page. "Whoa. Awesome."

"Those pictures aren't real, you idiot." Hal snatched the tabloid from Mick and tossed it back into the suitcase.

"How do you know?"

Hal gave him the look. *How do you think I know?*

"Oh. Yeah." Mick giggled until Hal closed the case and latched it. "Hey! I wanted to check out that issue of *Parrot World*. 'Courageous Quint—You Should See the Other Guy!' What other guy? Oh yeah, didn't he take a chunk out of y—" Mick flinched as Hal signaled him to shut the hell up. "But no one knows it was you," Mick whispered, "so how come it says 'you should see the other—'"

"It's an expression, you idiot. Get that back in there." Hal nodded toward the cabinet.

Mick dragged the case off the mattress, grunting. "Give me a hand with this thing, will ya?"

If Mick weren't the spitting image, Hal never would believe he'd sired him. He grabbed the suitcase from his son and hurled it deep into the cabinet.

"Who's gonna let me out of this thing?" Justin griped. "How many times do I have to say it?"

Mick's head swiveled. His malignant gaze narrowed on their client with the precision of a raptor homing in on a hapless chipmunk. This kid must never have had a mutt to kick around the yard. Hal watched him advance on Justin Wornak, still facing the corner, now struggling to make eye contact.

"Hey, how's it goin', man?" Justin offered Mick an affable smile; they were about the same age. Mick said nothing. "Yeah, okay, listen, I'm ready to get outta this thing." He jiggled his arms, to the extent they were jiggleable within the straitjacket. Mick remained mute. Justin's smile failed him. "Like, now?"

Mick turned to Hal, who'd joined them in the corner. "What's the deal with this guy?"

"Hannibal the Cannibal. Can't you tell?"

"How long's he been like this?"

Hal looked at his watch. "Ten, twelve minutes, tops."

Mick turned back to Justin. "You pussy."

"I'd like to see *you* tied up like this, see how long you'd last." Justin was getting shrill. "Listen, asshole, I'm the client. I paid for this shit. I say when it's over, okay? It's over. Take off these straps. Unbuckle this thing. Now."

"Unfortunately, Justin," Hal said, "that's not how it works. You met with our boss. You insisted on a specific brand of treatment for two full days. He got it all in writing. You signed on the dotted line."

Justin's elaborate eye-roll said he was dealing with simpletons. "Yes, yes, I signed on the dotted line and all that. Now I'm *un*signing. Your boss said

I could quit this anytime."

"Of course you can," Hal assured him.

"No prob, man." Mick gave him a couple of friendly thumps on the shoulder. "You're still a pussy, but hey, you're the one's gotta live with that, right?"

"So do it already. I'm waiting."

"I think you're forgetting something," Hal said.

"Huh?"

"The safe word?"

Their client frowned in puzzlement, then a spark of comprehension glimmered to life. "Safe word. Right. That guy Kitchen talked about a safe word."

"He made you choose a word," Hal prompted. "Told you not to forget it."

"I didn't forget it." Justin was perspiring now, reflexively jerking his limbs. Long moments passed as he sweated and twitched. "It's just not, like, on the tip of my tongue, that's all."

"You *forgot* your safe word?" Mick was clearly delighted by this turn of events.

"Wait, wait, gimme a chance to think. Oh yeah." Justin perked up. "I wrote it on my left wrist." Both arms were fully enrobed in the straightjacket. "Just loosen this thing, let me get a look at it."

Mick said, "Sorry, Hannibal, that's against the rules."

Which was bullshit, of course, but what did Hal care?

"Oh, come one, man . . ." Justin squirmed in his bindings. "Just one little peek. I've gotta get out of this thing."

"No can do, Hannibal." Mick shook his head sadly. "If we drop our guard even for a second, you might eat our livers with limas beans and Chianti."

"*Fava* beans," Justin said.

"What?"

"It's fava beans, not limas. 'I ate his liver with fava beans and a nice Chianti.'" He punctuated this quote with that creepy tongue-flapping thing from the movie.

"See?" Mick jabbed a stiff finger into his ribs, eliciting a wince. "That's why we can't loosen these straps, even a little."

"You people are nuts. Haven't you ever heard the customer is always right?"

Mick appeared to ponder that. "I don't think I ever heard that one. Have you, Ha—"

"Nope," Hal said. The moron had been about to say his real name. "Don't recall that one. I think Hannibal here's making it up."

"Oh God . . ." Justin blinked sweat out of his eyes. "Where's your boss? The one who signed me up? He won't be such a hard-ass."

"You mean Jack Crawford?" Mick poked him again, harder.

"Stop that. I mean your *real* boss. You know, Kitchen. The redhead. Get him in here."

"I don't think so." Poke, poke, poke.

This was getting old. "There is another way you can free yourself," Hal said. "You chose a gesture, too."

"I did?"

Was this guy really a Ph.D. candidate in physics? "You know, some kind of body movement to signal you're serious about getting free. Because as far as we're concerned, right now you're just *pretending* you want to be released. Understand? We let you go now and you could sue us for breach of contract."

Justin shrieked in frustration. "I don't know anything about any goddamn gesture. Get me out of this thing."

Mick turned to Hal. "So what was that mess over there all about?"

"I was *looking* for something?" Hal prompted.

Mick looked blank.

"Remember?"

A second passed, then, "Oh . . . right. Listen, that reminds me. Mom's not coming home today."

Hal stared at him, not daring to believe. "Why? What happened? Wait a minute." He crossed the room, shuffled through the hodgepodge of stuff in the cabinet, and produced the earplugs and ball gag. "Here we go, sport." He jammed the earplugs home, then unstrapped the faceguard.

"If you don't let me go," Justin screamed, "I'll sue your asses for every penny you're worth. Illegal imprisonment! Torture!"

Hal took advantage of their client's ranting to cork his mouth with the ball and secure the straps behind his head. Justin was crimson with rage. He bucked so hard, the handcart came close to toppling. Hal turned him around to face them, propping the cart into the corner for support. He pulled Mick aside. "What happened?"

"Look at him. Fuckin' loser. Hannibal Lechter my ass—"

Hal whacked the side of his son's head, then grabbed a fistful of the kid's T-shirt and yanked hard enough to secure his undivided attention. Justin had gone still, staring wide-eyed at his captors. "Your mother?" Hal growled.

"Oh yeah. She's not coming home today."

"Yeah, I got that part." He scooped the air in a gesture that said, *Let's have it.*

"Okay, well, uh, I think she's shacked up there in Barbados."

"Bermuda."

"Whatever. Some island."

"Shacked up with who?" Hal asked.

"She won't say, but it's Fergus, it's gotta be."

"That makes sense." Will and Gabby were of the opinion their friend had followed her to Bermuda. Like a dog sniffing around after a bitch, Hal thought. Guy couldn't get laid on the mainland? He released Mick, who stumbled back a step, smoothing his shirt.

Hal had been granted a reprieve: Judith would not be returning today. He felt energized, oxygenated, as if he'd just run wind sprints. She still didn't know he was a free man, much less that he was in cahoots with her son—*their* son—and that her brother had taken him in. He didn't know how much time he'd been granted, but it was more than he'd had just a minute ago. This was an offering from the gods, one he had no intention of squandering.

No more hide and seek. The presence of that suitcase was all the proof Hal needed. Will Kitchen had stolen two million dollars from him, and the time had come to get it back.

"My mom and that big mick." Mick sniggered, clearly tickled by this alternate use of his own name. "I was wondering when they were finally gonna hook up."

A soft whistling sound brought their heads around. Justin's eyes were closed, his nose piping a tune with every gentle exhalation. He'd fallen asleep. Mick started toward him—to kick him awake and inflict more torment, no doubt. Hal grabbed his son and hauled him back. He shot a glance at the open doorway. Cuba could return at any moment. "Where've you been the past few days? You didn't answer your cell."

Mick shrugged. "Battery died. I was with this girl in the city. Didn't have my charger." A greasy grin split his face. "This girl? She had a big can, but it was—"

"Your friend Joe paid us a visit."

"Joe who? I know lots of Joes."

"The Joe you blabbed to about our plans. Or does that still not narrow it down enough? Joe Silver."

Mick thought about it. "Don't know him."

"How about Archie Esterhaus? Big guy? You know who I'm talking about." Hal gave Mick a hard shove and advanced steadily as the kid backed up. "What the hell were you thinking? And giving him my real name?"

"I don't know what you're talking about," Mick squeaked. He'd backed up to the wooden straight chair, which he gripped like a lifeline. "I didn't talk to anyone. I told you, I've been—"

"I don't want to hear about your latest fuck-mate, I want to know exactly how much you told this guy." Hal's voice was low and controlled, his enunciation precise. "And do not even think about hosing me, Mick, because I will carve you like a grapefruit."

Mick's eyes were huge. "I didn't do anything," he blubbered. "I told you, I don't know any Joe Silver."

"I verified the name through his license plate. Did a little more checking. He's a school guidance counselor, like he says. Lives in Rockville Centre. Unlisted number. He knows about the two million, Mick."

"So?"

"He has your phone number."

Mick's brow creased as he tried to recall this Joe Silver. He was probably wasted when he ran his mouth to the man.

"I'll bet he tried to get through to you when your phone was dead," Hal said. "Did you charge it yet?"

Mick scratched his armpit. "Not yet."

"Do it. Immediately. When Silver calls, set up a meeting."

"Why? What's he want?"

"What do you think he wants?"

After a moment of deep cogitation, Mick's eyes widened. "No way. No fucking way is he getting a penny of that two mil. It belongs to you and me. An even split, like we agreed."

Dream on, kid. "You're the reason Silver came snooping around. He knows too much to just blow him off. I'll take care of him if I have to, but for now we'll play along, make him think he's riding the gravy train. Keep him quiet—you understand?"

Mick's eyes glittered. "What do you mean, 'take care of him'?"

"I mean a foot rub and a pedicure, what do you think?" Did this asinine kid really share his genes? "Tell him to go to that little park in Soundhaven. The one on Grove Street with the duck pond. Tell him to meet us behind the band shell."

"When?"

"Later in the week," Hal said. "Thursday or Friday. Make it Friday, two p.m. Then when Silver calls and says I'm here at the park, where the hell are you, tell him something came up and reschedule for a few days later. String him along. With any luck, I'll be long gone before he gets pissed enough to blow the whistle."

"*We'll* be long gone, you mean."

"You remember what to tell Silver?" Hal asked. "Where to meet us?"

"Yeah, yeah, the grove in the park. The park on, um . . ."

If he says, "Band Shell Street," I'll break all his teeth. Hal repeated the instructions several times, making Mick spit them back until it was branded into whatever passed for the kid's cerebrum.

The door opened. "I'm here to see Dr. Lechter." It was Cuba, making her wobbly entrance in low-heeled pumps a couple of sizes too large for her dainty feet. Her Clarice getup included a shoulder-length brown wig, charcoal-gray skirt suit, prim blouse buttoned to the throat, and leather attaché case. Plus a fake FBI badge clipped to her lapel. She'd completely transformed herself, right down to the subtle hill-country accent, which was spot-on. If you closed your eyes, you could convince yourself Jodie Foster was in the room. Boy, when this girl applied herself to something . . .

Hal gave her a reassuring thumbs-up. He liked Cuba. She reminded him a little of himself at that age.

Mick said, "You got decent legs, Cuba. Should let 'em out to play more often."

She addressed him coolly. "My name is Clarice Starling—Special Agent Clarice Starling, FBI."

"Dr. Lechter's with the Sandman at present," Hal said, "but he'll see you shortly." He plucked out Justin's earplugs and shouted, "Wakey, wakey, Hannibal. Look who's come to chat."

Justin jerked awake with a snort. He blinked at his surroundings until he spotted Cuba, standing straight and dignified before him. His eyes bulged. He tried to speak, but there was the little matter of the ball gag.

Cuba turned to Hal. Her accent never faltered. "Please remove Dr. Lechter's gag, Dr. Chilton."

"This is a very dangerous man, Miss Starling. He's already eaten a former patient, a policeman, a nurse, and, uh . . ." Hal had only seen the film once, in an overcrowded dayroom with raucous cons contributing knowledgeable commentary from start to finish. "And a few other people. I must insist he remain gagged."

Justin offered a garbled plea from behind the ball.

"I understand your concerns, Dr. Chilton, but I'm here on official FBI business," she said. "A serial killer is on the loose, and I need to get some advice from Dr. Lechter. I take full responsibility for my safety."

"All right, but don't say I didn't warn you." Hal removed the gag.

Justin gazed adoringly at Cuba. "I've been waiting for you, Clarice." He tried to do Hannibal Lechter as rendered by Anthony Hopkins, tried for that velvet voice and basilisk stare, but in the end he came across more Thurston Howell the Third.

Mick sneered, "Hey, Clarice, I can smell your—*oof!*" He doubled over from the accidental contact of Hal's fist to his solar plexus.

Cuba didn't miss a beat. "Dr. Lechter, the FBI needs your help."

"Why should I help the FBI, Clarice?" Justin asked. "What's in it for me?"

"I'm authorized to make you an offer. You must get awful tired of being cooped up in this cell all the time." She pulled a travel brochure out of her attaché case: Disney World and Epcot Center. "One week every year. All expenses paid."

Mick rubbed his sore midsection. "You look cute in that outfit, Cub—uh, Clarice." He wagged his brows. "Real strict."

She turned to Hal. "Dr. Chilton, it would be helpful if prisoner Miggs were confined to his cell during my discussion with Dr. Lechter."

"Mick." Hal jerked his head toward the door.

"Oh, come on . . ." Mick placed his hand on Cuba's waist, laughing when she threw it off.

Justin said, "Why don't you go swallow your tongue, man?"

"Just can't seem to tear myself away from Agent Starling here." Mick returned his hand to the small of her back, then slid it lower. With lightning speed Cuba spun, seized his index finger, and snapped it sideways.

Mick howled in pain. "You bitch!" He did a little rain dance, clutching the hand to his chest. "You broke it. Fuck!" He stomped in circles, eyes squeezed shut as if the agony were more than he could bear, and managed to hurl himself face-first into the wall. Hard. Another, shriller scream. "My *doze*!" Fresh blood poured from his snout.

"You know what they say, kid." Hal opened the door and booted Mick into the hallway. "Old enough to bleed, old enough to get your ass kicked by a girl."

21

THE NOISE COAXED Ricky out of his stupor. He was in some kind of box, and a million hammers were banging on the outside of it. The sound reverberated, echoed. And something else—someone was pounding a bass drum in a steady, thumping beat. Behind his closed eyelids was a glowing orange ball, which pulsated in time with the drumbeats. Those eyelids were indescribably heavy, but after a long while he managed to pry them open.

Darkness. He lay curled on his side, his cheek pressed to flattened shag carpeting that smelled like spoiled lunch meat and cigarettes. Something was crusted on his face. Dirt and tears and dried snot. The drumbeat grew more insistent, and now it pounded in his arm, his left arm, from the pinky finger right up to his shoulder. Ricky's wrists were bound in front of him. He began to roll onto his hands, intending to lever himself up. The orange ball detonated into an explosion of pain. He heard a scream and, suddenly alert, realized it had come from his own throat.

Ricky collapsed onto his back, releasing shrill cries with every gasping breath. The bass drum had multiplied a thousandfold, echoing the beat of his heart. But only in his head, he now realized. The drum, the orange ball, they were inventions of his muzzy, pain-fogged head. The hammers on the roof, though, they were real. He tasted blood, turned his head and spat. He'd bitten his lip.

It was rain. Not hammers. Rain on the roof, a hard, steady downpour.

But the roof of what? He still had no idea where he was being held.

Ricky felt the tight band around his eyes and knew he was still blindfolded. He lay there struggling to slow his breathing, to push back the pain, to compress the glowing ball into a fiery point. He tried to remember the last day or so, but it was all kind of a jumble. So much easier to forget.

In his head he heard his father's familiar exhortation. *Try harder. You're my son. Don't tell me you can't.* Auditions. Callbacks. Memorizing lines. Laughing on cue. Crying on cue. Struggling to please his acting coach. His voice coach. The directors. The executive producers. Never quite managing to please Dad.

I'm trying, he thought now, deliberately summoning his father's image, the man's flat, overenunciated baritone. *I'm trying to remember, Dad.*

The knife. He remembered the knife. And the plastic princess grinning down at him. After that, he couldn't be sure what was real and what was a dream. His little finger was gone; that part wasn't a dream.

There had been yelling. He couldn't say when, or precisely what they were arguing about, but there'd been a lot of yelling. His kidnapper and someone else. A woman. The man was saying a lot of bad words. It sounded like someone was getting hit. The woman was hysterical, screaming and crying. She said the same thing, over and over, in a hoarse shriek, more animal than human. *What have you done? What have you done?* Not long after that, Ricky smelled vomit. He knew he hadn't imagined that part, because the stink was still there, though fainter.

Later—he didn't know how much later—he felt hands on him. Not the kidnapper's hands; these were smaller, gentle. The hands pushed up the sleeve of his rugby shirt. He felt the stab of a needle, like when Dr. Lamstein gave him his booster shots. The hands began to peel away the cloth his kidnapper had tied around his left hand. The cloth was stiff now and stuck to where the pinky finger used to be. Ricky tried not to cry, but he couldn't help it, the pain was so immense. Someone said, "Shh . . . shh . . ." The fingers that stroked his head were cold and they shook.

Ricky began to feel strange, like he was there but not really. His breathing slowed, along with the tears. The nurse—is that what she was, a nurse?—carefully teased away the stiff cloth. It still hurt, but he found he could kind of wad up the pain and push it away from himself. The nurse wiped something cold and wet on his hand, especially where he'd been cut. *Don't cry,* he wanted to tell her. *It doesn't hurt so much anymore.* Then the winding of a bandage, the real kind, the kind that comes in a roll. Then he slept.

How much of that had he dreamt and how much had really happened? The medicine in the shot was real. He felt the lingering effects even now, lulling him back to sleep.

He *wanted* to sleep, wanted the oblivion it would bring, the respite from the pain and terror, however brief. It would be so easy. But instinctively he knew that someone bad enough to cut off a kid's finger wouldn't stop at that. He needed to stay awake, if only to know when the monster was coming back to do something else, maybe something even worse.

Ricky forced his heavy limbs to move. He shifted toward his right side, braced himself on his elbow. Every movement, no matter how slight, triggered flares of scalding pain. He used the pain to concentrate his depleted strength and sit up. He paused, listening. Just the rain pummeling the roof. Still, he couldn't be certain he was alone. His kidnapper could be a foot or two away. Watching him.

That was why Ricky had never dared to touch his blindfold, wondering what the monster might do to him if he did. He no longer wondered. He brought his bound hands to his face, panting against the pain. Using his good hand, he pushed the blindfold—a soiled bandana—up his forehead.

He'd taken a huge risk for no gain. His surroundings were pitch black; not one light shone. On the plus side, he had to assume his abductor wouldn't be sitting around in the dark. Most likely Ricky was alone. But who knew how long that would last.

Tentatively he groped the air in front of him, his hand still throbbing to the cadence of his heartbeat. Nothing. He scooted forward on his knees, reaching out in the dark, until his fingers brushed against something. It felt soft and springy, like a sofa or an easy chair. Leaning against it for balance, he struggled to his feet and began to shuffle through the space, feeling his way with his bound hands. His sneakered feet knocked against junk left lying around, stuff he imagined to be cardboard cups and burger wrappers and empty fast-food sacks.

There was more stuffed furniture and a low, cluttered table sticky with grime. He groped his way to the wall, hoping a door or window might have been left unlocked. There was a window, but not the kind he expected. It didn't have a real wooden frame, just metal all the way around. It was covered by a sturdy shade, which he yanked on repeatedly, to no avail. He took a breather, listening hard for sounds of footsteps or a door opening. All he heard was the rat-a-tat hammering of the rain. If anything, it was coming down harder than before.

He felt along the edges of the shade and discovered that, unlike conventional roller shades, you had to push this one down from the top. He figured out how to release the latch and inch the shade down. Weak light shone through the narrow gap. Ricky hadn't known whether it was day or night, and he still wasn't sure, so dark was the rain-swollen sky. Wherever his captor was, would he notice the gap in the window shade? It was another risk Ricky had to take.

He pushed it down a little more, just enough to peek outside. He glimpsed bare tree limbs. He risked another inch, two inches. This place was in some kind of wooded area, like the witch's cabin in "Hansel and Gretel." Ricky could see little besides the trees. He was about to search for the door and try to escape when a movement outside caught his eye.

He blinked, fighting to focus his vision through the driving rain and the lingering fuzziness from that shot. Everything kind of drifted a little. He squeezed his eyes shut and rubbed them, but it didn't help. He stared hard through the lashing rain. There it was again. Something dark in the distance. Man-sized.

His heart banged. They'd come for him. The police. But as he stared, the image resolved itself into a lone individual. Cops didn't do rescues all alone. On TV and in the movies, yeah, but he was pretty sure that in real life they did stuff like that in pairs and groups. Which meant this was his kidnapper out there in the rain. Ricky rubbed his eyes again. The man was covered in something dark, head to calves. A rain slicker, with the hood pulled down so low over his face, Ricky didn't have a prayer of seeing his features. What was he doing out there?

The wind shifted direction, affording Ricky a clearer view through the curtain of rain. The man had a shovel. He was digging next to a huge rock that from this direction looked like a tooth, the flat-topped kind in the back of your mouth.

Ricky stopped breathing. *My grave.* His kidnapper was going to kill him and put his body in that hole.

The man jumped into the hole and dug some more, tossing the dirt onto a pile. After a while he pitched the shovel aside, leapt out, and bent to lift something off the ground, something dark and rectangular that Ricky hadn't noticed before. It looked heavy. He dropped it into the hole and stood there awhile, looking down at it.

The man picked up the shovel and refilled the hole. Fast, like it was some kind of race. He tamped down the dirt, then kicked leaves and sticks on top of it so it wouldn't look like anyone had been digging there. The man straightened and looked toward Ricky, who ducked. After a few moments he risked another peek. The man was just a few feet away now, striding back with the shovel over his shoulder, his hooded head bent against the rain.

Ricky shoved the shade up and hurriedly groped his way back to the spot where his kidnapper had left him, barking his shin on the table and crunching litter underfoot. He heard a door start to open and threw himself to the floor, pulling his blindfold back in place and curling onto his side.

22

WILL SHIFTED THE bottle of wine to his left hand, rang Lucy's doorbell, and listened to the muted chime in the foyer of her home. The two of them had arranged this little assignation last Wednesday before she'd set out from his place, and he was *ready*. They'd been so close in his bedroom, almost *there*. And then that Esterhaus fellow had to go and spoil the fun.

Well, nothing was going to stop them today. Today it was just Will, Lucy, and a big, empty house.

The door was opened by a woman he'd never seen before. *Please, God, let this be the housekeeper,* he thought. And let her be on her way out. She was about his age and on the tall side, two or three inches shorter than his six feet. She had a bun in the oven, the blessed event advertised by a stretchy neon green top that displayed every maternal curve, right down to the outie bellybutton. A multicolored sarong was tied low on her hips. Price tags dangled from both pieces. She presented him with a side view. "Whaddaya think?"

"I think it makes your stomach look fat."

That elicited a jolly cackle. Will decided he liked this person, but he still wanted her to go away.

From inside the house Lucy called, "Who is it, Anne Marie?" She joined the other woman in the doorway, and he watched her expression morph from surprised to chagrined.

"I forgot." She looked genuinely contrite as she took hold of his forearm and ushered him inside. "I'm sorry, Will. It's just . . . there's been so much going on."

He forced a smile. "No problem."

"You met Anne Marie." She led them through the greatroom to the library, where a second Lucy sat cross-legged on the bare wood floor—Frank had liberated his big chair and his antique Oriental carpet—amid heaps of clothes.

Will glared at the irrepressible practical joker. "Hello, *Ethel*."

She glanced up from the slinky, royal blue cocktail dress she was examining, apparently unsurprised to see the man she'd hired to fake-kidnap her sister strolling into the place with a fifty-dollar bottle of pinot grigio. "How's it going, Will?"

"Smargin' peachy. How's it going with you?"

"Can't complain." She gave Anne Marie a thumb-up. "That outfit's a killer. Put it on the yes pile. Try this on."

"Like I have somewhere to wear a dress like that." Anne Marie started to untie the sarong. "Fair warning," she told Will. "This thing's about to come off."

He turned his back to her. "Looks like you ladies are busy. I'll leave you to it."

"No." Lucy still looked contrite, which should have made him feel better but didn't. In a low voice she said, "I really am sorry, Will. It's not like me to forget something like that. Things have been crazy."

Anne Marie said, "I'd love to see Frank's face when he gets the bill for all this."

"He can afford it," Ethel assured her, "no matter what he claims. Anyway, it's about time you had a few nice things."

"You can say that again. Is this the front or the back?"

"It's the back. Here, let's get it turned around."

It sounded like Lucy was buying her friend clothes on her estranged husband's credit. Will had thought she had more class than that.

She smiled knowingly, watching him. "You ready for this? Anne Marie is Frank's wife."

"Really. I didn't know he'd been married before."

"She said *wife*." Anne Marie joined the conversation. "Not *ex*. You can turn around."

Will did. The dress was as figure-hugging as the previous outfit, the neckline low enough to be interesting, the hem high enough to show off a pair of long, more-than-decent legs.

The women paid close attention to his reaction. "See?" Ethel said. "What did I tell you?"

"I'm going to burn all my old maternity stuff," Anne Marie said. "Just pile it up on the grill, soak it in lighter fluid, and . . ." She mimed tossing in a lit match. "Whoosh!"

"We'll go shopping again after the baby," Ethel offered. "Get you fixed up with a whole new wardrobe."

"Where will I put it all?"

"In the humongous walk-in closet in your new house." Ethel adjusted the dress to hide Anne Marie's bra strap. "The modern one with the attached greenhouse. Solar panels."

Anne Marie shook her head. "I like the big stone one with the playhouse that looks like the big house. And that fabulous pool. And the multi-tiered deck. Did you *see* that deck?"

Lucy explained. "Ethel and Anne Marie have been house-shopping on the Internet. The better Chicago suburbs. Anne Marie lives out there—she's been staying with me for a few days."

"Somebody going to explain this 'wife' thing to me?" Will asked.

"Frank married Anne Marie twelve years ago," Lucy said. "Only he neglected to inform me."

Ethel muttered something under her breath. Will thought he heard the words "lowlife" and "prick."

"I didn't know about Lucy either," Anne Marie said.

"Wait a minute." He shook his head. "April Fool's Day was a couple of weeks ago, ladies."

"The only fool here is me," Lucy said, "for not wising up sooner."

"So what does that make me?" Anne Marie turned and let Ethel unzip her.

Will presented his back once more. Frank Narby was a bigamist. He tried to imagine that gadget-happy dweeb behind bars. "Think he'll do time?"

"Oh, we're not going to report him," Lucy said.

"No need to get outsiders involved." Anne Marie's voice was muffled by whatever garment Ethel was tugging over her head. "This is a family matter."

"Not to worry," Ethel said. "By the time these two are finished with Frank, he'll *wish* they'd turned him in."

"How did you two find out about each other?" Will asked.

"I'll tell you about it. Later." Lucy commandeered the wine bottle and took his hand. "First there's something I want to show you."

This was more like it. As they left the library he heard Anne Marie say, "You have got to be kidding." He peeked over his shoulder to see her gaping down at herself in the maternity equivalent of a tube dress, the elastic material knitted in an exotic diamond pattern. She looked like a rattler that had swallowed a . . . well, a baby.

Ethel was wagging a pair of pointy-toed high heels at her. "Try it with the shoes before you say no."

Lucy deposited the bottle on the counter, then led him past the laundry room and half bath to the basement door.

Well, why not? He wasn't averse to a little subterranean slap-and-tickle.

She flipped on the lights and preceded him down the stairs and into a spacious entertainment room, complete with sixty-inch plasma TV, state-of-the-art sound system, cushy cream-colored furniture, and an ultramodern pool table made of cherry wood and brushed aluminum.

Will backed Lucy against the table and grabbed a double handful of soft, jeans-clad tush. "I hope you didn't bring me down here to play pool."

"Actually . . ." She pushed gently on his chest as he went in for the kiss. "I brought you down here to talk."

He sagged theatrically. She patted his shoulder. Why did women think maternal gestures like that *helped* at a moment like this?

"Really, Will, we have to clear the air about some things."

"We can do that after." He'd already learned how sensitive her throat was. Now he splayed his fingers in her hair, tipped her head back, and brushed his mouth from the tip of her ear to the place where her pulse fluttered against his lips.

Her thighs tightened around his hips, just a little, just enough to turn Mr. Happy into Mr. Happier. Suddenly it was hot as hell in that basement.

Will released her for the fraction of a second it took him to lose his jacket.

"Hear me out, Will . . . I've been thinking about this."

"So have I." He trailed kisses into the vee neckline of her taupe sweater, noting with satisfaction how her breathing quickened. "I've thought of nothing else for the past four days." He tugged down on her sweater and dipped his tongue into the newly minted cleavage. She smelled like her own delicious self and something else, some kind of fancy soap they didn't carry at the local supermarket.

"Don't do that," she groaned. "I can't think when you do that."

Good to know. Will dragged his mouth over the sweater and homed in on a nipple valiantly struggling to raise its little head through layers of lace and cashmere. Lucy's shuddering groan made him pull her even harder against him.

"We shouldn't do this." She pushed on his shoulders even as her legs closed pincerlike around his waist. "We aren't going to do this. Listen to me, Will."

He closed his eyes, struggling to rein himself in. "I'm listening. Talk fast."

Lucy scooted back and adjusted her sweater. "I know we got kind of, you know, frisky the other day in your bedroom."

Frisky? She could have been talking about a basketful of kittens. "If Archie's timing hadn't been so lousy," Will said, "you and I would've had sex."

"Well, maybe it was a good thing he showed up when he did. I've had second thoughts."

Will was going to kill the man. He was going to crash the International Beauty Show, hunt down Archie Esterhaus, and turn him into four hundred pounds of well-marbled hamburger.

"Lucy." He stroked her thighs. "I know what you're thinking. You're thinking you just came out of a long, miserable marriage. You're afraid of getting hurt."

"That's not it at all," she said. "I've got nothing against casual sex."

"So let's have some."

"It's not *my* expectations that are the problem here."

After a moment he said, "Okay, you lost me."

"I'm a lot older than you are."

"A lot? Six years. Five and a half. So?"

"And I'm so much more . . . settled. Twenty years in the same steady, monogamous marriage." She pulled a face. "Did I say 'monogamous'?"

"What's your point, Lucy?"

"Look who you've found yourself attracted to. A middle-aged matron in the midst of an absurdly complicated divorce."

"Forty isn't middle-aged."

She shook her head. "You asked what my point is. That's my point. You could hook up with some hot young thing half my age, but who do you pick?"

"A dried-up old crone like you. What was I thinking?" Will oozed his fingers under the hem of her sweater, slick as a Times Square pickpocket. Perhaps not so slick as all that, considering her expression of exaggerated patience as he groped her. It was a look that said, *Whenever you're finished . . . ?*

So much for distracting her. "I'm not attracted to you *because* of your age, Lucy, but *in spite* of it. Oh shit. That didn't come out right. What I mean is, the age thing doesn't matter. What difference does it make who's got a few years on who?"

"It's what you find appealing about me," Lucy said, "whether you realize it or not. That I'm this mature, maternal—"

"Whoa." He backed up a couple of steps. "Peter Pan, looking for a mother? Is that what you think?" Before she could respond, he added, "Because I *have* a mother, Lucy. What I want from you has nothing to do with mothering, trust me."

A disembodied male voice advised, "Go for it, Mom."

Lucy yelped as if she'd stepped on a scorpion. She buried her face in her hands as her ears turned purple. "Goddammit. I thought you were at the computer store."

"Changed my mind."

Will followed the voice to a closetlike room whose door stood ajar. The only items of furniture were a task chair and a compact computer desk supporting a desktop PC and printer. Books, files, and bound stacks of paper littered the floor. One wall was paneled in corkboard and studded with pictures cut from magazines—photos of actors, politicians, models, and just plain folks, each distinctive in some way, each bearing a handwritten caption: Wizard Wize, Gloriandra, Simon Z, Bloot, Johnny S. Characters from the Johnny Sherlock series. Will couldn't imagine Lucy's delightful children's books being crafted in this drab hole, but that was obviously the case.

The chair was occupied by a slim young man with short, dark, artfully mussed hair. He lounged comfortably with his feet on the desk and the keyboard on his lap. Will glanced at the monitor, which displayed a multicolumn list of song titles and artists. He noticed the iPod hooked up to the computer. "You've got some good tunes there."

"Thanks." The kid stretched out his right hand. "John. The son."

"Will. The kidnapper."

"How's it going?" John asked.

"It was going better before we discovered we weren't alone."

"Didn't sound like that from where I was sitting. Sounded like you were getting the brush-off."

"Your mom always overanalyze everything?"

John nodded. "Always. So you got a thing for old broads or what?"

"I can hear you," Lucy called. "Go upstairs, John. Get!"

"Sure do." Will answered John's question in a voice that carried. "I like 'em leathery as an old boot."

Lucy muttered something as she clomped up the stairs. It was just as well Will couldn't make out the words.

"So you're down for the weekend?" Will asked. "You go to Cornell, right?"

In a bored tone John said, "Go, Big Red," and offered a lazy fist-pump. He had his mother's coloring, right down to the dark-roast eyes. His mouth and the shape of his face were from Frank.

"Good school." Will leaned against the wall. "You have a major yet?"

"Classics."

Will offered a polite nod.

"Don't say it," John warned. "I *like* tending bar."

"You could always teach."

"I guess. Maybe I could teach bartending. The Cocktails of Ancient Greece and Rome."

Will looked the kid in the eye. "That wasn't cool, you know. Listening in on us."

"What would you have done?"

Will would have sat utterly still and eavesdropped, of course. At least John had made his presence known before things got too "frisky."

From upstairs, a burst of female laughter, muted by the floorboards. Will asked, "What do you think of Anne Marie?"

"She's all right. None of this is her fault. She didn't know about us, either." John gave him a speculative look. "So you were a child star, huh?"

"I was in a show called *In No Time.* Ran for two and a half seasons."

"I've caught bits and pieces channel-surfing," John said. "Time-travel, right? Kid goes into the future?"

"Into the past. Twenty-five years. He's from, well, now," Will said. "Finds himself stranded in the eighties. Him and his parrot."

"Oh yeah. 'I'm having conniptions.' Isn't that from your show?"

Will nodded. "The parrot learns all these uptight phrases from the mom in the family they live with."

"Weren't they worried about changing the course of history, all that stuff?"

"History, schmistory." Will shrugged. "It was a vapid sitcom. Can the laughter and sell the cat food."

The one thing everyone knew about *In No Time,* if they knew nothing else, was why it suffered sudden cancellation. Lucy's son had been brought up well. His gaze never strayed to Will's left pinky.

Lunch was Caesar salad with wild salmon prepared on Lucy's fancy indoor grill. Everyone partook of the pinot grigio except Anne Marie, who sipped Pellegrino and had a double helping of fish. By the time Will pulled into his driveway it was nearly four. Cuba was waiting for him in the foyer.

"I've gotta talk to you." She glanced around to make sure they were alone.

Will brought her to his office upstairs and closed the door. "What's wrong?"

"It's about Keith."

His nape tingled. "What about him?"

"I wasn't gonna say anything, but . . ." Cuba fiddled with the X-ray vision specs adorning the bust of Einstein on Will's desk.

"Cuba." He looked her in the eye. "Has he done something to you? Tried to do something?"

Her brow creased in confusion, but only for a moment. "No, no." She waved away the notion. "Nothing like that. He's not the type."

Will didn't think so, either. "Then what?"

"Well, it's probably nothing."

"Why don't you let me be the judge of that?" Listening to himself, Will did a mental eye-roll. All he needed was a cardigan and a pipe. At least he hadn't called her "young lady." "What happened, Cuba?"

"Well, I went to the Goo while you were gone to see if I could help out with the client. I know, I know." She raised a palm to forestall a lecture.

He sighed. "I've had some ideas about that. We'll talk about it later."

Her face lit up. "Let's talk about it now. Can I, Will? I was *so* good as Clarice. You should've seen."

"I said we'll talk later. And it all depends on how much your math improves." Before she could get permanently sidetracked, he steered the conversation back to Keith. "So you went to the Goo and what? Keith was with the client."

"Yeah," she said, "and the place was, like, a total mess. He pulled everything out of the cabinet."

"Keith did?"

Cuba nodded. "All this shit was lying around."

"Where was the client? Justin."

"He was in the corner. Tied to the cart. He was all right."

This didn't sound so odd to Will. He'd been to the room since then; any mess had been cleaned up. "I really don't think there's any—"

"So I'm, like, what's all this shit, Keith? And he's, like, I'm looking for something."

"For what? Did he say?"

Cuba shook her head. "Something to make Jason's stay more exciting or something like that. The thing is, he was acting nervous. I kinda surprised him. He was looking in this suitcase and he, like, slams the top down when I come in."

Will frowned. "The green suitcase? He was going through that?"

Cuba nodded. "What's in there?"

"Just some old papers. Nothing exciting." He placed a hand on Cuba's shoulder. "Thanks for telling me about this."

"I wasn't going to." She shrugged. "It's probably nothing."

"Probably, but I'm glad you did." Keith had seemed kind of nosy when he first arrived, which Will supposed was reasonable under the circumstances. When the questions veered in directions that were none of his cousin's business, Will deflected them easily. It was a skill he'd honed since he was nine. Then again, it worked both ways. Keith had filled in some blanks for Will about Great-Aunt Marguerite and her life after she left New York. But that still left an uncomfortable number of gaping holes. He reached across his desk for his laptop computer.

"I tried that already," she said. "There's nothing on the Web about Keith."

"No Web site? Nothing about his personal-training business?"

Cuba shook her head. "No Twitter, no Facebook. *Nada.*"

"All right. Don't mention this to anyone else, okay? Especially—"

"Gabby," she said. "I'm, like, way ahead of you."

THERE ARE MOMENTS in one's life when one can only wonder why, in the name of all that is holy, one has embarked on a particularly questionable, if not lunatic, course of action.

No one questioned the fact that something needed to be done about the leaking roof, and indeed, something had been done. Irving had positioned a lobster pot under the cataract pouring through the ceiling light fixture in his third-floor bedroom. As for the water streaming around the nearby window frame, every towel in the house had been pressed into service. That should have been a sufficient temporary solution until the afternoon thunderstorm abated and Will could inspect the damage under sane, sunlit conditions.

The problem was Ming-hua. Between her compulsive orderliness and her excitable nature, this leak was a disaster to rival the Johnstown Flood. The more her placid husband tried to soothe her, the more crazed she became. Gabby attempted to escort her downstairs for a sloe gin fizz, Ming-hua's poison of choice, but the old woman wouldn't budge. It didn't help that Quint had picked up on the tension in the household and was screeching and ringing his little bell nonstop. With Ming-hua on the verge of a meltdown and the storm showing no sign of letting up, Keith had driven to the local hardware store for supplies.

Which was how Will found himself on a pitched slate roof in the driving rain, holding a tube of roof caulk. Keith was up there with him, naturally. He was the handy one, the one who knew how to do this sort of thing. Will hugged a chimney and curled his sneakered toes into the ridges between roof shingles as the cold, wind-whipped rain swiped his ball cap and saturated his supposedly water-resistant windbreaker. He tried not to let his gaze drift toward the ground. It was a long way down.

Keith, meanwhile, appeared perfectly at ease, moving like a cat across the irregular roof, homing in on the source of the leak. The sky lit up with a deafening crack of thunder. Keith didn't so much as flinch. "Come take a look at this." He had to shout to make himself heard.

Shit. Will peeled himself off the chimney and gingerly groped his way over to his cousin. His knuckles were raw; he wished he'd worn gloves.

"Here's your problem." Keith ran his fingers over a strip of corroded copper flashing; he picked at a few flecks of loose slate. "How old is this roof?"

"Um . . . I'm not sure. Pretty old. We've had a few leaks over the years. I figure I'll need to replace it sooner or later."

"Maybe, but an expert might be able to save it. All new slate would cost a bundle. Meanwhile . . ." Keith took the caulking gun from Will.

"We can really use this stuff in the rain?"

"That's what it's for." With careless agility Keith shifted position on the steeply pitched slate as the rain pounded and their breath smoked. "You want to do the honors?"

"Sure." Like he wanted bleeding hemorrhoids. Will started to ease into the space vacated by Keith when a human head popped into view around the nearby turret, startling him. He lost his balance and started to slide southward. *This is it,* he thought, fumbling for a handhold. Maybe he'd be lucky and only end up paralyzed from the neck down.

His descent was interrupted by Keith's steel-band grip on his forearm, giving Will the precious second or two he needed to get his feet under himself and scramble back up. The pounding of his heart drowned out the rain, the wind, and whatever wry comment Keith made as he thumped Will's shoulder.

The disembodied head belonged to Ming-hua, nosing out one of the turret windows to assess their progress. Her precious perm was protected by one of those clear, accordion-folded rain bonnets. She called out, "You find hole?"

"Yes, ma'am." Keith said.

"Where?" She stretched farther out, craning her neck to see.

"Dammit, Ming-hua," Will shouted, "get back in there. I don't need you falling out the damn window."

"You no swear at Ming-hua. You fix hole."

"I'm fixing it, I'm fixing it," Will said. "Get back inside. *Irving!*" he hollered.

From the first floor Quint screamed, *"What!"*

"Ming-hua, we're on it," Keith assured her. "We need you inside to tell us when the leak stops."

"Okay. I watch. You fix hole," she told Keith. "Not that schmuck. He no good." She disappeared and slammed the window shut.

"Gee, Ming-hua," Will shouted, "thanks for the vote of confidence."

Keith offered the caulking gun to Will, who waved it away, muttering, "You do it. This schmuck is no good." He added, "Thanks for saving my bacon, Keith. I owe you one."

"Hey, if anyone owes anyone, it's the other way around." Deftly Keith began patching the hole. "After everything you've done for me?"

Will watched his cousin work. "How'd you get so good at stuff like this?"

"I did odd jobs for a contractor when I was in school," Keith said. "Picked up a lot of skills. And Mom's house always needed something done."

"Yet you ended up in personal training instead."

"Steadier work. Not as seasonal, and not as hard on the back and knees. I started out during the big fitness boom in the eighties. I've done okay."

"You work for yourself?"

"Yep." Keith examined the patch closely, squirted another blob of goo. "I like being my own boss. Give me that putty knife."

Will reached into his back pocket and handed it over. "Yeah, I like it, too—working for myself." Another thunderclap made him jump, but he plowed ahead. "It can be tough getting the word out, though. Do you advertise?"

"Some."

"I get a lot of business through my Web site," Will said. "What about you?"

Keith put the final touches on his repair. "Guess I should think about getting one of those. Back in Seattle, I got so many clients by word of mouth, I never felt the need."

After his conversation with Cuba, Will had performed his own thorough search. Even without a Web site, a successful personal trainer who'd been in business that long could be expected to have some presence on the Internet—mentions in fitness boards, blogs, that sort of thing. But it was as if Keith Kitchen, personal trainer, didn't exist. Not in Seattle, not anywhere in all of Googleville. He wasn't listed in the yellow pages either.

Keith grinned through the rain sluicing down his face. "You thinking of changing careers?"

"When I can bench two seventy-five like you, I'll consider it, Cuz." Watching Keith with the free weights was a humbling experience. Will reminded himself never to get on this guy's bad side.

He wanted to dismiss Cuba's concerns as the product of an overactive teen imagination, but for all her "Wednesday Addams on a bad day" posturing, Cuba was one of the most pragmatic, levelheaded people he'd ever met. He'd checked the green suitcase Keith had gotten into, the suitcase whose tinny lock he and Gabby had broken twenty years ago after digging it up and cutting off its plastic shroud. If any of the clippings in the case had been disturbed, Will couldn't tell.

Most of the money that had been buried in the suitcase rightfully belonged to him, of course. As for the seven hundred grand his father had been forced to kick in, Will had felt no compunction about keeping that, too, considering what the old man's miserly stubbornness had cost him.

Naturally, he'd tried to split the money with Gabby, who'd suffered plenty herself, but she insisted it belonged to him.

Which didn't keep her from accepting an absurdly generous salary as designer kidnapping associate and part-time French tutor for the kids. And he made sure she was well provided for in the event he ever fell under a bus. No one else knew Will and Gabby had found the money—no one but Fergus, without whose help they wouldn't have known even to look for it.

Will and Keith made their way to the ladder leaning against the house. Will descended first and held the ladder steady as his cousin swung his weight onto it. The wind shifted, blowing needles of rain into Keith's face. He squeezed his eyes shut and dipped his head. Will saw him blink several times, rub his eye, and blink some more. "You okay?" he called.

"Yeah, just lost a—" He cut himself off and started down the ladder. "Got something in my eye."

"I'll take a look when we get into the house."

"No, it's all right." Keith stepped off the bottom rung and hurried toward the back door.

Will followed him into the kitchen, where Gabby sat reading French *Elle* and digging into a bag of Ched'r Wheelz With X-treme Cheeze. "Did it work?" she asked.

"Yep, thanks to the cuz here." Will nodded toward Keith. "I wouldn't have had a clue where to begin."

Keith kept his face averted even as Gabby lavished flirtatious praise on him.

"He got something in his eye," Will said.

She leapt up from her chair. "I will look."

"No, it's okay." Keith waved her off, shielding his eyes with a hand.

"It could be a piece of the roof," she said, cutting him off as he tried to scoot past her. "Let me—"

"I said it's nothing!" He shoved Gabby away and bolted from the room.

23

"**H**ONEY, I'M HOME!"

Fergus's voice boomed through the cottage, a peach-colored nugget of Bermudan real estate he'd borrowed from a "mate" who was spending a couple of weeks in London. Judith had moved in with him three days ago, after the farmers market and their detour to the secluded cove. They were no less secluded here in this former gardener's cottage on eight acres of Bermuda's east end. The one-bedroom house sat tucked amid concealing trees, with a private beach and a spectacular view of the Atlantic.

Judith had returned to the hotel on Saturday, explained the situation to Roger—who took the news with his usual sangfroid, damn his civilized hide—and settled into prime waterfront domesticity with her big Irishman. Everything was perfect. Well, except for one irksome detail, and she was about to remedy that situation.

Fergus was—who suspected?—a gentleman. He'd given her the king-size bed and bunked down the past three nights on the pullout in the living room. He had this crazy idea that once they did the deed, the fragile accord they'd established would collapse like a bad soufflé. They were going to become lovers, he'd told her, it was inevitable. But first they needed to cement their relationship.

Fergus Dowd had to be the most touchy-feely spy who ever lived. Or IRA agent or gangster or whatever he was. Judith doubted she'd ever get a straight answer on that one.

And that was what really turned her on, she had to admit. The not knowing. Her imagination worked overtime to fill in the blanks, and her libido wasn't far behind. Judith had had this unwholesome thing for rebels ever since little Dickie Schneck, lunch-money extortionist and graffitist extraordinaire, had deftly unhooked her training bra right through her parochial-school jumper and starched white shirt. Sure, she'd managed to suppress that side of her nature for over half her life, to go cold turkey like a junkie, but she could no longer delude herself. Her brother was right. At heart she was a wild girl who craved wild men.

What would it hurt to indulge herself with a prime example of the breed like Fergus Dowd? Just for a few days before returning to her good works and her book club and her prizewinning roses.

And Roger. The good-natured schlub would take her back with no hard feelings, just for the asking. She had no doubts on that score.

No. No more Roger. No more Rogers or Donalds. Judith had had her fill of safe, respectable M.D.s. She'd rather spend the rest of her life in celibate isolation than settle for decades of soul-sapping boredom with Dr. de Rigueur.

As for Fergus's stated desire for an honest-to-God, hearts-and-flowers relationship, well, that had even less chance of happening. The junkie analogy wasn't far off. Bad boys were like heroin: incomparable for a quick high, disastrous for a long-term commitment. And that went double for this particular bad boy, who, though far from the worst example of the breed, happened to be best buds with her brother.

Which brought her back to that quick high. She needed her fix, and she needed it now.

Even from the backyard she could hear him moving around the kitchen, cupboard doors slamming, the contents of the refrigerator rattling as he put away the items he'd just purchased at the local market. She tossed aside the *New Yorker* she'd been perusing with half her brain, rolled out of the big hammock slung between a pair of towering palms, and strolled across the lawn and deck to the back door.

She wore only Fergus's soft ivory guayabera shirt, minimally buttoned and less than opaque. Her skin had begun to bronze during the past couple of days of less-than-fanatical sun protection, and she had to admit her thighs looked damn good below the hem of the shirt. She moved silently on bare feet, sneaking up behind Fergus in the kitchen just as he started to call out, "Did you go for a sw—" He broke off with a startled laugh as she slid her hands around his waist. He seized her wrists and hauled her into his arms.

Judith had never been kissed until Fergus. Oh, plenty of men had gone through the motions, of course, but none of them, not a blessed one, had known how to do it. She hadn't realized it then. She did now. The past three days had been enlightening, to put it mildly.

Soft, deep, endless kisses that made her head swim. Hard, possessive, take-no-prisoners kisses that tugged at her innards in a most agreeable way. Kisses as whispery-soft as a butterfly alighting on her lips, her eyes, her throat. The butterfly seemed to touch down other places as well—she could swear she felt it flitter over her body—but in fact, Fergus's talented mouth never strayed below her collarbone.

He was voracious now, they both were, their hunger feeding off each other. His hand slid down her back, over her bottom—

He made a little sound, a murmur of surprise. Judith was on tiptoes, her arms around his neck. The hem of the borrowed shirt had ridden up. And up. He broke off the kiss and looked at what she was wearing—and more to the point, not wearing—as his long fingers fondled the newly exposed lower slope of her bottom. They were both breathing hard.

"What are you doing?" he asked.

"I believe they call it an ambush." She flicked her last few buttons free and let the shirt drop.

"Lass . . ." His gaze never wavered from her body, even as he shook his head.

"You can 'lass' me all you want. It won't do you a bit of good." She'd studied her options, the various modes of seduction at her disposal, and in the end rejected them all. Subtlety was not going to work with this man. She needed to jump him before he had a chance to rally his defenses. A lightning strike.

She managed to pull his T-shirt over his head, but he grabbed her wrist when she went for the fly of his cargo shorts. "I don't think this is a good idea, la—Judith."

"Really?" Her free hand explored an erection of imposing proportions.

"Didn't your mama teach you never to lie?"

He gripped her hips as if trying to decide whether to push her away or pull her close. "Wait . . ." he groaned. "We need to talk first."

"Okay, let's talk." She shoved him against the counter and unzipped the shorts. "Do you like being on top or bottom?"

Within seconds she had him as bare as she, at which point Fergus muttered something in Gaelic and let his hands and mouth stray to those places he'd ignored for too damn long. Judith felt cold Formica at her hip; the two of them had somehow gotten turned around. She braced her palms behind her, boosted her fanny onto the counter, and locked her strong legs around his waist. Thank heaven for Pilates.

"I'm serious, darlin'." Fergus made one last valiant effort, holding himself stiffly away even as her thighs tightened inexorably. "There's something we must discuss. Then after, if you still want to—" He broke off with a full-throated groan as Judith grabbed a piece of prime Irish real estate and merged it with her personal portfolio. She cried out, the shock of pleasure so acute it rode the knife edge of pain.

This was what she'd been waiting for, she thought dully. All those years with her gentle, dutiful Donald. All those Saturday-night fumblings under 1,200-count percale, in the half-hour break between the local Long Island news and *Great Performances* on PBS. And all that time, this astonishing man had been living in her brother's basement. Hiding in plain sight as it were.

Fergus planted his feet and lifted her off the counter. They made their way through the small house to the sliding glass door in back, with side excursions to sofa, dining chair, window seat, floor pillow, and mirrored coffee table, ending up on the hammock in a postcoital tangle of sweaty limbs.

Fergus mumbled, "If you choose this moment to take up Demon Tobacco again, I'll pitch you into the ocean."

Judith did crave a cigarette, but not as much as she craved this man's arms around her, his chest hairs tickling her cheek. Groggily she lifted her head and offered a teasing smile. "Is this the part where I ask what you're thinking?"

"Go ahead and ask. I'll tell you."

"I thought men hated that—all those female questions. 'What are you thinking?' 'Can't we just be friends?' 'Does this hammock make me look fat?'"

He gazed down the length of her naked body, nestled so intimately against his. No use wishing he could have seen her when she was young and perky. She said, "Don't answer that last one."

He stroked her side. "You're more beautiful than I imagined. And I have a healthy imagination."

"And a healthy talent for Irish bullshit." Which was fine with Judith. She'd take a bit of blarney over the unvarnished truth any day, at least where her aging body was concerned.

"As for your second question," he said, "you and I have never been just friends. I've wanted you since the day Will introduced us."

"Donald and I had just gotten married," Judith recalled.

"It was lousy timing in more ways than one," he said. "I was the last man you'd have taken up with back then."

"How do you do that?" She raised her head. "Always know what I'm thinking?"

He shrugged. "A byproduct of my former profession."

There it was again, that buzz of excitement. The merest offhand mention of the mysterious "former profession" and Judith felt the hands of the clock spinning in reverse, felt herself turning back into some kind of giddy groupie.

"Why do you even bring it up?" She dropped her head to his chest again. "You're never going to tell me what you used to do for a living."

"Now, where'd you get that idea?"

"Oh, please." Idly she stroked her hand down his chest and over the sinewy contours of his hip. "It's always been this big state secret. Torquemada couldn't torture it out of you."

"You could try asking."

She snorted in derision. "I've been asking for, what is it, sixteen years? For all the good it's done me. And I can't get it out of my brother either."

"Will knows I'm private about my past," Fergus said. "He respects that. What I'm saying is—" he gave her bottom a light pinch "—you could stop dancin' around the subject and simply ask me. Maybe you don't really want to know."

She thought about it. *Had* she ever asked directly? Could it be as simple as that? Was she ready for the truth, now that she and Fergus were actually involved?

Where had that come from? They weren't *involved*, they were just . . . friends with benefits? Like a couple of rootless college kids? Lord, how she detested that phrase, the whole idea behind it, but wasn't that what she wanted from this man?

Judith was glad her cheek rested on his chest and she wasn't looking him in the eye. Her mouth was dry. "Okay," she said as casually as she could manage, "I'm asking. What, precisely, did you used to do for a living, Fergus?"

"I was a psychiatrist."

It took a moment for the unexpected word to register. Then her head whipped up so fast, she nearly strained her neck. "Bull*shit!*"

"I still have my med-school diploma around somewhere," he said. "I'll dig it up when we get back home. Johns Hopkins. You should be impressed."

Judith realized her mouth was hanging open. "No no no no no no no." She swung herself off the hammock and stood glaring at Fergus. "You were a spy," she charged. "Some kind of . . . some kind of, of double agent. Or an enforcer for the Mob. Something . . ." She windmilled her arms, groping for words. "Something . . ."

Fergus folded his hands under his head, crossed his feet at the ankles. "Something more irresistibly dangerous than an M.D."

"Oh my God," she groaned. An M.D. *Doctor* Dowd.

"You're pale, lass." Fergus patted the hammock and scooted over a bit, inviting her to snuggle with him again, but her feet were rooted in place.

"Another M.D." Her voice was small and breathy. "I fell for another M.D."

"We could discuss what that signifies."

"No." Judith backed up a step, her palm held out as if to ward off Nosferatu. "We aren't discussing anything. You *deceived* me."

Fergus spread his arms, all innocence. "That's a slanderous accusation. When have I ever lied to you?"

"Oh, don't give me that. You knew what I imagined about your past.

You could have disabused me anytime. A *doctor*." She put her face in her hands. "Oh my God . . ."

Fergus rose from the hammock and wrapped his arms around her. She didn't have the will to shove him away.

"This is what you wanted to talk about," Judith muttered. "When I jumped you in there. You wanted to get this out in the open before we did the deed."

His chest expanded against her cheek; his heart thumped harder. She lifted her face. "Wasn't that it?" He didn't answer immediately. Rarely had she seen him look so serious. "Fergus? What is it? What's wrong?"

She waited for him to say, *Nothing, lass. Nothing's wrong.* He didn't.

"Is it Will?" Now her own heart was galloping. "Has something happened to Will? To Mick? Tom?"

He shook his head. "They're fine. I assume they are, anyway. I've heard nothing to indicate otherwise. It's something else, Judith. Something I found out today." He lifted a beach towel off the grass and swaddled her in it, as if sensing how vulnerable she suddenly felt. "I've been lookin' into things. Like I told you I would."

Judith drew back from him. She pulled the towel more tightly around herself. "You've been snooping into my life."

"So I have. You need to know—"

"No." She spun away from him and stalked toward the house; her lungs felt starved for air. "I don't want to hear any of this. You had no right, Fergus. No right."

"Hal Lynch is out of prison."

She stumbled to a stop at the sliding glass door. His statement hovered in the air, just beyond reach. Her ears heard the words, but her brain refused to process them.

When she didn't respond, he added, "He was released earlier this month."

She shook her head. "Hal's in for life. What he did to his victim . . . They'll never let him out."

"Good behavior." Fergus's voice sounded closer. He didn't touch her, for which Judith was grateful; she felt as fragile as spun glass. "Lynch did twenty-five, the minimum, and made parole."

She continued to shake her head. "No . . . no . . ." This wasn't supposed to happen. She turned to face him. "How did you find out his name? I never mentioned it."

"You let the first name slip. And that he was at Attica. I cross-referenced arrest records, inmate lists. I had a little help. A former patient of mine works for the Department of Corrections."

"There must be a lot of Hal Lynches out there. It's not the same man."

"Harold Stuart Lynch." Fergus spoke precisely, patiently. "Born in Buffalo on January the twelfth, fifty years ago. Oldest of four delinquents. Family moved to Babylon, Long Island, when he was six."

"Stop it." Judith felt dizzy.

"He should've done brilliantly in school with an IQ of one forty-five, but when you throw drugs and sociopathic inclinations into the mix, you're not talking National Honor Society. Lynch dropped out of high school to play guitar full-time for a heavy-metal warm-up band called Puny Earthlings. At age twenty-five he was arrested for murder, following an anonymous tip, and held without bail—"

"Stop it, Fergus." She lurched through the house and into the bedroom, where she threw off the towel and dressed with desperate urgency, not bothering with underwear as she yanked on linen slacks and a striped blouse.

"Judith, listen to me." He tried to hold her, but she pushed him away and thrust her feet into beige leather slides.

"I've heard enough." She hauled her suitcase out of the closet and began tossing clothes and toiletries into it. "Take me to the airport. I'm going home."

"I'm not taking you anywhere until—"

"Then I'll call a taxi."

Fergus seized her upper arms, giving her a little shake as she tried to throw him off. "Stop and think about what you're doing."

"He'll come looking for me."

"I know. That's why you're going to stay put."

The flood of adrenaline evaporated as quickly as it had surged, leaving Judith depleted. She sank heavily on the edge of the bed and dropped her head into her hands. "*How* do you know?"

"What's that, lass?"

"That Hal will come looking for me, now that he's out. How do you know? Let me guess, *Doctor* Dowd." She made no effort to soften her bitter tone. "You figured out I was the one who ratted out Hal on the drug murder. Or maybe that was something else I'd just 'let slip'? I'm sure *he's* known all along—he's been waiting all these years to confront me."

"Sure, and that might make him pay you a little visit." Fergus squatted in front of her; he took both her hands in his. "But my guess is, it's about the two million dollars."

His words were an electric shock. Judith jerked back, but he held on. "What two million dollars?" she managed to ask. "I don't know what you're talking about."

"Yes, you do." His gaze never left hers. "He would've gone to collect the ransom money straight off, once he was out. And wouldn't he have been peeved to find it missing."

What ransom money? she wanted to demand. How on earth would she know anything about any two million dollars? She couldn't force the words past the knot in her throat. Shame and dread boiled within her, and she wondered if she was going to vomit.

In a raw whisper she asked, "Does Will know?"

Fergus shook his head. "No one but me knows you were involved in his kidnapping."

Judith squeezed his fingers so hard, she was surprised he didn't flinch. "He mustn't find out, Fergus. Not ever. Promise me you won't tell him."

"You're the one must tell him, lass, not me."

She didn't bother saying that would never happen, and not just for selfish reasons. She'd been responsible for Will's terror and pain all those years ago when he was a helpless child. Revealing the truth now would not only obliterate her relationship with her brother and his son, it would revive his grief and add a particularly brutal new dimension.

Your sister did this to you, Will. Your older half sister who was supposed to love you and nurture you and protect you from bad things.

She wanted to explain it to Fergus, to make him understand who she'd been back then and that that person had nothing to do with the woman she was now. But she couldn't even make herself look him in the eye. "How did you find out?"

"Partly it was the timing. Lynch was picked up for the drug murder shortly after your brother's kidnapping. Which was when *you* went from bein' the life of the party to hardworkin' single mom, overnight."

"'The life of the party.'" Her smile was sad. "You are kind."

"But mostly it's knowin' that Lynch is your son's da."

She should have been immune to surprise at this point, yet his words packed a wallop. "What did you do, find a photo of Hal?"

"His old mug shots. I could've been looking at pictures of Mick with long hair and a serious coke habit."

"Why do you say the money was missing?" she asked. "Hal stashed it in several banks—it would have to be there as long as he kept paying rent on the safe-deposit boxes, and why on earth would he stop?"

Fergus rose from his squat, perfectly at ease, it seemed, in his naked skin. "Is that what he told you? That he put it in banks?"

"Where *did* he put it? Since you seem to know everything."

"Not everything, but I'm getting there. He buried the two million. Five years later, your brother dug it up. I'm dying for a beer—satisfyin' a woman like you is thirsty work. You want one?" He headed out of the bedroom.

It took Judith a moment to shake off her slack-jawed astonishment, then she ran after him. "*Will* dug up the money?"

"Well, Gabby helped him." Fergus pulled two bottles of North Rock pilsner out of the fridge and opened them. "He was too young to drive. She drove him around for months, lookin' for the spot."

Judith batted away the beer he held out to her. "Fergus, what are you talking about? My brother never dug up his own ransom money. That's . . . that's absurd."

"Where do you think all his green stuff came from?"

"From the residuals. The reruns." In a weak voice she asked, "Didn't it?"

"The reruns never produced that kind of bread." He took a deep pull of his beer. "Just as well everyone thinks they did, though. Avoids awkward conversations."

Judith slumped against the counter, rubbing her temples, struggling to assimilate and organize what she was learning. "If Will knew where the money was buried, why did he wait five years to get it?"

"He knew, but he didn't know he knew. He'd been havin' a recurring nightmare, poor lad, from the day he was returned to his family."

After her father finally forked over the ransom, the family waited anxiously for instructions about where to find Will. Dad had been full of bluster and empty threats during those tense hours. If the kidnapper pulled a Lindbergh on him, he'd hunt down the cowardly cocksucker, shoot him in the balls, and watch him bleed to death. After he got his money back, of course.

It came at three in the morning, one last, brief phone call naming a lonely, winding road in the Catskills about seventy-five miles from New York City. A battery of police cruisers and choppers converged on the location, and within minutes the boy had been spotted, wandering dazed along the side of the road.

Judith said, "Ginny, his mother, sent him to therapy. I don't think it helped much." She followed Fergus through the sliding doors to the picnic table and chairs shaded by a khaki market umbrella. "Except for one thing. My father had fired Gabby immediately after the kidnapping. He accused her of negligence in letting it happen, even of being in on it herself, though of course, the police never took his ranting seriously. Anyway, Ginny had grown a backbone by then, and when one of the shrinks told her Gabby's absence was detrimental to Will's psychological recovery, she defied my father and hired her back."

"It was Gabby who finally decided to try hypnotherapy for him." Fergus set down his beer. "She read an article about it in the *Times* science section. That's where she got my name—they interviewed me for the piece. Will was fourteen then."

Judith's eyes grew round. "That's how you met? You were his shrink?"

"Number ten or eleven, something like that. None of them had been able to help him. The kid was still a sleepless wreck. Clearly, talk therapy was not the answer."

"You've known Will that long? I had no idea." Judith didn't meet Fergus until several years later when Will bought the property from the church. By that time Fergus had apparently given up the practice of psychiatry. "So you hypnotized him."

He nodded. "My Freudian colleagues had taken their best shots at interpreting the dream. The grave, the giant tooth, all of it. Then I put Will under and what do you know—it wasn't Death in a black cape with a scythe, after all, but a bad man in a rain poncho with a shovel. The giant tooth was a boulder—Lynch's marker so he could locate the cash again after everything cooled down."

"There was a boulder like that in those woods. How on earth did Will manage to see it, tied up like he was, and after all he'd been through?" Judith's throat clogged with emotion. "What a strong kid. I had no idea."

"We figured he was held in some sort of vehicle parked in the woods," he said. "A truck or camper. Something with a window."

"Lots of windows, actually. It was the Puny Earthlings' tour bus."

Fergus got that *aha* look. "Of course."

"How did Will know where to find that boulder, years later? I know for a fact he was driven there blindfolded in a van with no windows." She knew it because she'd been at the wheel of the van, a detail Fergus could no doubt surmise.

"Gabby guessed the tooth boulder would be within a few miles of where Will had been released. The two of them drove up there every weekend for months, in all weather, exploring back roads and wooded trails, markin' off where they'd been on a map. Their route looked like a rough spiral with little branches here and there. They became kind of obsessive about it, turned it into a hobby. Told the family they were fossil-huntin' or some such."

"And they found it. The boulder."

Fergus nodded. "They found it on a hot Sunday in August. Finally got to use the shovels they'd been haulin' around for so long. Gabby invested the money for Will until he turned eighteen."

"And the family had no idea." Judith shook her head in wonder. "Everyone assumed the kidnapper had gotten away with the ransom money. Well, except for me. I figured it would molder in those safe-deposit boxes until Hal croaked behind bars and the rental fees stopped. How did Will and Gabby know the cash would still be where he'd buried it?"

"They didn't, but they figured it was worth a try. Either way, it was good post-traumatic therapy for Will, takin' the active role, hunting the kidnapper's prize, just as the kidnapper had hunted him." Fergus looked directly at her. "Will said there was someone else in that bus. The nurse, he called her. A kind, gentle lady who gave him shots for the pain."

Judith looked down, fighting for composure. She didn't deserve the luxury of tears. "Morphine," she said quietly. "It was all I could do. That's probably why his memories got all muddled—he was high most of the time at that point."

"I know that wasn't your idea, Judith. Takin' the boy's finger."

"Hal didn't expect my dad to balk at the ransom," she said. "Neither did I. I should have, knowing how he was. Hal was the real wild card, though I didn't know that until it was too late. The whole thing was my fault. I was so . . . *stupid*."

"You came up with the idea to kidnap your brother?"

Judith nodded miserably. She reached for Fergus's beer bottle and took a healthy swig.

"You just went up to your boyfriend Hal one day and said, here's a way we can make some easy cash."

"Well, no, of course not," she said. "He knew I was concerned, though. Ricky was getting all the attention, and I was such a screw-up. I was pretty certain Dad had cut me out of his will."

"So how did you broach the subject to Lynch?"

"I . . . it wasn't exactly like that. Why are you harping on this? I'm not one of your neurotic patients, Dr. Dowd. I've had a long time to mull this whole thing over from every possible angle."

"I'm just curious."

"Yeah, right." She drained his beer.

"You weren't the first girl to gripe to her boyfriend about her family. But it's the rare boyfriend who suggests kidnapping and ransom."

"What can I tell you?" Judith said. "I know how to pick 'em."

"So it *was* Lynch's idea."

She gave an exasperated sigh. "Okay, technically? Hal was the first to voice the thought. I know what you're trying to do, Fergus. You're trying to absolve me of responsibility so you can persuade yourself you're not banging a felon."

"I appreciate your thoughtful analysis, Doctor Drinkwater, but allow me to offer my take on it. You've spent the past twenty-five years floggin' yourself over a criminal deed you neither initiated nor executed. Lynch recognized an opportunity. He exploited your weaknesses and manipulated you into thinkin' it was all your idea, thus ensuring you'd have a stake in seeing the thing through to the end and not squealin' on him. It's what sociopaths do. Well, that and maim innocent children. See, they don't have that pesky conscience tellin' 'em not to."

Judith opened her mouth to rebut his statement, but the words refused to form. Instead she said, "It didn't work." At his perplexed expression, she explained, "If that's what Hal was trying to do, to get me so inextricably involved I'd never blow the whistle, then he miscalculated."

"But you didn't blow the whistle. Not about the kidnapping, anyway."

"No, but he knew I was prepared to," she said. "It was after he cut off Will's finger. I had no doubt he was capable of worse. He even threatened to kill him. If you hurt my brother again, I said, just one little scratch, I'll have the cops on you before you can blink."

"But then he'd just turn around and squeal on you," Fergus said.

"Sure, I'd go to jail, too, but at that point I was beyond caring, and he knew it. All I wanted was for Will to go back home and for neither of us ever to see Hal Lynch again. I didn't want the money. The very thought of that money sickened me."

"You saved your brother's life."

"Oh, Fergus, please."

"You were willing to risk a kidnapping conviction to protect him."

"Sometimes I wonder if Hal hacked up that poor drug dealer out of frustration over not being able to . . ." *To do the same thing to Will.* She couldn't bring herself to say it. "Anyway, I saw my opportunity to put that monster away and I took it. I didn't think twice and I've never regretted it."

"Nor should you."

She leaned forward. "But now he's out. And the money's not where he left it. Fergus, I know this man, I don't care how many years have passed. He's not going to throw his hands up and say, oh well, these things happen, and walk away."

"That's why you're not goin' home," Fergus said. "Not until I've had a chance to track down Lynch and make sure he's not a threat to you. I'll grab the next flight—"

"Of course I'm going home."

"Judith—"

"Do you think I could sit here twiddling my thumbs while that maniac is running around loose, looking for me, looking for . . ." She grabbed his arm. "Fergus, what about Mick? If Hal comes looking for me . . . one look at Mick and he'll know he's his son. I was counting on them never meeting." She didn't say the rest, about how immature and impressionable Mick was, and how dangerous his father was. She didn't have to.

Fergus stood. "Does your cell have a charge?"

Moments later she was listening to her groggy son berate her for waking him; it was nearly noon, New York time. She grilled him on whether anyone had come looking for her, and got a lot of *whaddaya means* and *how the fuck should I knows* in return. She thought he sounded evasive, but how to distinguish between evasion and Mick's customary apathy and insolence?

"Listen to me, Mick. There's someone . . . there's a man who might show up. He's not a friend. Well, he used to be a friend."

"What kind of friend?" Insolence edged out apathy in his voice.

Judith's fingers tightened around the cell phone. "He's not to be trusted. He's about my age, a little older. Don't let him in the house. Let me know immediately if he shows up."

"Does this former friend have a name?" Mick asked.

Judith hesitated. Fergus signaled her to give him the phone. She shook her head and turned away. "His name is Hal Lynch. Harold. He might, um . . ." She swallowed hard; her hands trembled. "He might use a different name, though."

"What did this guy do that's got you so freaked?"

"I can't get into it right now. I just need you to watch out for him, okay? And if you could—"

"I gotta take a leak."

"Goddammit, Mick, listen to me." Tears of frustration welled in her eyes. "This is not a game. This person could be . . . He's dangerous, okay? I'll be home as soon as I can. I promise I'll explain it all when I see you, but in the meantime I also need you to keep an eye on your uncle Will's place in case Hal shows up there. Don't, um, don't discuss it with Will, though— no sense alarming him." She took a deep breath. "I'm trusting you to do this for me, Mick."

"Yeah, yeah, I won't open the door to strangers." Mick yawned. "I'll look both ways and cross at the light."

Judith slumped in defeat. Fergus snatched the phone from her and growled into it, "Listen, Mick, you haven't a clue what you're dealin' with if this fella shows up."

Judith shook her head violently and mouthed, *Let me handle it.* She tried to commandeer the phone, with no success. Mick said something that made the vein bulge in Fergus's forehead, and she knew it was about Fergus and her.

"You're quite the brave lad when you've an ocean at your back. Here's a bit of free advice, you mouthy piece o' shite. If you drop the ball on this one, don't be around when I get back."

24

I
T WAS NO longer about the money. Wesley flipped up the collar of his dark gray trench coat against the misty drizzle as he made his way from the little parking strip past the duck pond to the band shell at the rear of the park. It hadn't been about the money since the moment he connected Will Kitchen to Ricky Baines and the unsolved kidnapping that had nagged at him for twenty-five years. During the six days since he'd encountered Kitchen and that parrot, the case had dominated his thoughts.

Not that he'd forgotten about the two million. He was still curious about what had become of the ransom money, but only insofar as a means to solving the most frustrating unsolved case of his police career. As to how the cash might have ended up with the kidnap victim, Hal had promised to enlighten him on that point during this meeting. With any luck, Wesley would come away with enough new information to persuade the NYPD to reopen the cold case.

He still had a couple of buddies on the force, stand-up guys who never gave a shit about his sexual orientation, guys who'd stood by his side after he'd been outed. Friends like that, you don't burn off, and Wesley had kept in touch over the years. He'd been to Larry and Cliff's weddings, to their kids' first Communions and *their* weddings. And next December in Lowell they'd be watching him and Joe tie the knot at long last. And he'd get to tease Larry for squirting tears the way he always did at weddings, get to call him a big old girly-man.

The big old girly-man had come through. Just yesterday Wesley had been able to paw through the old case file and physical evidence in the Baines kidnapping. It was all just as he remembered it, but forensic science had advanced by leaps and bounds in the past quarter century. As Wesley stood in the police warehouse staring at the contents of that evidence box, specifically at the spots of crusted human blood on the towel he'd used to subdue Quint, the next step was obvious.

His stride slowed as he approached the ugly concrete band shell. He scanned his surroundings. The small public park was deserted; no surprise considering the shitty weather. It was just him and a few glum-looking geese who probably wished they'd waited another week or two before hauling their asses up here from Fort Lauderdale or wherever it was they spent the winter.

He slipped his left hand into his coat pocket and switched on the voice-activated recorder. A Glock nine-millimeter rested in the right-hand pocket. He preferred not to carry on the job, but he wasn't stupid. This Hal was a dangerous dude. He was also related to Will/Ricky in some way; the family resemblance was too strong for coincidence. Of course, the resemblance was actually to Will's nephew. Wesley had assumed Judith Baines's late husband was her kid's dad until he'd done a little checking and discovered Mick was seven when his mother had met and married Dr. Donald Drinkwater.

Which naturally made Wesley wonder whether Hal himself might be the proud daddy—a possibility he'd initially discounted, but now he wasn't so sure. If only he knew Hal's last name, even an alias, he could dig a little deeper and find out how he fit into the family. A check of Hal Baineses and Kitchens had turned up zilch. He'd also looked into friends and business associates of the family who were named Hal or Harold or anything close. No luck there either.

That train of thought led inevitably to speculation of Hal's involvement in Ricky Baines's kidnapping. If Hal was indeed Mick's father, that meant he'd been balling Ricky's half sister Judith at around the same time. Judith had been a loose cannon in those days, a spoiled girl testing every sort of limit, most notably her parents' patience. Wesley hadn't been the only cop back then to put forward the idea that the girl was somehow involved. Not that any evidence existed to directly link her to the crime. Chalk it up to the old blue sense.

Those suspicions vanished when the boy was reunited with his family. Wesley was present for the event and he witnessed Judith's emotional response. You can't fake something like that. Wesley would never forget the sight of the girl locking her arms around her little brother, sobbing uncontrollably and looking as if she'd never let go.

Cautiously he passed the band shell, eyes moving, ears straining for any sound not related to weather, waterfowl, or the distant midmorning traffic.

"LOOK WHO DROPPED a couple hundred pounds of blubber," Hal said as he and Mick joined Joe Silver behind the band shell. Trees and a high fence separated this patch of scraggly grass from the golf course next door. "That must've been some crash diet, Joe," he added. "You oughta write a book."

"Yeah, I could make a fortune." Silver did not appear amused. "Only, I got a better way to make a fortune, my friend, which is that you could stop dicking around and tell me what you know about the two mil." Even without the padded disguise, Silver was a big guy, but powerful, too, Hal could tell.

Mick stood with his hands jammed in his jeans pockets, shoulders hunched against the light rain, which was beginning to let up. His sullen glower raked Silver from head to toe. "I've never met this guy, Hal. Like I told you." He got in Silver's face. "So how'd you get my number, dickwad?"

"Drop it," Hal told his son. "We're all here now, all interested in the same thing."

Mick jabbed his splinted finger at Silver. "And you're not getting any. That money's ours. So just turn around and—"

"Shut up," Hal said.

"Who the fuck does this guy think he is, that he can just—"

"Did you not hear me?" Hal's voice remained calm; he simply gave his son the look. Mick shrunk back into himself, grumbling. He'd repeatedly warned Mick to keep his yap shut and let Hal do the talking. Judith must've had one hell of a time raising this kid.

"You're late," Silver said. "Your boy here told me two o'clock."

"He also told you Friday," Hal said. "You're the one insisted on moving it up three days. You should be thankful we even showed up."

"What did you think," Silver said, "I was gonna let you two jerk me around for who knows how long and beat me out of my share?"

Hal had had no choice but to accede to Silver's demand to meet on Tuesday afternoon. He didn't dare test the man's patience. He could spill the beans anytime, tell Will what his nephew and so-called cousin were up to. Plus, if Mick was that high when he talked to Silver, so out of it he couldn't even recall meeting the man, there was no telling how much he'd revealed. Silver might know enough to send Hal back to Attica for life.

"What makes you think Will got hold of the money?" Silver asked.

"Call it intuition," Hal said. "What does it matter?"

"What, little Ricky Baines fakes his own kidnapping, then hacks off his finger to make it look real?"

This scenario elicited a whinny of laughter from Mick.

"'Cause that's the only way I can think of for the money to end up with the victim," Silver said.

"You'll get your split as long as you keep your mouth shut," Hal said. "That's all you need to know."

"Did Judith know you were the one that snatched her kid brother?"

Before Hal could muzzle him, Mick answered. "You kidding? She was the one that thought it up." He moved fast, dodging the back of Hal's hand. "What? That's what you said."

"I also said, *shut the hell up.*" Hal seized a fistful of his son's leather jacket. "Is that so tough to remember?"

"All right, all right." Mick shot a self-conscious glance at Silver as he tried to squirm out of Hal's grasp. Hal shoved him away.

"So that's how it was, huh?" Silver asked. "You and Ricky's sister were in on it together."

"You're pretty damn nosy." The hairs on Hal's nape prickled.

Silver shrugged. "The whole world wants to know what really happened. I figure I got a right, seeing as we're partners now. What, like I'm gonna blab to my barber? After taking a cut of the dough?"

Mick was irrepressible. "Damn right you're not gonna blab."

"You were the one dressed up like a security guard," Silver told Hal.

"Bide your time for a few days, then make your move when the kid goes to buy his M&M's. Solo operation like that takes brains *and* balls. I thought so at the time and I still do."

"Shucks." Hal slid the .45 automatic from the back of his waistband, cocked it, and took aim at Silver's heart. "You're making me blush."

"Take it easy, my friend." Silver spread his hands. "We're just talking here."

"How'd you know about the M&M's, Joe?"

"Huh? The news. You know."

"The press never got hold of that detail," Hal said. All anyone knew was that the abduction took place at a vending machine. Early on, some TV reporter called it a soda machine, and everyone else took that as gospel. As far as the public was concerned, Ricky Baines was snatched while buying a frosty can of Coke. The powers that be at PepsiCo probably didn't know whether to weep or cheer.

"I know I read it somewhere," Silver said.

"Yeah, in a police report. Keep those hands up."

Mick's perplexed gaze bounced from one man to the other. "What's going on?"

"Our 'business partner' here is a cop," Hal said.

"Fuck. No way."

"You're nuts," Silver said. "I'm a guidance counselor, like I—"

"Only a cop would've known about the M&M's."

Hal squeezed the trigger just as Silver's hand darted toward his coat pocket. The round punched into Silver's chest at point-blank range. He dropped to the wet grass like a supersized sack of potatoes.

Mick's scream flushed a flock of birds out of the nearby trees. Hal pointed the gun at his hysterical son. Quietly he said, "I will shoot you if you don't stop."

Mick gulped air. He was bug-eyed and ashen. Hal moved to the corner of the band shell and peered into the park to ensure they were still alone. The rain had let up, but the sky was still swollen. Over his shoulder he said, "Check his pockets." Silver might have told someone where he was going today, who he was meeting. *If I'm not back by four, call the cops.*

As if that weren't bad enough, somehow Judith had found out Hal was a free man, according to Mick. She was freaking out, he said, warning Mick to look out for him, catching the next flight home. Was she nervous enough to confess all to her brother? To involve the authorities?

When he re-joined Mick, the kid hadn't moved a muscle; he stood staring at the corpse, at the sightless, half-open eyes.

"You're worthless, you know that?" Hal said.

"You killed him." Mick whispered it over and over like some kind of demented mantra. "You killed him. You fucking killed him."

"Yeah, and whose fault is that?" Hal squatted by the body. "If it wasn't for you shooting off your mouth, your buddy here wouldn't have come sniffing around in the first place." He reached into Silver's coat pocket and found the pistol the man had been going for. Wiping his prints off it, he said, "You happy now? That could've been you and me lying here."

"Let's get outta here."

Hal left Silver's gun lying by his body. He replaced his own weapon under his waistband where it was concealed by his lightweight windbreaker and checked Silver's other pocket. "What's this thing?"

Mick peered at the slim electronic device. "It's a recorder."

"No shit. Where's the tape?" He turned the thing around, inspecting it from all angles.

"There's no tape, it's digital. Come on, man," Mick whined, "let's go."

Hal studied the gadget. It was still going; must be voice-activated. He located the rewind button, then pushed Play. First came Silver's voice: *". . . Judith know you were the one that snatched her kid brother?"* followed by Mick's: *"You kidding? She was the one—"* Hal stopped the playback, figured out how to erase the recording, and slipped the device into his pocket.

"We gotta get outta here." Mick sounded like a little girl. "Come on, Hal, let's go."

"I'm not finished." Hal produced his switchblade and flipped it open.

"Are you fucking crazy?" Mick shrieked. "We gotta get outta here. You fucking *killed* a guy."

Hal studied Silver's face. There was the ideal spot to start, right there in front of the left ear. Hal smiled. *Ready for your face-lift, Joe?*

The first bead of blood appeared and Mick lost it. He seized Hal by the shoulders and, in an astonishing display of strength, threw him off Silver.

Hal sprang up, swinging the blade. Mick hopped out of the way. Hal was unprepared for the sneakered foot that flew at him. He watched his beloved switchblade bounce off the back of the band shell when he should have been dodging the fist Mick drove into his midsection. Hal doubled over, gagging, while the kid clutched his splinted finger and roared in pain.

Mick kicked Hal. "Get up. We're outta here *now*." Hal went for the gun in his waistband, but his son was faster. The cold barrel kissed Hal's temple. "I'm not gonna get caught out here 'cause you get your rocks off slicing and dicing. Move." He propelled Hal toward the corner of the band shell.

"My blade," Hal croaked. "Fingerprints."

Mick bent to retrieve the switchblade, which he folded and slipped into his own pocket.

Hal had always known he'd have to eliminate Mick. Until this moment, he hadn't been looking forward to it.

WILL RAISED HIS binoculars as Keith and Mick emerged from behind the band shell. The pair had left the house over an hour ago, supposedly headed for the local sporting goods store. Will had followed at a discreet distance in Irving's anonymous blue Chevy. He sat parked on a residential side street with a complete view of the park. His suspicions regarding Cousin Keith appeared to be founded. Whatever he was up to, Will's nephew was involved. He wished that surprised him.

Was it drugs? He wouldn't put anything past Mick, but Keith seemed too high-functioning for a guy with a habit. He'd told Will he'd done some stuff in his youth and that it was behind him. Will believed him. If not drugs, then what? Not some kind of sexual tryst. Keith and Mick were both a hundred percent hetero; he'd bet money on it.

Someone in the house Will was parked in front of probably thought *he* was up to something. Every once in a while a window curtain flicked, but no one emerged to question his presence in this nouveau riche bedroom community, so Will ignored it.

The term *nouveau riche* nudged his thoughts toward Lucy Narby. Also *bedroom.* Maybe he'd drive up to the North Shore after this, pay her a little visit.

Why? his sensible side grumped. So he could come *this close* again, only to be lectured about his Peter Pan tendencies or interrupted by her kid?

If it were any other woman, he'd say to hell with her and her hang-ups. There were plenty of other ladies who didn't turn all Dr. Phil on him and overanalyze mutual attraction and good, healthy sex. But the fact was, Lucy was different. He didn't obsess over those other ladies the way he was . . . no, not obsessing, simply thinking about Lucy. As in all the time.

Will forced himself to focus, visually as well as mentally, adjusting the binoculars to get a better look at his cousin and his nephew. Mick looked rattled. Keith looked rattled and pissed—and hyperalert, scanning his surroundings as the two strode toward Gabby's car, which shared the narrow parking strip with a white Maxima. Where was the driver of the Maxima? Will had a view of the entire park, and except for Keith and Mick, it was vacant.

After they'd driven away, Will stepped from the car and headed into the park. Maybe Keith and Mick had left something behind, some clue to whatever they were up to. He retraced their steps past the duck pond and around the band shell—and stopped dead in his tracks, staring at a body sprawled in the wet grass. A body clad in a charcoal gray trench coat with a hole in the center of the chest. That face. He'd seen that face before. He knew this person, but in his stunned state it took a couple of seconds to register.

What the hell was Archie Esterhaus doing here? Maybe it was the man's position sprawled there on the ground, or just Will's state of shock, but Archie looked like he'd lost a ton of weight since last week. Will approached the body, scrabbling for his cell phone before recalling he'd lent the phone to Cuba. Something shiny winked in the grass near the body. He picked it up. A pistol. Semiautomatic.

"Police! Drop the weapon!"

Will wheeled around and found himself face-to-face with two uniformed cops, a middle-aged Black woman and a young, crew-cut white man, their service weapons trained on him.

The woman sharpened her aim. "I said drop it."

Will tossed the gun and thrust his arms up. "I just got—"

"On the ground." Rough hands forced him facedown on the turf, cuffed his wrists, frisked him. The woman barked into her radio. Suspect in custody. Ambulance. Grove Street. Band shell. A fourth person arrived on the scene, a skinny older woman whose eggplant-colored jogging suit matched her puffy hair.

"That's him!" the woman shrieked. "That's the fellow that was peeking through my windows. With *binoculars*!"

"You're making a mistake," Will told the cops.

"Oh my *God*, he killed that man!" the woman screeched, as the cops ordered her back to her house. She stood rooted in place, a broken record stuck on *"Oh my God! Oh my God!"*

"Wait. No." Will tried to turn his head, but the crew-cut cop was having none of it. "The men who did this just left. They're driving a purple—"

"You're under arrest for murder. You have the right to remain silent. Anything you say—"

"Listen to me." Will struggled to turn his head; the cop slammed it back down. "They're on their way to my place!" he roared, spitting grass. "My son is there. You've got to—"

Another head-slam. "—can and will be used against you in a court of law. You have the right to an attorney . . ."

25

HAL ENTERED THE Goo, with Mick slouching in after him like a whipped dog. No, not whipped, not anymore, not since that thing with Joe Silver in the park. The whipped dog had turned into a feral pit bull, untrained and unpredictable. The kid had discovered something that passed for balls, and at the worst possible time.

Hal strolled into the social hall with as much cool as he could muster, considering the invisible time bomb strapped to his chest. Nassau County's finest might be on their way even now if Joe Silver did indeed have someone waiting by the phone for an all-clear. He started to send Mick outside to keep watch, then thought better of it. The kid was no longer under Hal's control; he might even come up with an idea or two on his own. Hal needed his son right here, where he could keep an eye on him.

Hal had checked the house first, looking for Will. No one was there. They passed through the social hall into the kitchen, where potatoes, onions, and carrots shared counter space with a thawing shoulder roast.

Mick whispered, "We don't have time for this, let's—"

"You want to walk away from your share, be my guest, my man. I've got no problem keeping the whole two mil."

Mick's conflicting impulses chased each other across his face. He squinted toward the outer door. No patrol cars screaming up the drive. Not yet anyway. "All right, all right. But then let's get the fuck outta here."

They followed the narrow corridor at the back of the building and emerged in the living room. Vacant. Ditto for the game room. Will had one kidnapping client in residence; he wouldn't have left him completely alone. The door to Room A stood open. As they neared it, Hal heard Ming-hua droning on in Mandarin. He peeked inside.

The client, a narrow-minded über-WASP who thought "melting pot" meant fondue, stood in the center of the room, his wrists bound overhead to a chain hanging from the ceiling, the ubiquitous duct tape sealing his mouth. Dave something. Dave looked miserable, and no wonder. Ming-hua sat on a hardback chair, reading aloud from the *World Journal*, a Chinese-language newspaper. Quint, perched on her chairback, appeared to be reading over her shoulder. Without taking her eyes off the paper, Ming-hua reached into the pocket of her housedress, extracted a red licorice whip, and handed it up to the parrot.

Hal planted himself in front of her. "Where's Will?"

Quint responded first, greeting Hal with his usual gooey affection: beak open in a hiss, eyes pinned, crouched and ruffled and spoiling for a fight. Ming-hua blinked at Hal over her reading glasses. "He go."

"When?"

Quint's enthusiasm rubbed off on Dave, who treated them to muffled imprecations and leaping high kicks that served only to launch him in circles. Mick sniggered at the spectacle.

Ming-hua rolled her newspaper into a tube. "You no move, Dave. You listen Ming-hua." She started to rise. Hal shoved her back down, causing Quint to lunge for his hand. Hal jerked it back just in time.

"When, Ming-hua?" he demanded. "When did Will leave?"

She gaped in startled outrage. Hal had never treated her with anything but gentlemanly respect.

He snatched the newspaper from her and tossed it aside. His voice was icily calm. "Answer me."

Her expression shifted as fear edged out anger. "One, two hour." Quint picked up on her distress. He swayed from side to side and screamed with renewed vigor.

"How long after I left?" Hal said.

"Right after. You go—he go right after. He take Irving's car."

Hal's scalp prickled. "Where? Did he say?"

She shook her head. "I ask. He say, 'Out.'"

Will had tailed him. Hal hadn't thought his "cousin" was on to him, not yet, but the past couple of days he'd seemed a tad more vigilant, more attentive to Hal's comings and goings. Gabby's purple Viper must have been laughably easy for Will to keep in his sights.

Hal pictured Will finding Joe Silver's corpse. Pictured him pulling out his cell phone and punching in 911.

Ming-hua's expression turned mulish. "You go. Will no here. You go."

The cousin act was officially over. Hal's fingers slipped under the back of his windbreaker and touched the place where his .45 should have been. He cut his eyes to Mick's jacket pocket. The kid had his blade, too. Hal wheeled on Ming-hua. "Can't you shut that bird up?"

"He no like you."

"No. Really? Where are the others? Gabby and Irving."

"They pick up kids at school. Take them for ice cream." Ming-hua glanced at Mick. "What that schmuck doing with a gun?"

Hal turned to see his son holding the .45 auto, the muzzle wobbling all over the place. "Put that thing away before you shoot *me*."

Mick gave Hal a flat, defiant stare. "Ask her where the money is."

"How the hell would *she* know where it is, you idiot? You want to shoot something, do me a favor and shoot the fucking bird."

"No!" Ming-hua pulled Quint into her arms, shielding his body with hers. She cursed Hal in her native tongue and the parrot followed suit, the two of them shrieking in Mandarin at the top of their lungs. Dave was clearly enjoying the drama. No doubt the idiot thought it was being staged for his benefit.

Hal clamped his hands over his ears. "Do it, Mick. Shoot the fucking bird!"

Mick squinted one eye closed, struggling to get Quint in his sights. The kid had probably never even held a gun before today.

"You've gotta cock it, genius." Hal went for the .45. "Give me that."

Mick held it away, fumbling with the slide. "No. I'll do it. You never let me do anything."

"I said give it to me. You don't know what you're doing."

The two struggled over the pistol, wrestling each other to the tiled floor. Hal had the advantage of raw strength, but his son had youth and dumb reflexes on his side. They rolled near Dave, only to have the grinning idiot and his Bruno Maglis join in the act. Hal finally managed to flip Mick onto his belly and twist his gun hand in a direction nature never intended. Mick howled and released the weapon. And howled again when the barrel ground into his ear.

Hal dug his knee hard into Mick's kidney. "I should kill you right now." He glanced toward Ming-hua, only to find her and the parrot gone. "Shit."

He leapt up and raced out of the room. Ming-hua had made it to the end-hall vestibule, cradling the bird to her chest, her plump little legs churning with surprising speed. She'd just reached the outer door when Hal caught up with her and spun her around—and came eye-to-eye with Quint, who sprang at him in a flurry of feathers and pure, savage instinct.

It was a replay of twenty-five years ago, round two in the man-versus-beast Mega Death Match. Hal stumbled backward, lashing out blindly as the creature went for his eyes. They fell against the U-shaped costume rack, which promptly collapsed, half burying them under an avalanche of clothing, accessories, and props. Through it all, Quint maintained his relentless claw-hold, landing punishing blows to Hal's head and arms with that hatchet of a beak. In such close hand-to-talon combat, Hal's .45 was useless. Ming-hua meanwhile had begun flogging him with an authentic World War I entrenching tool. Where the hell was Mick?

Hal rolled onto his stomach, squinting through a haze of blood, taking wild shots at his attackers. He heard the entrenching tool clatter to the floor and thought he'd hit Ming-hua, but her hysterical shrieks only increased in volume. Mick had gotten the old woman in a sloppy half nelson and was gingerly poking at Quint with a plastic Star Wars light saber.

"Do it, Mick." Hal wagged the pistol, offering it. "Shoot the fucking bird!"

Taking the gun would have required Mick to get within striking distance of The Beak. Instead, he shoved Ming-hua away, got a two-fisted grip on the light saber, and whacked Quint with enough force to send him flapping into a pile of wigs. Hal came shakily to his feet, swiping at the blood dripping from gashes in his scalp and face.

Mick stood gawking at Hal's injuries while Ming-hua made a beeline for the door. "Get her," Hal barked. "Bring her back in there." He pointed to Room A. In the end, it took both men and an entire roll of duct tape to restrain and muzzle the furious woman. Dave looked on with gleeful anticipation, no doubt wondering what other little diversions his captors had in store for him.

"We gotta get outta here now," Mick said. "The cops are prob'ly—"

"Not without my money. Or a hostage." Hal formulated the plan as he spoke.

"So take her." Mick pointed to Ming-hua.

"What, and hope Kitchen will cough up two mil to save her ass?" Hal shook his head. "It has to be someone he really cares about."

Ming-hua was the picture of mute indignation.

"Too bad Tom's not here," Mick said, echoing Hal's thoughts.

Sticky blood plastered Hal's hair to his skull. He felt it drying on his face and neck. His arms and hands had taken their share of abuse as well; his windbreaker was in shreds. He wiped his bloody palms on his jeans, grabbed the .45, and stalked out of the room.

"Where ya going?" Mick asked.

"Hunting."

Hal had expected to find Quint amid the heaps of costumes, where he'd left him. He should have known the bird wouldn't make it easy for him. Something on the floor caught his attention. He squatted to inspect a series of delicate red brushstrokes. Bird tracks, in Hal's own blood. The tracks led into the living room and trailed off through the open door of the game room.

Hal stood just inside the threshold of the onetime church sanctuary, alert for the slightest sound or movement. The only light in the room was a weak splash of watercolors through the abstract stained glass. Suddenly Hal was back at Holy Resurrection with his mother and brothers, his pale hair slicked back with Brylcreem, his face scrubbed raw with Ma's spit and a rough handkerchief. He was ten years old again, genuflecting, watching the censer swing. "Your Harold is so handsome." His mother's friends cooed over him as they milled about after mass. "He looks like a little angel."

Hal dragged in a lungful of air and swore he smelled churchy incense. His fingers tightened on the pistol grip. The cuts on his face and arms burned. "Where are you, you son of a bitch?" he whispered, advancing into the room. If Ma and Father Anthony could see him now, smeared with blood and stalking someone's pet with a powerful semiautomatic—in God's house. For the first time in decades, Hal felt an urge to cross himself.

He sensed movement out of the corner of his eye near the old-fashioned pinball machines. He swung his gun hand, squinting through the gloom. "You can't hide from me," he swore, turning his back just long enough to flip the wall switches. Light flooded the room, chasing Holy Resurrection and his ten-year-old self back to whatever mossy corner of his psyche they'd slithered out of. He looked under and around the pinball machines. Nothing. He should have killed that bird all those years ago, the first time it took a chunk out of him.

Hal heard a rustle near the model train on the opposite side of the room. He spun toward the sound, fingers cramping on the gun grip. The trains ran on an intricately constructed layout, an eclectic hodgepodge of mismatched landforms and historical eras crafted on twenty-four square feet of plywood bolted to an old dining table.

Hal bent to peer under the layout. Nothing. He circled the table, stared unblinkingly at it, though logically he knew a bird of that size couldn't possibly find cover behind one of Tom's plaster hills, much less inside a Lilliputian train tunnel.

A feral growl rumbled up Hal's throat. *"Where are you?"* he bellowed, and pumped four shots into the layout—*BAM BAM BAM BAM!*—taking out the water tower, the downtown shopping district, a string of Cotton Belt freight cars, and the electronic control panel, which exploded in a spray of sparks.

"You have fucking lost it, man."

Hal whipped around and trained the gun on Mick, who flinched and stumbled back, knocking over a card table and two folding chairs. The Scrabble board did a triple somersault. Dozens of little wooden tiles scattered. And Quint emitted a startled squawk.

The bird had taken refuge under the card table. Now he was out in the open, stranded by his bum wing, exposed but defiant.

Hal grinned. He took careful aim at Quint's feathered cranium. Mick snickered in anticipation. Hal fired the pistol, which responded with an anemic click. "Shit. Don't let him go anywhere, Mick." He ejected the spent magazine and replaced it with the spare from his jacket pocket. "Now. Where were we?" He aimed, started to squeeze the trigger—

"Anybody home? Will?" a female voice called from the vestibule. "The door was open. What happened here?"

Hal gritted his teeth and eased his finger off the trigger. At least it wasn't the cops. He turned to Mick and mouthed, *Get rid of her.*

Mick stared goggle-eyed at the gun. He pointed to his chest. *Me?*

Hal smacked the side of his son's head. He whispered, "Send her away, you idiot."

Hal and Quint glared at each other while Mick dealt with whoever had come calling. After a few moments he shambled back into the room. "You said I could get back at her. You promised. No way that's gonna happen now."

"What are you talking about? Who?"

"That Narby bitch. The one that did this to me." He indicated his nose. "You said—"

"That was Lucy?" Hal shoved the gun into his back waistband. He'd seen how Will behaved around her. *It has to be someone he cares about.* "You sent her away?"

"You told me to."

Hal bolted out of the Goo. Lucy was behind the wheel of her silver Volvo, backing down the driveway. "Lucy!" He sprinted across the lawn. "Lucy, wait!"

She slammed on the brakes just as he reached her. She stared at him openmouthed through the windshield, then leapt out of the car. "Oh my God, Keith, what happened to you?"

Hal feigned wooziness. Lucy was at his side in a heartbeat, supporting him, opening the back door of her car.

"You can tell me on the way to the hospital," she said. "Lie down in back."

Mick strolled across the lawn toward them. Lucy called out, "Why didn't you tell me Keith's hurt?" She ducked her head into the car and asked quietly, "Was it Mick? Did he do this to you?"

"No." Hal shook his head. "It was an accident. Fixing . . . something."

"I'm taking him to the emergency room," she told Mick, who slid into the front passenger seat uninvited. Lucy got behind the wheel and backed down the drive. "Thank God I showed up when I did."

Behind her, Hal smiled. "You read my mind."

26

AN ANVIL SAT on Wesley's chest, robbing his air, crushing him. He wanted to push it off, but every time he tried to raise his arms, someone pressed them back down. The pain was startling. He could barely breathe. He opened his eyes. He was on his back, in a moving vehicle. Somewhere nearby, a siren whooped. A face hovered above him, a handsome, young blond fellow with rimless glasses and an unfortunate mustache.

Wesley's voice was a rasp. "Wha—wha—wha—?"

"Take it easy, pal." The paramedic laid his hand on Wesley's bare shoulder. Wesley tried to raise his head to see what was compressing his chest, but the man wouldn't let him. He strapped Wesley down and gave him oxygen. "You've got a cracked sternum, for sure. You gotta lie still."

"Cra—cra—cra—?" The last thing he remembered was verbally sparring with Hal.

"Coulda been a lot worse. That vest saved your life."

Vest? It started to come together in Wesley's mind. He'd taken the precaution of donning personal armor under his trench coat before the meeting with Hal. He cleared his throat. Every breath was agony. "Sh—sh—shot?"

The paramedic nodded. "At close range."

Wesley scoured his memory. Bits of his conversation with Hal made it through the mental haze. Hal thought Wesley knew too much. He pulled a gun. "Th—th—th—" He fought the straps.

"Relax, buddy. You don't want to pierce a lung."

"The sh—shooter."

"High-caliber, for sure," the paramedic said. "You're lucky to be—"

"The *shooter*." Wesley forced out the words, each one detonating a little explosion in his chest. "H—His name—"

"Don't worry about that. The cops got the guy." The paramedic adjusted Wesley's IV bag. "Caught him standing over you, still holding the gun. Fucker's not going anywhere, believe me."

Thank God. Wesley collapsed against the stretcher as a wave of relief washed over him. So he got himself a cracked sternum. So what? They had the psycho that kidnapped Ricky Baines. Nothing else mattered.

"LISTEN TO ME!" Will's fingers cramped around the bars of the holding cell. He glared at the surveillance camera mounted four feet away, trying to make his voice carry down the corridor to the nearby squad room. "Detective Cullen, will you just *listen to me*? The man that did that shooting, he'll be coming after my family next. After my *son!*"

He didn't know who Keith really was, or what he was after, but one thing was agonizingly clear: Will had screwed up big-time the day he'd welcomed him into his household. Keith had shot that man, he was certain. As repugnant as Mick was, Will couldn't picture him pulling the trigger. Instinct told him Tom would be Keith's next target.

The officers had thoughtfully provided company for him. His cellmate squatted in a corner, scratching inside his clothing and examining his fingers. Will struggled not to gag on the man's stench, a piquant mélange of stale booze, Dumpster, and hazmat BO.

Detective Paul Cullen had tried to interrogate Will but had given up when his obviously guilty suspect remained uncooperative. Will kept insisting the real culprit was on the loose and that he had happened upon the scene just in time to be found with the proverbial smoking gun. Even to his own ears, it sounded like a desperate, spur-of-the-moment fabrication. The more Cullen rolled his eyes, the louder and more insistent Will became, until finally the detective had tossed him in this cage to cool his heels until he was ready to explain why he'd killed Wesley McIntyre.

Wesley McIntyre, a local private investigator. Not Archie Esterhaus, hair-care salesman from St. Louis. The PI had pretended to be a former resident of Will's house; he'd spent hours snooping around. But why? What was he looking for?

All the yelling had turned Will's voice into a painful croak, but he managed to crank up the volume. "I told you, Cullen, I had nothing to do with that shooting. It was Keith Kitchen. That's what he calls himself. He's been living at my place, pretending to be my cousin. Just go there and check it out."

Will's cellmate had begun peeling off the many layers of his dirt-stiffened clothing, starting with three pairs of institutional pajama bottoms, which he proceeded to stuff into the steel toilet. His stink grew fangs and claws, like something out of a B horror flick.

Will dropped his forehead to the cool bars, but only for an instant. He had no time to waste, not with Tom's safety at stake. "I want my lawyer. Do you hear me?" He waited a few moments, straining for the sound of footsteps, a door opening, anything.

"You've checked me out, I'm not in your damn system. I don't shoot people!" Will stalked across his cell, only to spin back around and slam his shoulder into the bars. Pain lanced his arm, but he paid it no mind. *"If anything happens to my boy,"* he hollered, *"you'd better find a way to keep me in here, Cullen, 'cause I will come after you, I promise you that!"*

"WHERE'S THE NEAREST HOSPITAL?" Lucy asked again. Maybe Keith and Mick hadn't heard her the first time. She glanced in the rearview. Keith was looking over his shoulder at the sparse traffic behind them. They were on a residential two-lane headed for the highway. She had to know which direction to go. "Mick?"

"Huh?" He was looking at her a little strangely. She hadn't seen him since her "kidnapping" ten days earlier. His nose was still swollen and bruised, and now he had a splinted finger as well. From another less-than-satisfied client?

"Which way do I go?" she asked. "To get to the hospital?"

"Fuck if I know." Mick turned toward the backseat. He gave Keith the kind of look that said, *What are you waiting for?*

Keith told him to turn on the radio. He added, "A news station, you idiot," when Mick started blasting hip-hop.

Lucy's nape prickled. "How did you get hurt?" she asked Keith. "You said you were fixing some—"

Keith shushed her and reached between the front seats to turn up the volume. The weather report was winding down. Fifty-seven degrees in Central Park. Scattered showers north and west of the city.

"Here we are." She spied a blue *hospital* sign directing her to turn right at the next major intersection, which she did.

Mick settled a little closer to Lucy, letting his arm drape the back of her seat. She tensed and was about to ask him to move it when his cell phone rang. As he pulled it out of his pocket, Keith said, "Don't answer it."

Lucy swallowed hard. Something was wrong. She'd drop them off at the ER and make an excuse to get away.

"Who is it?" Keith leaned forward to peer at the display on Mick's phone, which announced the caller.

"My mom."

"Where's she calling from? Her mobile?"

"The house," Mick said.

"Shit." Keith flopped back against the seat. "Let her leave a message."

What was that about? Keith didn't even know Will's sister. "It should be around here somewhere," she said.

"What?" Mick asked.

She glanced at him. No, she did not like the way he was looking at her. "The hospital?"

He tossed a smirk over his shoulder. "Hear that, Hal? We're almost at the hospital."

Lucy's hands tightened on the wheel. "Why did you call him Hal?"

Keith's breath was hot on her neck. "'Cause it gives me the creeps when he calls me dad."

Lucy willed her voice not to wobble. "What's going on, guys?" The hospital complex loomed on the left—at last. Lucy put on her blinker and started to edge into the turning lane.

"Changed our minds." Mick tugged the wheel to keep them on course. *"What are you doing?"*

"Where do you live?" Keith—or Hal—asked.

"Why?"

"That's where we're going," he said. "To your place."

"No." Lucy started looking for an opportunity to turn around. "I don't know what game you two are playing, but I want no part of it."

"Maybe not yet." This time Mick not only placed his arm on her seatback, he actually fondled her hair. "But you will. We're going to have some fun."

"Get your hands off me." She tried to jerk her head away. Mick laughed and yanked her back by the hair.

"Take it easy," Hal told Mick. "We don't need a fender-bender." He tapped Lucy's neck with something, something hard and cold. She flicked a glance at it, and every last scrap of air left her lungs. A gun. He lowered it, and she knew it was aimed at her back through the car seat. With his other hand he emptied her purse on the seat beside him and rummaged through the contents. "Here we go." He read from her driver's license. "Narby, Lucille M. Three Gloria Court, Crystal Harbor, N-Y." He whistled. "Nice neighborhood. You rich?"

He didn't seem to expect an answer, which was just as well. Lucy couldn't speak, couldn't think, as she struggled to make sense of what was happening. The last time she'd been this scared, it had turned out to be an elaborate practical joke. Mick's fingers slid down her side and over her khaki-clad thigh, which he squeezed.

No. Will would never subject her to this kind of "joke." She'd gone to his place to share her exciting news with him and Tom. In truth, if she hadn't had a legitimate excuse to see Will again, she'd have made one up. She couldn't leave things as they were, not after that frustrating encounter in her basement.

"Why don't you tell me what you want?" she asked Hal. "Maybe I can help you and then we can . . . we can put this behind us. Will doesn't have to hear about it."

She flinched as Hal lunged forward, cranking up the volume on the radio even more. *"—about an hour ago at the Grove Street Park in*

Soundhaven. No report yet on the condition of the victim, whom police have identified as Wesley McIntyre, a private detect—"

"Who?" Mick frowned. "That's not the guy's—"

"Shut up." Hal whacked the back of Mick's head.

"—arrest has been made in the case," the radio announcer continued. *"The suspect, thirty-four-year-old Wilbur Kitchen, was apprehended at the scene after a neighbor reported suspicious activity—"*

Mick hooted in delight. "How's it *feel*, motherfucker!" he yelled at the radio. "That'll teach you to fuck with m—Ow!" He grabbed the back of his head, casting a baleful look over his shoulder.

"Think, idiot." Hal kicked the back of Mick's seat. "How's Kitchen supposed to get me my two mil if he's locked up?"

"*Our* two mil." Mick rubbed his head. "Stop doing that."

Lucy drove on autopilot, staring numbly through the windshield. Wilbur Kitchen. Arrested at the scene. Victim's condition unknown. It wasn't possible. She *knew* Will. She'd almost *slept* with Will. Lucy Narby did not almost sleep with men who shot people.

And what was this about two million dollars?

Hal told Mick to turn off the radio. "Did she leave a message?"

"Who?"

"Your mother. Who do you think?"

"Oh." Mick checked the display on his phone. "Yeah."

"Play it. Put it on speaker." Hal leaned forward to listen as Mick tapped buttons. *"Mick, it's me,"* Will's sister said. *"I'm home. Call me when you get this message. Call me on my cell. What?"* A pause, an indistinct male voice in the background.

"Fergus," Mick said. Hal nodded.

"Maybe he's at Will's," Judith told Fergus. *"I asked him to keep an eye out there, remember? Mick, listen, it's really important that you call me. I need to talk to you. I need to know you're safe."*

Mick snorted his derision.

Judith's shaky voice got shakier. *"That man I told you about. Hal Lynch. He's dangerous, like I said. What I didn't tell you . . . he just got out of jail. For murder."*

Lucy's throat constricted. She forced herself to concentrate on the traffic.

"Hal's trying to locate some money," Judith continued. *"A lot of money that kind of . . . got misplaced a long time ago."*

Mick hooted in laughter. "'Misplaced.'"

"Shut up," Hal growled.

"He'll do anything to get it," Judith said. *"Please, please don't try to deal with him yourself. Just . . . call me, okay, honey? I'm going to Will's now, but my cell will be on."*

"WHO DID THIS to you?" Judith tore the duct tape off Ming-hua's mouth. The old woman didn't so much as blink. A rapid-fire string of Mandarin issued forth, punctuated by "Cousin Keith!" hurled like an epithet.

"Who?" Judith turned to Fergus, busy slicing the tape that bound Ming-hua to the chair. He shrugged. Neither of them had ever heard of a cousin named Keith.

"Keith Kitchen. He bad sheep." Ming-hua eased her cranky bones off the seat, then bent to check on Quint, who hunkered under the chair, preening his feathers and muttering to himself. She coaxed him out with a licorice whip, turning to wag her finger at Judith. "Your boy, too. Bad sheep. Two bad sheep find each other, they many times bad."

Judith had expected the worst when she'd seen the mayhem where Will's costume racks once stood, though that was nothing compared to her own home where they'd gone first, looking for Mick. If she weren't so accustomed to her son's slovenly habits, she'd have thought that was the crime scene.

Fergus jerked his thumb toward the man standing under the ceiling chain. "Who's this bloke, then?"

"Dave." Ming-hua dismissed Dave with a flip of her gnarled hand. "He no like Chinese come to U.S."

"Dave's a paying customer?"

Ming-hua nodded. She placed her hands on the small of her back and unkinked her spine. "Schmuck pay five thousand dollar cash."

Fergus peeled the tape from Dave's mouth. "Is it everything you'd hoped for and more?"

"Absolutely!" Dave's grin was ecstatic. "You're Irish, aren't you? Lazy, drunken parasites, the Ir—"

Fergus replaced the tape and gently patted it in place. "Hold that thought, Dave."

Judith touched Ming-hua's shoulder. "What did you mean, two bad sheep finding each other? Is Mick mixed up with this Keith?"

"Do it, Mick!" Quint squawked. *"Shoot the fucking bird!"*

"I'm goin' to call that a yes." Fergus lifted Quint to his shoulder as Ming-hua confirmed Judith's son was indeed mixed up with Cousin Keith. Fergus sent Judith a look that asked if she was thinking the same thing he was.

With growing dread she asked Ming-hua, "What does he look like? This Keith? Is he . . . How old is he?"

"Young, very young," Ming-hua said, and Judith began to sigh in relief until the old woman added, "Like you. Forty-five, fifty. Blond hair." She gestured toward her temple. "Some gray."

Fergus put his arm around Judith just then, as if he sensed how close her legs were to buckling. "What color are his eyes?" he asked.

"Brown. Light brown."

Hope stirred anew. Judith turned to Fergus. "Hal's eyes are gray. Like Mick's."

"Who Hal?" Ming-hua asked.

"We think this fella who calls himself Keith may be pretending to be Will's cousin," Fergus explained. "We think he may be someone Judith used to know, someone named Hal." To Judith he said, "Eye color can be disguised nowadays."

"No." Ming-hua gave a decisive head-shake. "Keith family. From Seattle. He look the same. Eyes, mouth, the same."

"Keith looks like Will?" Judith asked.

"No, not Will," Ming-hua said. "He look like Mick."

Judith couldn't say how she ended up on the chair recently vacated by Ming-hua, with her head between her knees. She heard Fergus speaking to her, felt his big hands on her head, her shoulder. She tried to rise; the room tilted sickeningly.

"Easy, lass." Fergus kept her pinned to the chair. "Give yourself a minute—"

"There's no time." She tried to throw off his hands. "Fergus, there's no time. Hal has my boy. That animal . . . Oh God." She cradled her head in her palms. "He knows. They both know." How could this have happened? How could any parole board have liberated a psycho like Hal Lynch?

Fergus pulled out his phone.

"Who are you calling?" Judith asked.

"The police. Who else?"

27

"**B**EEN A WHILE, McIntyre. Still a homo?"

Wesley, flat on his back on an emergency room gurney, squinted up at his visitor. Eight years evaporated in a heartbeat. "Hey there, Paulie. Still an asshole?"

A machine over Wesley's head dinged every few seconds. Behind the privacy curtain on the left, an elderly woman moaned and raved nonstop. From the right came cursing, some soft weeping—a teenage dog-bite victim, from what Wesley had overheard in the hour or so he'd been there. Hospital sounds, hospital smells. It sucked, but what were you gonna do?

"I thought you were dead." Paul Cullen looked around the minuscule ER stall as if expecting a La-Z-Boy to materialize. "Figured the AIDS woulda got you by now."

"It did. Can't you tell? I'm wasting away." Wesley patted the mound of belly fat under the thin hospital johnny. The last time Wesley had seen Cullen, they'd both been street cops in the 114th precinct. Now here was the smug SOB all these years later with a Nassau County detective's shield clipped to his suit jacket. "You the lead on this case or is this some new aversion therapy for homophobia?"

"Here's how I see it." Cullen stood with his hands jammed in his pockets, rattling his change. "You and this other fag hit it off, you tell him to join you there behind the band shell at the park. Lover boy shows up— only problem, he's not there to blow a pitiful tub of lard like you. Bang bang."

"Your powers of deduction amaze and thrill, Detective." Wesley wanted to laugh, but it would hurt like hell, so instead he asked the obvious. "If that's how it went down, why didn't lover boy liberate my wallet?"

"'Cause our guys showed up before he could."

"Why the vest?" Wesley tapped his chest. "What, the smell of Kevlar gets me off?"

A hint of uncertainty crept into Cullen's meatloaf of a face, but he was all bluster. "I were you, I'd wear a fucking suit of armor to go trolling those gay bars."

"Think you can stop fixating on the queer thing for a moment? Nah, probably not. You never could."

"What's that supposed to mean?"

Wesley shrugged—a mistake. It felt like a hot knife in his chest, even with the painkillers dripping into his IV. "As if you didn't know. I'm talking about your personal crusade to de-queer the department. All that time and energy devoted to snooping into my private life. Harassing me. Outing me. Turning the CO against me. Turning my *partner* against me."

Cullen crossed his arms over his chest. "Guys on the job gotta be able to trust their backup."

"Backup? You got some nerve, my friend, talking about backup." Wesley tried to lever himself up—another mistake. He collapsed with a grunt of pain. "Where was *my* backup when that domestic went bad in Jackson Heights? I almost bought it in that rat-hole 'cause I thought Jimmy had my back. I didn't know the rules were different for queers. Is it still that way, Paulie? You still setting up any guy that doesn't pass your sexual-orientation test?"

"Nobody set you up."

"No? What do you call it when you wait till a fellow cop's in a tight spot and make sure his call for backup goes unanswered?"

Cullen's neck turned an unbecoming shade of purple, but he managed to hold Wesley's stare. "The police force isn't for everybody, McIntyre. Someone shoulda clued you in before you entered the academy."

"Yeah, well, better late than never, right?" Wesley could never prove he'd been targeted by his brothers in blue. He could fight the bad guys on the streets or the bad guys on the force, but he couldn't fight both. He walked away with a partial pension and a nine-millimeter slug lodged between the major blood vessels in his neck, meaning it was his for the duration; the docs couldn't remove it without killing him.

"So that didn't work with Tina, I guess," Wesley said. "That cluing-in thing."

Cullen's glower hardened. "Who's been talking about my daughter? What did you hear?"

"She was a cute kid. And smart. I liked Tina, the one or two times we met. Her mom, too. Say hi for me, will ya?"

That purplish color had spread up Cullen's throat and turned his cheeks into big, overripe plums. Well, if he stroked out, he was in the right place. He took a menacing step toward Wesley. "I said, where'd you hear that about Tina? It's not true."

"Paulie, come on, I coulda told you when she was twelve. And anyway, you of all people should know how word gets around."

The detective shoved a stubby finger in Wesley's face. "I find out you're spreading lies about—"

"Hey, I don't gossip." Wesley spread his palms. "Not about folks' sex lives." He wasn't the one snickering behind Cullen's back, calling his little girl a buzz-cut drag king and worse. "Do the ballistics match?"

"Huh?" Cullen's simple mind struggled with the change of subject.

"The perp's gun and the slug from my vest." Wesley enunciated slowly, "Do they match up?"

"Why wouldn't they?"

"Have you checked?"

"You telling me how to do my job now?" Cullen sneered. "Guy was standing over you holding the weapon, for cryin' out loud."

"Don't take any shortcuts is all I'm saying. Do it by the book. This is a bad man, Paulie. If he walks on a technicality—"

"Don't get your knickers in a twist. He's not going anywhere."

"Who are we talking about?" Joe appeared at the foot of the bed, clutching a box of Krispy Kremes. "Who's not going anywhere? Besides you." He jiggled Wesley's big toe through the blanket. "Don't scratch that," he added as Wesley's fingers drifted to the Band-Aid in front of his left ear. He still wasn't sure how he'd gotten the small cut; must've happened when he fell.

Joe had driven into Oceanside to let Wesley's folks know what had happened before they heard it on the radio. This was not a chore that could be done by phone. Wesley's mother would be beside herself. To her, a hangnail was a crippling disability.

"Before you ask," Joe said, "your mom will survive. Your dad and I talked her down from the ledge and fed her a couple of Xanax. Eight chocolate and four original glazed." He plunked the doughnut box on the rolling table. "And only 'cause you're so pathetic lying there all helpless. Enjoy them, 'cause the instant you're on your feet again, it's Weight Watchers for you." He raised a palm, as if Wesley were in any condition to object. "I already paid for the first ten weeks, so don't even start. *You* look familiar." Joe swung toward Cullen, who flinched and mumbled his name. "Oh! I know where we met." He gave the detective's shield a playful pat. "You're one of Wesley's friends from the force." He squeezed Cullen's hand between both of his. "It is *so* good of you to show your support at a time like this."

Cullen grunted something unintelligible, his gaze shifting uncomfortably from Joe to Wesley to the box of doughnuts.

"Help yourself." Joe opened the box. "God knows Wesley doesn't need them all."

Wesley couldn't imagine eating even one, the way he was hurting. Maybe he should get shot in the chest on a regular basis. The .45-Caliber Diet.

Cullen backpedaled. "No, no, it's okay—"

"Oh, will you pu-leeeze?" Joe thrust an original glazed at the detective, who had no choice but to accept it with muttered thanks. "A cop turning down a doughnut. Tell me another one."

"You don't have to be nice to Paulie," Wesley said. "He just came here to gloat."

"Oh, no," Joe scolded, "oh, stop. It's the painkillers making you say that. Don't listen to this big grump, Detective. He doesn't mean it." Joe brushed doughnut crumbs off Cullen's jacket, pausing briefly to rub the material between his fingers. Cullen looked like a cornered rabbit. "Nice," Joe said. "Armani?"

"Uh . . . Penney's had a sale."

Joe leaned in confidentially. "You can't tell. With shoulders like yours, you could wear a flour sack and it'd look like it set you back a grand. Right?" This last query to Wesley, who sent him a silent communiqué: *Aren't you laying it on a bit thick?* Joe knew perfectly well who Cullen was and what he'd done to the man he loved. He was just having fun with the bastard.

Joe turned back to Cullen. "You are definitely coming to the wedding. It's in December. Do we have your address?"

"Wedding?" Cullen was about to ask who was getting married, Wesley could tell, but then his tiny detective brain filled in the blanks, leaving him blessedly speechless.

Any other time, Wesley would have enjoyed the spectacle of his lover torturing the malicious prick who'd driven him out of the NYPD, but at the moment he was in too much pain. Plus, he wasn't about to take a chance that the psycho who snatched Ricky Baines might walk.

"Hal really incriminated himself," Wesley said. "Did the recording come out good?"

It took Cullen a moment to realize Wesley was addressing him. "Who?"

"Hal? The guy that did this to me?" Wesley thumped his chest and instantly regretted it. "Your people must've found the voice recorder—it was in my pocket."

"Maybe he told *you* he was called Hal," Cullen said, retrieving his buzzing cell phone from a pants pocket, "but the shooter's name is Kitchen. Wilbur Kitchen. And there was no recorder."

It had to be the happy juice they'd put in Wesley's IV. He could have sworn Cullen said "Wilbur Kitchen." Wesley looked at Joe, whose perplexed frown told him he hadn't misheard.

Cullen, meanwhile, barked into his cell: "The perp's house? *Who* called?"

Why would they think Will Kitchen had shot him, unless . . . "Hal could've swiped Kitchen's ID. Hey, Paulie, what color is his hair?"

The detective shushed Wesley with a brusque wave as a nurse pushed past the curtain. She was a diminutive Hispanic woman named Carmen something, according to the nametag clipped to her scrubs. "*Who* tied up Kitchen's housekeeper?" Cullen demanded. "What the hell's going on?"

"You can't use that phone in here," Carmen scolded as the detective clamped a hand over his free ear, tuning her out. "And it's only one visitor at a time," she said. "You have to take turns."

Wesley pushed up onto an elbow as pain detonated in his sternum. "Someone tied up Ming-hua? That had to be Hal. Jesus, Paulie, you arrested the wrong man."

"Take that outside or turn it off." Carmen got in Cullen's face. "The rule goes for cops, too. You." She pointed to Joe. "Out."

Joe drew himself up. "I'm the *fiancé.*"

Wesley struggled to sit. "You've got the wrong guy. Paulie. Listen to me. You've got the *wrong guy!*"

"Oh no, you don't." Carmen tried to push Wesley back down. "Everyone—out."

Wesley brushed her off like a pesky fly. He swung his legs off the bed.

Joe folded his arms over his chest. "You are going to hurt yourself even worse, and if you think I'm going to go back to your mother and tell her—"

"He did the Ricky Baines kidnapping," Wesley shouted at Cullen, still huddled with his phone. "Hal did. The guy that shot me. And Will Kitchen, the one you arrested—he *is* Ricky Baines."

"Out. Both of you." Carmen yanked open the curtain. "Don't make me call Security."

"Are you shitting me?" Cullen asked the person on the other end of the line. "The Baines case is, like, twenty years old."

"Twenty-five," Joe corrected. "Oh my God. Don't do that!" he yelped as Wesley tore the tape off his IV and yanked the catheter out of his arm. Blood spurted from the punctured vein.

Carmen grabbed a pair of latex gloves, shouting for help to subdue her patient.

The old woman in the next stall yelled, "What's going on in there?" Curious eyes peeked past the curtains. Hospital workers stopped in their tracks to stare.

Wesley glanced around the little space. "Where the hell are my clothes?"

"Police took them. Evidence." Joe swung toward the gawkers. "Don't you have anything better to do than stand there with your mouths hanging open?" He wagged them away like the kids he dealt with every day at the middle school. "Shoo."

"What's that name again?" Cullen scribbled in a little notebook, cradling the phone against his shoulder. "Lynch, Harold."

"This Lynch guy. Paulie, listen." Wesley came unsteadily to his feet, heedless of the blood dribbling down his arm. "I know the man—he's one dangerous SOB." Cullen ignored him, having turned his back to focus on his call.

Carmen cursed in Spanish as she applied pressure to Wesley's arm. His hospital gown was liberally streaked with blood; he looked like the runner-up in a chain-saw fight. A pair of burly orderlies materialized, took one look at the patient, and started gloving up.

Cullen spoke into his phone, pen at the ready. "What's the address? I'll meet you there. Hey!" he snapped as Wesley grabbed the phone out of his hand and broke the connection.

"I know a shortcut," Wesley said. "Let's go."

Joe tried to bar his way. "Wesley, if you walk out of this hospital, so help me God, I will not be there when you get home. *If* you get home."

"Sure you will." Wesley gave him a quick peck on the mouth. The orderlies, who'd been about to pounce, exchanged a look and backpedaled to the glove dispenser to double up. Carmen tossed her own gloves onto the blood-spattered tiles and followed Wesley's exposed heinie through the ER and waiting room, out the doors to Cullen's gray Impala, ranting all the while about "liability" and "against medical advice" and foolhardy *payasos* who think they're indestructible.

28

AS USUAL, TOM'S comforter lay puddled on the floor, the top sheet heaped in the curve of one skinny, pajama-clad leg. The bottom sheet had come untucked, and the pillow had somehow landed several feet from the bed.

Will smiled and tilted his head to match the angle of Tom's in the near dark of the boy's bedroom. Tom lay sprawled on his side, mouth parted, a shadowy spot of drool soaking into the mattress pad. At moments like this, Will could detect a softer version of his own features in his son. He also saw Hope's influence and wondered for the thousandth time how any mother could willingly, even matter-of-factly, relinquish the child of her womb. For money.

He shook out the wadded top sheet and carefully smoothed it and the comforter over his sleeping son. All of which was wasted effort, but habit was hard to break, and tonight he didn't even try. His relief at finding Tom here, safe in bed where he belonged, was so intense it hurt. The surge of paternal love swelled Will's heart and spilled over into his brain; he was drunk on it.

As long as his boy was safe, nothing else mattered.

He let himself out of the room, feeling both weighted by exhaustion and buoyed by relief. Detective Cullen had released him a short while before, with no explanation aside from a gruff command to phone him immediately if he heard from one Harold Lynch, a.k.a. Keith Kitchen. Furthermore, Cullen was withholding the real shooter's name, as well as news of Will's release, from the media so as not to drive Lynch deeper into hiding. So Will had better keep a low profile. All of which meant Lynch was still at large, but at least now the cops were on the right track. More important, they knew Will wasn't the one who'd killed the PI.

Will hadn't lingered to press for details. The instant they let him go, he'd raced home to check on Tom, practically knocking over Gabby and Cuba in his haste as they greeted him on the porch.

Now, as he silently closed his son's bedroom door, the sound of muted conversation drew him to the kitchen. That and the need to pour himself a double Scotch. Or a triple. Seated around the tiled kitchen table were Gabby, Cuba, and Friar Tuck.

Will stopped and stared. The friar wore a brown, hooded, rope-belted robe Will recognized from his own costume collection. He leaned back in his chair, draining a bottle of beer, cradling an ice pack to his chest, and looking an awful lot like the late Wesley McIntyre.

"You're dead," Will said.

"Damn. If I knew being dead felt like this, I'd have tried harder to stay alive." Wesley wagged the beer bottle at Gabby. "You got another one of these?"

"No more for you." She plucked the empty from his fingers.

"Aw, have a heart."

Cuba looked up from stroking Hasenpfeffer. "It's that Vicadin she scrounged up for you. She's afraid you'll, like, stop breathing if you get loaded on top of it."

"It's tempting," he said, "considering how much it *hurts* to breathe."

"Seriously." Will pulled open cabinets, producing a bottle of The Macallan and a plastic Star Wars drinking cup. "I thought I was looking at a corpse back there in the park."

"Kevlar is cool stuff," Wesley said, "but a .45 auto is one serious weapon. The vest kept the bullet from penetrating, but it was kinda like getting kicked in the chest by a mule. Not that I remember the getting-shot part, but that's what it felt like when I came to." He shifted, wincing. "Still does. Lemme guess. Cullen didn't let on that I survived. No, of course he didn't."

"He let me believe I was going to be tried for murder." Will settled into a chair and filled the cup with Scotch. "After being caught standing over your lifeless body, holding—literally—the smoking gun."

"What a kidder, that Detective Cullen." Wesley's chuckle turned into a growl of pain. Gabby was on her feet in an instant, fussing over him, checking the ice pack, uncapping that second beer with a muttered *"Merde."*

He took a long pull from the bottle. "That 'smoking gun' was my own nine-mil. Hasn't been used since I took it to the range six, seven weeks ago. Lynch shot me with a .45. That's the reason they let you go," he told Will. "The ballistics. Oh yeah, *and?* Me telling 'em you were nowhere in the vicinity when one Harold Lynch, a.k.a. Keith Kitchen, pulled the trigger."

Gabby, Cuba, and Wesley brought Will up to speed on the goings-on at home while he'd been lazing around the slammer. They told him about Hal and Mick's confrontation with Ming-hua and the redoubtable Quint. He learned that Cullen and others from the NCPD had been all over the house, the Goo, and Gabby's Viper. They'd interviewed everyone about Hal Lynch and Mick. No one had any idea where the two were now or what vehicle they'd driven away in.

"Did anyone call Judith in Bermuda?" Will asked. "Does she know Mick is mixed up with this wacko?"

"Aunt Judy got back today," Cuba said. "The cops, like, interrogated her for a long time. About Mick, I guess. She's real upset."

"Can you blame her?" Will asked. "Did Fergus come back with her?"

Cuba nodded. "They're around here somewhere. She wants to talk to you. I don't know about what."

But Wesley did, Will sensed. It was something in the way the PI suddenly found the Pete's Wicked label of absorbing interest. "Wesley, what were you investigating that made you meet Lynch in that park," Will asked, "and pretend to be Archie Esterhaus so you could snoop around here?"

Wesley pushed away his beer bottle. He looked Will in the eye. "The Ricky Baines kidnapping."

Will was about to ask who would hire a PI to dredge up that old case when Wesley raised a forefinger and added, "Actually? When I came here in disguise that day, I didn't know you were Ricky. Not at first." He explained his hiring by Frank Narby. Yes, he and Joe were indeed the inept would-be kidnappers Will sent running from Lucy's kitchen that night. Wesley admitted scheming to extract a hefty service charge from Narby in exchange for keeping mum about the bigamy. He told how one greedy impulse led to another until ultimately it all became about closing an old, cold case that had eaten at him for the past two and a half decades.

Cuba lifted the bunny's floppy ears. "You following all this, Hasenpfeffer?"

"Mon dieu!" Gabby cried. "I knew you looked familiar, Wesley. You were a cop back then. You came to the hospital to see me. I was so worried for Ricky. You were very kind."

Even mentally exhausted and half-stewed, Will knew Wesley had danced around the most crucial detail. It was a detail Gabby and Cuba already knew, he was certain. A roiling sensation deep in his gut told him he knew it too, though a part of him wished he could remain in ignorance.

Will looked at Wesley. He could swear the man was reading his thoughts. "So Hal Lynch came here looking for the ransom money."

"That's right."

Will nodded, slowly. "Because it wasn't where he'd left it."

For a few moments no one said a thing. Will forced himself to think about it, forced himself to acknowledge the truth of it. This man, Hal Lynch. This man who had kidnapped, terrorized, and mutilated Will's nine-year-old self. This was the man Will had invited into his home, into his family. The maker of nightmares.

Gabby started to reach for him. Abruptly he stood and headed for the back door. "I need air."

Will welcomed the night chill. He needed to clear his head, to sort his thoughts. Harold Lynch. Keith Kitchen. Insinuating himself into Will's family. Sleeping in the same house as his son.

The backyard was shrouded in darkness except for a faint silvering of moonlight. Will shuffled across the grass, letting his eyes adjust. The cool breeze carried the scents of new growth, of renewal. Clean, green smells. Even the bare soil of the vegetable garden smelled clean in its way. Will tried to feel the sense of hope he'd always associated with this time of year, the sense of a fresh start, a clean slate.

Perhaps when the cops had caught up to Lynch and put him behind bars. Then it would be spring.

He paused at the empty rabbit hutch, ran his fingers over the new chicken wire recently installed by Hal Lynch. A movement drew his gaze to the small, fenced playground, a relic of the property's church days. He squinted and two pale figures materialized. Judith sat on a strap swing, her fingers wrapped around the chains. Fergus stood in front of her, his head tucked near hers, his arms draped protectively over her bowed back.

They didn't know Will was there. He stood watching them for a few moments. Despite everything, a smile tugged at his mouth. It had taken long enough for those two to connect.

Will approached the couple, who looked up in unison as he passed through the open gate.

Judith straightened. "Will. Are you all right?"

He took her outstretched hand, helped her rise—she felt boneless, worn down—and wrapped her in his arms. She trembled. "Of course I'm all right," he said. He knew what had to worry her the most, of course. Her son was mixed up in the park shooting and whatever other misery Lynch was perpetrating. "The cops are looking for them, Jude. Mick'll turn up soon."

She took a deep breath and said shakily, "I know."

"Did they tell you about Lynch?" he asked, and felt her stiffen.

She pulled away. "Yes." It was a whisper.

"What a gullible idiot I was." Will strode to the steel jungle gym and slammed it with his fist. The pain felt good; he deserved much worse. "Our *cousin*, he said. Marguerite's son. I let him bullshit his way into our lives."

Fergus spoke up. "Will, you can't blame your—"

"He's the one." Will held up his left hand, the stump of a finger. "All those shrink sessions with you? It's all in the past, you said, you'll never have to see him again, the nightmare's over. You remember saying those things?"

Fergus gave a single nod. Judith stood hugging herself, as if trying to hold herself together.

Will propped his butt on the jungle gym. He raked his fingers through his hair, then turned his face up to the night sky. It was a clear night, but he couldn't make out many stars. He never could around here: too much ambient light. He forced a long, slow breath, then another. "Okay. All right. The cops'll find him this time. This time it *will* be over."

"It will for certain," Fergus said. "Lynch left his DNA at the scene all those years ago. A bloody towel, according to Wesley. He sent it to the lab. I thought you'd want to know."

Will offered a weak smile. "You were right. Thanks." He turned to Judith. "Cuba said you wanted to talk to me."

She looked at Fergus, who put his arm around her. Her voice was barely audible as she told him, "Maybe you should wait inside."

Fergus searched her face in the gloom. "Are you sure?" She nodded. He seemed about to say something to Will, before changing his mind and walking back to the house.

Will gestured for Judith to join him, scooting over to make room next to him on the jungle gym. They sat in silence for several minutes. Finally she said, "This is hard, Will."

He stared at her shadowy profile, then enclosed her icy hand in both of his. "Jude. I've already figured out Lynch is Mick's father." She looked at him. He offered a tired smile. "Why do you think I bought his bullshit about being our cousin? He *looks* like family."

Judith said nothing. She did not appear reassured.

"Does Mick know?" he asked.

"I don't know. I assume so, now that they've met. I never told Hal about Mick. He was . . . I never wanted him to find out. But one look at each other . . ." Her words trailed off.

No wonder Judith seemed half in shock. Today she'd learned that one of her former lovers, or one-night stands or whatever, was the monster who'd kidnapped and brutalized her kid brother.

Will squeezed her hand. "So. You had a fling with this guy—no one warned you he was a psycho—and when he found out you came from money, he cooked up a kidnapping scheme. It's not your fault, Jude. You had no way of knowing Lynch's true nature. If he hadn't met you, he might've gotten the idea any number of other ways."

Judith pulled her hand away. She shook her head, staring at the ground. But no words came.

Will rubbed her back, his palm moving in lazy circles over the cable-knit pullover she'd obviously borrowed from Fergus. The sweater ended near her knees; her fingertips poked out of the rolled-up sleeves. "One thing that has me stumped, though," he said. "Why did it take him twenty-five years to come looking for the money?"

"He was in prison. Attica."

Will had considered this possibility. "For . . . ?"

"Murder," she said. "Unrelated to the kidnapping."

"Jesus."

She turned to face him, her arms banded around herself once more. Her voice quavered. "I had no idea what he was capable of, Will. I want you to know that."

"I do know that, Jude. Isn't that what I just said?"

"No, but—"

"Hal Lynch's actions had nothing to do with you," Will said. "You didn't know it was him. He acted on his own. Don't—"

"He didn't act on his own." Her anguished face was inches from his. "That's what I'm trying to tell you. It's not . . . it's not that simple."

Will's overtaxed brain struggled to incorporate this new information even as he told himself it wasn't what it sounded like. It couldn't be.

"I was a different person then. You know that." Judith's eyes swam with tears. "I had no idea what I was setting into motion. If I'd known . . ." She shook her head miserably. "Please believe that, Will. If I'd known how it would be for you—"

Will shot to his feet. He took three long strides from his sister, then stopped in his tracks and returned to stand over her. "What did he make you do?"

"He didn't make me do it. We . . . we planned it together—his cover as a security guard, the place in the woods where he took you . . ." She was shaking hard. "I drove the van."

Will's head swung from side to side in denial, as if of its own volition, as if unable to absorb this spectacular blow after a day of unwelcome surprises.

Judith looked up at him, her face streaked with tears. "I'm sorry, Will. I'm so, so sorry." She reached for him. He backed away.

"Why?" Will barely recognized his own gruff voice.

"Money."

Of course. What else could it be? It was the reason she'd married Don

Drinkwater, after all. All those years positioning herself as the country-club wife and civic volunteer, the coiffed church lady in pearls and sensible pumps. Just one more performance Will had readily fallen for.

"How could you do it, Jude?" he asked. "Your own brother. Half brother. I know you hated me back then, but—"

"I didn't hate you, Will." Judith pulled herself to her feet, clinging to the jungle gym for support. "I was confused."

"Not too confused to plan and execute a felony."

"Will—"

"Do the others know?"

"Just Fergus," she said. "And Wesley figured it out on his own. But he didn't tell the police. I think maybe because I cleaned up my act after the kidnapping. And because it's, well, it's been so long and it would tear our family apart."

"You didn't need any help to do that." Will's tone was flat. He ignored his sister's quiet sob. "Leave my home, Judith. I don't ever want to see you again."

"Will, please—" She reached for him. He seized her wrists, holding her at arm's length.

"Don't call or e-mail me," he said. "If I find out you've contacted Tom, I'll turn you in to the police myself."

"Listen to me." Judith wrenched herself from his grasp. "Just listen for a minute, Will. I know how this must seem to you—Will!" she called as he turned his back and stalked to the house. "Let me explain—please."

On the back doorstep he shoved past Fergus, who tried to speak to him, to halt his progress. His friend and former shrink wanted to talk sense to him, no doubt, wanted to help him put things in perspective: the perspective of the woman Fergus was currently balling. No, thanks. His anger felt good, it felt cleansing. After twenty-five years he had a face to put to his misery—*two* faces.

Will charged through the kitchen, ignoring Wesley and the others as he headed for his bedside phone. He felt a visceral need to hear Lucy's voice, to talk to her about his arrest, about Lynch and Judith and the rest of it. The urge to connect with this woman was bone-deep—and alarming, because it wasn't just about sex.

In that instant he knew he wouldn't call her. Not tonight. He was simply too fried, too liable to blurt out something he'd regret. Maybe tomorrow, when he was rested, more in command of himself.

"I'm going to bed," Will said over his shoulder. "Wake me if you hear from the cops. Or Lynch."

29

"**W**HAT'RE YOU PUTTING in there?" Hal hopped off the center island in Lucy's kitchen, reached her in two long strides, and snatched the bottle of Frank's Hot Sauce out of her hand. She watched him read the label and sniff the contents. And all the while that big gun of his remained trained on the star atop the Christmas tree crudely fabric-painted onto her bib apron. A gift from John when he was eight.

He slammed the bottle onto the counter. "Hurry up. I'm starving."

She shook sauce onto the mound of ground sirloin in a mixing bowl and reached for the pepper mill. "It wouldn't take so long if I didn't have to stop every few seconds so you could make sure I'm not poisoning you. As if I keep bottles of strychnine on hand just for situations like this." She had to speak up to make herself heard over the countertop radio, tuned to one of the local news stations. "Here, have another brownie." She'd made dessert before starting in on dinner; Hal had already scarfed down four triple-chocolate brownies.

"You gonna take that shit from her?" Mick demanded, his diction marinated in Gran Centenario Añejo tequila recently liberated from Frank's liquor cabinet. He sat on the granite floor tiles, legs splayed, back propped against the dishwasher, a bag of frozen mango chunks tucked against his balls. His lip was split and swollen. Livid bruises bloomed on his jaw and under one eye. And—surprise, surprise—fresh blood snaked from his nostrils.

Mick had jumped Lucy the instant they'd arrived at her house four hours earlier. If he'd thought she would wilt in the presence of a handgun, he must have forgotten how he'd first come by that busted schnoz. And if he'd thought his father would back him up, or join in raping her, he must have underestimated how distraught and distracted Hal was.

Lucy was prepared for Mick's attack; he certainly hadn't been coy about his intentions. Recalling what a mewling crybaby he was, she went for the nose first, following this attention-getter with a good, old-fashioned knee to the *cojones*. Pop pop pop, her fists found a variety of tender targets in rapid succession as Mick shrieked at Hal to get the crazy bitch off him.

Instead Hal told Mick to shut the hell up so he could hear the news. He prowled around the house peering around closed drapes and blinds, tuning TVs and radios to various stations, pacing between the sets, getting more worked up by the minute. He ordered time out for Mick and Lucy, separating them like sparring kindergartners. "I can't *think* with all this noise," he griped. "I've got to *think*."

So Lucy had sat where Hal told her to sit, and spent the idle hours wrapping her brain around her predicament. The shooting in Grove Street Park was getting less and less airplay. The victim had survived, the shooter was in custody—the *alleged* shooter—and there had been no new developments since the arrest.

Will was no criminal. She'd known it for sure after listening to Hal fuss and mutter to himself. Hal had shot that PI in the park, no doubt with the very weapon that now seemed grafted onto his hand.

The grim truth was, no one would be coming to Lucy's rescue, not even her hapless almost-ex in his stupid camo and night-vision goggles. No one even knew she needed rescuing. Will was behind bars, and it was case closed as far as the police were concerned. Lucy had no one to rely on but herself.

When, after a couple of hours of butt-numbing immobility, she announced a need for the little girls' room, Hal went in first to remove anything she might fashion into a weapon. After an exhaustive search, all he found worth confiscating was a couple of disposable shavers. "Well, so much for scraping you to death," she told him. "It's on to Plan B—giving you a dry-cleaning bag to play with."

Alone in the bathroom, Lucy had done her own quick perusal, pausing at the can of style-and-scrunch spray. Hadn't she read a mystery novel in which the would-be victim foiled her attacker by getting him in the eyes with hairspray? Somehow she couldn't picture Hal standing still for a literal shellacking without sticking that big gun in her face and pulling the trigger.

Then she'd opened the medicine chest and forgotten all about hair-care products.

Now, as Lucy stood in her kitchen shaping the last half-pound hamburger under the watchful eye of her captor, she turned on the happy-hostess charm. "Are you sure you won't have some wine, Hal? Frank has a fabulous Cab in there." She nodded toward the built-in wine cellar. "He bought a case. There's only one bottle left. Someone ought to drink it up before he remembers and comes back for it."

"Stop trying to get me buzzed." Hal removed and discarded a pair of colored contact lenses, leaving his eyes their natural color, a striking silver-gray. "It's not going to work."

"You can get buzzed on one little glass of wine? Lucky you." Lucy lifted the basket of French fries out of the deep fryer and fired up the indoor grill. "So, Mick, how're your mangoes doing?"

"What the fuck do you mean by that?" He'd grown roots, sitting there against the dishwasher with his tequila and his frozen fruit, glowering all the while at Lucy.

"I just mean, those chunks must be thawed by now." As the burgers sizzled, Lucy started tearing up a head of lettuce. "You might want to swap them out for a fresh bag. I've got some ground nuts in the freezer."

"Shut up and cook." Hal was surfing stations on the radio, becoming increasingly agitated at the dearth of information. "When the hell are they going to let him go?"

"Who?" Mick asked groggily.

"It's been, what, six hours, seven." Hal switched the little under-cabinet TV to the local Long Island channel. "By now they've got to know the ballistics are wrong. Will and that PI, they'll be backing each other up, telling the cops how it went down. They'll let Will go and start broadcasting our descriptions, looking for us."

"Looking for *you*." Mick bestirred himself to gesticulate with his tequila bottle. "*I* didn't shoot anyone."

"Why's it taking so long?" Hal said. "I can't do a thing till he's out.

Can't contact him, can't tell him where to leave the money. Plus, he's going to need time to get that much cash together. What's that?" he demanded as Lucy whisked salad dressing.

She sighed. "Extra-virgin olive oil. Roasted peanut oil. White balsamic—"

"All right, all right. Just do it." He grabbed another brownie and started pacing. "Half my life, they took. I will not go back. Never."

He'd declared it repeatedly during the past few hours, and Lucy believed him. Hal Lynch would do anything to avoid returning to prison, and that, more than anything else, scared the crap out of her. It meant he had nothing to lose.

The front doorbell chimed. Lucy jumped.

Hal asked, "Who's that?" Mick, oblivious, was absorbed with extracting the last few drops from the bottle.

She shook her head. "I'm not expecting anyone."

He hauled her through the dining room and foyer, and peered through the peephole in the front door. He shoved her face at the peephole and whispered, "Who is it?"

"My husband. I don't know who the other one is." The man who stood with Frank under the porch light was a head taller and heavily muscled. He sported curly dark hair, a prominent brow ridge, and an impeccably tailored dark suit and tie.

This scary-looking gentleman had to be one of Anne Marie's brothers or brothers-in-law. Frank's post-bigamy lifestyle, as ordained by the two Mrs. Narbys, included a constant chaperone in the form of one of Anne Marie's numerous menfolk.

The chaperone nudged Frank, who stabbed the doorbell again.

"Don't answer," Hal whispered. "They'll go away."

"Frank has a key," she said.

They heard it then, the snick of the deadbolt. "Get rid of them," Hal ordered as he and his gun slipped behind the floor-length dining-room drapes.

The door swung open and Frank's expression went from put-upon to surly. "You *are* home. Can't be bothered to answer the door?"

The big man nudged him. "Be nice, Frank."

"I didn't hear the bell. I was . . ." Lucy indicated her apron. "I was in the middle of cooking."

"At this time of night?" Frank sauntered through the foyer into the greatroom as if he still lived there.

The big man followed him, smiling politely. "It smells delicious."

"Thank you."

He nudged Frank again, harder. "Introduce us, Frank. Where are your manners?"

Frank sighed. "Murray Saperstein, Lucy Narby. Lucy Narby, Murray Saperstein. There."

"I'm real pleased to meet you, Mrs. Narby." The hand Murray extended was the size of a grizzly's paw. "I've heard so much about you, I feel like we're family. Well, we are family in a way, am I right?"

"I guess so. It's, uh, nice to meet you, too, Mr. Sap—"

"It's Murray, come on." He pumped her hand. "Can I call you Lucy?"

"Well, of course. Listen. Frank." Lucy's heart was a jackhammer. "It's not a good time."

"Not a good time how? I told you I was coming."

"No, you didn't—"

"I left a message on your machine this afternoon," Frank said.

"Oh. I . . . well, I didn't get a chance to listen to my messages." She wiped her damp palms on her apron.

Murray's sharp gaze swept the room. "Everything all right here, Lucy?"

"Yes. Of—Of course it is." She considered shaking her head no, but then Frank would no doubt open his big yap and say all the wrong things. So she gritted out a smile and added, "I'm in the middle of something, I'm afraid. Some other time, okay?"

"What," Frank sneered, "you got someone here?"

"No, I mean . . . I mean yes, I, well, I do have someone here. Sorry." Another shaky smile. "This is kind of awkward."

"Not at all." Murray waved away her embarrassment. "You got every right. I mean, you and Frank here are practically divorced, am I right?"

They both responded without hesitation. Yes, they said. Yes, practically divorced.

"Well then," Murray said, "we'll get outta your way, Lucy. We just came by to give you this." He produced an envelope from his breast pocket. "It's your copy of the power of attorney, all signed and legal."

Lucy and Anne Marie, as part of their fiscal reorganization plan, had demanded Frank execute a durable power of attorney, granting his wife Anne Marie and soon-to-be-ex Lucy absolute control over all his assets, real property, future income: the whole ball of wax. Desperate to avoid prosecution for bigamy, Frank had capitulated.

The envelope in her hand gave her an idea. There was a notepad and pen on the little mail table in the foyer. It would take no time at all to scrawl *CALL COPS* or even a simple *911* and slip the note to Murray. She'd taken a single step toward the table when Mick staggered in from the kitchen. He stopped dead at the sight of Frank's brother-in-law.

"Holy shit. For real?" Mick's puffy eyes widened. "The Murminator. It's the fuckin' *Murminator!*" He looked around the room. "Hey, Hal—"

"Mick!" Lucy dropped the envelope and lunged for him. "I'd like you to meet my ex-husband, Frank. Frank, this is my friend Mick."

Frank gave the beat-up, bedraggled young man the once-over. "This is him?" he asked, with a snicker. "This is the best you can do?"

"Huh?" Mick squinted at Frank, then at Lucy. "What's he mean, the best—"

She silenced him with a quick kiss. An air kiss, really, as she couldn't bring herself to make contact with Mick's swollen, blood-smeared, tequila-reeking mouth. She slipped her arm around his waist. Mick caught on fast—too fast, grabbing her rump and testing it for ripeness.

"You never said you knew the Murminator, babe." Mick's grubby fingers traced a southerly route down the back center seam of her jeans. It took all Lucy's self-control not to knee him in the balls again.

"We just met," Murray explained. "How'd you get that shiner, Mick? Looks like you went a couple rounds with some big ape like me."

"He fell down the stairs," Lucy blurted. "Listen, I don't want to seem inhospitable, but our dinner's getting cold—"

"Yeah, but you aren't, are you, babe?" Mick was all hands. He half-leaned on Lucy, his voice slurred. "Your old lady, Frank, I'm telling ya, she's gotta have it all the time. Was she always this horny? Babe, I tell her, you're gonna wear it out." He grabbed his crotch for effect, and winced for real.

Murray managed to keep his expression neutral. Color flooded Frank's face as if a switch had been flipped. "You've got a big mouth, son," he said.

"Come on, Frank." Murray placed a giant hand on his charge's shoulder. "It's time we left." He sent Lucy a silent query, asking if she really was okay. She tried to summon another smile as she nodded yes, but it refused to form.

"Hey, stick around," Mick said. "We got plenty of food. And then after, we can *all* do her. Lucy won't mind." He slipped his hand up her side, only to be thwarted before he could grab a breast. "She told me she's always wanted to pull a train, isn't that right, babe? After tonight, you can cross that one off your list." He traced a big *X* in the air.

"That's my wife, you insolent little pissant—"

Murray pulled Frank off of Mick, hesitating just long enough to allow the outraged husband to land a solid one to the insolent little pissant's jaw. Mick stumbled into an ottoman and back-flipped with Olympic flair.

"That's enough, Frank." Murray escorted him to the door. "Nice meeting you, Lucy."

"Same here, Murray. Give my best to Anne Marie."

"Will do."

"Who the hell does he think he is?" Frank howled as Murray propelled him out of the house and down the porch steps. "Insolent little—"

Lucy collapsed against the closed door. A few moments later she heard their car pull away. "They're gone," she told the dining-room drapes.

Hal emerged from behind the drapes and stalked into the greatroom, his vulpine gaze fixed on Mick, now sitting on the carpet rubbing his face. With icy deliberation he strode to Mick and straightened his gun arm, the barrel mere inches from his oblivious son's temple.

Lucy's heartbeat faltered. "Don't."

"Huh?" Mick looked at her. "Where is he? Where's the fucker that sucker-punched me?"

The look in Hal's eyes. She'd never seen that kind of icy, single-minded fury, as if he were more animal than human.

"Turn around, Lucy." Hal never took his eyes off his target.

She *wanted* to turn around. She couldn't bear to watch him do it. But she stood her ground and said, again, "Don't."

Mick now stared slack-jawed at the gun barrel almost touching his face. Hal's trigger finger began to move.

"He's your son," Lucy said, prompting a bark of derisive laughter from Hal. She added, "You'll never forgive yourself."

She doubted that was true. This man was unlike anyone she'd ever known. He was missing some part of his essential makeup, some part that separated men from beasts. The part, perhaps, that kept human fathers from killing their young. Still, she had to try to get through to him. Mick sat paralyzed by fear, blubbering like an infant.

"Hal," Lucy said. "That man in the park lived. You haven't killed anyone. Don't do it now."

He swiveled, and Lucy found herself staring down the barrel of the gun. She hadn't even realized she'd taken a step toward him. "I've killed someone," he said.

She swallowed hard. "You paid for that murder. It's in the past. You wounded a man today. That's all they can get you for."

"It's called attempted murder," Hal clarified. "And then there's kidnapping."

"No." Lucy shook her head. "I won't say a word, I swear. It's not even really, you know, kidnapping, is it, if you invite someone to your house and make them dinner?"

Something in Hal's taunting smile made her shiver. "How about if I cut off your pinky finger, too?" he asked. "Would you call it kidnapping then?"

Lucy couldn't get oxygen, no matter how hard her lungs heaved. It took all her concentration just to remain upright.

His smile broadened. "Ricky screamed and screamed when he saw what I was about to do. He begged me not to. Pissed his pants. But hey, he was just a kid, right? He had more balls then than this one has now." He jerked his head toward his son but didn't glance at him. If he had, he would have known what Lucy did, that Mick had slunk out of the room the instant Hal's back was turned. She'd listened for, and heard, the faint click of the back door closing behind him.

"I didn't know." Her voice sounded disembodied to her own ears. "I didn't know it was you. Does . . . does Will know?"

"Nope." Still grinning. "It's our little secret, Lucy. Well, and his." Hal glanced over his shoulder, cursed, and sprinted toward the kitchen.

Lucy shot to the front door, yanked it open, and took off toward the driveway, reaching it just as her Volvo careened around the side of the house. She threw herself at the car, scrabbling for the back-door handle, as Mick stomped the accelerator. She landed hard on the cobblestones, rolled and went with the roll, springing to her feet and running full tilt for the inky woods, practically begging for a bullet in the back.

She made it past the tree line, stumbling blindly through brush, whipped by branches, deaf to everything but her own rasping breaths.

Then he was on her, bringing her down with a predator's easy grace, pinning her, his breath hot in her ear. He wasn't even winded. "You're worth nothing to me dead, Lucy. But I can make you wish you were. Never forget that." He hauled her up. She spat dirt and decayed leaves as he shoved her back the way she'd come.

30

JUDITH ACCEPTED A ride home from Fergus on the condition he make no conversational overtures. She'd managed to pull herself together, but her composure was a fragile thing, and all she wanted now was to lock herself in her bedroom and have a nice, private breakdown. Fergus steered his 1957 black-and-white Chevy Bel Air past the unmarked police vehicle stationed across the street and pulled into the driveway behind her Acura. He killed the engine.

"No." She opened her door. "You're not coming in. Good night, Fergus. Thanks for the ride." Wordlessly he accompanied her to her front door. "I mean it. Please respect me this much. I need to be alone."

He framed her face in his big hands, there under her porch light, a show for the watchful cops and her nosy neighbors. Mick's name had been kept out of the news, but it was a temporary reprieve. Sooner or later the whole ugly story would be fodder for gossip on her block, at her club, everywhere.

Judith didn't care. For the first time since becoming a card-carrying member of the upright citizenry, she didn't give a rat's ass what they all thought of her. She cared only about Mick's safety, and Will, and Tom, and the god-awful mess she'd made of everything.

"Judith," he said, so tenderly she very nearly lost it right there, "don't you know how much I respect you?"

His expression was so candid, so sincere, it hurt to look at him. Judith closed her eyes. Tears trembled on her lashes. He kissed them before they could fall.

"Call me 'lass,'" she whispered into the cool breeze.

"Lass." He planted a warm, healing kiss on her cheek. "My lass." He smoothed back her hair, kissed her temple. "My beautiful, fine, strong lass." His mouth found hers and she clung to him, kissed him shamelessly there in the spotlight on her doorstep for all the world to see.

When at last they separated, he took the keys from her fingers, opened the door, and ushered her inside, turning on lights as he made his way through the house. "I'll leave you alone as you wish. Only humor me—I need to make sure you're safe."

"There are two cops sitting outside waiting for my son to do something outrageously stupid like come home." Judith collapsed heavily onto her sofa, leaned back, and shut her eyes. "I've never been safer." She listened to Fergus move from room to room. After a couple of minutes she heard muted voices from the back of the house.

Judith opened her eyes and listened hard. She heard the word "fuck" in an unmistakable voice and sprang to her feet. She found them in the den. Mick was sitting on the daybed rubbing his eyes. It looked like someone had knocked him around; her money was on Hal. Her son was alive, though. Her greatest fear had been averted.

Judith didn't throw her arms around him—not that he would have let her. She didn't kiss him or coddle him or tell him everything was going to be all right. Everything was not going to be all right. Her son was no longer a child. He was an adult who'd squandered every opportunity presented to him and made uniformly self-destructive choices.

Mick was Judith's son and she would always harbor a mother's unconditional love for him. But it was past time for him to accept the consequences of his behavior. At this point she hadn't the desire, much less the power, to prevent that.

"I found him sleepin' here," Fergus said.

"Mick, there are police parked outside," Judith said. "How did you get past them?"

"You think I don't know what an unmarked car looks like?" He jerked his head toward the back of the house. "Parked over on Harrison. Snuck through yards and slipped into the sunroom."

Fergus towered over him. "Where's Hal Lynch?"

He snorted. "Like I'm gonna tell *you*."

"Mick." Judith took a step toward him. "This isn't a game. People have gotten hurt. You don't know this man like I do."

"Just 'cause you fucked a guy all those years ago doesn't mean you know him. Any more than you know *this* dickwad."

Fergus didn't rise to the bait. "Lynch is a dangerous man," he said.

"No shit." Mick picked dried snot and blood from his nose and flicked it onto the carpet. "He's my dad, though, you know? Like, my flesh and blood? Which you'll never be, no matter how many times you bone my mom."

"All right, lad." Fergus lifted Mick by his shirt and slammed him against the adjacent wall, just hard enough to secure his attention. Judith jerked in alarm but restrained her maternal protectiveness. Mick was wrong. She knew Fergus better than he thought, had verbally sparred with her brother's best friend for sixteen years. No goading on Mick's part would make him turn violent.

"I asked you a question." Fergus tightened his grip. "I'm still waitin' on an answer."

Mick peered around the big man. "Get him off me, Mom."

Fergus addressed Judith over his shoulder. "I'm goin' to ask you to leave us alone now, darlin'. Mick and I have a couple of things to discuss. Man to man. You understand."

Judith exited the room, closing the door behind her.

A ROUGH HAND shook Will's shoulder, dragging him out of a deep sleep. "Leave me alone." He didn't open his eyes, simply turned over in bed, giving his back to the intruder.

"Get up, Will." It was Fergus. "Lucy's in trouble."

Will bolted upright so fast, his head throbbed. He threw off the covers. "What happened?"

"Lynch has her." It was Wesley, still in the brown friar's robe, the only outfit in the place that fit him. He'd stuck around in case they got word about Lynch. Apparently they had.

Fergus and Wesley filled Will in as he snatched up his jeans from the floor. According to Mick, Lucy had shown up at the Goo and Lynch had talked his way into her car. He was holding her at gunpoint at her house.

Will didn't need to be told why. "He wants his money. It's what he's been after all along."

"In his eyes, you stole it from him." Fergus wore a faded dark green sweatshirt with the sleeves torn off, black jeans, and the heavy, scuffed motorcycle boots Will called his "hippie stompers."

"It'll take time to get the cash together—it's sunk into this place." Will zipped his fly and grabbed his shirt. "I'll need to borrow against the equity. The banks open at, what, ten?"

"I've got to tell you, lad, the bloke's wired, gettin' reckless—that's what I got from Mick." Fergus shook his head. "If it were just the money, Lucy's got family, too, but we've no time for that. And even if he gets his two million, that doesn't mean he's going to let her go."

Wesley agreed. "Anything could set him off. Guy's got nothing to lose at this point. Cullen's kept his name outta the news so far, but Lynch is no dummy. He's gotta know the cops are on to him."

"Cullen," Will muttered as he shoved his sockless feet into sneakers. "I hate to think of how that bastard is handling this."

Wesley and Fergus exchanged a glance. "We haven't called him," Wesley said.

"Yet," Fergus added. "We're leavin' that decision to you."

Will turned back from the doorway and stared at the two men, at their sober expressions. Both were clearly aware of something it had taken Will until this moment to admit to himself—that his feelings for Lucy Narby ran deep. He couldn't recall ever feeling this strongly about a woman. Which astounded him considering he'd known her for less than two weeks and had yet to talk his way into her bed.

And now Lucy was at the mercy of a monster, a desperate man with no conscience, as Will knew from firsthand experience.

"I worked with Paulie Cullen for years," Wesley said. "I can just see that puffed-up bully negotiating with Lynch. He'll bark some threats into a bullhorn and follow it up with firepower. You want your Lucy to walk out of there alive, that's not the way to go about it, is all I'm saying."

"From what I could tell about the man when he was here," Fergus said, "I've got to agree."

Will's insides roiled. He had to stay focused, for Lucy's sake. If only it were as simple as handing over a truckload of cash. He'd gladly beggar himself if it meant he'd get her back in one piece.

"We need a plan," said Wesley, the Voice of Reason, filling out the voluminous monk's habit and carrying, Will now saw, an antique but fully functional crossbow—from Fergus's personal cabinet of curiosities, no doubt. Will could only imagine what weird and wonderful implements the big Irishman had secreted on his person. A high-velocity slingshot, perhaps? A Taser? A handful of those scary-as-hell throwing stars?

Will headed for the door. "We'll figure out a plan on the way. I just have to run upstairs for—"

"Got it." Fergus handed him the SIG, along with 9-millimeter ammo from the office safe.

Will rammed the magazine into the pistol's grip. "All right, let's do it."

JUDITH'S HANDS SHOOK, but she managed to give Lucy Narby's front doorbell a few more stabs, followed by some vigorous thumping. "I know you're in there, Hal. Open up." She heard voices on the other side: fierce, muted conversation.

Judith prayed she was doing the right thing. She'd never met Lucy, but she knew how her brother felt about her; Fergus had filled her in on all that. Will's clueless ardor was a source of amusement to everyone who knew him.

Judith had no idea what rescue plot Will and Fergus were at this very moment concocting, but the fact was, only she knew Hal, knew the real him and what made him tick, despite the passage of years. No one else stood as great a chance of freeing Lucy. She had to try, whatever the consequences to herself. She owed her brother that much.

Judith's fist pounded the door in a bruising staccato. "I'm not armed, I swear. What are you afraid of, Hal?" This, she knew, would tweak his male pride.

Moments later, the deadbolt slid and the door swung open, and Hal

Lynch fixed her with his startling ice-gray gaze. The face had aged, he had more muscle and less hair, and he looked like he'd recently gone one-on-one with a wood chipper. But those eyes.

Judith forced starch into her wobbly spine and returned his stare. Hal held a woman—it had to be Lucy—in a headlock, a gun pressed to her temple. Lucy was an attractive brunette with dark, intelligent-looking eyes. Judith swallowed hard. "Let me in, Hal."

"You've gotten stupider with age." His gaze darted around the grounds. He peered down the shadowy driveway, squinted into the distant black-on-black woods. His entire body radiated tension. Mick was right: Hal was wound tight. "Did our darling little boy blab to anyone else," he asked, "or just you?"

"Just me—I'm the only one who knows you're here."

"Bullshit. Where are they, Judith?"

"Where are who?"

"The *cops*, who do you think?" He jerked his arm tighter around Lucy's throat; she emitted a strangled sound. "Don't lie to me. Do not fucking lie to me."

"I didn't call the cops, Hal, I swear. It's just me."

"Throw that inside." Hal nodded toward Judith's Burberry plaid shoulder bag.

"I'm not armed, I told y—"

"Do it." Hal grimaced for an instant, making Judith wonder if his injuries were more serious than they looked. She tossed her purse into the foyer.

Hal kicked it into the greatroom, scanned the grounds once more, then jerked his head, wordlessly ordering her into the house. He slid the deadbolt home, made Lucy sit on the mushroom-colored carpet, and treated Judith to a rough, sexless pat-down. Then he backhanded her hard across the face, leaving her sprawled next to Lucy.

Hal towered over her, gesticulating with the pistol. "Sit up."

She did, with Lucy's help. Her cheek was on fire; the room spun.

"What was that for?" Lucy glared up at him. "She didn't do anything to you."

"You're wrong there, Lucy." Hal's hard gaze never left Judith. "Your boyfriend's sister here? She stole twenty-five years of my life. Just like that, with one little anonymous phone call. That's what she does to the father of her child. Isn't that right, Judith? Look at me." He grasped her throbbing jaw, forcing her face up. "I said look at me. I was a young man when I went into the joint. Thinking about what I'd do to you when I got out kept me sane all those years. That and the money." He shoved her away and wiped the blood from her split lip on his jeans.

Lucy looked from Hal to Judith, no doubt wondering about their connection.

He peered around the window drapes, then returned to stand over them. "Here's how it works, ladies. The cops show up, you die. Either of you tries anything, you die. I don't like the way you look at me, you die." He stiffened, sucking in a quick breath, but recovered quickly. "Got it?"

Yes—Judith and Lucy nodded in unison—they got it.

Judith wiped blood from her mouth. "I brought something for you. It's in my purse."

Hal's eyes narrowed.

"I know, I know," she said. "I try anything, I die. Go ahead. It won't explode."

He knelt by Judith's purse, unlatched it, and dumped the contents onto the glass table. There were the usual items, and then there was the not-so-usual one. "What's in that?" he asked.

"Open it and see," Judith said.

Hal released the ties on the burgundy velvet roll and unfurled it to reveal a satin interior of zippered pouches. He unzipped the first one and pulled out a four-foot strand of plump pink pearls. He brushed a pearl against his tooth. "They're real."

"My grandmother's," she said. "Grandpa Will got them for her in Japan."

Hal opened another pouch. Big, juicy emerald-and-diamond drop earrings. He examined them closely, set them aside, and found the matching necklace in the next pouch.

"Holy cow." Lucy stared goggle-eyed.

"They're worth three point four million," Judith said. "All the pieces in the roll, that is. The appraisal is in the side pocket of my bag. There's an envelope of cash in there too. Twenty-seven hundred. It's all I had at home."

Hal unzipped all the pouches and shook the contents onto the inch-thick glass. Rings, bracelets, necklaces, and earrings tumbled out, much of it one-of-a-kind antiques and all crafted of precious metals and gemstones. Most of the pieces were heirlooms passed down to Judith and her late husband. Some were gifts from Don during their marriage. A ruby ring their first Christmas together. A diamond bracelet for their tenth anniversary. Judith used to assume these pieces would stay in the family, that someday she'd hand them down to her own child.

That assumption hadn't survived Mick's adolescence. Oh sure, she'd still prefer to keep these treasures in the family, which meant leaving them to Tom rather than Mick, who wouldn't think twice about using them to enhance his slothful, druggy lifestyle. But fate had other plans.

Hal studied a coral and diamond flower pin set in yellow gold, set it down, and picked up a diamond-and-platinum brooch shaped like a seahorse, with a magnificent black pearl at its center. He located the brooch on the itemized appraisal. "This won't fetch any forty-five grand once it's taken apart."

"Look, don't ask me what the individual stones are worth," Judith said, "but it's got to be more than the two million you're after."

"Oh, definitely." Lucy nodded with vigor.

"I don't want *any* two million." A vein bulged in Hal's forehead; he tapped his chest with the gun barrel. "I want *my* two million. I want the money your brother swiped—" He stopped, his lips pressed thin, fingers clawing his gut. "What did you put in that food?" he asked Lucy.

"You're kidding, right?" she asked. "You ate too fast. Seconds and thirds. Plus a panful of brownies. Can I help it if—"

"Shut up," he growled, still clutching his middle. "Just *shut up*."

"The cash will get you a plane ticket anywhere," Judith said. "And that's where you can fence those stones—anywhere in the world. It's the universal currency."

Hal was staring at the jewelry, poking at it with the barrel of his gun. That gave Judith hope. "I want *my* two mil," he grumbled to a sapphire circle brooch, but with less heat than before.

"See those diamond drop earrings?" Judith said. "Ninety-four thousand dollars. Look at the size of those yellow diamonds."

"All right, all right. Jesus." Hal kept glancing past the curving staircase, where Judith assumed a powder room beckoned. He was probably trying to decide how to control her and Lucy while taking care of business. He turned to Lucy. "You have any rope?"

Say no, Judith silently pleaded. *You have no rope, no duct tape, no belts, scarves, or panty hose.*

"There's some clothesline in the basement," Lucy said. "Will that do?"

Judith cursed silently. Her brother used to go for women with brains. What happened?

"Lead the way." Hal and Judith followed Lucy around the staircase, past the kitchen and laundry room toward the basement door. As they passed the powder room, Lucy slipped into it, slamming and locking the door before Hal could stop her. "Before you tie me up, I just have to pee," she called from within. "I won't be a sec."

"You'll have to hold it." He rattled the doorknob. "Get out of there."

"Just a minute," she trilled.

"I mean it." He pistol-whipped the door, holding his gut in a half crouch. Sweat misted his brow. "Open this door." He winced. "Now!"

"Paper ran out. Gotta find another roll."

"Goddammit, Lucy." Hal prepared to kick in the door, only to collapse against the opposite wall as another cramp seized him. He pointed the gun at the lock.

Judith screamed, "Lucy, watch out!"

BAM! The gunshot was deafening. The door slammed back on its hinges, a ragged hole where the knob and lock had been. An acrid smell hung in the air.

Hal didn't waste a second. He hauled Lucy out from under the pedestal sink, shoved the two of them to the floor of the laundry room where he could keep an eye on them, then dropped trou and enthroned himself in one swift, desperate motion. Judith tried to ignore the sensory input as he sought and found explosive relief from his overindulgence. Through it all, his gun hand never wavered. She didn't doubt that if either of them made the slightest move, he'd blow them both away.

Lucy tensed as if preparing to make a run for it. Judith's suspicions were confirmed when Lucy whispered, very quietly, "Get ready." She couldn't be serious. Did the woman have a death wish?

At last Judith heard the toilet paper unspooling. Seconds later, Hal muttered, "What the hell?"

"Now." Lucy jumped up, yanking on Judith's arm. "Come on!"

"Looo-seeeee!" Hal howled, pants around his ankles, struggling to push himself off the seat. *"What did you do?"*

BAM! Judith sprang up as a gunshot cratered the wall next to her head, and raced Lucy to the front door.

BAM! BAM! "You are dead, Lucy!"

Lucy fumbled with the deadbolt for an interminable two or three seconds before the door swung open. The two of them pushed through the doorway together and slammed up against a tank of a man in an Armani suit. Judith screamed.

"Whoa." The man steadied them. "What's goin' on here, Lucy? I heard shots."

"Murray!" Lucy clung to him. "Oh my God, it's Hal, he—he—"

"Back up," he said. "Who's Hal? What happened to that other one? Mick?"

"Mick is—is—" Breathless, Lucy wagged her hand to indicate Mick had vacated the premises. "Hal's the one that shot that man in the park today. He's holding me hostage and he has a gun, but he's stuck to the toilet. Superglue."

Murray took this report in stride. "I knew something was wrong. I told Frank we hadda come back and check it out." He led the women some distance from the house, where an errant bullet was less likely to find them.

"Do you have a phone?" Judith said. "Call nine-one-one."

"Yeah, I'm on it." He patted his pockets.

Inside the house, Hal had grown quiet. No gunshots. No ranting. Judith was not reassured. Neither, apparently, was Lucy. They exchanged a look.

"You *did* put something in his food, didn't you?" Judith asked.

"Ex-Lax brownies. Old family recipe. My sister, Ethel, made me a batch in the fifth grade. The glue stunt came from her, too. Timing's tricky on that one. You've got to do it right before the victim sits down." Which explained Lucy's sudden need to pee.

Murray was still hunting for his phone. "You always keep superglue in the john?"

"Of course." Lucy and Judith shared a *Who doesn't?* look. "For nail repairs. Where's Frank?"

"In the car." He jerked his head toward a gold Mercedes idling behind Judith's Acura. A figure sat hunched in the passenger seat. "He's pissed— 'scuse me, ladies, annoyed—'cause he's missing *Survivor*. Here's the darn thing." His huge hand dwarfed the cell phone as he squinted at the keypad.

"What's he doing in there?" Judith hugged herself, staring at the open front door. "It's too quiet."

Murray started patting his pockets again. "I got some reading glasses somewhere."

Judith grabbed the phone from him. Unfortunately, her middle-aged eyes weren't much better than his. She thought she'd punched in 911, but the phone's display informed her she was speed-dialing someone named Nick. She groped for the end button just as someone in the rear of the house hollered Lucy's name. It was a voice she knew, and it wasn't Hal's. "Will. Oh my God."

Lucy looked stunned. "But he's in jail."

"Will!" Judith sprinted across the lawn. *"Will, be careful, he's got a gun!"* She took the front steps three at a time and ran through the open front door into the foyer, only to be clotheslined by a sinewy arm striking like a cobra from the adjacent dining room. Hal jerked her hard against him, plucked the phone from her hand, and threw it against the wall. "You never could stay away from me for long."

31

WILL, FERGUS, AND WESLEY were picking their way through dense trees and underbrush, heading for the cluster of lights that was the rear of Lucy's house, when the first gunshot rang out. As one, they abandoned stealth and turned on the juice, tearing their way through the dark woods. A minute later, three more shots punched the placid spring night.

Lucy.

Was Will too late? Had he made a tragic mistake by not involving the cops? *Hang on, sweetheart.* He racked the slide on the SIG. *I'm coming.*

It seemed to take forever to reach the backyard. Will hadn't expected the injured, overweight PI to keep up. True, Wesley was huffing like the little train that couldn't, and every one of those breaths had to be agony to his cracked sternum, but he was right there with Will and Fergus, robe billowing, sandaled feet eating up the manicured lawn. The trio parted around the covered pool and convened close to the French doors that led into the library.

Fergus reared back to kick in the doors, freezing in place when Will produced a key. "From Ethel." Will unlocked the doors. "When she hired me." It was quiet inside the house now. Not good.

Will led the way, pistol at the ready. He'd never aimed a loaded weapon at another human being. Would he be able to shoot Lynch if it came to that?

Yes. He'd do anything he had to, to save Lucy.

Wesley held his crossbow loaded and cocked. Fergus had reached into his right hippie stomper and retrieved an antique dirk. Will recognized it as one of his friend's finer specimens, lovingly maintained and beautifully balanced. In a pinch it could double as a throwing knife.

They paused inside the library, straining their ears, but heard only the babble of a radio from the direction of the kitchen. It was a big house. Lucy could be anywhere. Lynch might already have fled, leaving her bleeding to death somewhere within these four walls. The time for skulking had come and gone. "Lucy!" he bellowed, gesturing to his companions to fan out and search for her.

They'd barely taken a step when Judith hollered from beyond the front door, *"Will, be careful, he's got a gun!"*

"Bloody hell." Fergus emitted an anxious growl. "I told the woman to stay put. Why can't she ever fekkin' listen to me?"

They charged into the greatroom just as Lynch lurched in from the foyer, naked from the waist down and towing Judith in a headlock. Her lip was split; a bruise was forming on her left cheek. Just then Lucy raced in, accompanied by a nattily dressed behemoth with no neck, the two of them skidding to a halt at the sight of Lynch and Judith. No Neck looked familiar somehow, but Will was too distracted to try and place him.

Though he was relieved beyond words to see Lucy unharmed, his relief was eclipsed by the sight of his sister with the barrel of a pistol pressed to her head. She'd run into the house trying to warn him away. Trying to protect him.

Lynch's deranged gaze jittered between the two groups of intruders. He ordered Will and his companions to drop their weapons and kick them to him, and all of them to line up next to the curved staircase, hands high. Wesley's outfit prompted a double take. "I get it." Lynch wore a mocking smile. "You *did* die, and were reincarnated as a giant turd."

"That's real funny, my friend," Wesley said, "comin' from a guy with a toilet seat stuck to his ass."

Okay, they all had eyes, but did Wesley have to come right out and say it? Will braced himself. He was standing right next to the loudmouth PI; he prayed Lynch was an accurate shot.

"*You* did this to me." Lynch's malignant gaze was aimed at Lucy. "You better be able to *un*do it. I don't have to tell you what'll happen if you don't." He jerked his elbow, snapping up Judith's chin.

Fugitives from the law generally tried to blend in. Not only was Lynch a mass of cuts and claw marks, thanks to Quint, but his getaway outfit consisted of navy polo shirt, white crew socks, and a peach-colored toilet seat, its lid flapping against his back with every step. How the hell had Lucy accomplished *that*? When Lynch had found himself stuck to the seat, he must have reached around with a coin and unscrewed it from the bowl.

"I'll get you your money, Lynch," Will said. "As soon as the banks open."

"You think I can wait for the goddamn *banks*?" Lynch was walking the razor edge of reason. His lips curled back like a feral dog's. "You think I've got that kind of time?"

"Hal, listen to me." Judith's voice was a strangled whisper.

"I've listened to you plenty." Lynch ground the gun barrel into her temple. She grimaced, and Will had to restrain an urge to pounce on him. "This is all your fault. Did you think of that? Huh?" Lynch squeezed her windpipe a little more, causing her to claw at his ropy forearm.

"Take it easy, Lynch." Fergus's voice was tight.

"You started it all, Judith, twenty-five years ago," Lynch persisted, "you and your kid brother. The little star. My partner here got cold feet," he told the rest of them. "Lost her nerve, so what does she do? Goes blabbing to the cops and gets me sent away for half my life."

This was news to Will. Judith had told him Lynch had done time for murder, but not that she'd turned him in.

Somehow she found the strength to shoot back, "You're delusional if you think anyone's to blame for all this but yourself." Before he could retaliate, she added, "Take the jewelry, Hal. Use it to start over somewhere."

Will followed Lynch's gaze to the glass coffee table and the pile of baubles that had escaped his notice in all the excitement. He recognized a couple of pieces that had belonged to his grandmother. So that was why Judith was here.

"Oh, I'll take the jewelry," Hal told her. "And you're coming along, too."

"No." Will and Fergus said it in unison.

Lynch gazed almost lovingly at Judith as he tapped her temple with the gun barrel. "Your sister and I have some unfinished business, Will. I've had plenty of time to plan how I'm going to repay her for all she's done for me."

Will could only imagine what gruesome form that repayment would take. Every muscle in his body tensed. No way was he going to stand by and let this psycho walk out of here with his sister.

"She'll be a liability," Fergus said. "On your own, you can slip out of the country, sell the stones, make a new life, like she says."

Lynch regarded Fergus. "You're the one that followed her to Bermuda, like a dog after a bitch in heat. Was she worth the airfare?"

Fergus didn't answer.

"I'm gonna put my hands down now," Lucy's neckless friend said. He lowered his thick arms with a groan, and suddenly Will knew where he'd seen him: on TV. Specifically, on those outlandish wrestling matches Irving made him watch. Will wasn't even going to guess how the Murminator got mixed up in all this.

"Keep 'em up." Lynch gesticulated with the gun.

"It's the joints." The Murminator rotated his shoulders; it sounded like corn popping. "Too many powerslams. All right, all right." He raised his hands again. "Listen, I dunno what-all's goin' on here. Well, I know some of it. Like that you shot that guy in the park today."

Wesley wagged one of his upraised hands. "That guy would be me."

"No kidding. Looks like you're doing okay, though."

Lynch said, "You don't need to know what's going on, pal. Just stand there and shut up."

"Well, it's just like, okay, I know you're the one with the gun and all, and trust me." The Murminator was the soul of sincerity. "I respect that, okay? But looking at these guys here, I can't help but notice, well, like this one over here." He indicated Fergus. "Fella with that kinda build, he wouldn't have to bulk up all that much to meet me in the ring, you know what I'm saying? Will looks like he's in decent shape. Even Mr. Private Eye here—you work out, am I right?"

"My line of work?" Wesley said. "Be stupid not to."

"And then there's me." The Murminator gave a look that said, *I'm not bragging, just stating fact.* "Lucy doesn't count. No offense," he told her.

"None taken," she said.

"Your *point*?" A tic jumped to life under Lynch's right eye.

"Only that you kinda got your hands full here," the Murminator said. "The four of us come at you, sure, you got time to get off one good shot. Take out Judith there, or maybe one of us. But then? You're back in the can, buddy, looking at life for sure."

Lucy spoke up. "He was in for murder before."

"Yeah? Then this'll be number two," the Murminator said. "So maybe it's the needle, am I right?"

The rest of them nodded. Yeah, maybe the needle this time.

"Or," Wesley said, "you can do the sensible thing, my friend. I dunno much about jewelry, but that stuff looks like the real deal."

Lynch's gaze kept straying toward the coffee table. It wasn't hard to read his mind. The instant he left with his loot, they'd have the cops after him. To Judith he said, "Go to the basement and get the rope—that clothesline. If you're not back in two minutes, I'm gonna begin shooting. Starting with your boyfriend here."

"You're not tying up anyone, Lynch." Will was itching to follow through on the Murminator's threat and rush the man, but that was a last resort. "You have my word that no one will call the cops for an hour and a half after you leave."

Lynch barked out a laugh. "You're kidding, right? Your *word*?"

"Take my car," Judith said. "It's inconspicuous."

"That'll give you enough time to park at JFK or LaGuardia," Will said, "and grab a flight. It doesn't matter where." He didn't bring up the sticky subject of passports or flight manifests. Even if Will were sincere in the offer of a ninety-minute head start—yeah, right—and even if Lynch made it onto a flight, the authorities would be waiting for him when he landed. He was betting on Lynch being too desperate and distracted to see that far ahead.

"Let Judith come over here with us," Fergus said. "Then we can work on gettin' that thing off you."

"Nail polish remover," Lucy said. "That'll do the trick."

"It's true," the Murminator put in. "That's the only thing that works." No one asked him how he knew.

"You better have some," Lynch said.

"Are you kidding? Of course I do." Lucy nodded toward the rear of the house. "In that little half bath. I'll go get it."

"No. She will." Lynch indicated Judith. "You come here." If there was one lesson he'd absorbed during the past few hours, it seemed to be: Never let Lucy near a bathroom.

Lynch grabbed Lucy and gave Judith a shove toward the powder room. "Same deal. You have two minutes."

"All my nail stuff is together," Lucy told her. Will hated seeing her with a pistol pressed to her head. The fact that she was forced into close proximity to Lynch's dangling dick made it all the worse. She added, "It's all in a hatbox on the—"

"What the hell's taking so long?" Frank demanded, stalking in from the foyer.

Lynch started at the intrusion. Lucy elbowed him in the gut, stomped his foot, and wrenched out of his hold. Fergus, meanwhile, moved like lightning, extracting something from his right hippie stomper and bringing it to his mouth. Will recognized the handmade bamboo blowgun.

Pfffffft! Lynch yelped as a steel dart punctured the meat of his thigh. Before he could react, Will and the others were on him as promised, disarming and subduing him in seconds.

The fight went out of Lynch quickly. He lay sprawled on the plush carpet, his back bowed by the toilet seat, his privates rudely elevated, the dart bobbing in his thigh. The others stood around him in a circle, everyone but Frank, who flopped onto the sofa and grumped, "Guess no one's going to tell me what's going on." He sifted through the stack of magazines on the lamp table and settled down with *Allure*.

Lynch's jaw was slack, his eyes at half mast—altogether a relaxed expression if not for the worried-looking brow twitches. His hands and feet jerked restlessly as he muttered a slurred, ". . . the hell . . . can't . . ."

He winced in pain when Fergus jerked the dart from his leg. "Anyone care to venture a guess?" Fergus asked, displaying the dart's business end— tinged with blood and traces of a dark, tarry substance—before sliding a protective cap over it.

Wesley raised his hand.

Fergus pointed to him. "The gentleman in brown."

Lynch's eyes were now closed, but Will doubted he was unconscious. His breathing was irregular, punctuated by diaphragm spasms and an odd snoring sound. Once in a while, a finger or toe twitched.

"Rattlesnake venom?" Wesley guessed.

"I am sorry, rattlesnake venom is not the correct answer, but I admire the workin's of your mind. Anyone else? You're disqualified, Will, you know me too well."

"Is it one of those, like, rhino tranquilizers?" the Murminator asked. "Like you see on Animal Planet?"

"No. Sorry. Here's a hint."

Lucy frowned down at Lynch, whose breathing seemed to be shutting down by the second. "Shouldn't we call nine-one-one?"

"I made it myself," Fergus said.

Wesley's eyebrows rose. "The poison?" Everyone appeared duly impressed.

"In the Amazon," Fergus added, with encouraging gestures that invited more guesses. "Come on, people. Okay, final clue. The Ketchwa natives took me under their wing and showed me how to find the vine, how to crush the roots and stems—"

"Curare!" Judith cried.

"Right you are, darlin'." Fergus gave his woman a proud wink.

Lucy was still staring worriedly at Lynch. "Is he dead?"

"Not yet. Technically, curare isn't a poison, it's a powerful muscle relaxant." Fergus squatted by the prone man. "It works by paralyzin' the entire body. Death results from respiratory arrest. Meanwhile the victim remains fully conscious. Hal can hear everything we're sayin'." He pinched the man's arm, hard. "He can feel pain, but he can't react. His mind is as sharp as ever, and he can see." Fergus pried open one of Lynch's eyes and addressed him directly. "You've probably noticed you stopped breathing."

"All right, I'm calling." Lucy hurried away.

"The medics won't get here in time to save you," Fergus told Lynch. "That's the bad news. The good news is, it's possible for you to hang on till then *if* one of us can be moved to do your breathin' for you. To give the kiss of life, as it's called." He looked up at the others. "How about it?

Anyone up for a little mouth-to-mouth action?"

The small group shared conflicted glances. None of them wanted to watch a man die, even a man as repellant as Hal Lynch, but they'd all be happier if someone else played hero. Frank never looked up from "Eyeliner Do's and Don'ts."

"Oh, for heaven's sake," Judith grumbled. "Like I could really go home and tell my son I stood by and let his father suffocate. Hope you enjoy this, Hal." She knelt by Lynch and tipped his head back. "It's the last kiss you're ever going to get from a woman."

32

LUCY PULLED GRANDMA Willie's quilt more snugly around herself. She stood flanked by the open French doors of the library, staring out at her dark backyard. She had to stop thinking of this room as the library. It was the sunroom now, as it should have been all along. Tomorrow she'd arrange to have Frank's prefab collection of great books shipped to Anne Marie. Let his wife decide what to do with them.

It was late. Two a.m., three maybe; she didn't know, didn't care. She could just make out Will's dim form out there, and Judith's. They'd taken a stroll after the police had left, long after the departure of the ambulance carrying Hal Lynch, shackled, intubated, awake and aware though still completely paralyzed. He would recover during the next few hours, according to Fergus. Lucy wanted to believe Lynch would spend the rest of his life behind bars, but the judicial and penal systems were less than predictable. Who could say for sure?

Will and his sister had been talking for a long time out there. Lucy couldn't hear what they were saying, but neither had stalked off yet. She watched Will take Judith's hands in his. A few moments later, their shadowy forms merged in an embrace. They stood that way for several minutes before ambling back toward the house, arms around each other.

Fergus materialized from the gloom at the edge of the lawn, startling Lucy. He must have been watching, too. Judith kissed her brother's cheek, and she and Fergus headed for her car. Will stood looking after them until they disappeared around the side of the house.

Lucy stepped onto the patio then, the slate cool and satiny under her bare feet, the grass cooler still as she closed the distance between them. Will turned as she approached. Even in the faint silvering from a crescent moon, she could see how exhausted he was, mentally more than physically, she suspected. His welcoming smile went no further than his eyes.

Clutching the quilt one-handed, she stroked his cheek, bristly with stubble. She brushed her thumb over his mouth. He caught her fingers in a grip so fierce, it was almost bruising.

"I went a little nuts when I found out he had you." His voice was hoarse. "It took everything I had to hold it together and . . ." He sighed from deep in his chest.

"You did a lot more than hold it together, Will." She smiled up into his tired eyes. "The men in my life seem intent on mounting their own rescue operations, the authorities be damned."

"I don't like the sound of that." At her perplexed frown he added, "The *men* in your life. I thought Frank was past tense. Is there anyone else?"

"Frank is most certainly past tense, and you know damn well there's no one else." She gave him a pointed look. "Does that mean you consider yourself *the* man in my life?"

Without hesitation he said, "Absolutely."

"Well, that's a relief."

"Why?"

"Because I would have done this anyway, but it only feels right doing it for *the* man in my life." Lucy dropped the quilt to the grass and stood before him in her birthday suit.

Will no longer looked tired. He simply looked. For a good long time before his gaze flicked to the house.

"The cops are gone. Everyone went home," she said. "We're alone."

It took a few moments for her words to sink in. Then he wore a goofy little smile. "Really?"

Her hands went to her hips. "Would I be standing here in the altogether if there was the slightest chance—"

"Point made." He slid his arms around her and pulled her close. His warm hands got busy. "You're cold."

"Not anymore." She pushed the hoodie off his shoulders, then tugged his T-shirt up.

He leaned in close to her ear as he shucked off the rest of his clothes. His voice was a seductive rumble. "You ever do it outdoors?"

That prompted a snort of derision. "Right. Frank wouldn't even let me open the bedroom windows in case, I don't know, we scared a squirrel or something." Lucy's nearest neighbor lived so far away, she could have howled in passion at the top of her lungs and never been heard by another living soul. Not that that supposition had ever been tested. Sex with Frank had been predictable in every sense. It was basically birthdays and national holidays, with the occasional exotic-vacation quickie thrown in.

Will's body pressed to hers felt like a furnace—a hard and sleek, virile, intoxicating, mind-blowingly sexy furnace. Lucy felt as if it were her first time. In a sense, it *was* her first time—the first time she'd had sex because she really, really wanted to. With Frank, she'd kept the goodies under lock and key until the wedding night, a strategic part of her cunning plan to wrangle herself an upstanding citizen and remake herself as Mrs. M.B.A. The good news? Her cunning plan had worked. Which also happened to be the bad news.

Will's talented hands and mouth abandoned her long enough to spread the patchwork quilt on the grass. She saw him lean in close to examine the oddly shaped patches by weak moonlight.

"My grandma Willie made it," Lucy said. "She's an original. Let's leave it at that."

He squinted closer. "Is that a little sock?"

She sighed. "One of my baby socks. If you keep on looking, you'll find Grandma's white gloves, Grandpa's sleeping cap, John's teddy bear pelt, Mom's first training bra, and Great-grandpa Max's last hankie. Among other family 'keepsakes.'"

He looked up. "You mother's *bra?*"

"Her first and only. She never wore one after that. Still doesn't."

"Sounds like quite a character." He pulled Lucy down to sprawl on the quilt with him. "I'd like to meet her."

"Isn't that a little serious for a free spirit like you?" She trailed her fingers through his springy chest hair. "Meeting a woman's family?"

"You weren't paying attention. I am serious, Lucy. *We're* serious." He stroked her breast, brushing his thumb across the nipple. "Besides, I've already met your twin sister. And your . . . what do you call your husband's other wife?"

"I call her my husband's other wife. Officially? She's my ex-husband's second wife. If you want to keep chatting—" Lucy arched against his hand "—you're going to have to stop doing that."

"Tough choice." His mouth followed his fingers, making Lucy truly thankful she had no neighbors within earshot.

They explored each other with the zeal of new lovers, rolling from Ethel's Christmas stocking to a scrap of Uncle Dave's baby blanket to the monogrammed napkin Great-grandma Mamie filched from the Hotel Ritz during her 1913 Paris honeymoon. The keepsake quilt had never been put to better use.

When finally they came together, Lucy couldn't believe how good it felt, how just plain right. Her new lover was enthusiastic. He was uninhibited. He was—thank you, Jesus—athletic. Clearly, this man loved sex. He loved the feel of it, the sounds of it, even the mess of it. Who knew sex could be so much fun? Will treated Lucy to three brain-sapping orgasms before he let himself go, then he did it all over again.

At last they collapsed in a boneless heap, Lucy's head tucked against Will's chest, his arm draped around her shoulder. She felt his heartbeat slow from a gallop to a sedate canter, felt his breathing turn deep and rhythmic. Soon he was snoring lightly. When their sweat dried, she reached around and dragged the edges of the quilt up, swaddling them in a tidy bundle: a double nookie burrito, heavy on the afterglow.

For several minutes she was content simply to lie there, relishing the feel of him, the heat and scent of him, the welcome soreness that reminded her how long it had been since she'd had any kind of sex, much less the vigorous, joyous brand of lovemaking she'd just been treated to.

The man in her life. She smiled. Then she remembered.

"Oh! Oh! Will. Wake up." She shook him.

"What!" He bolted upright, glancing wildly around. "What's wrong?"

"Nothing's wrong, I just forgot to tell you why I came to your house today. My news."

He grabbed his chest and collapsed onto the quilt. "Jesus Christ, Lucy, don't do that to me. Not after the day I've had."

"You'll never believe it." She leaned on a palm, grinning down at him. "Johnny Sherlock's going to be a movie!"

His eyes widened. "You're kidding."

"A producer optioned the first book years ago and just kept renewing it. I figured nothing would ever come of it. That's the way it usually goes." She couldn't help it, her grin was irrepressible. "But Johnny's been getting more popular all the time. Kids' book clubs have been picking it up. And anyway, today my agent called—well, yesterday, I guess it was—"

"And?" Will sat up.

"And they bought it! They're starting production, the casting and all that. Johnny Sherlock's going to be a movie!" she squealed.

Will swept her into his arms. He told her how happy he was for her, and how proud. Her lips were still sensitive from their high-impact aerobic workout. By contrast, this kiss was tender, lingering, spiritual. It was the yoga of kisses.

"I know one nine-year-old boy who's going to freak when he hears the news." He cocked his head. "How does it feel? Being the next J.K. Rowling."

"It feels damn good." She giggled like a schoolgirl.

He reached for his boxer briefs. "What I really want to know is, when can I order a Johnny Sherlock Happy Meal?"

She made a face.

"Are you kidding?" he said. "Every kid under twelve will be begging their parents for an authentic Johnny Sherlock action figure. Collect the whole set. Accessories sold separately. Hey!" She'd snatched his briefs as he started to step into them.

"You won't be needing these." Lucy started for the house, leaving Will to gather their things and catch up.

She'd never sashayed in her life. She hoped she was doing it right.

EPILOGUE

The New York Times Vows Section

Wesley McIntyre,

Joseph Silver

WESLEY CARSON MCINTYRE and Joseph Robert Silver were married yesterday in Southampton. The Rev. Lois Stryker and Rabbi Nathan Katz performed the interfaith ceremony at the South Fork Unitarian Universalist Church.

Mr. McIntyre, 43, is a private investigator in Nassau County and a former officer in the NYPD. He attended Hofstra University for two years before entering the Police Academy. He is a son of Richard and Doreen McIntyre of Brooklyn, who own and manage The Poseidon Seafood Grill in Oceanside, N.Y. His mother is a former Miss Rheingold.

Mr. McIntyre's first marriage ended in divorce.

Mr. Silver, 36, is a guidance counselor at Baldwin Middle School and also teaches Hebrew at Union Reform Temple in Freeport, N.Y. He graduated from the State University of New York at Stony Brook and received a master's degree in school counseling from Columbia. He is the son of Benjamin Silver of Manhattan, a professional poker player and host of the syndicated radio program "No Limit," and the stepson of Jeanne Kowalczyk Silver, a professional matchmaker.

The wedding and reception were attended by more than 300 guests. One notable guest was Wilbur Kitchen, better known to fans of 1980s sitcoms as Ricky Baines, the redheaded child star of the popular NBS program *In No Time* who was abducted and held for ransom during the show's third season. Mr. McIntyre was the first police officer on the scene of the kidnapping. Ricky Baines was ultimately reunited with his family, but the crime remained unsolved until last April when Mr. McIntyre reopened the case in his capacity as a private investigator. He succeeded in identifying and helping to apprehend the kidnapper, Harold Stuart Lynch, who had been paroled weeks earlier on an unrelated murder conviction.

During the kidnapping ordeal twenty-five years ago, NBS had offered a reward of $100,000 for information leading to a conviction in the case. In August a jury found Mr. Lynch guilty of the kidnapping, and Mr. McIntyre collected the award. Mr. Lynch is currently serving twenty-five years to life at Attica Correctional Facility.

ABOUT THE AUTHOR

Pamela Burford comes from a funny family. You may take that any way you want. She was raised in a household that valued laughter above all, so of course the first thing she looked for in a husband was a sense of humor. Is it any wonder their grown kids are into stand-up comedy and improv? Oh, and here's another fun fact: Pamela's identical twin sister, Patricia Ryan, aka P.B. Ryan, is also a published novelist. Patricia is the Good Twin, and yeah, Pamela knows what that makes her. But hey, Evil Twins have more fun!

It should come as no surprise that everything Pamela writes is infused with her own quirky brand of humor, from her feel-good contemporary romance and romantic suspense novels to her popular Jane Delaney mystery series, featuring snarky "Death Diva" Jane, her canine sidekick Sexy Beast, and a fun love-triangle subplot. Pamela's own beloved poodle, Murray, wants you to know that any similarities between himself and neurotic, high-strung Sexy Beast are purely coincidental.

Pamela is the proud founder and past president of Long Island Romance Writers. Her books have won awards and sold millions of copies, but what excites her most is hearing from readers. Swing by and say hi at pamelaburford.com.